A Place
in Your Heart

by

Kathy Otten

A Place in Your Heart

Cover Art by *Debbie Taylor*

The Wild Rose Press, Inc.
PO Box 708
Adams Basin, NY 14410-0708
Visit us at www.thewildrosepress.com

Publishing History
First American Rose Edition, 2018
Print ISBN 978-1-5092-2049-6
Digital ISBN 978-1-5092-2050-2

Published in the United States of America

"No. I want you to go home
before the death of that ten-year-old boy becomes so ordinary that one day you wake up and realize you no longer have the ability to feel."

She squared her shoulders and stepped toward him. "Me own husband was a doctor, sir. I've birthed babies and stitched wounds. I stood by William's side during surgeries and passed him instruments. I helped him clean the intestines of a man gored by a bull, before putting it all back inside that man's belly. Me delicate sensibilities did not send me into a swoon then nor will they here. I thank ye for yer concern, Doctor Ellard, but 'tis who I am. And by the saints, as long as I have breath in me body, I will feel, and I will care."

Their gazes locked in that moment and something flickered in his icy depths, overshadowing his usual cynicism with what she suspected might be admiration. The harsh lines of his face softened.

"Saint Jude must indeed be watching over you, Mrs. McBride."

"That he is, Doctor Ellard, that he is."

He gave her a brisk nod and opened the door. "You're not going home then, are you?"

She turned. "Ye know us Irish, Doctor Ellard. We don't know what we want, but we'll fight to the death to get it."

Kudos for Kathy Otten

A PLACE IN YOUR HEART is a Northwest Houston RWA Lone Star Historical Winner.

Another of Ms. Otten's books, *LOST HEARTS*, is a Utah/Salt Lake Chapter RWA Hearts of the West Finalist.

~*~

Other Kathy Otten titles
available from The Wild Rose Press, Inc.
Novels
A TARNISHED KNIGHT
LOST HEARTS
BETWEEN THE LINES
Novellas
ANOTHER WALTZ
AN ORDINARY ANGEL
A CHRISTMAS SMILE
Short Stories
AFTER THE DARK
SOMEONE TO THE SUNSETS
REDEMPTION OF A CAVALIER

Dedication

Kristie,
Someday, the Mütter Museum!
Love you.

Chapter One

Gracie McBride peered around her armload of clean sheets and blankets, trying not to bump into anything as she moved up the aisle of the hospital ward.

Ahead, Corporal Robert Reid leaned over a wounded private. Robbie, his right arm in a sling, struggled to remove the patient's shirt, soiled with breakfast spills.

"Robbie."

He looked up. His dark bangs fell across one blue eye.

"All that pulling and tugging cannot be good for yer shoulder."

A smile played at the corners of his mouth, forming a winsome grin that reminded Gracie of her youngest brother, Bryan.

She couldn't help but smile back. Her regular orderly, Tom Halleck, was on a month's leave, and Robbie had been acting in his stead. Though recovering from a bullet wound he received at Fredericksburg, Robbie was still willing to take on duties the regular orderlies wouldn't attempt without specific instruction from Doctor Ellard.

Gracie stepped between the beds. "Robbie, take these linens and let me do that."

"But, ma'am, Cap'n Ellard, he don't want ya—"

"By the saints, Robbie Reid, Captain Ellard be no

1

more than bellow and bluster. I spent me last two days in the storehouse doing inventories and organizing supplies from the Sanitary Commission. That task, 'tis finished. Here is where I be needed."

Robbie hesitated for a moment then stepped back. He extended his arm, and she reached to pass him the pile of clean linens. The stack wobbled, and he braced it with his injured arm.

She turned to the private, whose glassy eyes widened, as though mortified by the prospect of a woman seeing his bare torso. Unconcerned, she lowered herself to the edge of his mattress.

"Did ye see the snow this morning?" She picked up the clean shirt and dropped it over his head. "By the saints there must be two inches or more out there."

Reaching through the open yoke of the soiled shirt, she gently pulled the young man's arms from the garment. Next, she slipped her hand through the clean shirt cuff, backward through the sleeve. She grabbed the patient's cold hand and pulled it through. She did the same with the man's second hand. Before the private could rally the energy to protest, she'd tugged down the new shirt and whipped the old one over his head.

"And here was I, hoping to see some fine spring weather." Rising, she tucked the blanket high around him to ward off drafts and gave his shoulder a reassuring pat.

The bite of sour milk wafted from the dirty garment as she rolled it into a ball and dropped it on a pile of soiled sheets near the end of the bed. She couldn't help but notice the many faded stains and mended tears scattered throughout the thin flannel.

"When we finish changing the beds, why don't ye run to the storehouse for some o' the new shirts, sent down by the Sanitary Commission?"

"Ma'am, I did go there, whilst ya ate your breakfast, but Corporal Weston, he said the new shirts was all gone."

"What? Five thousand shirts, gone in two days?"

Robbie shrugged.

There were only a thousand beds in the whole hospital, and with the army in winter camp at Falmouth, the hospital wasn't even half full. Yesterday a couple of orderlies from other wards had each requested a hundred shirts, but by the saints, there should still be plenty in stock.

One of the first bits of gossip she'd heard when she arrived was how the previous ward surgeon had been arrested for being aware of, and not reporting, a ring of thieves who were not only stealing hospital supplies meant for the wounded, but selling them for personal profit.

She would have to address this shirt issue with Doctor Ellard. He wouldn't like it, but he was the new ward surgeon, and short of taking her complaints to the hospital's surgeon-in-charge, Doctor D. Willard Bliss himself, Doctor Ellard would just have to listen.

She and Robbie continued, moving from patient to patient, changing sheets, giving water, or an extra blanket where needed.

After smoothing a blanket over the top of another bed, she looked up and found Robbie with his gaze once again fixed on the door at the end of the ward. "Robbie, please."

She sighed. From the day she arrived three weeks

ago to replace one of the male nurses being reassigned, she and the tall, dark-haired surgeon had locked horns. Yet, despite their differences, if things ran smoothly Doctor Ellard had no complaints. Robbie needn't be so nervous.

She glanced at the watch pinned to the bodice of her black dress. Nearly time for that doctor to start his daily walk through the ward.

"Could ye pass me that red quilt with the embroidered border and let me worry about Doctor Ellard."

She'd been saving this quilt especially for the ill drummer boy whose bed was partitioned off behind a curtain at the end of the ward. She forced her brightest smile as she tucked the extra warmth around his shivering body and brushed back his damp hair. "There ye go, Gilbert."

That any mother would allow her ten-year-old child to march off to war was beyond her ken. She tamped down her rage at the insanity of it all before it paralyzed her.

"I'll be back later to help ye write a letter to yer mother."

He nodded and closed his eyes. She patted his knee, thin and bony beneath the quilt then hurried to the patients on the other side of the ward before the sting in her eyes could form into tears.

Robbie trailed along behind her. "Ma'am, maybe ya should hurry, so's Cap'n Ellard don't see ya when he comes through. Ya know he don't want ya in the ward."

"And where would he be thinking I belong? Back in Boston, scrubbing floors and polishing silver for the gentry on Beacon Hill? By the saints, if me lot in life is to do such work, then 'tis me choice to be doing it here."

She stopped at bed thirty-six then looked back. "For who would ye rather have nurse ye back to health, Robbie Reid, me or the lazy attendants stealing peaches meant for the wounded?"

With a wave of her hand, she gestured down the wide aisle toward the men playing cards around a table beside one of the stoves.

Robbie laughed as patients in nearby beds and chairs chuckled.

Gracie's cheeks grew hot as she recalled the ruckus from Wednesday night. "Now lads," she conceded glancing around. "Doctor Ellard had the right of it. I did go a wee bit too far, sneaking that purgative into those jars of peaches. But in me own defense, Dr. Ellard did refuse to believe me when I told him those men were eating the food meant for all ye fine lads. 'Twas the only way I knew to prove it."

"It was pretty funny," Robbie added. "Watchin' 'em moanin', all doubled over, pukin' an'…an'…" His cheek bones flared red.

She turned away, hiding a smile. Like her brother Bryan, Robbie was a brash, confident young man one minute, and the next, mortified by the idea that she knew anything of a man's bodily functions.

They moved on to Major Carlton who'd lost his leg at Fredericksburg. While most of the officers chose to pay for care in private homes, the major had chosen to remain here and pay for his meals until his family could come for him. She helped support him as he maneuvered into the wheeled chair beside his bed. After draping a clean blanket across his lap, she poured him a cup of water while Robbie continued talking.

"We was all worried about ya though, when Cap'n Ellard grabbed your arm an' dragged ya outta here the other night."

"An' I be telling ye true, Robbie Reid. Banishing me to the storehouse 'twas *all* he did. Doctor Ellard be a fine man. He'd not lay one finger on me."

Robbie glanced at the floor, as she yanked the linens from the major's bed.

"Well," Robbie whispered, leaning close to her ear. "Some a the men figgered he hurt ya, cause ya wasn't around fer two days. He's got a temper ya know and got himself demoted fer assaultin' some lieutenant after Fredericksburg."

"Robbie—"

"I know ya don't like hearin' gossip, but they say he had some kind'a breakdown durin' the battle. That he's a coward, that he abandoned his post, walked away from the field hospital an' when they found him—"

Raising her hand, she silenced Robbie. "Stories about the man are all I be hearing for nearly a month. Stories be not truth, and I'll not be spreading them behind his back."

Despite the gossip, she refused to believe a surgeon as fine as Doctor Ellard could have ever walked away from men who desperately needed his skills, no matter how tired and cold he'd been.

She'd heard the whispers among the patients about Fredericksburg. In wave after wave of frontal assaults against Confederates entrenched behind a stone wall along a ridge known as Mayre's Heights, whole brigades had been cut down by muskets and canister shot, including the 28th Massachusetts and her two oldest brothers.

One wizened old sergeant told her how they'd used pick axes to free the bodies frozen to the earth, which lay in heaps at the base of that high ground along the Sunken Road. A shudder rippled through her. She refused to picture Michael and Callum dying that way.

She rubbed her arms and shoved the images to that special corner of her mind reserved for dying drummer boys and brothers charging toward Confederate lines, cut down with the battle cry of the Irish Brigade still on their lips.

Faugh-a-Ballagh, be damned.

"Come, Robbie," she snapped briskly. "Let's give the storehouse another look. I saw to the unloading of the supplies from the Sanitary Commission meself, and by the saints, I know I entered five thousand shirts in that ledger."

Robbie followed her down the wide aisle toward the door which led outside. Ahead, a table and chairs had been arranged close to one of the stoves where the orderlies and recovering patients gathered to play cards.

Two of the attendants narrowed their gazes on Gracie as she walked toward them. They had both been recipients of her tainted peaches, and she bravely met their threatening glowers with one of her own. The first man, Sergeant Clive Paul, sat with his chair rocked back on two legs.

He didn't even rise as she approached the table, nor did he have the decency to button his coat. His slovenly appearance drew her eye to the front of his shirt and the familiar style of yoke and buttons she'd seen recently— five thousand times—over the past two days.

That louse! Pressing her lips together, she marched

straight toward him and grabbed his collar. Off balance, the chair tipped over, and Sergeant Paul fell flat on his back. Unwilling to release the shirt, Gracie landed right on top of him.

She held tight, nearly choking him as he tried to roll away. With her free hand, she grabbed the collar of his military jacket and tugged it half way down his arms.

She clung to him like a vine as he tried to crawl away amid the hoots and hollers of the patients. Once she'd tossed aside his coat, she pulled back the shirt and clearly visible were the inked letters U-S-S-C on the inside of the neck.

"By the saints, remove that shirt!"

He pulled free of her grip and pushed to his feet.

She reached out and grabbed his ankle.

He crashed to the floor.

Gracie crawled forward and latched onto his shirt again, this time pulling the hem from the waistband of his trousers. At the bottom of his shirt tail, again were the initials of the United States Sanitary Commission.

Sergeant Paul shoved her hands away, but she pushed him down and managed to sit herself on his stomach. Pulling and tugging, she yanked the shirt off his body then whirled it around above her head in triumph. The ward erupted in a thunderous chorus of cheers loud enough to rival an entire division of charging Rebels.

Suddenly a hush descended, as though God himself had entered the ward. Except God didn't wear shoes that thudded hollow against the wood floor, resonating the long deliberate stride of the man who approached.

Afraid of what Dr. Ellard would say this time, she

froze, hoping against hope, that he somehow wouldn't notice her sitting on a half-naked orderly in the middle of the ward.

The footsteps stopped behind her. She glanced at Robbie, but he'd averted his blue eyes, to stare shame-faced at the floor.

Without warning, strong hands slid under her arms and lifted her straight off the sergeant. She hung suspended for a moment, long fingers pressing into her ribs, her feet dangling above the floor. Was he about to shake her like a rag doll? Instead, he shifted and set her firmly on her feet.

Sergeant Paul scrambled to stand. "Sir, did ya see what that red-headed Irish wen—lady nurse did? Why it ain't decent, a woman actin' like—"

"Get out." Doctor Ellard's voice sliced through Sergeant Paul's tirade like a shard of glass through parchment.

Gracie smiled, feeling vindicated. Doctor Ellard was finally on her side. But when she glanced at the sergeant, he was looking straight at her. A smug grin curled back the edges of his mouth.

Puzzled, she turned. Doctor Ellard's ice blue gaze was narrowed right on her face.

"Me?"

"Yes, you. You have disrupted my ward for the last time, Mrs. McBride."

Drawing a deep breath, she planted her fists on either side of her apron's waist band. "Doctor Ellard, I did not spend two days o' me life bogged down with inventories and requisitions, only to be learning that the shirts and produce meant for the wounded have been stolen by these—"

"And what would you have me do, Mrs. McBride?" he fired back. "Poison every orderly in the hospital then strip them naked?"

Anger jerked her chin up. "No, Doctor Ellard, ye'd best be leavin' that to me."

A few snickers skittered around the room.

He drew a deep breath, as though he were about to give her a piece of his mind, but caught himself.

"I want you gone. Today. Now. Get your things and go." No emotion inflected his brisk directive. Dr. Ellard stood before her as cold and rigid as a tree coated in ice after a freezing rain, both beautiful and brittle.

"Why?" Her soft challenge to his authority burst unbidden from her throat.

He stepped toward her, his brow tugged together in a scowl.

She gulped but held her ground and his gaze.

Shadows darkened the hollows beneath his eyes and deep lines of fatigue bracketed his mouth, making his glower appear far more fierce than she believed it actually was. At least that was what she told herself.

"The paid nurses have gone. Ye need me. All yer patients like me. The other staff like me—"

Dr. Ellard's dark eyebrows arched in doubt.

Well, with the exception of the attendant she'd just pummeled. And his friend. And the others who had eaten the peaches. She crossed her arms. "They do not count."

"Good day, Mrs. McBride." He spun on his heels and strode back the way he'd come.

She stared after him for a moment, then drew a deep breath and followed.

He stopped near bed number seven. At the hollow

click of her heels against the wood, his broad shoulders stiffened. His chin dropped to his chest as if he were suddenly fascinated by the grain in the planks beneath his feet.

She stopped behind him. "Why?"

He swung around.

She gasped and jumped back.

"May I see you outside?"

Without waiting for even the slightest indication of her assent, he strode toward the door at the end of the ward. Sweet Mary Jesus the man was arrogant. 'Twould serve him right if she stayed right here. But after several seconds she hurried after him.

He opened the door and moved to the side with an after-you gesture of his arm.

They stepped onto the covered plank walkway which connected the eleven long white buildings which made up the wards and general office of Armory Square Hospital. Gracie crossed her arms against the cold, wishing she'd brought her shawl.

For several erratic beats of her heart, they studied each other.

"Women do not belong in war," he stated in the lofty manner of a lecturer behind a podium.

Gracie opened her mouth to argue, but she closed it under the censure of his narrowed glare.

"They are creatures of delicate sensibilities, easily frightened and excitable."

Dumbfounded, her mouth fell open again. He didn't believe this nonsense he seemed to spout from memory—did he?

"I have witnessed first-hand the evidence of your own excitable nature, and I do not feel your emotional outbursts in the ward conducive to the calm and restorative atmosphere necessary in a hospital filled with ill and wounded patients."

A snicker escaped her lips and she clamped her hand over her mouth.

He frowned.

Had a flash of hurt flickered in his pale eyes? She hadn't meant to offend him, but Sweet Mary Jesus, they worked so well together—as she and William had. She'd believed Doctor Ellard different from the other doctors, more forward thinking and progressive.

"While I find your patriotic spirit admirable, we would all be better served if you returned from whence you came. There your zealous nature might be better applied to rolling bandages and sewing. The devastation this war has wrought on our country, on the country side, and on the human body, can barely be endured by the men caught up in the horror. Go home, Mrs. McBride, before the pain of this place makes you another casualty."

Mouth agape, she stared at him in disbelief. Always so controlled and distant, Doctor Ellard did his job efficiently, but without much tenderness. Now she wasn't sure what to think, because if she heard him right, in some back-handed way, it sounded as if he cared—about her.

Any response she might have made was no longer relevant, for his hands wrapped around her upper arms. Their gazes locked. Heat flared in his blue eyes.

Begorra, was he about to—

He yanked her to him.

Her heartbeat quickened.

He wasted no time with sensual foreplay, by gently

nipping at her earlobe or teasing her with butterfly kisses until her lips parted. Instead, he shoved his way inside, his tongue as arrogant and dominating as he.

The pressure of his lips teased an ache, long dormant. She wilted, clutching his upper arms to keep from sagging on the walkway. Her fingers gripped him through the wool of his sleeves, through the cotton of his shirt, holding tight to the solid strength of his muscles. The odors of lye soap and ether wafted to her from the fabric of his military jacket.

And she responded, absorbing the morning flavors of coffee and bread as her tongue swirled around his, her body aching to be held again, to be desired, to be needed. But this was wrong.

She shouldn't have to tip her head back so far. The scent of pipe tobacco should linger in the air. His beard should tickle, not scratch the tender skin around her mouth. She pushed against him.

He groaned, and as suddenly as the kiss began it ended. He stepped back. Confusion played across his features as though he wasn't sure what had just happened.

Gracie blinked, crossing her arms against her waist. Three years had passed since she'd been kissed, and William had never kissed her like this.

Doctor Ellard's voice, when he spoke, was hoarse, but his intent was crystal clear. "Now, go home."

Every muscle in her body stiffened. The audacity! Who did he think he was? Her breathing increased, building pressure behind her breastbone like water in a kettle on the back burner of the stove. Did he believe that one kiss from the great Doctor Ellard would so overwhelm her that she would run to do his bidding, as though she were nothing more than a vapid-brained society debutante?

"Would ye have me go home to shop for bonnets and gossip with me morning guests, ignorin' that ten-year-old boys are being shot on battlefields? Do ye want me to stay unchanged, so that when I go home I can pretend none o' this ever happened?"

"No. I want you to go home before the death of that ten-year-old boy becomes so ordinary that one day you wake up and realize you no longer have the ability to feel."

She squared her shoulders and stepped toward him. "Me own husband was a doctor, sir. I've birthed babies and stitched wounds. I stood by William's side during surgeries and passed him instruments. I helped him clean the intestines of a man gored by a bull, before putting it all back inside that man's belly. Me delicate sensibilities did not send me into a swoon then nor will they here. I thank ye for yer concern, Doctor Ellard, but 'tis who I am. And by the saints, as long as I have breath in me body, I will feel, and I will care."

Their gazes locked in that moment and something flickered in his icy depths, overshadowing his usual cynicism with what she suspected might be admiration. The harsh lines of his face softened.

"Saint Jude must indeed be watching over you, Mrs. McBride."

"That he is, Doctor Ellard, that he is."

He gave her a brisk nod and opened the door. "You're not going home then, are you?"

She turned. "Ye know us Irish, Doctor Ellard. We don't know what we want, but we'll fight to the death to get it."

His lips twitched, but he didn't laugh. Instead he waited as she preceded him inside. Then he stepped past her and strode down the aisle to bed number seven. Seemingly oblivious to the stunned silence of the patients around him, he lifted the card off the wall then leaned over the soldier gazing up at him. He folded down the sheet and slid up the patient's shirt.

Gracie marched down the aisle to join him.

"Since Corporal Timon be late again, would ye like me to stand in as your orderly?"

He stilled for a moment, heaved a weighted sigh then passed her the card.

She dug a pencil and memorandum book from her apron pocket. The card read, *Ward E, Cot #7, Edward Benjamim, Company G, 154th New York, Shot through hip, wound probed to remove bone fragments and foreign matter.*

He pulled his stethoscope from the pocket of his coat and put the ivory tipped ear pieces in each ear.

"Change dressing, three times," Doctor Ellard dictated as he dropped the device to hang from his neck.

She jotted down his instructions.

"Pack with lint," he continued. "And bandage. Administer stimulants and Blue Mass for constipation."

They moved to the next bed, *Thomas Haley, Company M, New York Cavalry.* Then on to the next...*shot through lung...*

Doctor Ellard placed the black walnut cone to the man's chest and listened for a moment to the patient's breathing.

"For stimulants, whiskey and wine punch. For the lungs, turpentine."

The stack of cards grew as they moved through the ward in quiet synchronization, as if they'd done this together a thousand times. And while this man wasn't her husband, she felt closer to William here, just by being in this hospital, by doing what she did best, helping the patients and assisting Doctor Ellard.

Cot #19, Ezra Minch...Typhoid

"Fever, eyes glazed, breathing shallow. Administer stimulants. For diarrhea continue cotton felt bellyband."

When they reached young Gilbert, every muscle inside Gracie tightened. Outwardly, she forced an expression of calm efficiency.

Doctor Ellard bent over the drummer boy, poked and prodded his wound. The sour stench of dead flesh and bowel wafted from the boy's belly.

Gracie swallowed her urge to gag and forced a smile for Gilbert.

Still examining the wound, Doctor Ellard dictated. "Fever, chills, face waxy, breath shallow. Stimulants, wine punch. Keep comfortable." He pulled the sheet and embroidered blanket up to the boy's chin.

She stepped around the bed and placed her free hand on the boy's forehead. "Ye'll soon be right as rain Gilbert, and when I finish helping Doctor Ellard, I'll be back to write yer letter."

He nodded, his glassy eyes locked on her face.

"'Tis a brave lad ye are, and sure yer mother be proud."

She gave him a quick smile and hurried after Doctor Ellard. He stopped in the center of the wide aisle and turned to face her. Furrows formed above the bridge of his nose.

"You do a disservice to that patient by coddling

him and giving him hope."

Her spine stiffened. "Coddling?" she bit out in a harsh whisper. "That patient is a child, Doctor Ellard, and by the saints, there will always be hope."

"Private Franklin is in the army, and I will treat him no different than any other soldier in my care."

"Nor will I, Doctor Ellard. For to ease the suffering of these brave men 'tis the reason I've come."

He stared down at her, and she shivered under the intensity of his ice-blue eyes.

"That soldier will die, Mrs. McBride, and there is nothing you, or I, or the Great Jehovah can do about it."

Then before she could draw breath to argue, he moved onto Major Carlton. Without a word, Doctor Ellard tossed aside the blanket and pushed up the edge of the major's long white shirt. Focused on the wound, he removed the bandage wrapped around the stump of the major's leg. He peered critically at the many knotted silk threads dangling from each end of the newly formed scar. Most of the threads had come away, leaving only those which tied off the main arteries of the leg. Doctor Ellard tugged lightly on each one.

"No wound discharge. Patient reports no phantom pain. Gaining weight." He straightened and stepped back from the wheeled chair. "Find one of the stewards. Have them rebandage this leg."

"I can do it."

He moved to the next patient. "I thought I clearly explained to you the delicate nature of a woman's sensibilities. Find a steward."

"And did I not explain to ye, that me sensibilities be not delicate. I can bandage the major's leg and do a fine job of it too."

At the front of the ward the door opened, funneling a rush of cold air down the length of the long room.

"Sorry I'm late, Captain." Corporal Timon hurried toward them, pausing to toss his overcoat and hat onto the table which stood half-way down the ward.

"I will listen to your excuse later, Corporal—when I file my report."

The orderly's features tightened. For a moment he looked poised to argue, then he squared his shoulders. "Yes, sir."

Turning toward Gracie, he extended his hand for the composition book and patient card. She stared at his open palm, loath to surrender her responsibility to someone who didn't care enough to arrive on time.

"Come now, Mrs. McBride." Doctor Ellard blew out an impatient sigh. "I'm sure there are other duties you can attend to more suited to your tender feminine nature."

She glared at him. From the way he watched her, she knew he expected an outburst reflective of her excitable disposition. But by the saints, she would not give the oaf that satisfaction. Instead she lined up the corners on her stack of cards and turned away to readjust the patient's blankets.

"Pencil?"

She swung around. Corporal Timon stood with his hand extended again. She was tempted to walk away and let him fend for himself. If he couldn't come prepared, then he deserved the mental exercise of having to remember all the doctor's orders. But then, he'd likely forget half the instructions, and the patients would suffer.

Without a word, she dug into her apron pocket and

held out a pencil, barely longer than an inch.

With a whispered curse, he snatched the stub from her fingers.

A smile inched across her face. She turned and strolled up the aisle to her table.

Robbie sat in the chair, and as she drew close, he stood.

She picked up the orderly's overcoat and hat. "Could ye find a place to hang these?" She itched to toss them into the snow, but the corporal would likely take sick, and she'd be forced to nurse him.

"Yes, ma'am."

"And we have need o' more pencils. I be down to me last one."

"Sure." He took the coat then headed toward the end of the ward where a dining area had been partitioned off.

She lowered herself into the chair and read through the cards, preparing a list of medicines they would need from the dispensary along with another list of food for the Special Diets Kitchen.

Engrossed in her work, she wasn't aware anyone had approached her table until a shadow fell across her paper. Doctor Ellard stood in front of her, the rest of the patient cards in one hand, a single card in his other. Accepting the stack, she set them to one side. "Thank ye."

"Where is Corporal Reid?"

She frowned at his brisk official tone. She searched his face. It held the grim look of a man braced to deliver bad news.

Her heartbeat quickened. "He be off on an errand."

He passed her the single card, Robbie's name and

rank scrawled across the top.

"I'll stop back to give him a final examination, but I am discharging him. He'll be sent back to his unit next week."

"No." The denial burst from her lips and she sprang to her feet. She sought his gaze, her heart in her throat.

"You can't protect them all, Mrs. McBride," he stated. "Anymore than I can save them all."

"But Robbie 'tis needed here."

"Corporal Reid is needed with his unit. Such is the futility of war. Men die, and others are sent to replace them."

He turned and strode from the ward.

Chapter Two

Pulling the door closed behind him, Charles stood on the covered walkway and sucked a deep breath of cold air into his lungs before releasing it in a streaming cloud of white. He rubbed his hands together as though washing them with invisible soap, but the friction brought little warmth.

He said far too much around Mrs. McBride. There was something about her that drew words from him, made him spill secrets he normally would never have shared. Maybe ancient Druid blood ran thick in her Irish veins and she'd cast a spell over him, over the patients, over the orderlies—well, not all the orderlies.

He gave his head a slight shake. She was nothing like the genteel ladies of his acquaintance, nothing like the other lady nurses he'd met. He pulled his watch from its pocket and popped open the clasp. And Gracie was nothing like the image he carried of his beautiful, refined mother.

He couldn't imagine his mother or any of the women he knew facing the reality of war head-on the way Gracie McBride did. Maybe that was why on her first day he'd looked down his nose and *harumphed* at her instead of greeting her properly, or gushing over her the way the other doctors, orderlies, and nurses did, as though they were all at a Sunday social instead of a military hospital in the middle of a war.

Either way, she'd gotten her back up that day, and they'd been at odds ever since. Many of the lady nurses had come and gone. Even here, safe from any fighting, they didn't understand the toll. Illness, mental and physical fatigue, this was grueling work, and they shouldn't be here. Hell, none of them should be here.

He stared at the skeletal dome of the Capitol building, the framework black against the dreary backdrop of gray sky. He wondered how much money it would cost to finish it.

War.

A vicious cycle of weapons designed to end life while doctors futilely tried to sustain it. He cursed Claude-Etinne Minié for inventing the conical shaped ball, for current medical knowledge was inadequate to combat its damage. And he cursed a government that would spend so much on a fancy building while doctors in the field suffered without medicines and surgical instruments.

Hell, he'd never even seen an amputation before he enlisted, now...

He turned and followed the breezeway past the general office, which stood in the center of the wards, to Ward F, the second ward of patients for which he was responsible.

Squaring his shoulders, he entered the long, white building. Corporal Timon met him inside. Briskly they moved from patient to patient in the same manner with which he conducted his rounds in Ward E. As usual, Timon didn't write fast enough, and Charles not only had to repeat his instructions numerous times, he had to spell several words and medication names aloud. For a moment he missed Gracie's quiet efficiency.

Though everything was clean and organized, in this ward the nurses and attendants lagged behind schedule. Some of the men on special diets were still being fed while several patients lay waiting either to be bathed or for their dressings to be changed. His nostrils flared at the sharp stench drifting from bed pans stacked near the piles of soiled linens, some of which contained the rank excrement from dysentery patients.

His rounds finished, he headed to the general office to take his turn in the rotation as the officer-of-the-day.

A white picket fence surrounded the hospital, leaving the general office with the only entrance to the street so anyone entering had to come past him.

He placed the supply ledger he'd received from Major Bliss on the wide desk and slid his chair close. Major Bliss, the hospital's surgeon-in-charge, had asked Charles, because of his battlefield experience, to submit the new supply requisition forms. The hospital couldn't be caught short when casualties arrived from the spring campaigns.

Lee had been pushing north. There were even rumors that 1863 would see his army marching on Washington. That meant wounded—probably more than he could bring himself to project.

Don't think about it.

He dipped his pen into the inkwell and drew a deep breath. What happened at Fredericksburg might never happen again.

Ether, he wrote. They would need cases and cases of ether and chloroform and morphine. He listed them next.

An inky blob landed on the paper beside the word morphine. The black spot spread, seeping into the fibers, obscuring the 'e' and then the 'n,' transforming into a widening circle of red against white.

His skin went cold.

His breath escaped in short, rapid pants as his pulse thudded wildly through his body. The pen slipped from his fingers as he struggled to draw a breath. Heart pounding wildly, he shoved his chair back, the legs scrapping loudly against the plank floor. Sweat broke out across his brow, and he shivered. He leaned forward dropping his head between his knees. Tiny fissures of light danced around the periphery of his vision.

No, no, no! Not here.

The rational part of his brain reminded him it had only been ink on paper. But the other part, the disturbed part, the part he feared he couldn't control saw—

No! He reached out and snatched the paper off the desk. Viciously, he crushed it into a ball and slammed it into the empty wastepaper basket beside the desk.

Pressure grew behind his sternum, tight and painful. At the bottom of the basket, the ball of white paper coalesced into a form.

A man's head. Blood oozed out across the cobblestones like a long, dark tentacle.

His throat closed off, keeping any breath from going in or out. His pulse pounded in his head, roared in his ears. His chest hurt. He couldn't breathe. God, he was going to die. This time he was going to die!

No! Fredericksburg had been worse, and he hadn't died then. He wouldn't die today. He bent forward again, his head between his knees. Closing his eyes, he tried to focus on breathing. In. Out. In. Out.

Don't think about Fredericksburg and the soldier in the surgery tent. Don't think about his head wrapped in blood-soaked bandages, his heart and lungs not yet aware the brain was dead.

Imagine something pretty. Lilacs—on the bush outside the back door. Breathe. In. Out. The technique had worked when he was a boy. But not on that day. Fredericksburg had been the first time in years that he'd had one of these attacks. Until then he'd believed he'd outgrown them.

Gradually the white spots faded, and his breathing returned to normal. He raised his head and slowly straightened. He glanced toward the corporal dozing in a chair, tipped back on two legs against the wall.

He released a long sigh. At least this time no one had seen. He wiped his forearm across his brow and ran his palm over his face. Maybe going to war had not been a good idea. But he'd known he could save lives. Being a physician was all he'd ever wanted, what he'd trained to do.

His grandfather had even thought joining the army a good idea and leant his financial support when Charles enlisted.

Charles ran his fingers through his damp hair and drew a deep breath. Calm.

How long had the episode lasted? Five minutes? Ten? Without knowing when it began, checking his watch now would be moot. At least no one had come in, and the corporal had slept through it.

Slept?

Charles rose, straightened his coat, and stepped around the desk. Marching across the room, Charles stopped in front of the corporal and kicked the chair leg.

The man tumbled to the floor. Dazed, he scrambled

to his knees and looked from the floor to the chair to Charles' brightly polished boots. Slowly, the corporal's gaze traveled up until it collided with Charles'. Surprise widened his eyes.

"Stand up, Corporal," Charles ordered. "You are on duty."

The soldier jumped to his feet. "Sorry, sir." He righted the chair and came to attention beside it. "I was up all night, and I—"

"I'm not interested in excuses, Corporal. I am putting you on report."

"But, sir—"

"Corporal."

The man snapped to attention, his stare fixed on the opposite wall, his lips compressed in a tight line.

Charles stepped in front of him. "Perhaps some fresh air will clear your head. Take the trash to the incinerator."

"Yes, sir."

Charles stepped back, allowing him to pass.

The man snatched up the wastepaper basket then paused as he peered inside. He lifted his head and opened his mouth as if to argue, then snapped it closed.

"Now, Corporal."

"Yes, sir." The basket in hand he strode down the hall toward the back entrance and disappeared outside.

As the door banged closed, Charles released a sigh and unclenched his fingers from behind his back.

Calmed, he returned to his desk, opened the drawer, and removed a new requisition form. He picked up the pen.

The front door opened. A gust of cold air swirled around his ankles. He set the pen down and looked up.

A short, thin man stepped through the door. He stomped his feet, knocking loose bits of mud and slush. Removing his hat, he approached the desk. "Good morning, Captain," he said, peering over the tops of his spectacles, the lenses foggy white.

"Reverend." Charles turned the guest book toward the man and passed him the pen.

"I've come to pray with Corporal Winston Mercer in Ward C," he explained as he signed and dated the next available line in the book. "His wife is with child, and he worries that her worry for him will cause her to fall ill. All this worry." He chuckled as he set down the pen. "If only people would put their trust in our Heavenly Father." He pushed his now steam-free glasses up the bridge of his nose, gave Charles a nod, then hurried toward the back door which opened onto the walk connecting all the wards.

The clergyman greeted someone. The corporal's voice replied and the two men chatted for a bit.

Then the door shut and footsteps drew closer. Charles said nothing as he picked up the pen, and the corporal returned to his post near the door.

Charles dipped the pen in the inkwell, this time giving the nib a little tap against the inside of the bottle before pulling it out all the way.

Ether. He swallowed then carefully printed a large capital 'E' on the first line.

The door opened again, and two ladies bustled in, their lively voices chattering at the same time, whether to each other, to the corporal who closed the door for them, or to him, Charles couldn't be sure.

He set down his pen and stood. "Ladies." He gave them a slight bow. "How can I help you?"

He lost sight of their faces, unable to see below the brims of their bonnets, until they stepped up to his desk and tipped their heads back.

The shorter of the two spoke first. "Good day, Captain." A forthright smile pushed back the wrinkles of her papery face. "My name is Mrs. Boggs, and this is Mrs. Nash. We are from the Episcopal Church in Georgetown." She switched her attention to her friend. "Show him the bag, Vivian."

"Yes, of course." Mrs. Nash reached inside her pelisse, withdrew a folded piece of white canvas, and handed it to her companion.

Mrs. Boggs passed it to him and continued, "Women from sister churches all over our great country have joined together in sewing these for the wounded."

Charles gave it a cursory glance then passed it back. It looked like a ditty bag with fancy stitching.

"If you ladies will please sign in, you can go through and distribute them."

Mrs. Boggs picked up the pen, her flowing script took up two full lines. Mrs. Nash carefully confined her signature to the allotted space.

"Captain." Mrs. Boggs lifted her gaze to meet his. "Would you be able to spare a man to help us deliver these to the patients?"

"Corporal," he snapped.

"Yes, sir?"

"Help these ladies carry their box of—"

"Boxes."

He frowned, and Mrs. Boggs continued undaunted. "Yes, we have several large boxes secured on the back of our carriage. As I explained, ladies from our sister churches all over—"

"Fine. Corporal." Charles sighed. The man was engrossed in conversation with Mrs. Nash.

"The men'll be right proud to have these."

"Rather ingenious, are they not?" Mrs. Nash pointed out the flap on the back. "Mrs. Carter designed them based on the beds she saw at the Union Hotel Hospital in Georgetown. You see, with this flap buttoned securely around the bed frame, each man can keep at hand his toiletries, a book, letters from home, a deck of cards…"

"Corporal."

"Yes, sir. Sorry, sir."

"Please escort these ladies around to the supply entrance and assist them in whatever way they require."

With a smile, the man dutifully ushered the ladies from the office.

Grateful for peace and quiet once more, he studied the single *'E'* he'd written at the top of the paper then added…*t-h-e-r*.

On his left lay the ledger from the quartermaster, listing the supplies used by the hospital during the fall campaigns. Antietam, Fredericksburg—

He blew out a breath and reached for the sheets of inventory completed yesterday by Mrs. McBride. The familiar, neat flowing script, so much a reflection of the woman who penned it, somehow calmed him.

He had no idea what possessed him to grab her and kiss her earlier, though he had no regrets. He had however, fully expected her to chastise him for taking liberties. Instead she'd kissed him back.

The corner of his mouth twitched. Gracie McBride never behaved as he expected. He wondered what drew him to her when he'd always been attracted to well-mannered young ladies who came from respectable families, women more like his mother had been, accomplished in music and conversation.

The back door opened and closed. Heavy footsteps thudded against the wood floor, growing louder as someone moved up the hallway to the front office.

Charles looked up.

A broad shouldered, robust man stopped in front of the desk. His open coat framed a white apron which sported an assortment of stains across his ample waist.

"Captain, you have to do something about this." He waved a sheet of paper in front of him as though it were a telegram of vital importance.

"And what would that be, Sergeant?"

"This is the third time this week."

"What is the third time this week?"

"The milk, sir."

Charles sighed. "Explain."

The sergeant drew himself up and took a deep breath. Droplets of melted snow slid down his forehead from his bald pate. He swiped away the annoyance. "The lady nurse in E is using all the milk. Near every day she orders extra milk. I only got so much, sir. If she keeps taking it, I'll report her to Major Bliss. Women ain't got no business—"

"Sergeant." Charles snapped, cutting off the man's words. He held out his hand, and the sergeant passed him the paper. In very familiar handwriting, the words, *Ward E Special Diets,* were written across the top.

Charles read each item on the list, recalling every single instruction he'd dictated to both Gracie and Corporal Timon. He next quickly calculated the exact quantity needed for each food Gracie had listed for those patients too ill to eat in the dining area of the ward.

He pulled out a clean sheet of paper and wrote *Ward 'E' Special Diets* across the top. A few minutes later he scrawled his signature across the bottom and handed it to the sergeant.

The man's eyes widened as he read the list. His nostrils flared as his gaze shot to Charles, but he didn't say a word.

"Take that list," Charles gestured toward the offices behind him, "straight to Major Bliss and report me. If you run out of milk, let me know. I'll buy you a cow."

The sergeant stared at him through narrowed eyes. Charles wasn't sure if the man wanted to say something but couldn't find the words, or if he had the words and struggled not to say them.

"That will be all, Sergeant."

The man glanced at Charles's list once more then snatched up the original list, whirled, and strode from the room. The door slammed. The wind could have done it, but Charles didn't think so.

A bugle sounded in the distance.

Wounded at the steamboat landing. He hoped there weren't too many. This time of year, the only patients they received here in Washington were those men too ill to remain at the regimental hospitals in Falmouth, where the Army of the Potomac had their winter camp.

He rose, paced to the door, to the desk, and back to the door. There were empty beds in his wards. Would the men be sent to E or F?

He strode back to the desk, shoved the inventory list inside the ledger, and slammed it closed. He'd think about this later.

At the front window, he gazed through the archway at the end of the front walk. The white picket fence stretched in either direction. Beyond the fence stood a lamp post and hitching rail. Trees lined the wide, muddy street, their dark branches starkly outlined against the bleak sky. Tiny buds had formed on their tips. He used to welcome them as a sign the long winter was ending. Now they were a precursor to armies on the move and the start of the spring campaigns.

****

The clatter of numerous feet against the planks of the walkway grew louder then stopped just outside the ward. The wide door at the end of the long building opened.

Gracie closed the medicine chest, gave the key a turn, and dropped the loop of string from which it hung, over her head. She tucked the brass key behind the bib of her apron and positioned herself beside her table, neatly arranged for the weekly inspection.

Sunday mornings were not for worship services, but for a full inspection walk-through of the hospital by Doctor Bliss and each doctor and cadet surgeon under him.

This was her fourth inspection, and today everything was in perfect order. She and Robbie had replaced the patient cards over each bed. Leticia had collected the soiled linens for washing. Harvey and Micah, the new attendants assigned to her ward, had bathed and dressed each patient. The ashes had been cleaned from the stoves, the fires relit, bed pans emptied and rinsed, the floors swept and mopped, and all the beds had been made.

Mingled with the uniformed army medical officers were the civilian doctors in their black double-breasted frock coats and black trousers. The swarm of nearly two dozen medical professionals milled like giant ants converging on a crumb at the end of the ward. On either side of where they stood, areas had been partitioned off for bathing rooms, dining, and Gracie's sleeping quarters. Their low voices blended with the stomping of shoes as they removed their hats and reorganized themselves.

She easily recognized Doctor Ellard as he moved to the front of the formation, not because he wore military dress, or because he was taller than the other doctors, or that he was the only man without facial hair, but because he had presence. An aura of confident authority surrounded him, so that however quietly he might enter a room, people noticed him.

Slowly the group moved up one side of the ward. Each man listened as Doctor Ellard recited an update on each patient. He knew each man by wound and prognosis without having to refer to the cards. Nods and murmurs followed, and then it was on to the next bed.

As they approached the patients across from her station, it became easier to understand what the doctors were saying.

"And what of this young boy?" asked a young medical cadet at the back of the group—a man Gracie hadn't seen before. "An abdominal wound. Is there no chance?"

Gracie gasped. While Gilbert had been sleeping most of the morning, he was awake at this moment. She charged around the table.

"Now this amputation over here," Doctor Ellard

said loudly, ignoring the question, as he moved away from the curtained area to the major sitting in his wheeled chair.

Gracie stopped.

The group shuffled past the drummer boy.

Why he'd done it Gracie couldn't tell, but at least for that moment, Gilbert was spared.

Doctor Ellard continued addressing the group. "Secondary hemorrhages have ceased. Only ligatures belonging to the larger vessels remain. Continuing with dressings. Patient is ready for discharge and further recuperation at home."

"When was the leg amputated?" Piped up the cadet, who for some reason seemed determined to challenge Doctor Ellard.

"December thirteenth."

"And he's been here all this time?"

Across the distance Doctor Ellard stiffened. "The patient suffered from pyemia and surgical fever, with secondary hemorrhaging."

"Which begs me to ask, was the amputation actually necessary?"

At the question, Doctor Ellard turned his head toward Major Carlton and met his gaze. Something unspoken passed between the two men, but Gracie couldn't guess what.

"Yes." Doctor Ellard answered the cadet's question, though he spoke to the major. "It was."

"What are your thoughts," the young upstart persisted, "on the horrendous number of unnecessary amputations performed by surgeons in field hospitals? I understand the public regards these men as little more than butchers."

Sweet Mary Jesus, did he know nothing of Doctor Ellard's temperament?

Doctor Ellard's gaze narrowed on the young man. "And who deemed them unnecessary? You?"

As he strode toward him, the other doctors parted like the Red Sea before Moses.

Doctor Ellard reached out, wrapped his long fingers around the man's neck cloth, then turned and dragged him like a recalcitrant puppy on a leash back to Major Carlton and gave the cadet a shove. The young man stumbled back against the bed and dropped heavily onto the mattress.

"Have you ever been to a field hospital, *cadet*?"

Weakly the man shook his head.

"No? Then ask Major Carlton here what it's like, or any of these men. Because until you've operated with only the instruments in your field pack, your fingers stiff from cold, smelled the powder and the blood, seen a man torn in half by cannonade or witnessed what a Minié ball does to bone, I'll thank you to keep your Goddamn opinions about field surgeons to yourself."

A blast of Artic wind seemed to blow through the ward, freezing everyone in place. The patients lay in their beds or sat in chairs, unmoving and silent. All eyes fixed on Doctor Ellard as he stepped around the end of the bed and resumed his summary of the next patient.

"Dysentery, recovering slowly." He moved on. The group scuffed along behind him. "Perforating gunshot wound of the abdomen..."

The medical cadet rose from the bed, adjusted his clothing, and with his gaze fixed on the floor scurried down the aisle to the back of the group.

"Holy mother of—"

Gracie swung toward the familiar voice behind her.

Red-faced, Robbie stammered, "Uh, I—s-sorry, ma'am."

Gracie smiled. "I thought ye'd be out enjoying yer day off."

"I am, ma'am. But boy, that Cap'n Ellard, ain't he somethin'? I thought sure he'd deliver a real facer to that fellow." He made two fists and feigned a couple of punches. "Cap'n Ellard would'a showed him, just like he done that officer at Aquia Creek who wouldn't send down stoves to for the wounded after Fredericksburg." His voice lit with the eagerness of a boy in the schoolyard.

Gracie sighed with a shake of her head. And men wondered how this war came to be.

"Robbie, is there something ye be needing?"

"Yeah, I come to tell ya that the Sisters of Charity brung a melodeon to C and Sister Mary says to come. They's gonna have a hymn sing at two o'clock."

"A melodeon. What a fine thing." She flashed him a smile. "We'll come for certain."

Robbie gestured toward the tall cupboard against the wall behind them. "Last week I seen there was a fiddle on the shelf an' I wondered could I borrow it for a while?"

"I did not know ye played."

He followed as she stepped toward the cabinet.

"I'm from Broken Creek Hollow, Virginia. I got kin all over the state, and when we get together all we do is play music. I can fiddle and play banjo and spoons."

She withdrew her key and opened the cabinet.

"Now that Doctor Ellard said I can use my arm, I reckon I'd like to practice up some."

She shoved aside several jars and rolls of lint. "Here it is." She carefully lifted out the violin and passed it back.

His eyes widened like a lad on Christmas morn, and he took it from her hand. "Do you play an instrument?"

"No, but I can sing a ballad or two." She grabbed the bow and passed it to him. "And I can kick up me heels to an Irish jig, balancing a cup o' water on me head, and not spill a drop."

He laughed. The full-throated sound carried through the ward, and without even a glance in Doctor Ellard's direction, she felt his narrow-eyed censure.

"Off with ye now, Robbie Reid." She waved her hands at him in a shooing motion. "Rosin up yer bow, for I be eager to hear ye play."

He grinned, then swung around and dashed toward the door at the end of the ward.

The doctors continued their inspection, traveling down the opposite row of patients. Several minutes later, they moved outside and onto the next building filled with sick and wounded.

Gracie and the new attendants set up for Sunday dinner, then Harvey and Micah left to pick up the special diets.

At one o'clock the visitors drifted in. A local reverend came to read from the scriptures and pray with the men. Some patients had family staying in Washington, and as they arrived Gracie made sure to invite them to the hymn sing. Two ladies from one of the relief societies brought the patients a box of puzzles and games.

Gracie took one of the puzzles and sat beside Gilbert. He wasn't interested in trying it himself but seemed content to listen as Gracie shared stories of her childhood while she struggled to transfer a disk from a loop of cord hanging from one side of a small wooden yoke, onto the second loop. After several minutes Gilbert fell asleep. However, believing she almost had the puzzle solved, Gracie continued to pull, flip, and push at the simple looking contraption.

As the hour approached two o'clock, she was forced to leave the yoke and rings on the small table beside Gilbert's bed and help the attendants ready any patient who wished to attend the singing.

Major Carlton wanted to go, and Gracie pushed his wheeled chair down the boardwalk to Ward C.

"Have ye anyone coming to take ye home?" Gracie asked as they slowly bumped along.

"My brother Sam is coming this week."

"Ye must be happy to finally see yer family again."

He gave a noncommittal grunt and shrugged. After a long moment he said, "I understand there is to be a lecture at the Smithsonian on Tuesday evening."

"Would ye like me to take ye over?"

Again he said nothing, then, "I would like you to accompany me," he whispered.

She stopped pushing and stepped to the side of the chair. She didn't really want to go with him, but he sounded so unsure she feared he'd be too hurt by her rejection to ask someone else. He was leaving in a few days anyway.

"And do ye know what the lecture is about?"

"Glaciers."

"Glaciers?" She smiled. "Oh it sounds grand. I'd be proud to go with ye, Major."

His smile was hesitant, but he did smile, and suddenly she was glad she'd agreed to go.

"Please, call me Win. It's short for Winfield. And it's what all my family and friends call me."

"Then ye must call me Gracie."

His smile broadened. "I'd be honored, Gracie. Shall we go in?"

In front of the small piano, rows of chairs had been placed for the patients, while everyone else stood. Gracie accepted a hymn book from Sister Mary. Standing beside Major Carlton's chair, Gracie held the book low and turned to the page for the first hymn.

Her voice started out soft, but as she grew more confident with the melody, her high, clear notes soon lifted to the rafters.

Robbie was in his element, and she was awed by the joy which radiated from his heart to the strings. He even improvised during the pauses and bridges in the music, making each song his own.

Eventually the group drifted away from the spirituals and joined together in a rousing chorus of the *Battle Hymn of the Republic.* From there Sister Mary asked for requests, and the rest of the afternoon flew by.

Invigorated, Gracie found herself humming Irish folk songs through the five o'clock pass of medications, through the evening meal, and through rounds at nine with the night orderlies.

Before heading to her own bed, she stopped again to bid goodnight to Gilbert.

"You sound like an angel," he said as she sat on the edge of his bed.

"Me brothers and sisters tell me I screech like a stomped-on cat."

A small smile momentarily brightened his pale face. "Can you sing for me tomorrow?"

"Aye. Think of your favorite songs tonight, and I'll sing for ye when I bring yer breakfast."

He nodded as she brushed back his bangs, resisting the urge to kiss him good night. Doctor Ellard's words echoed in her head. *Private Franklin is a soldier, and I will treat him no differently than any other soldier in my care.*

With a final good night, she headed to her small sleeping area at the end of the ward.

When she first arrived, she'd shared a corner of Ward A with Sister Mary and two other lady nurses. Because the hospital had not been built to accommodate female nurses, they'd had to sleep in small partitioned areas at the end of each ward. Leticia, one of the laundry girls who slept in the corner of E, hadn't been comfortable so close to the men, and when she mentioned her fear of being ravished, Gracie petitioned Doctor Bliss for an order allowing them to switch.

Recent rumor claimed that three hundred dollars had been donated to build a separate house on the grounds for all the lady nurses, but until the weather permitted its construction, Gracie was content to stay near her patients.

Exhausted, as usual, she burrowed under her covers, and no sooner had her head hit the pillow than the sharp blasts of a bugle blared out the quick-beat notes for reveille.

She groaned. Six o'clock came much too early. Though it was tempting to pull the blankets back over her head, she tossed them aside. She hurried through her toilet and tidied her space.

Pulling on her cloak, she stepped outside, greeted by the darkness and another layer of snow. It hardly seemed possible that April would be upon them in less than two weeks. As she hurried to join the other nurses for breakfast, she tried to decide if March was supposed to go out like a lion or like a lamb.

She wrapped her cinnamon and raisin muffin in a clean handkerchief and slipped it into her pocket. Gilbert had taken less than half of the beef tea she offered him last night. If she soaked the muffin in a bit of milk, maybe she could tempt him into eating.

Humming to herself, she returned to her ward, hung up her cloak, and tied on her apron. Though she gotten good at walking on her tip-toes, her leather soles still tapped against the wood floor as she hurried up the aisle.

"Gilbert, I've a fine surpri—" She stopped.

Cold washed through her body. She stood stupidly in place staring at the empty bed as though she'd never seen one before. The red embroidered blanket was gone. In its place across the mattress, lay one of utilitarian gray, the ends tucked in neatly at the corners. A crisp starched sheet folded down like a shirt cuff over the end and a fluffed white pillow sat where Gilbert's head was supposed to be.

She clamped her teeth over her bottom lip to keep the sob at the back of her throat from escaping. How could she not have known? How could she have slept through the footsteps of the night attendants when they carried Gilbert past her room, the glow of their lamp illuminating the ceiling above the partition?

"I'm sorry, Gracie."

The major had come up beside her. She should have been happy to see him upright supported by a crutch, but at that moment there was only intense pain in the center of her chest, as if the bone pressed into her heart.

"He must have died in his sleep," the major continued. "That's something anyway."

****

"Gracie he's gone." Callum stopped half way down the stairs.

Gasping for her next ragged breath, she looked up searching her oldest brother's pale face. Wind drove the rain through the open front door behind her.

"No. I found another doctor. He's coming. He said he'll try." She pointed without turning, into the darkness behind her. Her heart should be slowing its rhythm now, not swelling painfully behind her breast bone.

"Gracie…"

"No." She gathered her skirts high and hit the first tread.

Callum turned, pressing his back tight to the wall as she raced past.

At the top of the stairs, she whirled to the left, into the bedroom she shared with William.

He lay as though sleeping, his lips slightly parted, except soft snores didn't rumble in his throat. His chest didn't rise and fall. He was too still, too pale.

"Where have you been?" Michael rose from the chair on the other side of the bed. Accusation tightened his words, tears filled his eyes. "He was asking for ye."

"A doctor," she said stupidly, tugging free the

ribbons of her bonnet and yanking it from her head.

He stepped around the footboard. He swiped at his eyes and shook his head. "'Twas too late. William knew it, too. Gracie ye cannot fix everything. William needed ye, and ye were not here."

****

She managed a slight nod for Major Carlton, afraid if she opened her mouth to speak she'd start crying. Her throat tightened, and she swung away and hurried through the door at the end of the ward.

She gathered her skirts with both hands and ran. Off the covered breezeway into the slop of snow and mud churned up by horses, wagons, and ambulances, she slipped and slid past the wards and out buildings, studiously avoiding even a glance toward the dead house, until her mad dash was cut short by the back fence.

She grasped the wooden pickets, squeezing tight, and gazed past the open ground to the dome of the Capitol building which rose above the distant tangle of barren tree branches. The yawning hole of the unfinished dome made the building look like its own casualty of war, as though it had been ripped through by a massive artillery shell.

A light rain-snow-mix fell around her, melting on her cheeks, mixing with the tears that spilled from her eyes and dripped from her jaw.

She cried for all of them. For Michael and Callum, who would never come home or tease her again. For Gilbert, who was just a little boy and should never have seen the face of war.

And her tears fell for William. She'd loved him with all her heart. She should have been there for him when he lay dying, calling her name in the night. Instead, she'd been trying to find one more doctor who might find a way to save him.

She purged it all with each breath-stealing sob, washed it from the corners of her mind where she stored painful things, until the dark sky lightened to gray and there were no more tears.

She hadn't heard him come up behind her, but she felt him with that odd sense that had developed over nearly a month together.

"Ye've no need to lurk back there like a leprechaun waiting to do mischief."

A soft snort huffed at the back of her ear, as the heavy weight of his coat dropped around her shoulders. The warmth of him enveloped her, and she closed her eyes, pressing her chin against her own shoulder, pretending it was William's coat, that it was the warmth of his body which chased away the cold.

She rubbed her cheek against the fabric and bumped the rigid corner on the shoulder strap of his captain's insignia. Damp wool and cigar, not pipe, wafted from the fabric. With a sigh she opened her eyes and raised her head. William was gone. There was only—

"Come now, Mrs. McBride you can't cry over all of them."

She sniffed but didn't turn around. "Do not tell me who to cry for."

"You knew that soldier was dying."

"Gilbert 'twas no more than a lad, far from home and afraid."

She turned and looked up at him through disheveled strands of hair that stuck to her forehead and cheeks. "I should o'been there to hold his hand, to pray for him, to comfort him so he would not have to die alone in the dark."

She swiped a strand of hair from the corner of her mouth. "But 'tis not something ye understand, is it Doctor Ellard? Ye with yer cold heart and icy ways. Ye think 'tis wrong for me to care, but patients be more than wounds and illnesses. They be people. If ye cannot concern yerself with the feelings of yer own brethren, then 'tis ye who will one day die alone in the dark."

She shrugged off his frock coat and thrust it against him. Without waiting to see if it fell to the ground, she snatched up her skirt and marched briskly back toward the ward.

Chapter Three

Snow continued to fall. Each large flake so unique, its lacy pattern could be seen for all but the briefest of moments before it dissolved against the muddy ground.

Charles leaned over and picked up his coat. Her cutting words had stabbed him like an icicle to his heart. The wound hurt more than he wanted to acknowledge, even to himself. He gave his coat a shake and raised it to his nose.

He inhaled, hoping to catch a whiff of her, but all he smelled was stale cigar and wet wool. Shrugging into the garment, he slowly buttoned.

He'd wanted to kiss her again. With the wild bits of hair stuck to her face, the dull auburn was the only bit of color in a dreary landscape of gray, white, and brown. His fingers had tingled with the urge to brush her hair aside, slip to the back of her neck, cupping her face while his thumb brushed over the porcelain skin of her cheek.

Then she'd spoken, and cold doused that impulse right down to his groin.

Taking a deep breath, he walked back to the wards. Deciding to put some space between himself and Gracie McBride he began his rounds in Ward F.

With the armies still in winter camp, the hospital received only a few patients here and there, mostly dysentery, typhoid, measles, and illness too severe for the hospital at Falmouth.

Arriving in E, he began at bed seven with his orderly Corporal Timon taking notes. Mrs. McBride was busy at the opposite end of the ward, the gangly puppy Corporal Reid trotting along behind her.

There was another one to whom she'd grown excessively attached. If something happened to Reid would she again run off alone to cry her heart out? How many times could she endure that kind of pain before something inside her died?

When he finished rounds, he dismissed Timon and approached her table. She continued to write without looking up, no doubt deliberately ignoring him.

He handed her the patient cards.

"Thank ye, Doctor." She accepted them but didn't meet his gaze. Instead she resumed her list as if it were a vital set of surgical instructions.

He easily read the upside down words.

Take extra newspapers to K
Brush out dress
Small cake for Sister M.'s birthday
Trade books with F

Though he didn't believe he'd done anything wrong, he felt the need to make up to her somehow.

"There is a lecture on glaciers tomorrow evening at the Smithsonian. If you would care to attend, I would be pleased to escort you."

She looked up.

His heart skipped a hopeful beat.

"I thank ye, but…"

He stiffened. A tiny stab of pain pricked at the wound she'd inflicted earlier.

"I've promised to go with Major Carlton."

Major Carlton. Charles had overheard conversations about the two of them. How perfectly they sang together yesterday, how they'd laughed and brightened the hearts of all the patients.

Charles might have gone to the singing, but he'd been in surgery with Major Thomas and Doctor Greene, amputating a hand that had gone gangrenous. The hand should have been taken off in the field, but the surgeon had probably hesitated, hoping for the impossible.

He searched her face. Did she care for Major Carlton, or was she merely being polite? Did she kiss the major the way she'd kissed him?

"He only has one leg," he began then realized his blunder the moment the words were out of his mouth, the moment Gracie jumped from her chair and nearly vaulted over the table.

Before she could give him a dressing down in front of the men, he swung around and strode from the ward. He didn't have to glance back to know she followed. He almost winced in sympathy for the floor as it withstood the impact of each sharp click of her heels against the planks as she marched after him.

Once outside he kept walking, trying to get someplace more private before she caught up to him. He almost made it to the storehouse, before he felt the tug on his sleeve. He stopped and turned.

"Sweet Mary Jesus, Doctor Ellard, how could ye say such a terrible thing?" For emphasis, she poked him in the center of his chest.

Her hair was dry now, as bright a fiery red as the temper which flared gold in her large brown eyes. Her spirit warmed his heart. She was so unlike the mother his grandfather had told him about, so unlike any woman he knew. He shouldn't want her, but he did, even though she'd called him cold. Maybe if he smiled.

"And ye have the nerve to be laughing about it?"

"I am not laughing."

"The corners o' yer mouth be turned up."

"When I laugh, Mrs. McBride, you will know it."

"Then why would ye say such a thing?"

"While I do admit I may have begun badly, you did not allow me to finish."

She crossed her arms. She was probably mad, and cold, but for a moment he missed watching her bosom rise and fall with each angry breath.

"What then did ye intend to say?"

"I want to know your intentions with the major."

"My intentions? My intentions are none o' yer concern."

He sighed not knowing how to explain himself without making the hole he stood in any deeper.

"I was there, Mrs. McBride, at Fredericksburg. I remember Major Carlton. He pleaded with the other doctors not to take his leg. They consulted with me, and when I saw the damage, I made the decision. He begged me not to make him half a man, but I wouldn't change my mind. He hates me for it, but I…"

He sighed and gave himself a mental shake.

"Don't lead him on, Mrs. McBride."

She stared up at him, her lips temptingly parted for speech, though she uttered no words. Her brow furrowed in thought as if he were some sort of puzzle, more challenging to solve than she originally believed.

Gradually her expression softened, and for a moment he thought she saw beyond his rank, beyond his profession, to him, Charles Ellard, the man.

"I won't," she said, then turned away.

"Wait." Of its own volition his hand reached out and grabbed her arm.

She swung around.

Their gazes collided. Her brown eyes widened with surprise.

He wanted her, in his arms, in his life, but this war left no time for dancing, for Sunday carriage rides, and summer picnics. So he stepped close, and wrapping his hands around her upper arms, he leaned down and kissed her.

As she had the other day, she kissed him back, slipping her hands to his waist, absorbing his aggressive assault. He didn't temper himself for fear of overwhelming her. She was strong enough to match him, to take from him as he took from her. She was warm, and alive, and tender, and he needed her. But the moments of pleasure, the synchronized rhythm of breath and tongues didn't last.

Her hands slipped between their bodies, and she pushed against the front of his coat.

Reluctantly, he stepped back.

"Ye can be as arrogant as an English landlord, Doctor Ellard." Her reddened lips pursed in disapproval. "'Tis flattered, I am by yer attention, but I fear I may be leading ye on by allowing ye to kiss me. Me husband has been dead now these three years, and there be times this woman's body does ache for what we shared.

"Ye be a fine man, but if ever I decide to accept the suit of another, 'twill be someone of a more gentle nature, prone to laughter and compassion, who sees me as more than a woman to clean his house and bear his children."

Mercifully, her voice trailed off. He squared his shoulders. "Do forgive me, Mrs. McBride, for taking such liberties. I'll not impose on you again."

He stepped past her and strode to the general office, managing not to glance back even once. He'd be early for his meeting, but he would not return to the ward.

He stomped off his boots the best he could on the plank walkway then entered and removing his hat, walked straight to the desk he'd occupied on Saturday.

"Captain Ellard to see Major Bliss."

The Officer-of-the-Day, Major Fenton, glanced at the appointment book and nodded to the orderly. "Corporal, go tell Major Bliss, Captain Ellard is here."

"Yes, sir." He walked past and returned a minute later.

"The major said to go on in, sir."

Without a word, Charles stepped into the hall and after a cursory knock on the door, turned the knob and entered the office of the surgeon in charge of the hospital.

"Have a seat, Captain." Major Bliss gestured toward one of the leather chairs in front of his desk.

Charles sat and crossed his legs.

Major Bliss rested his forearms on the surface of the desk and leaned forward. "I think you know why I called you in here today."

"Yes, sir." While Charles wasn't positive of the reason, he'd made an educated guess.

Major Bliss picked up a sheet of paper and extended it toward Charles. "Having personally witnessed this incident between you and Medical Cadet

Emerson in Ward E on Sunday past, I will concede that Emerson, behaved in a manner unbecoming both a medical professional and a gentleman."

Charles reached for the paper and gave it a quick read.

"However," Bliss continued. "This is a military hospital, Captain. You are an officer. You cannot vent your frustration in front of the patients like an Irish rabble-rouser at the corner pub. Emerson does have cause to press this assault charge against you."

Charles leaned forward and set the page on the desk.

"Despite your attack on that officer after Fredericksburg, I expect better of you, Captain." The major lifted the paper and glanced over the report. With the backs of his fingers, he stroked his dark sideburns which stopped just short of his chin.

"You are as bold and rapid an operative surgeon as any I've seen. Your record shows you to be conservative in your treatments and seldom mistaken in your diagnosis. Therefore, I've decided this report ends here, at my desk. To send a surgeon of your caliber to Old Capitol Prison is in my opinion the greater crime."

He set down the report, and Charles met his steady gaze across the width of the desk.

"Thank you, sir," he replied, watching as Major Bliss picked up his pen and quickly scratched something across the bottom.

When he finished he opened his desk drawer, slipped the paper inside, and withdrew another, neatly folded into an oblong tri-fold. He slid it across the oak surface to Charles.

That the writing had been so discreetly hidden

caused a frisson of unease to quicken his heartbeat.

"I believe a man of your bold temperament is better suited to the duties of a field surgeon…"

Slowly Charles opened the sheet of paper, recognizing immediately the military letterhead. Feeling strangely detached, he skimmed over the page, certain phrases capturing his attention.

Assistant Surgeon, Captain Charles P. Ellard, 69th Pennsylvania…assigned temporary duty…Armory Square Hospital at Washington, D.C.…hearby directed to report for duty on April 1st to Major Curtis Bannister, 69th Pennsylvania, 2nd Brigade, 2nd Division, 2nd Corps, at Falmouth, VA…

"…and I'm sure you will be much happier once you report back to your regiment."

With steady hands Charles refolded the orders and slipped them inside his uniform, his body too numb for his fingers to even quiver at the news.

"I trust there will be no more outbursts during this last week of your service here." Major Bliss pushed back his chair and rose.

Charles came to his feet.

"And if I may offer a bit of advice," Major Bliss tempered his words with a quick smile. "A friendlier manner and less of an inclination to put people on report, might take you a little further in life. These are dark times. Don't alienate those who stand beside you."

Charles gave him a curt nod then strode from the office, strode down the hall, around the corner to his quarters. Though tempted to slam his door, years of lectures on gentlemanly conduct won out. He closed the door with a soft click, draped his hat and coat across his desk, and opened his trunk. Shoving aside *The Army*

Surgeon's Manual and *Elements of General Pathology*, his fingers brushed the neck of the bottle he'd been hunting for. He wiggled free the cork and downed a healthy swallow of whiskey.

He would be fine. He responded to that foolish thought with a derisive snort.

He took another drink and returned the bottle to his trunk. With a shaky sigh, he stretched out on his bed, stacked his hands behind his head, and stared blankly at the whitewashed rafters.

Seven damn days.

****

"Ma'am, are these the newspapers and books?" Robbie asked setting a large crate beside Gracie's table.

She glanced across the ward from where she collected Gilbert's few personal effects. "Aye, the newspapers be going to Ward K and the books to F. Maybe ye best make two trips. I do not want ye straining yer arm."

"It ain't heavy," Robbie maintained as he lifted the crate again. "'Sides, it ain't far. I'm only goin' over one." He started toward the door.

She called after him, "And Nurse Sarah will have books to trade for those."

"Yes, ma'am," his voice drifted back.

She would miss Robbie. With a sad sigh she checked over Gilbert's area one more time. The puzzle she'd played with last evening still sat on the small table between the beds. She picked it up.

Both wooden discs now hung from the same loop of cord. The cord fed through a hole in the center of the wooden yoke. Someone had solved the puzzle during the night. Assuming they hadn't untied and retied the cord, how in the world had they moved that disc? Had Gleason, the night orderly, solved it? Major Carlton?

For the next several minutes, she pulled and turned and flipped the cord, trying to get the disc back on the original loop.

Frustrated, she dropped it into her pocket, intending to return it to the cupboard. Then gathering Gilbert's hair brush, the last letter she'd written to his mother, and the drumsticks he'd been so proud of, she headed to the knapsack room where every patient's belongings were wrapped, tagged, and stored.

She'd send the drumsticks with a new letter to the boy's mother in the morning mail, expressing her deepest condolences and asking if she wanted to come to Washington to claim her son's body or make arrangements to have him sent home.

Keeping her words properly sympathetic had been more difficult than Gracie expected, for what she wanted to do was rail at the woman for allowing her son to march off to war.

Gilbert suffered no longer, and Gracie could almost imagine Callum, Michael, and William greeting the drummer boy at the Pearly Gates, welcoming him into Heaven with a pat on the back, a good joke, and a pint raised in salute.

Robbie returned with new books to pass around, and Gracie found herself reading aloud to him and a half a dozen patients. The high seas adventure, *Two Years Before the Mast*, was so engrossing she hardly noticed how quickly the afternoon flew by until her voice grew too scratchy to continue.

She closed the book and checked her watch. Nearly five o'clock, time to begin her evening medication pass.

She set the book on her table and unlocked the medicine chest. The steward who had been assigned the medication duty had had difficulty adding and subtracting the fractions necessary to correctly calculate the doses. When Gracie offered to assume the medication duty, he'd gladly surrendered the key.

Doctor Ellard had been oddly absent all afternoon. She worried that she'd been to blunt and had hurt his feelings. He did seem to be the sort of man who preferred to deal with things in a straightforward manner. However, in looking back she may have said those things more to remind herself of the reasons Doctor Ellard would not suit.

While he had been shockingly forward in presuming to kiss her, she never should have kissed him back. Her behavior had been improper and had undoubtedly led him to believe she returned his affections.

There was no doubt she was attracted to him physically, but it was just as she'd told him. She missed William, the way he used to come up behind her, hook his arm around her, and kiss the side of her neck. She missed lying beside him, wrapped in his arms while they whispered and laughed together in the night. And she missed the taste of him, the tingle of his callused hands sliding over her flesh, and that sense of completeness when she held him inside her as they made love.

A sigh escaped her lips, and a smile tugged them up at the corners.

Doctor Ellard's kisses were nothing like William's. They were a full-on assault to her senses, and while they stirred a dormant need inside her, after sharing two of them she wondered if the man even knew how to be gentle, if he knew anything of consideration, of giving instead of taking.

While she knew his views on the place of women in this war were no different from that of every other man and even many women, for some reason she'd foolishly expected more from him.

What she'd had with William had been special. He treated her as an equal at home, in bed, and in his practice. He'd been her best friend, and she knew now she would never have that with another man.

At least she felt closer to William here. The great ache in the center of her chest didn't hurt as much among the patient cards and bandages. And while she no longer expected him to walk through the door, as she did when she was home, at least here she had the feeling that William was proud of her, that he was happy she was using the knowledge and skills he'd taught her.

She stopped at bed twenty-four and smiled at the blond man lying there. Corporal Nathan Bennett, camp fever. "How are ye feeling, tonight?"

"Better, ma'am."

"Less pain?"

He nodded.

She checked his forehead. "Ye seem a bit cooler." Still, she gave him the ordered opium pill and replaced his cold compresses. "And be sure ye eat a bit o' something tonight."

With a smile, she gave his shoulder a pat and moved on with her medicines.

Camp fever and dysentery seemed to be the most common diseases of the patients in her ward. While she'd yet to experience the flood of wounded after a battle, she heard about the chaos from hospital stewards, orderlies, and the male nurses that still remained.

"Ma'am," Robbie called out as he hurried up to the bed where she was changing the dressing of a patient with an inflammation of the hand. "Ya gotta come."

Instead of seeing the usual exuberant boy, at this moment, Gracie caught a glimpse of Robbie the man, his grim expression every bit as intense as Doctor Ellard's.

She shoved the bandages into her pocket, locked the medicine chest, and hastened down the wide aisle beside him.

"It's Uncle Mark, ma'am, he cain't breathe. It's bad, it's real bad."

Robbie's uncle, Sergeant Mark Baker had arrived on Saturday afternoon with a high fever and suffering from quinsy.

Now each wheezy gasp for breath could be heard before they reached his bed. "Go find a doctor," she whispered urgently. "Then fetch Doctor Ellard. Hurry."

"Yes'um," Robbie replied and dashed toward the door.

Gracie stepped up beside the sergeant's bed. His whole body seemed to rise and fall as he struggled to find air. She reached toward him, intending to brush the hair from his forehead in a comforting gesture that had become automatic. Instead his broad hand grabbed onto hers and squeezed with the desperation of a drowning man.

She met his gaze, his eyes wide and terrified. Her heart raced. He was dying and looking to her for help.

What to do? What to do?

Leaning over, she lay her hand against his bristly cheek and forced what she hoped was a reassuring smile. "Ye'll be fine. The doctor's coming." Though the man was older than Doctor Ellard, she talked to him in the same low, soothing tones she'd used with Gilbert, as she loosened the first few buttons of his shirt.

"Now, let go o' me hand. I need to grab ye an extra pillow."

Carefully, she pried loose from his grip. Reaching behind his head with both hands, she yanked up the mattress frame, pulling against the sergeant's weight to raise the head of the bed upright and lock the bar in place. Turning, she grabbed pillows from the closest beds. Around her, the growing crowd of ambulatory patients had formed a semicircle.

She slipped her arm beneath the sergeant's shoulders and jammed in the pillows to support him fully upright.

Behind her came the hurried footfalls of two people. With a glance over her shoulder, she spotted an older doctor in a black frock coat.

"Out of my way," he snapped as he pushed through the men. If she remembered his name correctly, it was Colfax. He had his own practice in Washington somewhere and worked in the hospital a few days a week. Behind Doctor Colfax trotted the young medical cadet, Emerson, who'd foolishly challenged Doctor Ellard on Sunday morning.

"Having some breathing trouble?" Doctor Colfax asked as he stepped up to the bed and shooed his hand at Gracie with an impatient gesture to move aside.

She rose and tried to step away so the doctor could

examine the sergeant, but Robbie's uncle grabbed her hand and wouldn't let go. She was not about to force him. The poor man's lips had turned purpley-blue, and he was now only able to draw short, hiccupping breaths.

Doctor Colfax felt around the man's throat for a moment. "Open wide," he said.

The sergeant raised his helpless gaze to Gracie, his fingers squeezing the circulation from hers.

"I do not think he can, Doctor."

From the other side of the bed, Cadet Emerson said, "There seems to be an obstruction in his throat."

Help him! Gracie wanted to scream.

The sergeant kept his gaze locked on Gracie's. His brown eyes widened. The muscles of his face tightened, and the cords of his neck stood out as his tiny gasps grew more shallow.

She forced a half smile and wrapped her other hand around his. Tears burned at the back of her eyes, but she would not let go. Sergeant Mark Baker would not die alone.

"You should have been quicker to summon me, nurse." Doctor Colfax stepped back.

"Yes, nurse," Cadet Emerson parroted. "You should have called us sooner."

The sergeant drew one more tiny gasp then stopped breathing.

In the background she heard the long deliberate stride of Doctor Ellard, quickly drawing close. She glanced back. The group of patients parted. Robbie, close in height to Doctor Ellard, mirrored him stride for stride, as though he were his shadow, a small wooden case in his hands.

"You're too late," Cadet Emerson stated smugly. "He's not breathing."

Doctor Ellard fixed his icy blue glare on the young medical cadet and shoved him aside. "My patient needs air, and you're using it. Get out."

"Now see here," Doctor Colfax sputtered.

"Get the hell out of my ward." Doctor Ellard waved Robbie forward as he removed his heavy blue frock coat and tossed it onto the nearby bed.

Robbie set the case on the table between the beds and stepped back, bumping into Cadet Emerson. The medical cadet shot Robbie a dirty look, but Robbie replied with his own icy blue glare.

Doctor Ellard slipped his arm behind the sergeant, supporting his limp torso as he dropped the bed level. Gracie snatched away the remaining pillows, and Doctor Ellard lowered the sergeant flat on the thin mattress.

Then opening the wooden case, he withdrew from the red velvet lining a small knife and a silver tube. Extending his arm across the sergeant, he passed Gracie the tube.

Blowing out a long breath, he stared at his outstretched fingers. They trembled slightly. She'd seen his hands shake one other time, right before he cut away some dead tissue around a poorly healing head wound.

Now he opened and closed his fists a few times, then exhaled again.

Catching the scent of whiskey, Gracie frowned. She hadn't believed him a drinking man, but before she could think any more about it, Doctor Ellard had taken the knife and made a vertical incision from the middle of the sergeant's throat to the base.

"You're making that cut to low." Doctor Colfax hovered behind Gracie. "Protocol dictates the incision be made higher on the throat."

Ignoring him, she watched with fascination as Doctor Ellard held the skin open with his thumb and forefinger and made another smaller horizontal cut inside that opening.

Colfax leaned over Gracie's shoulder. The man snorted derisively. Gracie rolled her shoulder against the huff of breath that fanned her ear. He was a fine one, to offer advice now, to the only man who even tried to save Sergeant Baker.

"This procedure is nearly futile under the best of circumstances, and you're cutting between the second and third ring. If there is to be any hope you must be above the fifth."

Gracie pulled some extra sponges from her apron pocket and captured the blood which flowed from the wound. She tried to block out the annoying man the way Doctor Ellard had, so focused on what he was doing, he didn't appear to even hear what Colfax said.

"Most all these patients die, fracture of the tracheal rings, loss of airway, or hemorrhage."

Before Doctor Ellard could ask, she passed him the silver tube. The moment he slipped it into the hole she heard the unmistakable escape of breath and the sergeant's chest began to naturally rise and fall.

Her own breath caught, awed by the miracle Doctor Ellard had just performed. She lifted her gaze to his face, but his expression remained preoccupied as he grabbed her hand and tugged it close to the tube.

"Hold this."

Her fingers tips wrapped around the blood-slicked metal.

Reaching into his box, he withdrew a chamois cloth poked through with various needles. Quickly threading one of the small curved ones, he stitched the wound closed around the tube.

Gracie blotted away as much of the blood as she could with the bottom of her apron. When he knotted the last stitch, he gave her a nod, and she slowly lifted her hand away from the tube.

"Corporal Reid," he called, closing up his case.

"Yes, sir?" Robbie stepped forward.

"Find a stretcher and some attendants and transport this man over to surgery immediately. I'll meet you there."

"Yes, sir." He swung around and darted into the crowd.

Gracie stood, wiping her hands on her apron. She passed him an eight-yard roll of bandage from her pocket, and he wrapped it around the sergeant's neck.

When he finished tying the ends, he lifted his head, and their gazes met. The normal icy glint in his blue eyes melted, and he gave her a nod that somehow warmed her spirit like the highest praise.

She smiled back so elated by what they'd just shared, that she nearly threw her arms around his neck and hugged him.

But the sergeant lay between them, and a crowd of patients surrounded them, so she continued to wipe her hands, reminding herself that Charles Ellard wasn't William.

"I could have performed that operation," Doctor Colfax declared. "If I'd had my tracheotomy tubes."

Doctor Ellard shot the man a disbelieving glare. He slipped on his coat, tucked his case under his arm, and shouldered his way between the unyielding bodies of Emerson and Doctor Colfax.

The patients again quietly stepped aside for Doctor Ellard to pass. All heads turned to watch him walk up the aisle. The thud of his boot heels against the floor was the only sound as his long deliberate stride took him to the end of the ward and out the door.

As soon as it clicked shut, the ward erupted with the buzz of conversation.

"Arrogant ass," Doctor Colfax muttered under his breath.

Gracie gasped.

Doctor Colfax swung toward her. "He's not God, you know."

"Aye. But he be a closer relative than you."

He inhaled a sharp breath of air, then spun around and pushed his way through the gathered patients, Medical Cadet Emerson trailing in his wake.

Chapter Four

Robbie returned a few minutes later with a stretcher and men to transport the sergeant to the surgery. Gracie grabbed the blanket from an empty bed and tucked its extra warmth around the man before the attendants carried him from the ward.

Once they left, she hurried to her room to wash the blood from her hands and change her apron. Before tossing it into the pile of soiled linens for the laundry, she checked the pockets—a pencil, a length of bandage, and the puzzle.

Someone had sat beside Gilbert that night and solved it. She pulled the cord until it formed a large loop then slipped the yoke through the loop, but the disc remained on the same loop. Frustrated, she carried the puzzle back to the cabinet behind her table and tossed it into the box with the other puzzles.

****

Robbie was collecting dishes, and Gracie was spoon-feeding beef tea to a sick corporal, when the sergeant was returned to the ward and tucked into bed. Doctor Ellard checked the thick bandage around the man's throat then made a few notes on the patient card.

When the broth was gone, she carried the dishes to Robbie and started down the aisle. Doctor Ellard met her half way and passed her the card.

"I removed his tonsils. The tube is gone, but make

certain the night orderly knows to send for me immediately if there is the slightest problem."

She nodded and glanced at the card for instructions as to diet and medicines. The handwriting was barely legible, but she was able to decipher his scrawl.

Silence stretched between them. At that moment she wished they were arguing again.

She glanced up.

He looked poised to say something then seemed to change his mind. "Good evening," he said instead.

Disappointed that he didn't want to stay and talk, she moved aside as he stepped past her. Her shoulders slumped. She released a weary sigh and stared after him as he continued through the ward and out the door.

Returning to her table, she recopied the medication notes for the steward to pick up the medicine from the dispensary. Setting down her pencil, she rose and stretched her lower back.

Across the ward, Gilbert's bed stood empty. It had been such a long day she'd hardly had time to think about the poor child. How could she have forgotten him so quickly?

She'd only known him a few weeks, but he had touched her life. She glanced up and down the ward. Half the beds were empty right now, but once the spring campaigns began, more men would arrive to fill them. No one stayed. They passed away, went home, or returned to the war. It did her no good to get attached. Maybe Doctor Ellard had the right of it.

Gleason arrived, and she gave him the key to the medicine chest. They briefly discussed Doctor Ellard's notes on the sergeant, and she headed to bed.

As she passed the sergeant, she saw his eyes were

open. Stepping close beside his bed she smiled.

He silently mouthed, *Thank you*. He lifted his hand, and she wrapped her fingers around his icy digits.

"Are ye warm enough? Maybe we can move yer bed closer to one o'the stoves."

Soundlessly he drew both their hands closer to his throat and mouthed, *Thank you*, again.

She shook her head. "'Twas Doctor Ellard saved ye."

He gave his head a slight shake and squeezed her hand.

Tears filled his eyes.

Her eyes stung as she accepted his gratitude for her small part in saving him. She bit her lower lip then nodded. "Ye are welcome."

Holding his hand, she sat beside him and remained in the chair by his bed, long after he fell asleep.

****

She missed breakfast the next morning, so exhausted she hadn't even heard the bugle blow reveille. Tying on her apron, she hurried from her room at the end of the ward, down the wide aisle, to her table.

Doctor Ellard had already begun his rounds, Corporal Timon following behind jotting instructions in his notebook.

Robbie sat in her chair examining two odd-shaped blocks of wood. He stood as she approached. "I was wonderin' if ya was all right."

"A wee bit tired is all." She glanced around. "Have the men all had their breakfast?"

"Yes, ma'am. Me and Micah and Harvey got all the beds changed, too."

"Ye did a fine job, Robbie. I'll sorely miss ye when

ye go back to yer regiment."

He picked up the wooden blocks, studying them intently as he spoke. "I ain't much for letter writin' and such, but I'd be right pleased iffen you'd write to me."

She smiled, smoothing the back of her skirt before lowering herself onto the chair.

"O'course I'll write. I be as fond o'ye as me own brother." She withdrew a pencil from her pocket along with a small notepad. Carefully she wrote, *Cpl. Robert Reid*, then waited.

"Seventh West Virginia, Second Corps at Falmouth," he added. "Reckon it'll get to me."

"I'll send ye all the news from Armory Square."

Robbie brought the blocks in his hand together, turned one, and held them together again.

"What have ye there?"

"Micah found it by Uncle Mark's bed. I mean Sergeant Baker. It was together. He took it apart and reckoned he could put it back again, but he couldn't do it. He give it to me, but I cain't do it neither."

She watched as Robbie made several attempts to fit the halves together. The puzzle hadn't been there when she'd gone to bed in the early hours of the morning. Perhaps Gleason, the night orderly had cleverly worked this puzzle as well as the yoke and disc puzzle.

Each block was identical, with sloping sides. Each side had pegs and hollows which slid back and forth, so when the pegs and hollows came together correctly, they interlocked, joining the halves.

"Micah says iffen ya put the two pieces together it makes a pyramid." He shook his head and set the blocks on the table. She picked them up and tried putting them together, but couldn't figure it out.

From down the ward, Doctor Ellard barked something at Corporal Timon.

Robbie leaned close and whispered, "Cap'n Ellard ain't in a very good mood. He already put Harvey and Micah on report an' he's been yellin' at Corporal Timon since he got here."

"Why don't ye check the linen room for me and pick up some lint and bandages." She jotted the quantities on a piece of paper and passed it to him. "Take yer time, and when ye get back, Doctor Ellard will be done his rounds."

Robbie snatched the paper from her fingers with a grateful smile and hurried off as Doctor Ellard approached the table.

He passed her the stack of cards. "You were late."

Despite the frown marring the line of his brow, she met his pale blue gaze and flashed her brightest smile. "I be sitting up with Sergeant Baker last night and overslept." She took the cards and set them beside a blank sheet of paper.

"Coddling the patients again? It won't do, Mrs. McBride."

She searched his face and wondered if he was deliberately picking a fight.

"It will do, Doctor Ellard. Sergeant Baker nearly died, and he rested easier knowing there be someone beside him in the dark, knowing he wasn't alone if his breathing stopped again."

"The orderly was given instructions to come and get me, was he not?"

"O'course."

"Then he would have been fine."

"He was afraid."

"He is a soldier."

She shook her head at a loss for words to counter his argument. Did the man possess even one ounce of compassion?

"If you exhaust yourself staying up all night with one patient, the efficiency of this hospital is compromised, and likewise the quality of care the rest of the patients receive."

She pushed to her feet. "After I give instructions to the orderly at nine o'clock, me time is me own. And I'll be spending it where I will."

He placed his hands on the table and leaned closer. "Not if what you do affects this hospital and my patients."

Gracie planted her fists on the table and leaned toward him so that mere inches separated their noses. "On me sainted mother, ye know nothing I've done has hurt the patients. Ye be no more than an overgrown bully, Doctor Ellard."

His nostrils flared, and his clear blue eyes narrowed. In the late morning light, each dark hair of his beard was visible, and she clenched her fist tighter, angry with herself now for wanting to trace his jaw-line.

"I, a bully?" He bit out each word with disdain. "It is you lady nurses who are bullies."

She drew an indignant gasp.

"None of you belong here. You waltz into the hospital with your smiles and blushes, exciting the patients. Then you hang curtains and pictures and rearrange the wards. Next you quietly change my orders, because your grandmother's herbal recipe is better than the medicine I've prescribed…"

Some of the tension eased from her shoulders. At least he wasn't talking about her. She'd heard that Nurse Sarah in Ward F, constantly changed the orders on the patient cards.

"…then you run to Major Bliss and use your womanly tears to manipulate him in your favor." He leaned in closer.

She didn't back away, even as his nose just missed bumping hers.

"I am not an ogre, Mrs. McBride."

The warmth of his breath brushed across her mouth. She stared at his lips, so temptingly close. "I know," she whispered.

Her tongue flicked out to moisten her suddenly dry lips, and her heart beat quickened. She ached to feel the power of his kiss, the unique taste of—

No! These feelings were wrong. William couldn't be replaced by the first man to stir her senses in three years. And while Doctor Ellard might be attracted to her, he didn't respect her as a nurse.

Besides they were in the middle of the hospital ward with more eyes on them than she cared to think about. She straightened, her fingers gripping the edge of the table.

He seemed to draw into himself then, stepping back from the table, his stiffened spine making him appear taller. With a curt nod, he swung away and started down the length of the ward.

She released a long breath and dropped heavily into the chair. Sweet Mary Jesus, could the Father in Heaven have created a man any more powerful than Charles Ellard? He drained her emotions and left her exhausted every time she stood in his presence.

Scooting forward she picked up the cards, trying to remember what she needed to do.

She snapped her fingers and jumped to her feet—*Sergeant Baker.*

"Doctor Ellard," she called grasping her skirt and darting around the table. "Doctor Ellard, could ye wait, please?"

He stopped but didn't turn around until she stood behind him. Frost once more edged the blue of his eyes.

Squaring her shoulders, she raised her chin. "I only want to ask ye about moving Sergeant Baker closer to the stove."

"No."

"But there be a chill there, near the side door."

"No. I'm not switching his bed assignment. Give him an extra blanket."

"'Twould only be a simple changing o' the number on his card."

"Are you trying to prove my point?"

Her fingers itched to rub away the ache forming across her forehead. "The best interests of the patient be all I'm trying prove."

"You are a tease, Mrs. McBride. You look at me with want in your eyes, then push me away. And now, when I can't stop thinking about kissing you, you try to manipulate me into changing a bed assignment."

Planting her hands on her hips she took one step closer. "Ye are an arrogant ass, Doctor Ellard. I do not manipulate ye. I be asking ye straight out, not going behind yer back. I be not the kind of woman to tease a man with waving fans and batting eyelashes. If I want to kiss ye, Doctor Ellard, I'll grab ye by yer cravat and pull yer mouth down to mine."

He took a step toward her and leaned forward, his mouth close to her ear. "I don't think so, Mrs. McBride."

Goose flesh rippled over her body.

"Because if I ever see that hungry look in your big brown eyes again, my mouth will devour yours before your fingers have a chance to touch my cravat." Then he spun on his heels and continued toward the door.

Gracie rubbed the tickle from her ear wishing she had something to throw. She stomped her foot instead. And though she heard no laughter, she was certain the infuriating man was smiling.

****

Charles lay staring at the rafters above his bed, or what would be the rafters if there'd been enough light to see them. While the dark suited his mood, if he had something to look at, he might have been able to block the picture he held in his mind of Gracie McBride dressed in lavender.

That was the color he'd buy, if he ever had the right to purchase a dress for her. His mother had loved that color.

"My dress isn't purple, sweetie, it's lavender like the lilacs outside the back door." Except he couldn't remember there ever being lilacs outside the back door.

He'd only known Gracie a month, but the black she constantly wore was depressing.

He'd watched her earlier, doggedly pushing Major Carlton's chair across the wide street. Navigating around the green, now patched with snow, Gracie and the major continued toward the Smithsonian.

They hadn't been aware Charles had stood there at the corner of the fence, beside the tree, wrapped in the evening shadow. He'd held a cheroot in his fingers but hadn't lit it until they were absorbed into the silhouette of the castle-like building.

As he exhaled a stream of smoke, the faint lilt of feminine laughter drifted to his ears. Was it Gracie? Had the major said something clever? Charles had heard her laugh on the ward many times, but he'd never been the one to inspire it. All he managed to do was arouse her anger.

He'd drawn on his cigar a few more times, until night shrouded the brick spires and his toes grew numb inside his boots. Then he'd turned and reluctantly walked to his quarters.

Preparing himself for bed, images of Gracie McBride replayed behind his eyes, like the melody of a song he couldn't forget. His eyes perceived his desk, his trunk, the small commode with the pitcher and basin, yet his mind still saw the way Gracie floated above the sidewalk, her bell-shaped crinoline hiding all movement of her lower limbs.

Last week he'd caught a surprising glimpse of those limbs as she'd rolled around on the floor of the ward with that thieving attendant. Her legs had been encased in black wool stockings and tangled in layers of petticoats, but his eye had been drawn straight to her narrow ankles and the shapely curve of her calf. He'd never be able to erase that image, even if he wanted to, for beneath her serviceable charcoal dress, Gracie McBride had worn a red petticoat.

Rolling onto his stomach, he tried to squash the growing ache in his groin, the growing ache in his heart. He gripped the pillow with both hands and asked himself why any of it mattered. In five days he'd be leaving for Falmouth.

He certainly hadn't endeared himself to her in any way over the past twenty-nine days, especially when he kissed her. She'd responded as though she wanted him, but that was where he'd made the mistake. She liked the way he'd claimed her mouth, brushed his lips against hers and caressed her tongue with his, but she'd made it clear she didn't like the man who kissed her. Maybe if he could make her laugh, she would find him more tolerable.

A joke. He needed to think of a joke so funny it would bring a smile to her lips every time she remembered it, and cause her to think of him long after he was gone.

He sighed and burrowed his face deeper into his pillow. The tension in his shoulders eased then returned as he searched futilely through his mental file drawer for an amusing anecdote. He must have heard a joke or two in his life, but he'd be damned if he could recall a single one.

There had been a classmate at school who had found almost everything around him funny. Harry's laughter was so contagious that even if Charles had been sprawled on his bed immersed in a book, he'd find himself snickering without even knowing why.

There were no chuckles when Harry laughed, no hoots, or snorts, or giggles, just full-throated laughter which rose straight from his diaphragm to fill the room, or rooms, or the dormitory's entire first floor and maybe even the second floor. It was deep and rumbling like a fog horn in a lighthouse or the blasting of a bugle. No, not a bugle, a trombone maybe.

Wait—bugle? Bugle meant wounded.

Charles blinked against the darkness. The trumpeting sound came again as the general ward master announced wounded at the steamboat landing.

Damn, it wasn't a dream. He shoved his face deeper into the warmth of his pillow. Would he ever get a full night's sleep? The night surgeon and orderlies could deal with the latest arrivals. The new patients might not even be assigned to his wards. Except that his wards held the most empty beds and the most critical patients.

He should at least get up and check. If it was nothing but dysentery and measles, he'd come right back.

Shoving aside his covers, he rolled to his feet and without bothering to light a lamp, stepped into his trousers and boots by rote. He pulled his suspenders over his shoulders and headed outside. Cold air drove the sleep from his eyes while his long legs took him swiftly down the plank walk.

An ambulance stood backed up behind Ward E. The horses stamped impatiently in their harnesses. The attendant jumped from his seat beside the driver and darted around the vehicle to open the back of the ambulance.

The sour stench of urine and gangrenous flesh wafted out. The attendant turned his head away, gagged, and swung back to his duty as though fighting waves of nausea was an experience he'd dealt with countless times before.

Charles grabbed the end of the closest stretcher and helped move the patient inside.

They lowered him to the floor, and Charles hunkered down for his examination.

A dark splotch covered one side of the thick bandage which wrapped around the man's head.

Charles' heart began its frantic rhythm. He swallowed and tried to draw a deep breath. He could do this. This wasn't Fredericksburg.

The yellow stripe of cavalry traced the outside of the wounded soldier's pant legs above his boots. Possibly a saber or pistol wound.

Charles struggled against the image in his mind of a blood-soaked head, of blood pooling in a dark puddle on the cobblestones.

Fabric whished, and in his periphery he caught a glimpse of black skirt as Gracie stepped close beside him. He raised his gaze to her face. He would focus on her. Not think about the head wound before him.

She offered no smile as she stood poised with her pencil, new cards, and her memorandum book. She merely acknowledged him with a slight nod before she fell back into the quiet efficiency that was Gracie McBride.

The attendant and Micah set down a second wounded man.

Gracie knelt beside him, checking the card pinned to his uniform.

Lamp light flickered like gold in her auburn hair. Her single long braid traced the length of her spine from the top of her collar to the bow of her apron ties. No doubt she too had been sleeping. A fleeting image of her dressed in nightclothes, with that glorious red hair spilling across the white of her sheets and pillow, had him drawing a deep breath before turning his attention back to the head wound.

"They told me at the steamboat landing," the

attendant offered, "that there was a cavalry skirmish on Tuesday at Kelly's Ford. Reckon these fellows were too bad off to stay at Falmouth." He pointed to the patient he'd just brought in.

Charles nodded and leaned over the man who lay on the floor in front of him. "Bring that lantern closer," he snapped to no one in particular. "And get me some clean bandages."

A whish of fabric and a small white hand held the light close.

His hands visibly shaking, he clenched them into fists and glanced at Gracie.

She met his gaze and gave him a slight nod.

Encouraged, he knelt and carefully untied the end of the thick dressing then slowly unwound the cloth from the patient's head. His pulse raced and a crushing weight pressed against his chest.

Gracie gasped.

He struggled to breathe.

Wide laceration across the scalp, skull fractured—

Though it was dark, tiny white spots like stars on a summer night filled his vision. He squeezed his eyes tight for a moment and gave his head a shake. Focus.

—depressed area approximately two by two—

He struggled to breath. Each breath was like trying to draw air through a pillow.

—bone splintered, brain matter exposed.

The ward tilted. Instinctively, he put his hand out to steady himself. The world spun crazily. Sweat dampened his clammy forehead.

Not now!

A hand pressed down on his shoulder.

"Doctor Ellard? What's wrong? Are ye all right?"

The hand slid lower, following the length of his spine, rubbing up and down between his scapulae. He closed his eyes and concentrated on that hand, Gracie's hand, moving up and down, up and down. The warmth of her palm, heated his tense muscles through the linen of his shirt. He tried to match his breathing to the movement. Gradually, his brain focused on her words.

"If there is naught to be done for the poor soul, let me rewrap the wound with a fresh bandage."

What was wrong with him? He was a surgeon. He was in charge. He was supposed to have the answers. How could he ever open his eyes and face her?

He shrugged away from the comfort of her hand.

"Are ye better now, doctor?"

Ignoring her, he drew a deep breath and wiped his damp palms down the front of his thighs. He focused his attention on the brain injury before him.

The surgeons at Falmouth evidently decided the delicate removal of shattered bone would be best performed in a hospital. Aside from making this patient comfortable, there was nothing more Charles could do. Not without a repeat of the fiasco at Fredericksburg.

An orderly returned holding clean white bandages. Though it felt like an eternity as he'd struggled to breathe, evidently not much time had passed. Had anyone besides Gracie noticed his silent struggle?

Charles accepted the width of rolled cotton from the orderly.

Gracie touched his arm and held out her hand.

Without meeting her gaze, he passed it all to Gracie.

If the patient was still alive later, he'd take him to the surgery and check for any bone fragments and hair the field surgeon might have missed.

"Be careful with this man," he told the attendants. "When Mrs. McBride has finished, cut off this filthy uniform and put him to bed, down on the end, behind the curtain. And mind his head. Then find Major Greene. Have him take a look and decide what's to be done."

"Can ye not tr—"

"No."

He moved to the next stretcher leaving the head wound to Gracie's care.

Aside from his previous attack at Fredericksburg, it had been years since he'd experienced an episode so debilitating.

He'd been slow to mature, and the other boys at school taunted him mercilessly for his youthful voice and his lack of body hair. To avoid confrontations, he bathed early in the morning and always used the dormitory's back staircase to and from classes. Returning late from the library one evening, he'd found Randall Graham crumpled at the bottom, his head and face covered in blood from a skull fracture.

Charles had been so overwhelmed and unable to breathe from a nervous attack he'd been powerless to even call for help. Another student had come upon them and summoned aid.

The incident hadn't improved his relationship with the other boys, and like Fredericksburg the episode only served to generate whispers behind his back.

Shaking off the unpleasant memories, he focused on the patient.

Carefully he pulled back the soldier's bloody coat and shirt, revealing a blood-soaked bandage wrapped around the soldier's abdomen. The sour bite of sweat and urine filled Charles' nose, and he frowned. Unconscious. High fever.

Air had stiffened the cloth so that Charles was hesitant to pull it off, knowing he'd start the wound bleeding again.

"Scissors."

As if speaking the word conjured the instrument, they appeared in front of him inside a pool of lantern light. Without a thought to their appearance, he accepted them from the outstretched hand and snipped away pieces of bloody bandage, which disappeared before he had a chance to toss them aside.

Carefully, he pulled back the rigid cloth to reveal a small entry hole a few inches to the left of the man's navel. The lantern light moved closer, illuminating the soldier's abdomen. Peering close, Charles inspected the entry wound.

Taking hold of the man's hip and shoulder, Charles rolled the man onto his side.

Gracie shifted around and tugged the man's coat, vest, and shirt up, holding them while Charles cut away the rest of the wrapping.

Carefully, he lifted off a palm-sized patch of bloodied linen which covered another small hole in the lower back. Thin watery discharge oozed from the wound, and Charles' nostrils flared in response to the foul coppery odor.

A simple in and out, probably the round ball of a horse soldier's pistol. If there hadn't been too much damage to the internal organs, the man might make it. Abdominal wounds from a round ball, rather than the conical ball, had a greater chance of survival.

But something nagged at him. He stared at the small wound and rather than rebandage, he leaned closer. Without the brightness of daylight, it was difficult even if he'd known what he was looking for.

A swath of lantern light suddenly bathed the area. Frowning, he stared at the wound and sniffed. Gunpowder, not necrotic tissue, discolored the rim of the tiny hole. And like the opposite wound, the edge of the skin was inverted. The skin of an exit wound would be flared out, the hole larger.

Damn it, had the surgeon at Falmouth looked for two bullets or had he just assumed an in-and-out, bandaged the man, and sent him on his way? Charles eased the patient onto his back. Just to be certain, he checked the size of the wound in the front to be certain it was also an entry wound.

"This man needs to get to surgery." He straightened, and his gaze fell to Gracie, holding the lantern. The yellow up-light deepened the shadows beneath her eyes and created a ghostly cast to her face. This was why women didn't belong here. They were suited for the task of caring for a family and home, not an entire army.

"Don't come to the ward tomorrow," he said. "Take the day off."

She met his gaze as he stood. Shoulders back, she drew a breath as if to speak, but he cut off any possible argument.

"Sleep late, go shopping for bows and ribbons, before this place crushes your delicate nature."

A bright pink blush swept across her cheeks.

Error, the small voice inside his head warned.

She planted her fist on her hip then drew herself up

so that if he hugged her, his chin would rest nicely on her head.

"My nature be no more delicate than yers, Doctor Ellard. Me family come from famine to carve out a new life in this country. As a young lass, I worked for me wages, and I'll not have you treat me like a spoiled society miss. Ye'd be further along in this life, Doctor Ellard, if you spent less o'yer time with silly girls and more of it with real women."

He'd done it again. Made her mad, when all he wanted was to protect her from becoming fatigued, from letting this place destroy her passion for life, from becoming as damaged as he. Once again, he asked himself why her opinion of him mattered. He didn't care what anyone else thought of him, why her?

"Suit yourself, Mrs. McBride," he said then turned away and headed to the surgery. As he walked, he wondered if any of the booksellers in Washington carried a book about jokes.

Chapter Five

Gracie hated to admit it, but Doctor Ellard had been right in recommending a day away from the hospital, although it probably wouldn't hurt for him to follow his own advice. He always seemed so confident, so in control of every aspect of his life, it had thrown her off balance to see him nearly faint last night.

The head wound had been horrific, and she'd nearly lost her dinner when the bandage had been removed. But to see Doctor Ellard so vulnerable had shaken her sensibilities more than the sight of the actual brain.

She tried not to think about him or the hospital as she and Sister Mary walked to the capital to listen to the debates in Congress. Later they perused the overflowing shelves of a small book seller's shop before eating dinner in a restaurant.

Gracie was reluctant to let Sister Mary pay, but her friend insisted. Her parish had sent the money for Mary's personal use to supplement the forty cents a day the army paid them to administer to the sick and wounded. No one would mind if Gracie used some of it to purchase a bar of scented soap, a tin of toothpowder, and a jar of honey for her tea.

Returning to the hospital that evening so mentally refreshed and invigorated, Gracie took a long stroll around the hospital grounds. Awed by the vast expanse of stars in the clear black sky, she stopped near the general office and tipped her head back. She'd heard the sky went on forever, that it had no end. How could scientists know for certain? Although if there actually was an end, what existed beyond that, and beyond that? And where was Heaven? Could William see her? Or Callum or Michael?

"Good evening, Mrs. McBride."

Gracie gasped, jolted back to earth. She took a step to keep from losing her balance as she sought the person with the voice she didn't quite recognize.

"Beautiful sky, is it not?" Doctor Bliss walked up beside her. "I bet it's even prettier away from the city lights."

"Yes, sir."

"I'm glad to see you finally took some time away from the hospital. As I told you when you arrived, a day to yourself each week and a daily walk is strongly recommended."

"Sister Mary and I had a lovely time."

"Good, glad to hear it. It will be a good thing for you lady nurses once the new quarters are built. The funds have been donated, so hopefully construction will begin as soon as the weather warms."

"I do not mind being near the patients."

"Yes, well…" His voice trailed off as he seemed to search for what he really wanted to say. "If you have a few minutes, I'd like to discuss something with you."

"Certainly."

He gestured for her to accompany him inside the building, and she followed him to his office. He held the door for her then left it open as she took a seat in front of his desk.

She tried not to fidget, but she wondered what she'd done wrong. Had Doctor Ellard made a complaint? Had he been upset to learn she'd adjusted the knots on the T-bandage used to hold Private Morrison's catheter in place? William had taught her how to do it. She'd noticed they were loose when she changed his bed the day before. Normally, it was the steward's job, and the man had been angry when he learned what she'd done. Said he was a medical student, she was only a woman, and that he was registering a complaint with Doctor Ellard.

William had given her life purpose beyond that of childbearing and tending house. She'd come here to help, to do good with all that he'd taught her, but her skills and insights were constantly rejected, merely because she was a woman.

Doctor Bliss seated himself behind his desk and absently stroked his thick sideburns. "You've been here nearly a month. How are things going for you?"

"Fine, Doctor." She laced her fingers together in her lap and rubbed her thumb against her palm.

"You and Captain Ellard seem to get on well together."

She nodded. "Doctor Ellard be a fine surgeon."

"I know he can be somewhat abrasive in nature and he, well…let's just say he can drive grown men to either tears or thoughts of murder."

She snickered. "They be thoughts I've had me own self."

A quick grin tugged up the corner of his mouth. "You work closely with the man every day, yet you are the only person at this hospital who has not registered a complaint about him."

"Any issues I be having, I take straight to the man. You can be sure, nary a day passes we don't have words, but we understand each other. He is a fine doctor, and I'd want no other for me or mine."

He chuckled. "Glad to hear it." His posture stiffened slightly, and his smile faded. "As I said, I receive many, many complaints about Doctor Ellard, so many in fact that it becomes difficult to separate the wheat from the chaff as it were."

Gracie's thumb pressed deep against the center of her palm. A quiver of dread rippled through her stomach.

"Captain Ellard will know nothing of our conversation tonight. I will keep everything between us completely confidential, so please answer truthfully, Mrs. McBride."

Sweet Mary Jesus, what had the fool man done?

"What do ye need to know?"

"To the best of your knowledge has Captain Ellard ever been drunk while on duty?"

"No, Doctor, never."

"And you have never smelled alcohol on his breath then known him to operate in that condition on a patient?"

Icy cold slid to the base of her spine, as though Callum had shoved a ball of snow down the back of her dress. The truth stuck in her throat. If she said yes, would Doctor Ellard be brought up on charges? Would he lose his rank, his ability to practice medicine?

She met Doctor Bliss' gaze across the width of the desk. The truth was there, in his eyes. He already knew the answer, now he was waiting to see if she would lie about it.

"Sunday past be the only time I ever caught the scent o'whiskey on Doctor Ellard's breath."

Doctor Bliss scribbled something on the sheet of paper in front of him.

"But he was not on duty at the time." She quickly added. "I sent Robbie to fetch him. And to be sure, he wasn't drunk when he arrived. His hand was as steady—"

"Excuse me, you said you sent for Captain Ellard. Why? According to my notes here Doctor Colfax was on duty at the time."

"The patient could not breathe. I sent Corporal Reid for the closest doctor. But Sergeant Baker be Doctor Ellard's patient. I thought he ought to know."

"So you summoned Doctor Colfax…" Doctor Bliss repeated as he wrote. A moment later he looked up, locking his gaze on hers like a cat waiting to pounce.

"Mrs. McBride, did Doctor Ellard, in a drunken state, physically shove aside Doctor Colfax and Medical Cadet Emerson, preventing them from performing their duty, then cut open the patient's throat with hands shaking from drunken tremors, putting that patient's life at risk by performing the procedure incorrectly?"

Stunned, Gracie could only blink stupidly at the man for several moments. Then gradually the anger rose inside her at the audacity of the man she knew had made this allegation. "Are ye wanting the honest truth, or have ye already made up yer mind?"

Doctor Bliss drew himself up indignantly. "I *have not* made up my mind, and I'll thank you to extend me the courtesy of the truth."

"I'm sorry. Ye have the right of it. I've always seen

ye as a just man, but if ye want the truth then by the saints ye shall have it." She drew a breath and continued.

"Doctor Colfax and Cadet Emerson do not belong in a hospital. Sweet Mary Jesus, the patient had fair turned blue, and they did naught, but tell me 'twas nothing to be done. If Doctor Ellard had not shoved them aside, I would have.

"He may have had a sip or two o'whiskey, but he was not drunk."

She stood, and Doctor Bliss was forced by decorum to rise as well. Stepping close, her thighs bumped the edge of the desk.

His eyes widened, and his brows rose. He likely imagined she was about to climb over the desk after him.

Neglecting to speak of the tremors she'd seen in Doctor Ellard's hands, she pressed her finger tips against the wooden surface and leaned forward.

Doctor Bliss pulled back.

"I cannot speak to the placement of the tube, high or low, but Sergeant Baker be alive today because o' Doctor Ellard," Gracie continued. "I cannot believe that jealous, spiteful old goat and his toady dared to twist the truth then make report of it."

He glanced down at the papers in front of him for a moment. "Well then, Mrs. McBride." He looked up. "I thank you for your time and your input into this matter."

"Ye are welcome, Doctor Bliss."

"And remember this conversation is confidential. No one should know what we discussed here tonight."

She nodded and stepped to the door.

"I hope he appreciates you."

Confused, she turned back.

Doctor Bliss gave his side burns a thoughtful stroke. "Since Captain Ellard arrived at this hospital in January, I have never seen anyone rise to his defense the way you have. Unusual, don't you think, coming from someone who admits to arguing with the man every day?"

Unwilling to consider the implications of his observation, Gracie left the office and hurried to her room.

****

She tried not to watch Doctor Ellard the next morning as he made his rounds, but her gaze continually wandered in his direction. Doctor Bliss' comment continued to drone on in the back of her mind, forcing her to ask herself what it was about the rude, condescending, yet brilliant surgeon that had inspired her to defend him so vehemently. Each time their eyes met, he seemed to draw further into himself, making that invisible wall around him a little more impenetrable.

There was nothing remarkable about his appearance, except that he was so much taller than everyone else, and his eyes were a striking shade of crystal blue, like sunlight streaming through an empty bottle of camphor. His angular features were rather plain, aside from the bump distorting the line of his nose, and the thin white scar which cut across the corner of his chin. He frowned more than he smiled, but when he was amused, his mouth quirked up in a shy, almost endearing way.

Yet, while his physical attributes were no finer than

90

those of any other man, there was something about Charles Ellard that had roused in her such loyalty she'd lied for him. Not a lie exactly. An omission of truth. That his hand shook had nothing to do with any whiskey he may have had. She was certain. It was something much deeper, and something Colfax and his minion had no need of knowing.

He carried himself with such an extraordinary sense of presence he automatically commanded respect every time he entered the ward, yet there was something private and vulnerable about the man.

"Is Cap'n Ellard mad at you?" Robbie asked.

The food for the special diets noon meal had arrived, and she and Robbie portioned it according to the list she'd made after morning rounds.

Beef broth spilled across her hand. Startled back to the present, she set down the cup and ladle then gave her hand a shake to whisk away the hot soup, before wiping her fingers dry with her apron.

"No, 'tis all fine," she replied hastily. She grabbed a rag to clean up the puddle.

Across the table, a quick derisive snort rumbled from the back of Robbie's throat.

She looked up to meet his gaze. "If ye have something to say, Robbie Reid, then ye'd best spit it out."

He shifted his weight back and forth and toyed with the spoon in his hand. "Well, I reckon we'd all like it better iffen he was."

"What are ye going on about?"

"I—I mean we all noticed how you both been lookin' at each other, but ain't said two words all mornin'. An' Cap'n Ellard ain't yelled at Corporal

Timon one time. Well, if that's how it is when he ain't mad, then I reckon we all like it better when he is."

"Are ye saying our disagreements be fodder for yer entertainment?"

"No. Well, yeah, I reckon. But it ain't like ya think. I mean, look around. It's purt near as quiet as the dead house."

Gracie turned and let her gaze travel around the ward. The patients were either lying silently in their beds or talking in whispers. The usual buzz of conversation and occasional bursts of laughter were absent. Then again, they had gotten wounded men the other day. Gracie just assumed the unusual stillness was out of respect for their comrades.

"All the men like ya a lot," Robbie continued, setting down the spoon and tearing a piece of bread from the loaf. "And there ain't no doctor better than Cap'n Ellard. The men feel safe knowin' come hell or high water, he'll do all he can to save 'em. And when you two start scrappin', well, 'scuse me ma'am, fer sayin' it, but it's funny. Goin' toe to toe with the man like ya do gives the men somethin' to talk about, to look forward to, so's they got somethin' else to think on, 'sides how much they hurt, and how sick they feel, and how far away home is."

An odd pressure swelled inside her chest. While it hadn't been so very long since Robbie had lain wounded in one of these beds, shame washed through her for not noticing what her young orderly had so easily perceived.

Her gaze swung around the ward again, except now it was as if the smudges had been wiped from a window pane and she could suddenly see the large room through clear glass. Robbie even appeared more mature.

She gave him a nod. "Ye are a wise man, Robbie Reid."

The tension eased from his body, and he flashed his usual crooked grin.

"But who amused ye before I come? Did Doctor Ellard argue with the nurse who worked before me?"

Robbie shook his head. "I ain't even sure what his name was." He ripped bread into small pieces and dropped them into a bowl of milk. "Peter, maybe, but he never argued with Cap'n Ellard, he was too scairt. He was always droppin' things though. We used to have a bettin' pool fer how many things he'd drop, 'specially when Cap'n Ellard was around. I even won a couple a dollars a few times." Picking up a spoon, he pressed the small pile of bread down into the milk.

"I don't remember who was the nurse a'fore him, and 'fore that there was a different doctor."

Gracie began matching the special diets with the bed numbers. "I thought Doctor Ellard had been here a long time."

"No, ma'am. The battle of Fredericksburg was in December, a week or so a'fore Christmas. 'Member I tolt ya, Cap'n Ellard went looney—"

She held up her hand, halting his words. Maybe she should have let Robbie continue so she could finally learn what had happened. Had it been something similar to the other night? Or had it been something worse? Then again, maybe it was better this way. It might be harder to argue with the man if she saw him as vulnerable.

Maybe, like Doctor Ellard, she preferred the invisible wall around him to remain intact. Doctor

Bliss' words echoed inside her head once more. Shoving them aside she said, "We best get these men fed. Where have Micah and Harvey gone?"

"Micah went to fetch clean bedding for Harvey." With a vague gesture of his hand, Robbie pointed down the ward. "Harvey's changin' bed twelve. That feller what got shot in the stomach pissed himself..." his voice trailed off and his face turned red. "Sorry, ma'am, in...inter...intercontinent..."

"Incontinent, and 'tis fine, Robbie. I would not be here if a bit o'coarse talk could send me into a swoon."

He laughed. "No, ma'am, I reckon not."

They each took a tray and starting at opposite ends of the ward, fed dinner to those men unable to eat a regular meal or make it to what the men called the grub room.

Part way down the ward, she spotted Major Carlton sitting in his wheeled chair, while another man in civilian dress packed up the major's few belongings.

As she approached he turned and smiled. "Good afternoon, Gracie."

"Are ye leaving us now, Major?"

His smile faded when she used his rank instead of his given name.

She liked him, she really did. He was a nice man, sensitive and funny, and he loved music as much as she. But after they'd gone to the lecture the other night, she sensed he wanted to move their relationship beyond the casual into something more like courtship. Maybe Doctor Ellard had the right of it after all.

The major nodded. Instead of the eagerness she expected to see in his face, his smile seemed forced, his eyes shadowed with apprehension.

"I'd like to introduce you to my brother, Samuel. Sam, this is Nurse McBride. She's the wonderful nurse who made this place bearable."

Heat spread across her cheeks.

Sam smiled and bowed.

With her hands full, Gracie could only return his greeting with a nod. "A pleasure to meet ye."

Before the major could say more than she wanted to hear, she nodded toward the bed across the aisle and a few spaces down. "Excuse me, but I must be about me duties."

The major pressed his lips together in a bitter smile but gave her an accepting nod.

Guilt tweaked her heart. She really did like him, but William was the only man she'd ever love. "Don't ye worry now, I'll not let ye leave without saying goodbye."

The rigid line of his shoulders softened a bit. "Good, because I have something I want to give you."

"I'll not forget." She smiled and turned away, ashamed for wanting to escape the man.

When she reached the patient with the abdominal wound, she set her broth cup and spoon on the small table beside a wooden pyramid puzzle. Obviously, someone had managed to do what Robbie and Micah could not.

Glancing at the card above the bed, she noticed someone had finally written in the patient's name. The night orderly must have gotten it during his shift. While Gleason was obviously clever with puzzles, his penmanship needed a great deal of improvement. Aside from the clearly printed capital S and B, she could only blink at the rest of the barely legible scrawl as she tried to form the lines and bumps into a name that made sense.

"Private Bragg?" She pulled the wooden chair, already positioned between the beds, as close to him as she could. "Simon?" she prodded gently.

He opened his eyes and fixed his glassy brown gaze on her face. He blinked as though surprised to find her sitting there.

"Are ye thirsty?"

Fever reddened the cheekbones of his otherwise pale face.

Without waiting for a response, she levered the head of his bed up a bit, then carefully spooned broth between his dry lips until the cup was empty.

She rose then stretched the ache from her spine. "I'll be back with a cool cloth for yer head."

Leaving Micah, Robbie, and Harvey to finish up the meals, Gracie filled a basin with cold water and returned to bed twelve. Wringing out several cloths, she lay one across his forehead, slipped one behind his neck, and tucked two more inside each armpit.

"I'll come back later with fresh water." She adjusted his blanket then picked up the basin. Mindful of spilling the contents, she maneuvered carefully around the chair, took two steps forward, and slammed into something solid.

The enamelware basin hit the wooden floor with a clang that echoed through the ward as the basin wobbled in circles for several seconds like a spinning top about to fall on its side.

"By the saints, can ye not look where yer going?" Pinching the bib of her apron, she held it away from the bodice of her dress as she quickly pulled free the pins that secured it. Looking up she could only sigh, wondering why she was even surprised to find him there.

"I was not going," Doctor Ellard pointed out. "I was standing."

"Well, ye should not have been standing." Reaching behind, she tugged free the ties of her apron. "Ye should've stepped aside for me to pass." Rolling the garment into a ball, she used the dry end to blot at the wet spots on her dress.

"I assumed you saw me."

"How could I be doing that with me head down, making certain I'd not spill the water?"

She glared at him, expecting him to at least pick up the basin. Then with a frustrated sigh, she dropped to her knees and using her apron, mopped the puddle. As she rose she snatched up the basin and slapped the wet apron inside. When he didn't move, she side stepped around him.

"Mrs. McBride, wait."

She swung around and narrowed her gaze on his face. He drew a breath as if he were about to speak then said nothing.

She waited.

"A king was asked," Doctor Ellard began. "Why in some kingdoms he could be crowned at the age of fourteen, yet not be allowed to marry until he was eighteen."

Baffled, Gracie stared at him. Had the man gone daft? He looked perfectly serious however, as though he were carefully repeating the memorized passage of a book.

"'Because, answered the king, it is easier to govern

a kingdom than a woman.'"

Every muscle in her body stilled. She wasn't even sure she remembered to breathe as she stared at him. A joke? Was that a joke?

She drew a deep breath. "Ye'd best thank the Heavenly Father that he made you a brilliant surgeon, Doctor Ellard. For if ye had to make yer way in this world as the writer of comedies, ye'd starve."

Then taking the basin and apron, she upended them against his chest and marched straight down the center of the wide aisle.

As she passed her work table, she saw Robbie watching her with a crooked grin on his face.

"Are ye happy now, Robbie Reid?" she asked, then continued to her room at the end of the ward.

****

Charles stared after her for several seconds. He'd made a fool of himself again.

Across the ward he noticed Major Carlton and a man who looked like his brother, laughing together while stealing glances his way.

His ears burned, but he glared at them as though being humiliated didn't matter. They quickly returned to their packing.

The man with the major picked up a book, and when he transferred it to the major's knapsack, a piece of paper dropped to the floor near the end of the bed. A moment later the man pushed Major Carlton up the aisle.

Casually, Charles crossed the distance, retrieved the paper, and returned to bed twelve. Setting the basin Gracie had shoved at him on the small table, he tucked the note underneath.

98

He then positioned the chair so that as he checked the patient's wounds he could watch the major at the nurse's table. Gracie joined them tying a fresh apron on over her dress. Though this dress was black it was one that had once been plaid for there were several shades of black lines in varying widths woven through the cloth.

The major said something, and she laughed.

Regret swelled inside him, pressing heavily against his chest, filling his stomach and hurting his heart. He thought he'd outgrown the pain of being the outcast, of not being included with his classmates at school, or even later at medical college. The pretty girls he'd met at parties and gatherings had never been interested in him. He'd been awkward and clumsy in their presence. He couldn't sing or play an instrument. His long legs tangled like a gangly colt, which added dancing to a long list of social skills he could never master, so that even the wallflowers refused to talk with him.

A minute later, the brother returned to the major's area and searched beneath the cot, the table, and the empty beds on either side. He even looked under the pillow and behind the table. With a shake of his head and an exaggerated shrug, he rejoined his brother and Gracie.

Charles knew he should feel guilty. When he was a boy, his grandfather would have taken the belt to him for stealing. Maybe he'd put it back later, where she could find it. Maybe.

She walked with them up the length of the aisle and continued out the door. Once they'd gone, he glanced around to see if anyone watched him, then he pulled the paper from beneath the basin and unfolded it.

You are a single candle in the dark of night,
The sound of your laughter makes my sad days bright.
Your eyes are as soft as a little brown wren,
And your hair like autumn, takes me home again.

~*~

With a voice like an angel that carries on high,
I'm drawn from despair, and given hope to try.
You're a woman, a nurse, an angel of mercy
You're all that I need, you're my sweet girl Gracie.

Charles swallowed the lump in his throat and blinked. Nothing but poorly written sentimental drivel that belonged in the trash. Refolding it, he slipped it into his pocket instead. He hadn't thought Gracie McBride to be a flowers and poetry sort of woman.

Shifting his attention to his patient, he unwrapped the bandages and checked both wounds.

As expected they were red and swollen, oozing the predictable laudable pus. Abdominal wounds were nearly always fatal. He'd just hoped the slower velocity round balls had done less internal damage. Rising, he strode to the closest linen cupboard.

His joke hadn't made her laugh. Maybe he should try a poem. Distaste twisted the muscles of his face into a grimace. A dose of castor oil would be more palatable.

He grabbed a few rolls of bandage and returned to twelve. The book of jokes held one hundred, twenty-eight pages of humorous anecdotes and jests. Perhaps he should choose another.

Working quickly, he applied the new dressing and tossed the soiled bandages into the basin. Finished, he carried it up the aisle until he spotted one of the attendants.

"Here," he said as he strode past, and thrust the basin at the startled soldier who instinctively grabbed it before it fell to the floor.

Gracie entered the ward and started down the wide aisle. She had nearly reached her table when he stopped and blocked her way.

She dropped her hands to her hips and raised her chin to meet his gaze.

Reaching into his pocket he pulled out the poem. "I found this by the major's bed."

The fiery challenge in her eyes dimmed to a sparkle. She gave him a quick smile and took the paper from his outstretched fingers. "I thank ye, Doctor. Major Carlton was upset when he could not find it."

Charles half hoped she would read it now so he could see her reaction, but she tucked it away in her skirt pocket. She would probably take it to her room to read in private then slip it under her pillow so she could lie in bed and dream about the man. Tomorrow she'd show the poem to her lady nurse friends, and they'd giggle and swoon over how romantic the fellow was.

"Was there something else ye be needing, Doctor?" She stared up at him with a puzzled frown.

"Mercy doesn't rhyme with Gracie," he blurted out—then with his ears burning he strode to the end of the ward and into the cold.

Chapter Six

You're behaving worse than a foolish school boy, he told himself as he checked his patients in the next ward.

He should have just kissed Gracie McBride and been done with it. Except, that hadn't worked too well either.

Aside from the few kisses he'd stolen from the young women his grandfather had arranged for Charles to court, he hadn't had much practice. He could have visited a whore, but while he had no qualms about treating one, the idea of lying intimately with a woman who had been with so many men and transmitted diseases that could kill a man was horrifyingly repellent.

Once more, he asked himself why it mattered so much what Gracie thought of him. He was leaving in three days.

Of course he hadn't told her yet. He hadn't told anyone, not that there was anyone to tell. On Monday morning he would be on his way to Falmouth and Doctor Bliss would assign the responsibility of wards E and F to someone else.

Maybe he should let her know. Would she fear for his safety? Would she be as upset as she'd been when she learned young Reid was going back? Would she run to Doctor Bliss demanding that he stay? He had no idea. Her reaction was as uncertain as this March weather.

And what if all she said in response was, *Goodbye and take care?* He would much rather spend the rest of the war imagining what might have been. He could always write to her. Then again, what if she never wrote back?

Finished with his duties in F, he walked to his quarters. He didn't have time to moon over Gracie McBride. Good Lord, he was worse than Major Carlton. Forcing himself to focus on the requisition list Doctor Bliss had asked for, Charles spent the rest of his afternoon hunched over the quartermaster's ledgers from the fall campaign.

Taking the numbers in the book, Charles simply increased all the surgical supplies, bandages, and bed linens by twenty-five percent and the rest by twenty. This war was going to get worse before it got better.

A chill rippled through him. He couldn't conceive of anything worse than the fighting along Antietam Creek, or worse than Fredericksburg. Enemy shells bombarding the hospital, wounded lying on pine boughs, ten men to a tent with nothing but blankets for warmth. Days standing in the cold, the blood freezing his clothes stiff as he stood beside the surgical table, his numb finger barely able to wrap around the end of his long amputation knife. Feet, hands, arms, legs, cut, toss, sew—

He shoved away from the tiny desk and paced the confines of his room. He jammed his hands into his pockets and clenched them into fists. What if it happened again like it had at Fredericksburg? The night before last had been frightening enough, and only

Gracie had seen him lose control. He'd be committed to an asylum for certain this time, instead of being transferred to Washington to rest. His grandfather wouldn't be able to save him a second time.

God damn, how was he going to do this?

Turning to his trunk, he threw back the lid and dug to the bottom for his bottle of whiskey. Popping the cork, he slammed back a healthy swallow. He raised the bottle to eye level. He should probably pick up another one before he left, maybe two. Three would be better. God, at this rate he'd be a drunken sot by the end of the war.

He recorked the bottle and returned it to his trunk. As he drew the lid closed his gaze fell upon the red book covered with laughing faces, like an audience at a crowded theater. His fingers quavered as he reached for the slim volume. Then, lowering himself to his bed, he stretched out and began to read.

****

"A farmer who lives on a hill called 'Hard Scrabble,' said that owing to poor land and the drought last summer, the grass was so short he had to lather it before he could mow it."

Gracie stared at Doctor Ellard as he stood looking down at her from across the table after his morning rounds.

Another joke? This one might have been humorous if he hadn't delivered it in such a clinical manner as though he were presenting a lecture from the podium at a medical college.

"Are you amused?" he asked, the tone of his voice lightened with hope. His earnest expression touched her more than his joke.

Nodding, she clamped her bottom lip between her teeth. "Ummm hmmm." To burst out laughing now would hurt his feelings.

His brow furrowed skeptically then he passed her the patient cards.

She searched his face as she accepted them, trying to understand why he suddenly felt the need to tell her jokes.

For a moment she thought he might say more, but he closed his parted lips and abruptly swung on his heels.

Staring at the cards, she listened to him go. His long stride lengthened, each thud of his heels against the floor like a child taking giant steps.

She took out a sheet of paper to create the list of food for the special diets and suddenly recalled what she'd wanted to ask him.

Paper in hand, she shoved back her chair and hurried down the aisle, catching up to him on the covered walkway just outside the ward.

"Doctor Ellard," she called.

He turned. Expectation raised his brow.

"I wanted to ask ye again about moving Sergeant Baker from the side door."

He sighed. "Did you give him an extra blanket?"

"Yes, but the draft cannot be—"

"Has he complained?"

"Nay, but the man cannot speak."

"He stays where he is."

As though the matter were settled, he inclined his head in a slight bow and started to turn.

"Then I wonder if ye might do me a wee favor?"

He heaved a heavy sigh that seemed to carry the

weight of the world. That implacable mask was back in place, and Gracie suddenly wished she had laughed at his joke. "Tomorrow be Sunday and 'tis Robbie's last day with us before he must return to his unit." She held out the blank paper and a pencil.

"Could ye send a note to the cook in the kitchen allowing me to bake a cake later today."

"No." He ignored the paper and pencil.

She raised her gaze to meet his. "But the cook would not have to bake it. 'Tis I'd be doing all the work."

"No." Ice rimmed his hard blue stare.

"But Robbie be doing so much around the hospital—"

"He draws pay from the army."

She crossed her arms refusing to take back the paper. "Payment be not the issue. 'Tis a gesture of appreciation, a way to wish him well and—"

"Do other men get cakes?"

"I'll be making it large enough, so all who might want a piece—"

"Do other men get cakes before they leave here and go back to their regiments?"

"No, but Robbie is—"

"Corporal Reid is no different than any other soldier doing his duty. There are no parades, no parties, and no cakes. You go where the army commands and pray to God a Confederate twelve-pounder doesn't take off your head." He shuddered at the image he'd conjured.

"Ye are a cold and heartless man. I do not need your per—"

"If you think to take this to Doctor Bliss—"

"Sweet Mary Jesus, will ye let me finish a sentence?"

She shoved the paper and pencil into her pocket. "Fine. I'm letting ye know I've the sudden need for an afternoon off. And if the Sisters from Our Lady of Charity be coming round tomorrow with a cake for the poor wounded boys in our care, I'll thank ye not to stop Robbie from having a piece."

He narrowed his gaze and took a step toward her. "I have come to believe that there is much truth in jest, and that a country truly is easier to govern than a woman."

The paper crumpled inside her fist. Her breast heaved with each angry breath as she fought to keep herself from taking a swing at the egotistical, bigheaded ass.

"May all the goats in Gorey chase ye to hell, Charles Ellard. If ye ever think to leave this place, do not expect me to bake ye a cake. And I hope ye choke on the piece I cut for ye on Sunday."

"It will not be a problem, Mrs. McBride, for I will not be here. I have better things to do with my free time than to waste it singing and eating cake. Good day."

He swung around and strode off.

Frustrated, she stamped her foot against the plank walk. "And next time," she yelled at his back, "I'll thank ye not to be reading poetry meant for another!"

She watched him until he turned out of sight between two buildings. Then mortified by the realization she'd been screaming like a fishwife on hospital grounds, she went in search of Sister Mary.

****

Back in his quarters, Charles removed his coat and

vest and rolled up his sleeves. *A cake.* He flopped backward onto his bed and stacked his hands beneath his head. Cause for cakes and celebration would be when this war ended, for those who made it out alive. Not now.

Despite how fond she was of the young corporal, Reid was no more special than any one of them.

He wondered again what she would say if he told her he was leaving. She wouldn't bake him a cake, but would she say goodbye?

Reaching for the book on his bedside table, he propped it open on his stomach and began to read. Out of all the jokes and amusing anecdotes in this book, there must be one that could make her laugh, just one that would endear him, just a little bit, to her heart.

Someone knocked on his door.

"Come."

Slowly the knob turned, and the door creaked inward.

"Sir, you have a visitor." The sergeant spoke through the ten-inch opening between the door and its jamb.

"Get in here, Sergeant," he ordered. "Stop that goddamn lurking." From the way people tiptoed around him, one might believe he was more intimidating than a rebel cavalry charge. He closed the book and rolled to his feet.

The sergeant stepped half-way into the room. "You have a visitor, sir."

"Who?"

"He didn't say, sir, but it's an older gentleman. Finely dressed."

"Very well." He slipped on his waistcoat and

grabbed his coat from the hook on the back of his door, leaving the sergeant to close it behind him as they left the room.

Charles' long legs took him quickly to the front office.

A short man stood before the window, just a silhouette in the beam of sunlight, until he stepped forward.

Charles froze, his coat half way up his arm. The sergeant bumped against him. Startled from his daze, Charles drew a deep breath. "Hello, Grandfather."

The old man walked closer. Each gray hair lay neatly in place, his black trousers and frock coat, dust free and finely creased. Even his shoes gleamed—the mud and slush not daring to mar their pristine perfection.

Charles shrugged into his coat. Gathering his patience, he pushed each of his nine brass buttons through their corresponding holes.

His grandfather extended one hand in greeting. In the other he held both his hat and that damned walking stick. "Good morning, Charles." His shrewd gaze roamed from the top of Charles' head to the toes of his scuffed boots. A frown turned down the corners of Grandfather's mouth. "This slovenly appearance is how you present yourself to me?" He gave his head a slow shake. "Your mother would have never approved."

Charles didn't attempt to apologize or explain. He only knew he was not having this conversation in front of the sergeant, the office clerk, or the officer-of-the-day.

He hastily finger combed his pillow-mussed hair. "It's good to see you, sir. May I show you my quarters?" With a sweep of his arm, he gestured toward the hall.

As his grandfather passed by, Charles clearly heard a soft, derisive, "Harrumph." Ignoring it, he led the way to his small room toward the back of the building.

Tap. Step. His grandfather followed with his walking stick.

Just inside the doorway, his grandfather stopped. His disapproving gaze roamed from the mountain of medical reports, which Charles needed to finish and organize, to the stack of notes and medical books being used to write his paper on *Pymeia and Surgical Fevers,* to the Quartermaster's ledger and the supply requisitions for Doctor Bliss.

"You always did accumulate clutter."

There was no point in trying to explain that this was all work. His grandfather never understood. Books were to be kept neatly on the library shelves, not stacked in piles around a bedroom.

"Now when your mother was a girl, her room was immaculate. Nary a hair brush out of place. Extremely organized."

"Why are you here?"

The one blessing to being in the army was that he didn't have to listen to his grandfather's veiled criticisms any longer.

"Do I need a reason to come see my favorite grandson?"

"You shouldn't, but I expect you have one."

His grandfather raised his walking stick and poked Charles in the center of his chest. "You are still too much the smart aleck. I should have taken you over my knee a few times. I don't know where such disrespect comes from. Your father was too meek and your mother too much a lady."

Charles moved toward his desk and pulled the chair around. "May I offer you a seat?" he asked, dropping his gaze to his grandfather.

The older man stepped beside the bed, and reaching down, lifted the book Charles had been reading. "Jokes and Jests?" With his walking stick, he gave the room a haphazard wave. "This is what comes from reading such frivolous nonsense."

In one quick stride, Charles was across the room. He snatched the book from the old man's hands. "'Tis for research," he said, and took it to his desk, shifting the piles of books and papers around until the volume was buried.

"'*Tis*?" his grandfather repeated with slow, appalled distaste. "Has your diction also lapsed?"

Staring at the floor, Charles tried to replay in his head the words he'd just uttered. Had he actually said 'tis? He closed his eyes and clenched his teeth as his grandfather continued to rant.

"Here it is eleven o'clock in the morning, and your bed is a mess. I believed the regulation of army life would be good for you. That is why I encouraged you to enlist, but from what I've seen, this place lacks both structure and accountability."

Remaining in this room for a polite visit was no longer an option. He was thirty-two years old, yet he felt as if he were ten, called into his grandfather's study to be disciplined for spilling milk or receiving a ninety-three percent on his report from school. What was the old man's motto? Ah, yes, spare the walking stick and spoil the child.

"Would you like a tour of the hospital?"

"I suppose I ought to see what you do all day."

Quickly, Charles ushered his grandfather out the back door of the building onto the covered plank walkway which connected all the wards.

To accommodate the shorter man and his walking stick, Charles held his hands behind his back and curtailed his normal stride into tiny, mincing steps.

Tap, step. Tap, step.

"I hope this negligent attitude of yours doesn't carry over into the hospital and your duties there."

Charles tightly squeezed three of his own fingers. "This is a new hospital, built specifically to meet the guidelines of the U.S. Sanitary Commission for optimal ventilation and hygienic behaviors."

"Then why is the death rate so high?"

"Excuse me?" Charles turned to face the man who raised him, the man whose gray eyes lit with challenge.

"My friend in the Senate shared some interesting statistics last night over dinner." His grandfather continued up the walk. "Of all the hospitals in Washington, and I believe he said there were over fifty facilities being used right now, Armory Square Hospital has the highest number of deaths. Is this a reflection of the attitude I see from you here today?"

Fury roiled inside Charles like water in a whistling tea kettle. For a moment, he literally saw red. His fingers ached to wrap around the old man's throat.

Nothing he did was ever good enough.

Charles had graduated from Jefferson Medical College when he was just twenty-one, then gone to Europe for three years, continuing his studies in Edinburg, London, Paris, and Vienna. He'd even started his own small practice before enlisting. Yet, not one accomplishment rose high enough to meet his grandfather's standard of perfection. Charles clenched his teeth against all the vicious words rising in his throat, things he longed to scream right into his grandfather's face.

He drew several deep breaths until he was certain he could speak in a concise, level-headed manner.

"What your friend in the Senate neglected to take into account when he spouted those facts is that this hospital is the closest, both to the steamboat landing at the end of Seventh Street, and to the line of the Washington and Alexandria Railroad."

Tap, step. His grandfather ambled slowly along.

"Because of this," Charles continued. "We receive the worst cases of wounded, the men who won't make it to any other hospital. And we receive the soldiers who die en route."

At the entrance to Ward E, he turned to his grandfather. "The staff in these wards work hard to provide the best care they know how to these wounded men. I will thank you to address any disparaging remarks you may feel compelled to utter, only to me."

"Disparaging remarks?"

Whack!

His grandfather's walking stick slammed against Charles' shin. He gritted his teeth against the pain which radiated up to his knee and down to his ankle. Thank God he at least had on leather boots.

"How dare you disrespect your elder in such a manner? I can see this whole military idea of mine has been a mistake. You've been here two years and instead of creating a future political candidate, the army has corrupted you."

"I have not been corrupted."

"You say not, yet you deserted your duty as a physician on the battlefield and assaulted a superior officer, which resulted in a demotion from major to captain. Without me you would have spent the war rotting in Old Capitol Prison. Military life is obviously not for you. I will see what I can do to get you relieved of your duties and you can move back home to Philadelphia."

"Grandfather, the army has no plans to discharge me. They need all the surgeons they can get. In two days I'll be going back to my regiment to resume my duties as a field surgeon with the 69th Pennsylvania."

His grandfather emitted a soft grunt then tugged thoughtfully on his snowy beard. "Going back into battle?"

"Yes, sir."

His grandfather's narrow shoulders hunched as his head slowly moved up and down. "That might be the best thing for you. Get you away from this place. Give you some discipline. Then if you don't have another breakdown, we'll explore your political possibilities when this rebellion nonsense is over."

Charles closed his eyes and drew deep calming breaths, quelling the urge to bang his forehead against the wall of the building. If he had his way, he'd never go home again.

He turned the knob and pushed open the door. "Welcome to Ward E."

For a few minutes, his grandfather amicably strolled along as Charles explained rounds and medication passes, the jobs of the nurses, attendants, stewards, and orderlies. For a few minutes, Charles warmed toward the older man, who seemed eager to learn everything Charles had to share.

As they approached the nurses' table, Gracie looked up, pen in hand, from one of the many sheets of paper spread before her. She gave his grandfather a puzzled glance then switched her attention to meet his gaze.

"Doctor Ellard, if ye have a minute, could ye check the wound in Private Bragg's lower back? When Harvey changed the private's dressings, he be noticing gray around the wound and a discharge thicker than normal."

Charles nearly asked her which patient was Bragg, then remembered that Bragg was the new admission from whom he'd removed two bullets the other night.

He started down the aisle then glanced back to see if his grandfather followed, but the man seemed content to wander on his own.

At bed twenty-three, Charles pulled the chair close then lowered his rangy body so he was nearly level with the patient.

Bragg opened his eyes for a moment then closed them.

Carefully, Charles rolled the man onto his side, lifted his shirt, and peeled back the bandage.

His nostrils flared at the sour smell which wafted from the wound. He studied the heavy yellow substance on the pad then poked at the necrosis creeping around the edges of the wound. A steady, clear, even slight yellow discharge was expected, but when it crossed into pymeia paired with a high fever, he believed things had taken a turn for the worst.

He pulled a pencil and note pad from his pocket, focused on recording every detail of the patient's condition for his paper. Both doctors and medical texts encouraged laudable pus as a sign the wound was healing. But Charles found it to be the antecedent for pymeia and gangrene, which is why he'd needed further data to complete his paper and see it published. He wished he knew how to use photography equipment to visually document the progression of the septicemia.

After easing the man onto his back, Charles reached for the patient card and began to write. *Change dressing every two hours. Report all discharge. For fever, cold compresses.*

"Cap'n Ellard!"

Charles glanced up frowning at the disruption.

Corporal Reid hurried toward him, waving his arm in an urgent, *come-here* manner.

Baffled, Charles stood and immediately recognized the raised voices of Gracie McBride and his grandfather. As he stepped into the aisle, he saw the two of them in front of his tracheotomy patient.

His grandfather held fast to the silver head of the walking stick and Gracie, swearing at him in Gaelic, had hold of the opposite end, each trying to wrest the stick away from the other, with the pull-tug motion of loggers using a two-man saw.

Extending his stride, Charles was there in moments.

In what had become a familiar maneuver, he wrapped his arm around Gracie's waist and lifted her off her feet. With his free hand, he pried her fingers from the walking stick.

His grandfather staggered backward, but young

Reid and one of the attendants each grabbed an arm to keep old man from falling.

Despite the way Gracie squirmed and pulled at his arm, Charles still managed to point toward the nurses' table and chair. "Grandfather, please wait for me over there."

If his grandfather argued, Charles didn't wait to hear it. He swung on his heels and marched from the ward, a squirming, swearing Gracie held tight in front of him.

"Stop kicking," he whispered harshly, "or I swear to God I'll throw you over my shoulder."

She stilled in his arms. "Put me down, Charles Ellard."

"No."

"That old goat be hitting me with his cane, and by the saints he's going to know the feel of it."

While he could certainly understand her sentiment, hitting an old man in the middle of a hospital ward was not the way to handle it.

Once outside, he lowered her to her feet.

She tried to dodge past him.

He sidestepped to block her from reaching the door.

She feigned to the left and rushed to the right, forcing him to continue the game through several more attempts.

With a frustrated cry, she whirled on her heels and marched off down the walk.

He glanced over his shoulder, wondering what additional havoc his grandfather had wrought. He should check. Gracie seemed fine—angry, but fine.

"Oh hell," he muttered and started after her.

Several moments passed before his long stride caught up to her double-time quick march, the heels of her shoes sounding click, click, click against the wooden planks.

"Go away," she said as he came up behind her.

Was that a catch in her voice? "Do you want to tell me what happened?"

"No." She stepped off the walk onto a gravel path.

He stepped off right behind her. "Tell me."

"Then will ye go away?"

"Perhaps."

She stopped abruptly in front of the chapel.

He tried to move in front of her, but she turned, keeping her back to him.

Her shoulders heaved as she exhaled a loud sigh. "He was bothering the patients, walking up close and staring at them, like they be here for his entertainment. Then he asked Sergeant Baker what was wrong with his neck. The poor man cannot even talk."

She sniffed and raised her hand to her face for a moment.

Was she crying? His chest tightened, and his stomach gave a tiny flip. "Did he hurt you?"

She sniffed again, and her hand moved up to her face even as she shook her head. "'Tis fine. I've hit me shin harder on the end o' me own bed."

There was a distinctive catch in her breath. "You are crying."

"Go away."

He couldn't just walk off. He had to fix this somehow. "Don't cry."

"I'm—not," hiccup, "crying."

"Of course you're crying."

"Doctor Ellard, just leave me be."

"He hurt you, and I need to see the wound."

There were a few more sniffs. "'Tis not a wound that ye can see. Now go away."

A chill washed over him. God, where had his grandfather hit her? He never should have brought the old man to the ward. Charles had behaved like the coward he was purported to be, using the tour to avoid facing the litany of his grandfather's criticisms back in his quarters. And maybe some small part of him hoped that when his grandfather saw how fine a hospital Armory Square was and saw what good work they did here, that maybe, just for once Grandfather would be proud of him. He should have known better.

He tried again to see her face, but she neatly turned away.

"Gracie, you must tell me what he did." He couldn't believe his grandfather would strike a woman, then remembered that in his grandfather's world, Irish weren't good enough to be servants. "I need to see. I am a doctor and even if it might be embar—"

She whirled around. "Ye great oaf, he called me a whore."

Tears streamed down her flushed cheeks from brown eyes all red and puffy.

His shoulders sagged with relief. The tightness in his chest eased so he could breathe normally again. At least his grandfather hadn't hurt her. Not really. For a moment he had visions of the old man poking her with his walking stick and leaving bruises on her breasts, or lower, on her abdomen, or lower.

Stop! He ordered himself. He shouldn't be thinking of Gracie McBride naked, of roaming his hands over her body as he checked for injuries. He gave his head a shake. "At least you're not hurt."

"I be not a whore," she declared as more tears slid down her cheeks. She swung around to face the steps of the small white building.

"No, of course not." All this crying couldn't be healthy. The last time he tried to comfort her, she accused him of having ice in his veins and had thrown his coat on the ground. Hands behind his back, he stared through the branches of a small tree planted at the corner of the chapel. There must be something he could say, something that would distract her from her tears...

"Two neighbors," he began, "having gone shares on the purchase of a pig disagreed as to the time when it should be killed. 'Well,' said the one of them, 'you may kill your half when you like; I shall kill mine now.'"

She whirled around, her face blotchy. "A joke!" She stepped toward him, planted both hands on the center of his chest and shoved.

His boot heels skidded on the gravel, forcing him to step back into the grass.

"Ye stand there and think to tell me a joke?"

"I thought to make you laugh."

"That old goat called me an Irish wench, he said I be nothing more than a camp-follower, no better than a whore...right in front of the patients...the men I've come to tend and care for.

"I loved me husband. 'Twas never a finer man than William McBride. All I learned o'medicine and nursing come as I stood equal by his side. He'd not want me to stay in Boston scrubbing floors and polishing silver. I come here to honor his memory, to share what he taught me, and that devil's spawn…

"And ye? Ye stand there and tell me a joke?"

"My intention was for you to stop crying."

"Ye don't tell me a foolish joke, ye give me a hug!"

A hug? That was rather a simple solution. His arms already ached to wrap around her, to hold her close, to kiss her. He stepped forward. His fingers brushed her shoulders.

She stiffened and shoved him away. "Do not touch me."

Baffled, he stared at her. "You said…

She heaved a weighted sigh. "Not like that. Have ye never hugged a woman? Ye stand right where ye are, hold out yer arms and say, 'Ah, Gracie-lass…c-come h-here.' "

Her hand clamped over her mouth. Her eyes welled with fresh tears.

He extended his arms. "Gracie, come." It must have been wrong for she stood there staring at him wide-eyed. She made a loud choking sound behind her hand and fat tears spilled from her eyes.

She rushed forward, colliding against his body. Her hands wrapped around his waist, tugging on the back of his coat as she grabbed fistfuls of wool.

He wrapped his arms around her and rested his chin on top of her head, not sure what else to do.

Great wrenching sobs shook her body. "Why did he have to d-die?"

Charles stiffened. Despite the warmth of the sun on his shoulders, cold washed through him.

"I m-miss him so much. I want him back. I want what we had back."

He flinched. The kiss he'd thought to press against her hair vanished with his gasp of breath as the pain of her words pierced his heart.

What had he been thinking? He would never be her William. Perhaps it was just as well he was leaving.

Not knowing what else to do, he let her cry a bit longer then gave her back a couple of awkward pats.

Gradually, her body stopped shaking. There were a few more sniffs then she pushed away.

Keeping her head lowered, she slipped her hand into her pocket and withdrew a lacy white handkerchief. She blew her nose a couple of times then shoved the wadded up cloth into her pocket.

"I'm sorry," she said, sniffing again. "A lady should not be blowing her nose in front of a gentleman."

"No need to apologize, Mrs. McBride. And fear not, there has never been the hint of doubt in my mind that you are anything but a lady."

Glancing up, she gave him a quick smile. "Thank ye, Doctor Ellard."

Well, at least he'd finally done something right. She'd smiled—at him.

"I did not mean to weep all over ye. 'Twas only that the old goat riled me temper so I could think o' nothing but rapping him over the head with his cane." She turned and seated herself on the chapel steps.

"I've had that same thought many times."

She swiped her fingers across her reddened cheeks. "Ye have? Grandfather ye said?"

"Former Pennsylvania State Senator Foster Harrison. My maternal grandfather."

"I'd not have thought. Ye look nothing like him."

"I suppose I must take after my father."

"Ye don't know?"

He shook his head. "He died when I was seven."

"And yer mother told ye naught about him?"

He almost smiled at the trace of outrage in her voice—outrage for an injustice done to him. "She died as well. There was a typhus outbreak in Philadelphia in thirty-seven."

"I'm sorry. Do ye miss them?"

"I never knew them. I used to wonder what it might have been like not to be alone, to grow up with parents, and maybe brothers and sisters. I want a real family someday. If I'd had one perhaps I wouldn't be…"

He gave one shoulder a quick shrug. "But all I had were stories my grandfather told of my mother when she was a girl. I carry her likeness. Do you want to see?"

He slipped free the buttons of his coat and removed his watch from the small front pocket of his waistcoat. He popped open the cover, glancing at the tiny painted miniature of someone more girl than woman, with blonde hair and blue eyes, who must have been younger than Gracie at the time it was painted. He passed it down to her.

The gold chain pooled in her palm, and she cradled the open time piece in her hands as though she were afraid she'd break it. "She's very pretty." Reaching out her finger, she lightly traced the image. "And ye've no notion o'yer father?"

Charles shook his head. "He was alone in the world when he married my mother. Anytime I asked about him, my grandfather said he didn't know. He did work in a bank. My grandfather gave me his watch so I'd at least have something of him."

Carefully Gracie closed the two halves and turned it over. She lightly traced the words engraved in the silver. "Peter," she read aloud. "All my love, Julia.

"'Tis a fine name, Julia." Gracie stood then and passed him the watch. "I'd best get back. 'Tis near time for the medication passes."

He returned the watch to his pocket and pushed the end of the chain through the button hole of his waistcoat, then buttoned his coat. He offered his arm, surprised when she actually slipped her hand through the crook of his elbow and rested her palm on his forearm.

"He's not that bad," he said as they started walking.

She shot him a sideways glance, one auburn eyebrow quirked dubiously.

"He's always tried to control my life, but since I moved into my own rented rooms, I think it's gotten worse—and so has his inclination to wield that walking stick."

They stepped onto the plank walkway together.

"Maybe the army should be putting him and his cane on a horse and let him direct the battles."

He chuckled at the image. How easily she moved from tears to laughter. Nothing held Gracie McBride down for long. Of all the people he'd known in his life, Gracie he would truly miss.

"Pay him no mind, Mrs. McBride. He is an old man, and lonely, and I am all he has left in this world. He does care for me in his way. When I was a boy and ill with fever, he sat by my bedside until I was well. He delayed my start of school and hired a tutor because he thought me too small for my age.

"Then after the boys in school had beaten me for the second time"—Charles pointed to the scar on his chin and the bump on his nose—"he insisted I take boxing lessons. He longs for great-grandchildren to fill that empty house. And I'd like to give them to him."

"Please, Doctor Ellard, ye are making me feel sorry for the old goat."

"Believe me, my grandfather is the last person in the world you need to feel sorry for, but a little understanding and a bit of patience would be appreciated."

"Me Da always says, 'Tis better to quarrel than be lonesome. Maybe that's his way."

He glanced down and met her gaze. A slow smile tugged back the corners of his mouth. "Yes, in my grandfather's case I dare say that's true. Don't worry. He won't be staying long. We'll be going out for dinner soon. I may see him back to his hotel afterward. Don't look for me until tomorrow."

"I'll be going out as well. Sister Mary and I be—" She cut off her own words, leaving nothing but the sound of their footsteps against the planks.

"Ah, your cake," he said as they continued and approached Ward E.

Sudden tension radiated from her body as though she were poised to argue.

"I still hold to my opinion," he said before she could open her mouth. "There will be no celebratory cakes in the ward tomorrow and the tracheotomy case remains where it is."

He stepped forward to open the door.

She squared her shoulders as though preparing for

battle then marched past him into the ward.

He smiled to himself as he watched her go. President Lincoln was wrong. He shouldn't have chosen Joseph Hooker to replaced Ambrose Burnside and lead the Army of the Potomac. He should have appointed Gracie McBride.

Chapter Seven

With her back ramrod straight and her head up, she almost glided down the aisle. Without a hoop beneath her skirt, he could watch the natural sway of her hips. For a moment he wished he could again see that long rope of braided hair, tracing the line of her spine. He'd wrap his hand around it and hang on, letting her lead him into her world filled with people and laughter.

But convention and practicality held her beautiful red tresses inside that white linen cap, pinned in place at the back of her head.

He tried to capture this picture of her with his mind, the way a photographer captures an image on a glass plate, that he might remember her during the lonely nights ahead, the same way he easily recalled pages of printed text.

Again he questioned why he didn't tell her he was leaving, but down deep inside he knew the reason.

Fear.

Had she heard the whispers? She must have after all these weeks. What did she really think of him?

He'd bet William McBride had never walked away from a patient, terrified, sick, and shaking like a baby. Certainly Major Carlton had never been charged with dereliction of duty or assaulting a superior officer.

Any dreams his grandfather held with regards to Charles' future political career were as fragile as soap bubbles in his palm, bursting into droplets with one simple word.

Crazy.

****

Silverware clinked against china and low male voices rumbled through a restaurant filled with attorneys, congressmen, and senators. Dark paneling, leather chairs, and pristine linen tablecloths filled the room. Instead of savoring the luxury, it chaffed against Charles like a wool collar at the back of his neck.

"Grandfather, it must have crossed your mind, at least once, since I began attending lectures at Jefferson Medical College, that I have no interest in politics."

Patience and understanding, he'd repeated those words to himself countless times since he and his grandfather were seated.

He set down his fork and sipped from his water glass. He'd never had what people called a hearty appetite, and years of army fare turned his stomach against the meal of crab and oysters his grandfather had ordered for each of them.

"A medical profession is fine for now. It should keep you safe, yet create that heroic image you'll need when you run for office. Yes, the military is an excellent foundation for a career in politics. Look what it did for Washington and Jackson. The people loved them."

Picking at his food, Charles half-listened while his grandfather rambled on making plans for a future that would never be.

"I'm selling the house."

The abrupt announcement jerked Charles' attention from the patterns his fork made in the clarified butter to his grandfather's shrewd brown eyes. "Pardon me, did you say you were selling the house?"

"Yes. It's too big for one person. And there are too many stairs. My knees can't endure all that climbing up and down."

Charles had always pictured his grandfather living in that brick row house until he died. For a moment he wondered why the news left him feeling so detached, why he didn't feel sadder at the thought of losing such a significant part of his life.

"I hadn't planned on selling. I assumed you would have married by now and populated the place with children. You're thirty-two years of age. What are you waiting for?"

What could he say? *I don't know how to talk to women? Women aren't interested in me? Or that the most beautiful one I know wishes I was someone else.*

"And don't even think about bringing home that Irish wench."

Charles' backbone snapped to attention. The cords of his neck stiffened. "Never," he snapped, "disparage the good name of Mrs. McBride with that despicable term again."

"No!" His grandfather slammed the palm of his hand against the tabletop, rattling the silverware and drawing stares. "I saw the way you watched her." Instead of pointing his cane, the old man leveled an accusing finger. "This woman may be an adequate hospital nurse, but she is Irish. Any alliance with her will ruin your career. *I will not have it.*"

Charles' pulse beat against his eardrums. Breathe, he told himself. None of this mattered. After Monday he'd never see Gracie McBride again. Let the old man

have his plans. Once his party cronies saw Charles'
military record they'd withdraw any support. His
grandfather would have no reason to interfere with
Charles desire to practice medicine. If the damn war
ever ended.

"I will select a young lady for you. Do you
remember Miss Adelaide Emmerson?"

"Who?"

"Her father is a retired senator. Her brother has a
seat in the House. She is beautiful and well connected.
She would be perfect for you."

Perfect? The sort of wife Foster Harrison would
deem perfect was likely an insipid blonde with money
and political connections. A wallflower who knew
nothing of life, and with whom he could only expect an
existence of polite indifference. Forcing himself to
appear calm, Charles reached for his water glass, leaned
back in his chair, and crossed his legs. He glanced at his
grandfather, who seemed mollified by his grandson's
tacit agreement.

"I've been going through the house, deciding what
to keep, what to throw away. It's been difficult. Your
mother's things. I wouldn't have to sell if you were to
marry and fill the house with children."

How many times, as a boy, had he wished his
parents had lived? How different would his life have
been? Would he have learned to laugh, wrestle with his
brothers and tease his sisters, spent his life creating
memories with people instead of stacks of books?

"I have an old hat box for you at the hotel," his
grandfather said. "You left behind a few of your
childhood toys and books. You must have attached
some importance to them as you'd stored them in the

bottom drawer of your wardrobe."

Charles had always intended to collect the hat box. However, once he returned from Europe and found a place to set up his practice, the only time he'd gone to the house was for Sunday dinners, and he was usually so furious by the time he left, he never remembered the box.

"That old stuffed toy is in there. The one you used to carry everywhere. Screamed your head off when you didn't have it. Glad I took the damned thing away or you'd have taken it off to school with you. Probably still be sleeping with it."

Bunzy.

Those big soft ears had wiped away many tears in the middle of the night when he'd awoken terrified and struggling for breath, when the boys at school had teased and bullied him, or when he'd just wished for his mother.

He could never remember how Bunzy's ear had gotten ripped. He only remembered stitching it closed. He couldn't have been more than seven, but it had been his very first surgery. Afterward, he was careful never to carry Bunzy by his ears.

Charles crossed his knife and fork on the plate and leaned back in his chair. What little appetite he had was gone. He'd once told the stuffed rabbit all his secrets. There had never been anyone he could trust more.

Bunzy doesn't have a mouth. He will never tell.

A sharp pain stabbed like a needle through Charles temple. Wincing, he pressed his fingertips against his head, rubbing hard tight circles as the pain eased.

"Charles, are you listening to me?"

"Yes, sir," he replied automatically, lowering his

hand to the napkin in his lap.

The old man frowned, his disbelief evident. "I asked if you wanted to come get the box or shall I have it sent to the hospital?"

"I won't have the time to see you back to your hotel. I need to start my rounds soon. Just send it when you can."

"All right then." His grandfather laid his napkin on the table and pushed to his feet.

Charles stood and handed the man his walking stick. "It was good seeing you again, sir."

They made their way outside. Charles hailed a cab and helped the older man inside.

"Thank you," his grandfather murmured and settled himself on the seat. "I assume your regiment will be the same as before? Sixty-ninth Pennsylvania?"

"Yes, sir, at Falmouth."

His grandfather reached into his coat and withdrew a black purse. "Take it." He leaned through the door, extending his hand to Charles.

Charles shook his head. "Hooker got us all our back pay. I'll be fine."

His grandfather shoved the purse against Charles' chest until he had no choice but to accept the money.

"Nonsense," he snapped. "You're too thin. You'll need funds to buy food from the suttler, and you'll need to acquire a horse."

Resigned, Charles slipped the purse into his pocket, "Thank you, sir."

"You shall hear from me soon."

Charles merely nodded, then stepped back, signaling the driver to move ahead into traffic.

He watched the departing cab for several seconds

then started back to the hospital.

****

Doctor Ellard said little during Sunday morning inspection. Gracie wasn't sure if he was being stubborn over the issue of the cake or if something else bothered him.

When Gracie approached Sister Mary, with the idea of baking cakes, she had been sympathetic to Doctor Ellard's position that no one soldier be singled out above the other. Conceding the man had been right, Gracie decided to compromise and suggested they bake loaves of gingerbread for all the wards. The Sisters at Our Lady of Charity thought it a marvelous idea as gingerbread was a favorite among the men. Not only did the nuns allow Gracie and Sister Mary to use their kitchen, they all pitched in to help.

When the nuns swept into the ward that afternoon with several loaves, Robbie had no idea that he'd been the inspiration.

With the fiddle on his shoulder, he walked up and down the ward playing requests for most of the afternoon.

"Why don't ye take the instrument with ye?" Gracie suggested as they prepared the evening medications.

He shrugged. "It'd be great to have, but I got no place to keep it. 'Sides the rain and cold will ruin it, and I'd have to worry it don't get broke."

"Then I'll be keeping it safe till ye return."

He nodded. "Don't fret, I'll be back."

"Ye're so tall, promise me, ye'll keep your head down. And no foolish frontal assaults at Marye's Heights."

He rolled his eyes and grinned. "I'll be fine. Reckon I survived this long..."

She glanced pointedly at his shoulder.

"Hell," he said with a shrug, "they was so many bullets flyin' around that day, I don't think it was even a Reb who shot me."

His bizarre logic baffled her. Shot was shot, and dead was dead. What did it matter where the bullet came from? She set her bottles, ointments, and lists on her tray. Then again, what did it matter if he needed to believe the lie?

"Ye best go on and get your supper, now."

He moved off down the aisle as though he hadn't a care in the world.

Gracie had saved a thick slice of gingerbread for Doctor Ellard and planned to offer it to him along with her apology when he returned to the ward that afternoon, but he never came through.

That night, Robbie made sure he said goodbye. She hugged him, and though he blushed, he seemed grateful to have someone close by to wish him well. He sat and talked to his uncle Mark for a while. Then with a wave, he left the ward.

That night after she enjoyed her own slice of gingerbread with her tea and a spoonful of honey, she prayed to the Virgin Mary to keep Robbie safe and that she'd see him again.

****

The next morning Micah acted as her orderly. He was nice enough, but he didn't have Robbie's enthusiasm and quick wit. Her regular orderly, Tom Halleck, was supposed to be back from his leave next week, and hopefully things would return to a regular routine.

She was stacking the dishes from breakfast when Micah approached her table.

"Do you know how to do this?"

Glancing up, she saw in his hand, the puzzle with the yoke and rings that she'd left beside Gilbert's bed the night he passed away.

"Sorry." She shook her head. "I could not get it. Ye might ask Gleason, the night orderly. He discerned how to move the ring and how to do the pyramid puzzle too."

Micah shrugged. "I did, but he didn't know how. Said they made him so mad he wanted to smash them."

She chuckled as Micah tossed the puzzle into the cupboard. The door at the end of the ward opened, and she heard Corporal Timon's voice. Turning, she reached past Micah and grabbed the slice of gingerbread she'd wrapped in a handkerchief and saved for Doctor Ellard. She half expected him to refuse the peace offering and tell her he didn't like gingerbread.

Smiling to herself, she swung around and started down the aisle. She took several steps before she realized the doctor with Corporal Timon was too short...and too gray...and too...

The doctor looked up, and their gazes met. She stared at Doctor Colfax in disbelief, the wrongness of his presence freezing her feet to the floor.

Her stunned brain tried to rationalize what she saw, or who she didn't see. Charles Ellard had conceived another jest. That's what had happened; he wasn't really gone. He must think scaring her with Doctor Colfax to be funny. For a moment she understood Robbie's desperation to believe he hadn't been wounded by a confederate minié ball.

Then she noticed the smug curl of Doctor Colfax's lips as they stretched toward his thick pork chop sideburns.

Well, Gracie McBride would not be laughed at by the likes of him. Snapping her spine straight, she shoved the gingerbread into her skirt pocket, and marched down the aisle.

"Where is Doctor Ellard?" she demanded before Doctor Colfax had a chance to say a word.

He took so long responding, she almost expected him to rub his hands together with dastardly glee.

"Captain Ellard has gone back to his regiment."

Gone? He left? But he hadn't said a word. Something wasn't right. She narrowed her gaze on Doctor Colfax. "Ye pompous old sawbones. Ye did this, telling yer lies and making yer reports."

"If those charges were dropped, Mrs. McBride, it was because you lied, not me."

She spun around and headed for the door, the click of her heels louder than usual in the suddenly quiet ward.

****

"Ah, Mrs. McBride, you're just the person I wanted to see."

Puzzled, because she had come to see him, she stepped into the doctor's office.

Rising, he gestured toward one of the chairs in front of his desk then waited until she sat before he too, lowered himself into his chair.

"You've worked with Captain Ellard for over a month now, and I'm hoping you can help me with something." He leaned to the left and rummaged through one of the drawers.

Gracie leaned forward. "Doctor Ellard be the reason I've come to see ye."

"Now where did I put it?" He pulled open another drawer. "The captain handed it in last evening, where did it go?"

"Doctor, I be wanting to know where Doctor Ellard—"

"Here it is." He straightened, raising the brown file folder then stretched across his desk and held it toward her. "I would appreciate if you could take a moment to read this for me."

Baffled, she accepted the folder and laid it open on her side of the wide desk. The sheets of paper looked like an inventory of sorts, maybe a requisition.

She studied the hand writing, knowing she'd seen this illegible scrawl somewhere before.

"Can you read it?" he asked eagerly.

She stared thoughtfully at the top of the first sheet.

"Acetate lead, alcohol, alcohol…extract of…bell…belladonna—"

"Excellent. Try reading another page."

She flipped ahead and read aloud a few words here and there. "Artery…forceps. Bullet probes, bone wax…"

Where had she seen this handwriting before? A capital 'B' followed by letters nearly impossible to decipher. "Bow saw, silver urinary staves…"

And the 'S,' printed and capitalized like the 'B' while the rest of the word was scribbled in that rushed script, as if the writer was too impatient to take the time… Wait. Bragg, Simon, Private. The unknown patient who'd received the two bullet wounds. Gracie had assumed Gleason, the night orderly had been the one who sat up with Bragg and learned the private's name while putting together the pyramid puzzle.

Every muscle went still. The word forceps, blurred on the paper.

Doctor Ellard.

It was his handwriting which scrawled Private Bragg's name across the top of the card. Doctor Ellard stayed up all night with that patient and never said a word, even as he'd lectured her for wanting to sit with Sergeant Baker. Doctor Ellard must be the mysterious puzzle solver, completing the pyramid while he sat beside Sergeant Baker as well as the yoke puzzle while he sat beside—

Sweet Mary Jesus, Gilbert. Her heart warmed at the picture that formed in her mind of Charles Ellard sitting in the dark beside the boy, talking to him so he'd know he wasn't alone, brushing the hair from his brow...

Then before that image could fully form, anger washed it from her mind along with any tenderness she'd begun to feel toward the man.

Why the conceited ass, he'd seen her crying. He knew it had broken her heart to think of Gilbert alone in the dark, dying and afraid. How could he have just stood there and not said a word?

Did he think a show of compassion to be weakness? Hadn't he realized that knowing he'd been with Gilbert for his last breath would have been meant far more to her than his arrogant kisses and ridiculous jokes? Her fingers tingled with the need to wrap around his throat.

"Mrs. McBride, are you feeling all right?"

Gracie blinked and looked up. "Yes, Doctor, I be fine."

He studied her thoughtfully for a moment as he cupped his chin and stroked his sideburns. "I only ask because you were smiling, and that was not the reaction I expected when I asked if you could recopy the whole requisition."

Heat flooded her cheeks. "Recopy this? To be sure, 'tis not a problem." She squinted at the page. Did that say three, or five, or eight thousand blankets? "And if I have doubt about these numbers Doctor Ellard can clarify them for me."

"I'm afraid Captain Ellard is no longer here."

"Excuse me?"

"Captain Ellard left this morning for Falmouth."

Falmouth? He was gone? Really gone? She thought he'd been assigned to another ward, which is why she'd come to see Doctor Bliss.

"For how long?"

"Fortu—er—unfortunately, it's permanent."

"Can ye not get him back?"

"I'm sorry, Mrs. McBride, but there is nothing I can do." Doctor Bliss pressed his fingertips together and leaned back in his chair. "Captain Ellard was only assigned to this hospital temporarily while he recovered from his…er…illness. It was always intended he return to his regiment."

"But Doctor Ellard be a fine surgeon and needed here."

"There is no doubt that he is a good doctor, but a man with his skill is better served closer to the battle where he can care for the wounded as they come off the field, not when they arrive here days or weeks later."

"''Tis not right, to be giving the man no notice."

"He's known for a good week now."

A week? He'd known he was leaving for a week and hadn't said a word? Maybe she hadn't mattered to him as much as she thought. Then why the kisses? Many people thought nurses no more than immoral, loose women. Is that why he'd kissed her? Had he been looking to her for a dalliance? Then good riddance.

Why did she care anyway? Charles Ellard was no William McBride. Not with his notions of a woman's delicate sensibilities.

Doctor Bliss pulled open the top drawer of his desk and withdrew a folded piece of paper. "He asked me to give you this."

Gracie reached out and accepted the note. Was this his way of saying goodbye? She turned it over, tempted to break open the wax seal and read the contents. "Thank ye," she said instead, then slipped it into her pocket.

"I believe you have a good twenty minutes before the boat leaves." Doctor Bliss gave a nod toward the mantel clock on a side table. "If you hurry, you might be able to catch him."

Realizing she'd been dismissed, she came to her feet. Doctor Bliss did the same.

"You are an excellent nurse, Mrs. McBride. Make the best of it and try not to antagonize Doctor Colfax."

Too late for that, she thought then thanked Doctor Bliss and hurried back to her room.

Should she go down to the steamboat landing? She picked up her shawl and swung it around her shoulders. The better question was why? Why did she *want* to go?

Because wishing him well was the polite thing to

do after all they'd shared the past month, and because she did still have that wrapped piece of gingerbread in her pocket. She glanced at the watch pinned to her bodice.

Only fifteen minutes. She needn't hurry, she told herself, though her feet were nearly running as she passed the long picket fence which separated the front of the hospital from the sidewalk. It wasn't *that* important to catch him, but her pace only quickened.

She gathered her skirt in her hands to keep from tripping as she hurried down Seventh Street and crossed the muddy intersection. Only six blocks to go.

Horse hooves squished and sucked behind her.

"Nurse McBride. Gracie."

A buggy rolled alongside. Her pace slowed as she turned toward the vehicle in the street.

Major Carlton leaned out. "May we drive you somewhere?"

The word 'no,' nearly crossed her lips. "Aye, I would be thankful for a ride."

Before the major's brother, Sam, could rein the horse to a complete stop, she hiked up her skirt and scrambled into the buggy, nearly tumbling into the major's lap.

"So sorry." She quickly apologized as she righted herself. "Did I hurt yer leg?"

The major slid closer to his brother allowing her more room on the seat. "No, not at all. I'm fine. Where are you going?"

She pointed straight ahead. "To the steamboat landing at the end o' the wharf, but I don't mean to take ye out of yer way. Drop me as close as ye can, 'twill be fine."

"We were on our way to the train station, but we've plenty of time."

"I didn't know ye were still in Washington," she said, tucking her skirt close. "I thought Sam had come to take ye home."

"He wanted to remain a few days to see the sights."

She nodded and mumbled something appropriate, wondering why Sam didn't urge the horse to move faster. She'd been walking more quickly than this on the sidewalk. The thought crossed her mind to jump out, but the major would probably be mortified, and she'd likely end up twisting her ankle.

She glanced at her watch. Sam must have felt her anxiety, for he clucked to the horse and it moved into a trot.

A few minutes later he stopped the buggy at the first of three, side-by-side warehouses which ran parallel to the Potomac River. Again she chafed at the protocol which made her sit in the seat and wait for Sam to come around and assist her from the buggy.

"Would you like us to wait for you?" Major Carlton asked.

She smiled up at him. "I thank ye for yer help, but I do not want ye to be missing your train."

"As I said, we have time."

She glanced down the wharf, her eyes sorting through the forest of masts from three tall ships, docked at two of the piers which jutted into the river. Workers transferred wooden boxes from wagons onto the boats.

A small steamboat chugged past on the river. The longest of the four piers which jutted into the water was crowded with soldiers and at the end sat a large, two story steamboat. "Excuse me, Major. I thank ye for the ride, but I must go."

A wave of guilt washed over her for being so abrupt, but the crowd of soldiers had begun making its way up the gangplank, and she didn't have time for pleasantries.

She waved goodbye to the major and his brother then moved forward, focused on finding Doctor Ellard. Barrels and crates stacked as high as her head were being loaded into wagons. A team of horses clattered up behind her, and she had to hurry off to the side so the wagon could pass.

If Gracie had known what it meant to quit, she would have turned around and walked the ten blocks back to the hospital.

Unable to see beyond the wall of men in front of her, Gracie elbowed her way to the warehouse closest to the river. Beside a pyramid of barrels, at the corner of the building, she climbed onto a wide flat cart like the ones used for moving luggage at the train station. Balancing herself with one hand on the clapboard wall, she scanned the heads of anyone wearing a uniform who stood taller than the rest.

Gulls screeched overhead then swooped down to hop around the ground inspecting for bits of food, before taking flight once more.

Young boys with eager expressions darted in and out among the crowd and the wagons. A row of ambulances stood off to the side. Horses stomped their hooves, their harnesses jangled as their heads bobbed with their efforts to escape the boredom of standing still.

Soldiers shuffled toward the steamboat at the end of the crowded pier. In one hand they each carried a rifle. On their backs, bulging packs topped with a rolled blanket. These men were healthy, but thin, with deep lines of fatigue etched in their faces.

The shrill blast of the steam whistle overwhelmed the sounds of the dockside bustle.

What if Doctor Ellard had already boarded the boat? There were so many people…

"'Scuse me, ma'am?"

She glanced down. A young man wearing a black wool cap and jacket stood looking up at her. "You have to get off there. It ain't safe."

"One moment, please."

She scanned the soldiers one last time. There, way down at the opposite end of the platform, she spotted him. She'd forgotten that aside from being tall, he had that invisible wall around him which kept him isolated from others and now parted the flow of boarding soldiers around him like a rock in a stream.

"Doctor Ellard!" she called out hoping to be heard over the din. "Doctor Ellard!"

Several men glanced her way then returned to their own business.

"Ma'am, you have to get down."

At least she had a fix on his position.

The dock worker extended his hand. She placed her fingers in his rough, calloused palm and stepped off the cart. "Thank ye," she murmured absently, already making her way toward the end of the long pier.

"Excuse me…pardon me…" She kept up the litany as she pressed her way through the congestion of stevedores and military men. "I'm sorry," she added when she bumped into men or stepped on toes.

She'd nearly reached the end of the pier when she

spotted Doctor Ellard moving up the gangplank. The green sash of the medical corps tied around his waist distinguished his uniform from every other man in blue. "Doctor Ellard! Charles!"

The whistle blew again. Without pause, he stepped onto the boat.

Shoulders sagging, she heaved a defeated sigh. Oddly, her eyes began to sting.

Tobacco smoke, she told herself, as she waved away the smelly cloud wafting from the cigar clamped between the teeth of the sergeant in front of her. She wasn't crying. Pressing her index fingers against the inside corners of her eyes, she blotted away the moisture.

She might as well carry on. Besides, she still had his slice of gingerbread in her pocket.

"Excuse me," she said again, weaving her way forward until she reached the end of the gangplank.

"Halt, please, ma'am."

She stopped and turned. A clean-shaven, older man stood watching her. He wore sky-blue military pants and jacket. Three chevrons had been sewn on the sleeves of his upper arms and on his chest was pinned the badge of the Provost Guard.

"Pass?"

"'Tis someone on this boat I be needing to find."

"This is a military transport going south, ma'am. No civilian gets on without a pass from the Provost Marshal."

"'Twill only take me a minute or two."

"Not without a pass." Tight furrows appeared above the bridge of his nose as the boredom in his face shifted to irritation.

"Please, Sergeant."

He crossed his arms. His jaw thrust forward, his silent reply, firm and unyielding.

The crowd of soldiers had quickly dwindled to a few stragglers. Gracie tried to dart around the guard.

He immediately blocked her way.

She tried a different tactic. "Then can ye go on board instead, and ask for Captain Ellard to come out here?"

When he only glared at her, she stepped to the side of the gangplank and searched the faces of the soldiers standing along the rail of the deck. Behind them a row of windows framed the faces of more soldiers, and above those windows were the windows of an upper deck.

"Doctor Ellard," she called. "Does anyone know Doctor Ellard?" In response all she received from the soldiers were enthusiastic waves and several men claiming to be Doctor Ellard.

Frustrated, she approached the sergeant again. "Please?"

He shook his head.

Discouraged, she slipped her hand into her pocket and withdrew the gingerbread wrapped in her handkerchief.

"Then can ye at least go on board and give this to Captain Charles Ellard? Tell him 'tis from Gracie McBride." She passed it to the sergeant.

Yelling from one of the soldiers caught her attention, and she turned toward the boat.

A soldier leaned over the rail and waved his cap. "Who are you looking for?"

The chugging of the steamboat engine grew louder.

"Captain Charles Ellard!" She yelled over the noise.

The man cupped his ear and shook his head.

"Captain Charles Ellard! He's a doctor."

"Ellard?"

"Yes!"

Two of the crew approached the gangplank and lifted it away from the steamboat.

A dockworker stepped up beside her. "Ma'am you'll have to step back."

Reluctantly, she moved away from the edge of the pier so the two men could move the gangplank aside.

The men on the boat closed the gate over the opening as the steamboat, which had been docked pointing up river, now slowly backed away from the landing.

She searched the men at the rail one more time. The boat slowly turned, until the bow pointed down river and the large round paddle wheel faced her. Big blue letters spelled out the name *John Brooks*. She waved one last time then turned away.

The sergeant was still on the dock—eating her gingerbread.

She lunged for him, knocking his hand away from his mouth. The last bite flew to the ground. "How dare ye!"

A smirk flattened his lips and turned up the corners of his mouth. "You gave it to me."

Her hands curled into fists so tight her nails dug into her palms. "To be giving to another."

He shrugged.

Frustration and anger crested inside her like breakers off the Cliffs of Moher. She drew back her fist and swung.

Expecting her knuckles to connect with some part of his person, Gracie gasped when strong fingers wrapped around her forearm and halted its forward motion.

For a moment she struggled to free her arm from the grip of the unknown person.

"Gracie. Nurse McBride."

She turned toward the voice of the man suddenly beside her. Major Carlton, leaning heavily on one crutch, gradually eased his hold on her arm as he looked down his nose at the sergeant as though inspecting a green recruit.

Instinctively, the sergeant snapped to attention.

"Is there a problem here?" Major Carlton asked.

"No, sir. The lady was trying to board the transport. I was only doing my job by stopping her."

The major switched his attention back to her. "Are you all right? Did this man upset you or behave in any manner inappropriate for a gentleman?"

"No," she replied, though she wished the gingerbread had been laced with one of her purgatives.

The major's shrewd gaze darted between them, but all he said was, "Very well, Sergeant, you are dismissed."

The man moved on down the pier as the *John Brooks* headed south.

"Do you want to tell me what happened?"

She shook her head, wondering if she'd ever see Charles Ellard again.

"Well, whatever the issue between you, you cannot hit a provost guard, unless you want to go to jail."

"I'd not have hurt him."

"Yes, well…"

"Why are ye here? I thought ye'd a train to catch."

"I was not comfortable leaving you unprotected among all these men."

They slowly walked back down the length of the pier toward the warehouses. Sam waited with the buggy.

"I can take care o'meself, Major."

He sighed. "I thought you were going to call me Win."

"I found the poem ye wrote for me."

"Really?" His gaze brightened for a moment then lowered to the wide planks beneath their feet. "It wasn't very good."

"'Twas a fine poem and so sweet o' ye to write it special for me."

He stopped and glanced up expectantly.

She met his gaze, but unsure of what to say, she added, "I'll treasure it always."

"But…" He shifted his weight on his crutches. "You don't return my affections."

"Ye are a kind, sweet man, Winfield Carlton. I enjoyed talking with ye and singing with ye, but—"

"But you have feelings for Captain Ellard."

"No."

Major Carlton smiled sadly.

"I still mourn me husband, Major. What we had together was special. No other man will ever hold my affections."

He nodded, though doubt shadowed his face.

They continued toward the buggy.

"Might we offer you a ride back to the hospital?"

"I thank ye, but 'tis a fine day for a walk."

He inclined his head. "Then I wish you well, Mrs.

McBride."

Sam stepped forward to assist Major Carlton into the buggy and reined the horse around. Then with a final wave, Major Carlton and his brother headed to the train station.

Gracie swung back toward the river. Crossing her arms, she tried to rub away the chill. Gradually the stacks of the *John Brooks* faded from sight. The black smoke that poured from them turned to gray and drifted away to blend with the clouds. That was that. He was gone.

From her pocket, she withdrew the note he'd left for her with Doctor Bliss. *Mrs. McBride* had been scrawled across the front. Was this a farewell? He'd kissed her twice and held her while she cried. Did he care for her the way Major Carlton did? Were his parting words a declaration of his affections?

Turning the letter over, she ran her finger across the bumps and ridges of the blue wax seal. The letters C-P framed a larger letter E. She slid her finger under the edge of the paper careful not to break the wax. Drawing a breath, she unfolded the note. A few, nearly illegible lines had been scribbled across the center of the page.

My grandfather is sending a box from his hotel. When it arrives could you care for the contents? I will write again when I better know my situation.

In disbelief she stared at the note. She read it again, just to see if she'd misunderstood the inked lines, curls, and bumps. Did he mean more than he was saying?

No. There was no other way to interpret the handwriting. After working closely for a month, after life and death, tears and kisses, he wanted her to keep a box?

Her fingers tightened, crinkling the sides of the paper. No goodbye, just a box. She lifted her gaze to the river. A breeze carried in the salty scent of the distant ocean over the river where it blended with the smell of muck and dead fish.

She sighed. A box. At least he hadn't declared any amorous affections. She certainly did not want that, but a goodbye would have been nice.

For a moment she wondered what kind of note Charles Ellard would pen if he ever fell in love. Would it be as blunt and socially inept as the man? Did he even know the niceties of courtship?

She hoped one day he would find a woman who didn't expect such things as flowers and gentle words, that she would appreciate his intelligence and realize he was the kind of man who sat quietly beside his patients, working his puzzles, keeping vigil in the middle of the night so no one in his care had to die alone or be afraid.

She smoothed out the wrinkles, refolded the paper and slipped it into her pocket. Slowly, she walked back to the hospital. At least she'd hear from him again.

Chapter Eight

"Look, there. See that pretty gal waving."

"She's waving to her sweetheart.

"Wave to me, darling."

Charles lowered his long frame onto the end of the bench seat. The two men who occupied it slid toward the outside wall of the boat to give him room. His knees bumped into the back of the man in front of him, who turned and gave him a quick look of disapproval.

If Charles could have moved he would have, but as it was, men were already sitting on the floor. Besides, he was an officer. The corporal in front of him had no right to complain.

"What's she doing now?"

"Yelling someone's name."

Eager for a glimpse of the woman on the pier, men crowded the windows along the dock side of the boat, waving and calling to her through the glass. No doubt a woman of low standing. He couldn't imagine any woman of his acquaintance who would have yelled and waved at a group of strange men like a common street walker.

The engines chugged as steam pressure built and the boat began to slowly back away from the dock.

"Yell my name, darling."

"Yo, Freddie, look at that red hair."

The words punched Charles in the chest. He

stiffened under their impact. No, his mind immediately denied.

A few men moved away from the windows searching for their seats, while others continued to crane their necks as the boat moved back. "I seen her somewheres."

"Yeah, she's one of the nurses."

Charles pushed to his feet. It couldn't be, but he had to know. Shoving his way between the men, he climbed the steps to the deck and found an opening among the soldiers nearly hanging over the side. One hand on the rail, the other gripping a rope that hung from one of the unused yardarms, he leaned out trying to sort through the congestion of faces on the dock.

He'd stupidly waited to board the steamboat while others filed on ahead of him, some schoolboy fantasy keeping his boots planted on the wooden pier, hoping she'd come.

The logical side of his brain reminded him that he'd never told her he was leaving. He should have let her know, but he'd feared the disappointment he knew he'd feel if she didn't come to wish him well. So he'd stood there looking foolish, knowing she'd probably noticed his absence by now, wistfully hoping to see her one more time.

In his fantasy she kissed him and waved goodbye. She'd give a token, a ribbon, some fringe from her shawl, or a lock of her hair.

A lock of autumn red hair he could carry in his watch with his picture of his mother. He could take it out and inhale that slight scent of lye, trace her snip of hair over his lips, and remember. In his mind it would be his talisman, that special thing to hold onto, something to keep him sane amidst the chaos, reminding him there was still something pure and beautiful in this world.

But she hadn't come, because he hadn't told her. So he'd boarded the crowded boat and found a seat.

Now renewed anticipation kept him searching.

One of the soldiers had mentioned red hair. If it was Gracie that meant she'd been in a hurry to get here and hadn't worn her bonnet. He searched the thinning crowd for a woman without one, but the boat was turning and he had to fight his way to the other side. He stretched out over the rail. The boat picked up speed and he had to hustle to reach the stern.

There. He leaned out farther. A woman without a bonnet or hoops. His heart lifted and a smile tugged at the corners of his mouth. She had come.

She stood near the edge of the pier her hand raised to shield her eyes from the sun as she gazed toward the boat moving into the center of the river. Beside her stood a soldier on crutches, his leg amputated just above his knee.

Charles' heart plunged into his stomach, displacing the breakfast he'd hastily eaten. He straightened away from the rail and stared blankly at the dock, watching the people grow smaller, watching the foamy wake, churned up by the paddle wheel, as it rolled away from the boat toward the banks of the Potomac.

The Washington skyline faded until all that was left was the skeletal dome of the capitol building and that ragged, half-finished marble obelisk. He turned away, searching among the soldiers for a place to sit. Near the bow he wedged himself into a small space among a group of young soldiers and lowered himself to the deck. He drew up one knee and extended his other leg. The sole of his boot bumped against a private in a brand new uniform. Charles glared at him, shutting him up before he could utter the smallest sound of complaint.

His gaze passed over each excited face. How long before the same jaded hardness which had slowly seeped into his bones since Manassas, obliterated the eagerness in each expression? How long before one of them died and how long before one of them lay on his table waiting for his bone saw.

****

Sergeant Baker's fever was lower this morning, and he smiled as Gracie helped him to the chair next to his bed.

"Feeling better, are ye now?"

Though a thick bandage wrapped around his throat, he managed a slight nod.

A soft breeze wafted through the area. She glanced toward the side door and inhaled the fresh scent of spring.

So much better than the sour bite of sweat and urine, and putrid flesh, which permeated the wards, her clothes, and her hair so that she hardly noticed the fetid odors until moments like this. This morning's breeze so clean and pure she'd yet to detect even the faintest whiff of the garbage and dead animals which often floated in the muck of the nearby canal.

"But there be a chill there, near the side door."

"No. I am not switching his bed assignment. Give him an extra blanket."

She tucked a blanket around Sergeant Baker's waist and draped a second over his shoulders.

"Most all these patients die…" Doctor Colfax's smug declaration echoed in her head.

Was that the reason Doctor Ellard assigned Sergeant Baker this bed? Had the cooler air kept the sergeant's fever at bay? Had the flow of fresh air from outside kept the miasma away? Could the arrogant man ever explain himself?

Trying to understand the workings of Doctor Ellard's brain was more difficult than one of the cursed wooden puzzles, made even more frustrating now that the man was gone.

Sergeant Baker's brow furrowed.

She forced a bright smile. "Soon ye'll be ready to go home and won't that be fine?"

Turning her attention to the bed, she yanked the sheets from the mattress, rolled them into a ball, and tossed them on the floor. Grabbing a clean sheet from her stack on the bedside table, she spread it over the mattress, then folded and pulled tight the corners.

The sergeant whispered something, but his voice was so faint, Gracie couldn't make out his words.

"Ye should not talk. Yer throat has not healed."

Giving the blanket a hard snap, she waited for it to float down then smoothed it out across the sheet. As she stepped around to tuck in the other side, Sergeant Baker grabbed her hand.

"Doc…" he whispered, though she could barely understand the word.

"Are ye in pain? Do ye need the doctor?"

He shook his head. "Ta…him."

She strained her ears, confused by what he wanted until he pointed to his throat.

Assuming he wanted to thank the surgeon who'd

saved his life, she explained. "Doctor Ellard is not here any—"

He cut off her words with a wave of his hand. "Doc…Re…"

She frowned, not certain what he'd said after the word doctor. "Doctor Colfax will be back later."

He shook his head. "Reee," he rasped.

"Robbie?" She smiled as much as she could with a pillow tucked under her chin. "The lad has such skill in his work he could well be a doctor one day. Did he not tell ye he's gone back to his unit at Falmouth?"

Sergeant Baker heaved a weighted sigh as he gave his head a vigorous shake. He touched the wound at his throat. "Doc Reee."

She dropped the pillow at the head of his bed before lowering herself to the edge of the mattress.

He tried to speak again, but his words became trapped inside his swollen throat. His shoulders drooped and he shook his head.

Reaching out, she gave his hand a motherly squeeze. "'Tis naught to be frettin' o'er. Maybe ye be thinking of yer doctor at Falmouth, before ye come here. We can talk later if ye've a mind, and yer feelin' more yerself."

She left him sitting beside his bed then walked to the table at the center of the ward. Micah leaned on the end, focused on the two halves of the pyramid puzzle. He straightened when she approached and set down her pile of sheets.

Moving to the cupboard, she searched through the musical instruments, books, stationery, and puzzles inside. She withdrew a deck of cards and held them out to the tall attendant. "Might ye take this to Sergeant

Baker? I fear the man has become bored and will try to talk before his throat is healed."

"Yes, ma'am." Micah set down the puzzle and accepted the cards. "Sergeant Cole at the general office said something came for Doctor Ellard. He wondered if you knew of any kin he could send it on to, or should he ship it down to Falmouth? And Major Bliss wants to see you when you're not busy."

"Thank ye, Micah. I'll see to it in a minute. Just be sure to stow all the soiled linens in the bags before Leticia comes to collect them for the laundry."

Gracie dropped into her chair and picked up the puzzle. How easily Doctor Ellard had fitted the halves together. And the other puzzle with the yoke and rings.

Why couldn't he have told her he'd sat up with Gilbert the night the boy passed away, or that he'd stayed with Sergeant Baker the night he'd nearly died?

And why hadn't the insufferable man told her he was leaving?

The door opened at the end of the ward. She glanced up. For a half a second, she expected to see him striding down the length of the aisle.

She'd done the same thing after William's death, lifting her gaze to the door at six o'clock, expecting him to walk into the kitchen for supper, or rolling over in bed and being surprised to find his side empty and cold.

Standing, she opened the cupboard and tossed the puzzle halves on the shelf beside the violin. It was William she missed, not that lanky doctor and his ridiculous jokes. Slamming the cupboard shut, she turned and headed to the general office to find out what Doctor Colfax had made complaint about this time.

****

"Ah, Mrs. McBride, come in." Doctor Bliss gestured toward the chairs in front of his desk.

She lowered herself onto the edge of the leather cushion and folded her hands together.

He too, sat. The wheels of his chair rumbled across the wood floor like distant thunder as he moved close to the desk. He thumbed through one of the paper piles stacked around his desk top. He removed a sheet then put it back before pulling out another. "Here we are."

Gracie tensed, wondering what she'd done wrong now. In the four days since Doctor Ellard left for Falmouth, Doctor Colfax had registered four complaints with Doctor Bliss regarding both her behavior and her performance.

"Sergeant Folsom, the cook in the Special Diets kitchen has submitted a complaint regarding the amount of milk you request for your ward."

She stiffened. "'Tis no more than usual."

"I spoke to Doctor Colfax, and he seems to feel that you may have continued to submit your special diet requests, based on Doctor Ellard's recommendations."

Gracie ground her thumb against the center of her palm. "Doctor, some of the men we have be very ill. Milk sops and milk punch be excellent for nourishing patients whose conditions be most critical."

Doctor Bliss leaned forward and leveled his most direct stare on her. "I would like to remind you that you are required to heed the orders of the physician in charge of the ward. In this case Doctor Colfax. He is far more knowledgeable in all aspects of medicine than you. If he prescribes wine punch that is the order you will follow."

Her pulse thudded against the side of her neck. She

swallowed against the tightness in her throat and dug her thumbnail into her palm. "Yes, sir," she whispered.

"Very good. Now there is just one more thing. Have you had a chance to copy that supply requisition?"

"'Tis only the numbers I be having a wee bit o' trouble deciphering."

"Do you think you could finish it up this afternoon? We are already into April. In a few weeks, the armies will be on the move. We can't afford to be caught without vital supplies."

Her palm hurt from the pressure of her thumb and nail pressing into the soft center. She nodded. "Yes, sir."

Charles Ellard was a smart man. Why couldn't he learn to write legibly? The large capital letter at the start of each word was fine, but the rest of the letters were scrawled in a rush, as though his brain had jumped to the next word before his hand could finish writing the first.

Doctor Bliss bid her good day.

Leaving his office, she picked up the expected package. *Ellard, C.P., Surg. Capt. 69th Pennsyvania, Armory Square Hospital, Washington, D.C.* had been precisely printed across a tag tied to the handle of a brown leather hat-box, the kind used for travel with a hinged back and three clasps to secure the lid. An oval name plate engraved with the initials *J R H*, lay beneath the curved handle.

Returning to her room, she set the box on her bed and sat down beside it. He'd asked her to look after it, so it was only right that she know what was inside. Besides, she was entitled to satisfy her curiosity after the torturous hours she spent trying to decipher pages of illegible handwriting.

The lock above the handle appeared to be broken. The tab which normally snapped into place above the key hole was missing. She clicked open the two brass clasps on either side of the box and lifted back the hinged lid. Pretty pink and blue paper with red roses and green leaves lined the interior. In the center of the lid was a faded label for a hat maker in Philadelphia and the name Julia Rosemary Harrison printed on the line beside the words—*Property Of.*

A stuffed rabbit caught her attention next. It lay atop a pile of children's toys and books. She lifted it out smiling at the expressionless face. Some of the fuzz had been worn away on the ears, where tiny hands must have constantly held it tight.

Had the rabbit belonged to Charles? He was always so controlled, so sure of himself, she found it difficult to imagine him as a child. Her brothers had been rowdy and full of laughter whether running the streets, stealing pies, or building a raft to sail in the bay.

Charles would have had bright blue eyes, a mop of dark hair, and knobby knees with skinny limbs that were always longer than his clothes. Had this rabbit been his daytime playmate, his nighttime protector, guarding him from monsters beneath his bed?

She gave the soft ears a quick stroke and spotted the tiny row of neat black stitches where the left ear had been reattached to the top of the head. Had his mother lovingly repaired the toy for him before she died?

She set the rabbit on her small bedside table, next to a photograph of William taken when he graduated from the Royal College of Surgeons.

The daguerreotype was taken on their wedding day. Gazing at the black and gray image inside a silver oval frame, it was hard to believe ten years had passed. She'd been just sixteen, but she'd felt so mature standing before the priest with William beside her. He had just started his practice in East Boston, and they'd naively believed that as long as they were together they could conquer the world.

How could she know a pain in William's side would take the only man she'd ever loved? If only she'd been able to find a physician able to save him.

At least coming here to Armory Square Hospital had given her the opportunity to use all William had taught her for good. And though Doctor Ellard constantly reminded her women did not belong in war, that she did not belong in war, he did allow her to help without too much argument.

She closed the lid of the hatbox, shutting away the carved animals, spelling blocks, and books. Rising from the bed, she shoved the box into the corner underneath the tiny table she used as a writing desk. Repositioning the chair she sat, picked up her pen, and went back to the task of transcribing Doctor Ellard's hospital supply requisition.

****

The sharp cadence of a bugle blaring reveille jolted Charles from a sound sleep. He sniffed through his cold nose and burrowed deeper beneath his blankets, hoping to enjoy their warmth for another five minutes. Wind snapped at the tiny log and canvas hut the way it snapped the lines of wet sheets strung around the laundry.

Across the width of their tiny quarters came the

thump, thump of Major Dennis stomping into his boots.

Charles opened one eye. Just once he'd love to sleep past five a.m. He tossed back his covers and set his stocking feet on the plank floor. Cold seeped through his wool socks. He shivered.

"Looks like it snowed," Major Dennis said as he hooked his suspenders over his shoulders.

Charles pulled on his pants and glanced toward the front of the hut where frosty wisps of white clung to the cracks between the logs. Stepping to the small commode, he poured water into the basin and bent forward to splash his face with icy wet. A chill rippled through his body.

"Where's that private with the wood for the fireplace?"

"We're leaving anyway. You really going to have him build a fire?" The major frowned as he buttoned his coat. "Besides he's probably already cooking our breakfast."

Charles leaned close to the tiny mirror and rubbed his hand over his jaw. "I hate shaving with cold water."

"Washington made you soft, Ellard." The major pulled on his gloves. "If you don't like it, grow a beard like mine." He set his hat on his head and opened the door. "Hey, it did snow. Should melt though, as soon as the sun comes up."

The small shaving mirror reflected the gray dawn outside and the snow which covered the ground and other tents. Great. He never should have complained about the dust, because now all that had been dust for past three days would be mud.

A gust of wind blew through the opening before Major Dennis pulled the door closed behind him.

Charles dipped his shaving brush in the water then set it in the mug against the disc of soap and tried furiously to whip it into a lather.

He hated it here. Cold, mud, rain, and monotony. Despite being surrounded by a hundred and thirty thousand men, he was lonely.

He should be used to the feeling, having been the odd man out his entire life, but Gracie McBride had briefly filled that aching emptiness. They'd connected. She'd made him smile. In four short weeks entering the wards had become something he anticipated. He appreciated her quiet efficiency and found himself eager for the stimulation of their verbal sparring matches. Like an intricate puzzle, she'd challenged him. Now he was alone again.

He winced as the blade cut into the thin skin at the back of his jaw. He pressed his index finger against the wound, pushing hard against the bone. Searching his face in the mirror, he watched blood ooze around his finger and mixed with the soap, creating a thin pink trail down the side of his neck. A dab of witch hazel would stop it. He dug through his ditty bag, but the bottle wasn't there. Frustration rumbled in his throat.

Crossing to his trunk, he lifted the lid and pulled down the set of drawers and compartments. His eye went straight to the section where he stored his shaving kit. Empty. Had Major Dennis been using his things again?

He heaved a weighted sigh and began a thorough search, assuming the bottle had somehow become mislaid. Locking the top compartment back in place, he studied the neatly organized contents, mentally recalling where each one of his belongings had been placed. He slid his arm into the depths between his clothing and the outside wall of the trunk, following it around in a circle.

His fingers brushed the cool glass of his whiskey bottle. It crossed his mind to have a drink, but thought better of it and continued probing. The hard edge of a book was his next non-clothing encounter. Odd, because he'd placed all his medical books at the bottom. Curious, he lifted it out.

Beeton's Book of Jokes and Jests. He'd planned to leave it in the ward with the other books, but at the last minute, he'd shoved it into his trunk.

He studied the group of laughing faces on the cover. When he'd purchased it, he'd assumed it would be filled with amusing anecdotes which would surely make Gracie smile. And while that hadn't happened, for some reason he couldn't part with the ridiculous volume.

He'd yet to write to her and ask if she received the box from his grandfather. He could include a joke. Perhaps they were more humorous when he wasn't telling them. But what if she hated the written version as much as those he recited aloud? What if she didn't continue the correspondence?

He tossed the book on top of his frock coat and slammed the lid. He no longer needed the witch hazel anyway. At the mirror he scraped away the last of the drying soap, brushed his teeth, and finished dressing.

He didn't care about breakfast. All he really wanted was a cup of coffee. He headed between the tents toward the morning cook fire.

Laughter rang out.

Someone said, "Yeah, the majesty of those

shoulder straps seems to have conveyed to his brain the idea he lords over the rest of us."

More laughter.

He turned the corner. Major Dennis sat with a few other medical officers in front of a fire where two privates cooked breakfast. Conversation stopped.

Disregarding the silence, Charles approached and the orderly assigned to Major Dennis wordlessly handed him a tin cup.

Charles accepted it with a nod and took a sip of the bitter liquid, grateful for the warmth which slid down the back of his throat and spread through his stomach. He savored another swallow then uncomfortable with the prolonged quiet he gulped downed the rest of his drink, ignoring the heat against his tongue and the roof of his mouth.

He passed back the empty cup and turned away. He'd only gone a few paces when the low murmurs of their conversation began again. Why it bothered him now, when being excluded had never bothered him before, he didn't know. With a sigh, he dismissed the maudlin sentiment and went on his way.

The regimental hospital was little more than a grouping of several large tents set up over wide, log dug-outs. A small cabin held the medical supplies. To alleviate the slop of deep mud, corduroy roads and walkways had been constructed by lashing logs together like an endless maze of river rafts twining between the camps and the main thoroughfares. The area in front of the hospital tents was covered by one of these corduroy walkways, now nearly as muddy as ground around them.

Men reporting for sick-call stood along the walk, a

seemingly endless line of frayed, dark-blue sack coats and light blue wool trousers, stained and sagging. Some men left their pants to hang over their shoes. Others rolled them to their ankles to keep from being splattered with the red clay.

The line wasn't too long, and a small group of men stood clustered around another man leaning on a crutch.

"Yes, when the Rebels whack us," he recited in a deep sing-song voice, "You are always ready with your traps, To mangle, saw, and hack us."

Laughter burst from the group.

"I got another one. Ho! Ho! Old saw bones, here you come…"

Charles stopped behind one of the men and waited. Across the circle one man looked up. His eyes widened. He snapped to attention and saluted.

The other men turned toward him as one and raised their right hands, palms out, to the visors of their caps, their elbows at proper shoulder height. Charles returned their salutes and continued past to the front of the surgery tent.

The regimental surgeon, Major Balch, sat before a table, examining a bloody gash in the forearm of a young sergeant. An attendant stood off to one side recording the name, rank, company, and medical complaint of each man in line.

Charles quickly surveyed the men waiting to be seen, then checked the list the attendant had completed. Glancing around, he spied an empty ammunition crate. He picked it up by the cleanest side and set it on end, near the table where Major Balch cleaned the wound of the young sergeant.

The makeshift stool wobbled when Charles sat, but

he braced his heel against one of the lashed logs and called for the next man on the list.

Charles pulled his stethoscope from his pocket and placed the bell end against the man's chest.

"Cough."

The wheezy rattle was quite clear through the instrument as the soldier coughed and breathed.

"Inflammation of the bronchia," Charles dictated to the attendant. "Write him a pass excusing him from drill for the next two days."

The attendant filled out the form, then handed it to Charles who quickly added his signature.

Charles slipped into the log building and returned with a bottle of quinine. He shook a tiny tablet into the soldier's palm. "Take this then come see me on Tuesday. Sooner, if you feel worse."

"Thank you, sir." The corporal swallowed the pill, accepted the pass, and turned to go.

"Get some sleep," Charles added.

The next two cases were dysentery and the following one of scurvy. Charles had the attendant take the men to the second of the hospital tents. This was the fourth case of scurvy he'd seen since he arrived. The army needed to provide these men with more vegetables and fruit.

He gestured the next man forward. The poet from earlier limped slowly toward Charles, carefully placing his crutch, taking short measured steps as he maneuvered across the logs.

Charles glanced over at Major Balch, who carefully pushed a length of silk thread through the eye of a curved needle. The thought crossed his mind to suggest Balch use a Glover's suture so it wouldn't leave as noticeable a scar but thought better of the idea. For some reason the other doctors didn't seem to like it when he offered advice.

Turning back to his approaching patient, he watched as the man hopped forward, repositioned the crutch, and hopped forward again.

Charles stood and gestured for the private to take the seat. The man wore no shoe and had sloppily wrapped a dirty gray cloth over his foot and around his ankle.

"What is wrong with your foot?"

The man shook his head. "I don't know, Doc. Hurts somethin' terrible. I reckon I must'a broke it or somethin'."

Charles hunkered down and rested the man's leg on his thigh. He unwound the bandage and peered closely at the ankle. "Does this hurt?" Charles turned the foot left.

The private stiffened and sucked in his breath.

"How about this?" Charles rotated the foot toward the right.

The private reacted with another sharp intake of breath.

"I'm going to press on it in different areas," Charles explained as he searched for signs of discoloration. "Tell me if it hurts."

The man nodded.

Charles pressed and poked the inner and outer ankle bones, across the arch, around the heel, and against the ball of the foot.

The private cringed and winced each time, pairing every flinch with either an, "Owww," or an, "Oooh."

"How did you say you injured it?"

"Don't know. We had picket duty a couple a nights ago. We had to march for miles. We was awake all night and had to march back. I must a tripped and twisted it or something. I can't march no more."

"And why have you not come to see me before today?"

"Reckon I thought it'd get better, but it ain't."

Charles set the man's foot down, bunched up the old bandage, and tossed it into the private's lap.

"Take yourself back to your tent, find your shoe, and prepare for drill."

The private glanced at his foot then up at Charles. "What?"

"There is nothing wrong with your foot."

"But there is. You seen how bad it hurt ever'time ya touched it."

"Yes, you apparently have some mediocre acting ability." He gestured with his arm for the private to move along.

"You gotta treat me."

"Come back when you have something for me to treat and I shall."

"I ain't fit for duty. You gotta discharge me. It's in the regulations."

"I believe what you refer to are paragraphs 150-167 of the Army Regulations, which reads, '...*every man laboring under any physical infirmity which is liable to unfit him for bearing...fatigues and hardships of a soldier's life in the field, should be promptly discharged from the service by his commanding officer on a surgeon's certificate of disability.*' "

Charles pulled his notebook and pencil from his overcoat pocket.

"I assume that is why you're here. You have heard the rumors that we will soon march, and you came expecting me to present you with a certificate of disability. I think not. You private, have a responsibility to the men of your regiment to present yourself as fit for duty and stand with them."

"I hear that rule don't apply to you." The private mumbled, then wadded the wrapping from his foot into a ball and slammed it down against the walkway.

If the ball of cloth had been rubber, it would have bounced higher than Charles' head.

"Consider yourself on report, Private."

The private seized his crutch and stood. Without shifting any weight onto it, he clenched the length of wood, his knuckles white. A sneer pulled back one corner of his mouth.

Charles moved toward the insolent fool, grateful at this moment for his extra height and thanks to his grandfather, years of boxing lessons. He stared down into the man's narrowed eyes.

The private's lips compressed into a tight line.

Charles took another step, close enough now so the brass buttons of his coat were mere inches from the private's nose. "You raise that crutch one inch, and I will have you brought up on charges." From his peripheral vision, he saw Major Balch step toward them.

"Is there a problem?"

"Yeah," the private spoke quickly backing away from Charles. "The doc says there ain't nothing wrong with my foot, but it pains me terrible. He says I gotta report for drill, and I cain't even put weight on it."

Charles lifted his gaze to the regimental surgeon,

who with a jerk of his head bade Charles follow him as they moved away from the annoying louse of a private.

They stopped beside Major Balch's patient, who sat with his newly stitched arm extended on the table.

Major Balch seated himself across from the young sergeant and picked up a rolled bandage. "I trust you have an explanation, Captain Ellard. From what I overheard it sounded as if the patient was in a great deal of pain."

"It did sound that way. However, I assure you, this man here is in far greater pain, yet I heard nary a peep as you stitched his laceration closed."

"Some men have a greater tolerance." Major Balch wound the bandage around the arm.

"The amount of pain the private expressed was inconsistent with the alleged injury presented." Charles watched the doctor tie off the ends of the bandage. His fingers tingled with the urge to wrap the wound a few more times. The sergeant would surely bump that arm when he moved about camp. He hoped the major would at least isolate the limb with a sling.

"Captain, I hope you based your diagnosis on something other than pain tolerance."

Charles blinked and refocused his attention on Major Balch, frowning at the condescension in the other doctor's voice.

"Neither his foot nor his ankle presents any redness or evidence of contusion. There are no areas of swelling or heat. Nor is there an indication of a lack of circulation. As the private approached me and was not focused entirely on his alleged injury, the man, seventeen times, touched the toes of that foot to the walkway before advancing his crutch, yet he did not wince or exhibit any physical sign of pain. However, the moment I began my examination, he moaned and groaned and flinched and winced. I've seen men with entire limbs amputated take on with less caterwauling."

The young sergeant snickered.

Major Balch scowled at the man. "That will be all, Sergeant."

Rising, the sergeant stepped to the side and rolled down the sleeve of his shirt. Blood soaked the entire forearm. The brightness glistened stark against the white.

"Captain Ellard." Major Balch slid his needle back through the chamois cloth of his needle case. "The line is relatively short this morning. President Lincoln will be arriving in the next day or so for a full review of the troops. Perhaps you could get an early start on the daily kitchen inspection before you report for ambulance drill."

Charles raised his chin. His nostrils flared as he drew in a deep breath. Calm, he reminded himself.

"Sir, I have been in this since the beginning. I know when someone is playing the *old man*. No disrespect, but you have only been here since January and have seen merely those malingerers attempting to avoid drill. We are about to march into—"

"Captain Ellard." Major Balch stood but couldn't come close to Charles' imposing height. "Need I remind you that I am the Regimental Surgeon and you, my *Assistant Surgeon*. Nor are you any longer a major."

"Sir, that man is my patient, and I have made my diagnosis."

"You have been given your orders, Captain. If you have a problem with that, feel free to take your complaints to the Corps medical director, otherwise you may find yourself spending the rest of the war back in Old Capitol Prison."

"Yes, sir," Charles hissed through clenched teeth. He swung on his heels, his long legs taking him quickly along the walk.

"Captain!" A voice called out behind him. "Captain Ellard."

Charles stopped and turned. The young sergeant hurried to catch up. From elbow to wrist, the sleeve of his coat was dark with blood.

"I know you don't know me," the young sergeant began, then in an afterthought he raised his hand to salute.

Charles responded in kind.

"I don't know if you're the right Captain Ellard, but did you come down here from Washington a week ago on the *John Brooks*?"

"Yes," Charles replied slowly, wondering if Doctor Balch had excused this man from drill. He'd obviously lost a good deal of blood. The bandage wasn't thick, and he'd certainly bang it with his rifle.

"Me too. I was on board waiting to come down to Aquia Creek Landing, and this pretty woman with red hair—"

Charles stilled. He drew a deep breath and waited.

"She was yelling for her beau, a Doctor Ellard, Charles Ellard. I remember 'cause I asked her to repeat the name. Is it you she was trying to find?"

His chest tightened. Gracie had called for him specifically? He inclined his head. "My name is Charles Ellard, but I can't imagine why the lady you mentioned would be looking for me." His heartbeat quickened for a moment then—"I believe she already has a beau."

The sergeant shrugged. "I didn't see nobody. She was trying awful hard to get on that boat, but the provost marshal wouldn't let her—Wait. There was someone, a fellow on crutches. He stopped her when she took a swing at the provost marshal."

The sergeant chuckled. "Never seen a lady fly at a man the way she done. Too bad she didn't get to talk to you."

The corner of Charles' mouth twitched. Moral outrage had driven Gracie to fly at that orderly in the ward. Had the denial of the provost marshal to let her say goodbye to him triggered that same outrage? That she would fight for him the same way she'd fought for the patients that day...

But why had Major Carlton been there? Had he merely been her escort, or had it been something more? Had he also glimpsed the turn of her ankle, her red petticoat?

"Yes, well, thank you, Sergeant, for sharing that information with me."

The man nodded. "I figured. I'd want to know if my sweetheart came to see me off."

"Thank you, Sergeant. And come find me before taps and roll-call. I'd like to check your arm."

The sergeant glanced toward the hospital tents and nodded. "I will." Then he swung on his heels and headed back the other way.

Charles continued to the regiment's hospital kitchen, to make sure the cooks were properly washing the pots and the soups were cooked for the required amount of time.

These were the same men, who like all but a few in

the regiment, saw little need to void their bladders in the trenches dug for the express purpose of keeping human excrement away from both the camp and the regiment's hospital kitchen. With just himself, Major Balch, and Major Dennis to inspect the kitchen, sanitation became a daunting task.

Chapter Nine

That evening, Charles sat on a stool in the corner of a hospital tent. A light rain pelted the canvas like tiny pebbles tossed from Heaven. Using an empty haversack as a desk, he composed his concerns to Doctor Letterman in Washington. He took his time forming every curve and line so each individual letter was legible. Carefully, he detailed the numerous cases of scurvy then requested an increase in the vegetables of each man's ration.

Setting that letter aside to dry, he removed a blank sheet of paper from his stationery box, picked up his pen and held it poised over the paper.

Taking a deep breath, he wrote—
Dear Gracie McBride,

Frowning, he slashed a line straight through the center of the salutation.
My dearest Grace,

No. Another line.
Dear Mrs. Grace McBride,

Line.
My dear Mrs. William McBride,

No.
My dear friend Gracie...

****

Dear Mrs. McBride,
I trust you received the box from my grandfather.

Thank you for keeping it.
Sincerely,
Charles P. Ellard, Capt.
Assistant Surgeon
69th Pennsylvania, Second Division

Gracie turned the paper over. Blank. Then again, why was she surprised? This brief note, obviously written when he was busy, was just like him—quick, to the point, and dismissive. At least now she knew where to write, to reassure him his box of childhood toys was indeed in her possession. And if she included a few anecdotes about life here at Armory Square, that only meant she was being friendly.

"Ma'am?"

Gracie shoved the letter into her pocket and looked up. Her orderly, Tom Halleck, stood in front of her table.

"Sergeant Baker asked me about the other doctor again."

She sighed. "All ye can do is remind him that Doctors Ellard and Colfax and Medical Cadet Emmerson be the only ones attending him that day. If he be thinking 'twas another, 'twas naught but his feverish dreams."

He nodded. "And Corporal McAuley puked his lunch."

Gracie started down the aisle toward bed six. "By the saints, I knew it would happen."

Micah was already there changing the corporal's shirt and bedding.

She swung around and nearly slammed into Tom. They sidestepped each other for a moment, then once again, Tom fell in line behind her as she marched back to the table.

"The poor man's stomach can handle naught but beef tea." She crossed her arms and lifted her gaze to Tom.

"Did ye have the chance to go and ask the Special Diets cook to give ye some?"

Tom shifted his weight and glanced down at the floor. "Yes, ma'am. But soon as I said it was for Ward E, he said, no."

"Sweet Mary, Jesus, and Joseph, is the man's pride so stiff, he'd see poor Sean McAuley perish rather than spare a quart o'beef tea?"

"Excuse me for saying so, but I don't think that cook likes you much."

"Aye Tom, ye have the right of it now." She frowned and gnawed on the inside of her cheek. After a moment, she squared her shoulders and gave Tom a quick smile. "Then he'll think no less o' me if I go over there and get it meself."

"You're going to steal it?"

She grinned. "We be in the army, Tom. 'Tis called foraging."

His eyes widened, and he snickered. "Then you'd best hurry, ma'am. The cook is likely still taking his noon break."

****

Gracie cautiously pushed one of the two wide barn-doors inward. She listened. No voices, no pots clanging or vegetables being chopped, only silence filled the large open building along with the savory aromas of onion, celery, and beef.

She released a breath and made the sign of the cross. Lifting her gaze to the rafters, she whispered a quick, *thank you*. Not even the stewards were here.

There probably wasn't much time. She slipped inside and peeked around the long row of shelves filled with over-sized pots and pans, large spatulas, and ladles. She sidled along the wall and around a wide butcher block, its surface sloped from many scrapings. The large stoves and work tables in the center of the cavernous building drew her attention. Since beef tea usually simmered for hours, she focused on the huge pot on the back of one stove.

Carefully, she moved to avoid passing in front of a window, and even though she walked on tip-toe, each tap of her leather soles against the brick floor sounded three times louder to her sharpened hearing.

A quilted pot holder had been tossed on one of the wide tables that divided the work space. She grabbed the thick calico pad, swung toward the stove, and lifted the lid.

A misty cloud of steam swirled around her face. Moisture dampened her cheeks as she leaned close and inhaled the scent of beef. A tangy hint of bay leaf teased her senses. Perfect. She lowered the lid and scanned the room. A row of shelves filled with glassware, plates, serving platters, and soup tureens captured her attention.

Her heart rate accelerated, and she rubbed her palms down the front of her apron. She had to hurry. A couple of the quart fruit jars on the third shelf would serve her purpose. One in each hand, she carried them back to the stove and set them on the most level corner of the butcher block while she hunted for a ladle.

Outside the planks of the walkway creaked. She jumped. Her mouth went dry. To her heightened senses, the low murmur of voices echoed like a cacophony of angry rabble.

Her gaze shot to the stove. She could do this.

A faint whiff of cherry tobacco drifted through the kitchen. Whoever was smoking didn't seem interested in coming inside—yet.

She dipped a ladle into the broth and filled the jars. After she screwed the zinc lids on tight, she dashed across the room to the side door and pulled it open.

A wall of white, splattered with grease and splotches of food, blocked her way.

"What the hell are you doing in my kitchen?"

Gracie's breath caught in her throat along with her reply. She lifted her gaze to meet his frowning, sweat-dotted face.

He glanced at the jars in her hand and didn't even wait for her to fabricate an explanation.

"That's it. Major Bliss is going to hear about this. That crazy doctor ain't here no more to protect you." He swung on his heels and marched off toward the general office.

****

"Stealing food, Mrs. McBride?" Doctor Bliss asked from where he stood in front of his desk. Cradling his elbow in the palm of his opposite hand, he thoughtfully stroked his porkchop sideburns with the backs of his fingers.

"How is it stealing if I be giving it to the men 'tis intended for?" Gracie hugged the fruit jars tight to her bosoms.

"Because it ain't all intended for you." The sergeant shot an accusing glare toward Gracie.

She shrank back a step, as though protecting an

infant in her arms.

Major Bliss straightened and stepped around his desk. "That will be all, Sergeant."

"What about my beef tea?"

"I will deal with this." He nodded toward the door.

With a low grunt, the sergeant left the office. Doctor Bliss gestured for her to take a seat.

She frowned and lowered herself onto the edge of the chair, keeping her back straight and her fruit jars close.

Doctor Bliss took a seat behind his desk and leaning back, pursed his lips as he studied her over the tips of his steepled fingers.

"Mrs. McBride," he began. "Can I assume Doctor Colfax did not order this beef tea and that you have once again taken it upon yourself to defy his orders?"

"Adding a bit o' beef tea to his list 'twas all I be doing. I do not know why, but 'tis the only thing Corporal McAuley can keep in his stomach. Doctor Colfax refuses to prescribe it. 'Twas the only order I be changing."

"You are an excellent nurse, and what perplexes me is that you got on so well with Doctor Ellard."

"He be a fine doctor."

"And he would be the first one to remind you that it is not your place to change any order he'd given."

While it was true, she also knew Doctor Ellard would have likely prescribed beef tea in the first place. The words danced on the tip of her tongue, but she pressed them to the roof of her mouth and shifted the weight of the jars in her arms.

"There is another matter I wish to address, concerning a..." he rifled through his papers and pulled a single sheet from a pile on the left side of his desk.

He ran his thumb down the dark mutton chop width of hair on his cheek as he glanced over the page. "A complaint was registered by a Mrs. Prescott, the founder of the Ladies for the Betterment of War Society."

"The betterment of wa—"

Doctor Bliss cut her off with a sharp glare.

"It seems, Mrs. McBride, that you failed to distribute the apples she brought for the men."

"And which o' the men would I be giving them to? We've only the worst cases sent up from the winter camps, men suffering from abdominal wounds, gangrene, typhus, dysentery, small pox, and measles."

Doctor Bliss gave his sideburns another stroke. "She also claims you were insolent and threw her out of the ward."

"I give her me thanks for bringing them, and Tom, me orderly kept one box on the table. But she followed me around, waiting for me pass them out. 'Twas making the patients uncomfortable, her staring at them, asking if they be wanting any apples. She might have at least brought applesauce or compote. If she come to sit with the men and read to them, or write their letters, 'tis fine. But I cleaned house for her sort, and she be the kind o' woman to give large, anonymous donations to the church that turn out to be not so anonymous."

Behind his desk, Doctor Bliss momentarily closed his eyes and gave his forehead a rub. Then meeting her gaze he said, "But did you have to shove her out the door? She is the sister-in-law of a congressman. I have enough trouble getting my requisitions filled without now having every order scrutinized."

"I did not shove her out the door. I be asking her to leave, but she be not the kind of woman to take direction from the likes o' me. So I be pointing to the door and give her a wee push."

Doctor Bliss groaned.

Gracie wasn't sure if the sound was good or bad, but at least he seemed willing to let her keep her jars.

He rolled his chair close to his desk and rested his forearms on the green felt blotter. "When you have a problem such as the one you describe, you are to take it to the ward surgeon, Doctor Colfax, or to myself, or to another doctor at this hospital. Let a man handle it."

Gracie sucked in a breath and opened her mouth to argue, but Doctor Bliss hastily continued.

"To be honest with you, Mrs. McBride, I have considered transferring you to another hospital, but I don't know who would replace you. Most of the military nurses have gone to Falmouth, and the nuns who serve here seem given to prayer at the most inopportune times."

He reached for a piece of paper from a pile on his left. "So I would like to offer you the opportunity to renew your perspective. There is a boat leaving for Aquia Creek Landing a week from today, with food and medical supplies from the Sanitary Commission. Volunteers are needed to help distribute those supplies. I suggested you."

"Ye want me to go to Falmouth?" She shot to her feet.

He stood. "You would only be gone a few days. I realize this decision is entirely yours, but I believe time away from this place will do you good."

Gracie stared. She felt like a worn-out shoe.

Though she served a purpose, she was still unwanted. This trip to Falmouth was only to put a bit of polish on the scuffed leather.

"When you return, the new dormitory for the lady nurses should be complete, which will afford you the opportunity to escape each day from the dreary atmosphere and smell of the ward. I can only hope that a fresh outlook and renewed spirit will make life here more agreeable, and you will no longer feel the need to challenge every order."

Heat surged through her body. Her nostrils flared, and she pressed her lips together. Struggling to hold back the curses she ached to spew at the man, she swung around, and chin high, she marched from his office, down the hall, and out the door.

The discordant pounding of multiple hammers echoed between the buildings. This morning she thought the activity exciting, now it seemed ominous. Each thud of hammer to nail was like the echo of her mother's voice inside Gracie's head, *"Ye be a woman, and ye're Irish. Remember your place. Remember your place."*

It had only been once Gracie left her job as a maid and married William, that she'd gained the freedom to speak her mind, to develop a skill, and use it to help others. She'd lost that after he died, and she'd been forced back to work on Beacon Hill.

Even Doctor Ellard, for whom she had the highest regard, firmly believed this place too rigorous for a mere woman and constantly suggested she return home.

A lump formed in her throat, and she swallowed. Would she ever have the kind of relationship she'd had with William? He'd been the love of her life with his easy laughter, and his low tones rumbling the endearment, *Gracie-lass*.

And while the lonely woman inside her was attracted to Doctor Ellard, his views on women and their place in society constantly reminded her that the mutual respect and easy camaraderie she'd had with William was something she'd never have with Charles Ellard, no matter how much she missed the man.

At least Doctor Bliss hadn't sent her away permanently. *Remember your place.* She'd managed to tamp down her feisty spirit before, she could do it again.

****

Inside the ward she set the jars of beef tea on the table.

Tom sat beside one of the nearby patients, writing a letter. He rose and joined her. A grin spread across his face. "Ya got it. Did ya get caught?"

Still feeling the sting of anger in her eyes, she kept her gaze averted. "Aye." She nodded. "Though neither the cook nor Doctor Bliss are too fond o' me now." She jotted the corporal's name on a piece of paper and slid it under one of the jars.

"Ye best keep this for Corporal McAuley. Give him a wine glass full every two hours. And if Doctor Colfax will not write it on the list himself, we'll not be getting more."

"Yes, ma'am."

As she straightened, she met Tom's gaze. Older than she by a several years, Tom's shrewd brown eyes studied her with a wisdom that Robbie, with his enthusiasm for life, had not yet acquired.

Replying to his silent question, Gracie offered a

half-smile. "'Tis no more than a headache. A nap 'tis all I be needing."

"Yes, ma'am," he said, though a shadow of doubt remained.

"I'll be back to help with the medication pass at five."

He nodded, accepting her excuse. "Ma'am, for what ya do for the men…well, they all know how hard ya try. They…we…we all appreciate it."

Tears stung her eyes, and she pressed her lips together for a moment. "Ye be a fine man Tom Halleck, you and Micah and Harvey. 'Tis proud I am, to be working with ye every day."

"Thank you, ma'am," he said, studying the pencil in his hand.

"Go on with ye, now, and finish yer letter."

He replied with a nod and a quick smile.

She made a shooing gesture with her hand, and though he hesitated a moment, Tom whirled and hurried back to the patient.

With a last glance at the jars, Gracie turned away and headed to her partitioned room at the end of the ward.

As much as she longed for a door to slam in frustration, she could only yank the curtain closed instead. It wasn't fair. She paced the confines of her space, her shoes silent on the rag rug she'd found in a donation bin.

Frustration and anger welled in her eyes, and she pressed the heels of her hands against the sting before the tears spilled over and her sobbing could be heard by the patients.

The stuffed rabbit watched in silence from the

nightstand. "I only want to help," she whispered to the toy, with its big ears for gathering secrets and no mouth to share them. "'Tis not fair to be punished for wanting to ease the suffering o' these brave men."

What was she to do? Spend a few days distributing supplies for the Sanitary Commission, then return here to a different ward where she would have to meekly remember her place, or return to Boston and clean houses for rich pretentious women with boxes of apples? Why did William have to die? Having tasted independence, to lose her freedom now was worse than never experiencing it.

She grabbed the rabbit by the ears and hurled it with every ounce of rage inside her. It hit the outside wall with a thud and fell to the floor. Then she threw herself on the bed and cried.

Keeping her face buried in her pillow to muffle her sobs, she let the tears flow. Doctor Ellard had been with her the last few times she'd cried. At least when he wasn't trying to kiss her or tell her a foolish joke, his warmth and awkward pats had offered a measure of comfort.

Maybe she should go to Falmouth. She could find Doctor Ellard and…what? She didn't know, but suddenly it was where she wanted to be. Maybe Doctor Bliss was right. And if she ran into Doctor Ellard…at least he was a friend.

Wiping her eyes, she sat up. The rabbit watched her from across the room, where he leaned crookedly against the white-washed wall.

She rose and stepped over to pick it up. One ear had torn away from the head and dangled down to the seam where the arm met the body. Guilt washed over her leaving her ashamed for having hurt the poor thing. She held the damaged ear upright. But something poked from the sawdust inside the rabbit's head. Curious, she pulled out a tightly rolled piece of paper about two inches long.

She smiled to herself, wondering what sort of secret message Charles the boy had hidden. Tucking the rabbit under her arm she unrolled the yellowed paper.

mY nam is JaSon
CharelZ is ded
I wesh I WaS tO

She blinked and stared. Her breath caught in her chest and lodged there until the pain reminded her to take another.

Cold washed through her insides the way it had when her brother Callum told her William had died. She shivered. Her knees gave out, and she dropped to the floor, sitting back on her heels, her hand clamped tight against her mouth. Her fingers trembled.

The childish scrawl made no more sense to her numb brain now than it had a moment ago.

Had Charles written this? Maybe this toy had once belonged to another child. But who was Jason? What could be so horrible that such a young boy would wish for death?

An idea took root in her mind, even as she denied its growth with a slow shake of her head.

No. Charles could not be Jason. Impossible. Because for that to be true someone would have had to... No. That couldn't be right. Jason was not Charles. Charles was not Jason.

She rolled the note up and shoved it back into the rabbit's head. Then she pushed to her feet, tossed the rabbit into the corner, where it landed on top of the hat box. Sad and silent, that rabbit had just shared his deepest secret.

She grabbed her shawl and tossed it over the rabbit and hat box. Next, she grabbed her coat and threw it on top. Still the pain of that long ago child called to her.

My name is Jason. Charles is dead.

She backed away from the mountain of box and clothing—away from the rabbit. She couldn't stay here.

Tom glanced up when she strode past but didn't say a word. She grabbed a book from the cupboard behind her table and headed to the end of the long room where she usually read to the patients. She chose *The House of Seven Gables* by Nathaniel Hawthorne, partly because reading aloud would drown out the haunting words that reverberated in her head and partly because Doctor Colfax had decreed that the story of ghosts, murder, and witchcraft too stimulating for the men.

Harvey pulled chairs around some of the bedridden patients who wished to hear the story, and he and the other orderlies assisted those who needed help to find seats.

Gracie read until mental pictures of the Pyncheon house overshadowed the haunting images of a stuffed rabbit and a child's words printed on yellowed paper.

Her voice grew hoarse, and she closed the book. Some men stayed to talk to each other, and others went back to their beds.

"Please, ma'am." Sergeant Baker asked as she walked with him back to number thirty-six. "Any...car's?" After two weeks his voice was still barely more than a harsh whisper.

She went to the cupboard and grabbed the last

deck.

"Here you go, Sergeant."

He sat waiting for her in a chair positioned alongside his bed.

"Thank...you," he whispered as he accepted the cards.

"Ye are welcome, but ye really should be careful not to be straining yer voice."

"Try. Wish I...thank doc...tor...saved life."

"I know ye do, and I'll pass along yer thanks in me next letter to Doctor Ellard."

"No." His raspy whisper was far less emphatic than his accompanying head shake. "Reee."

Gracie sighed and dropped to sit on the edge of his bed. It had been a long day, and she didn't have the energy for this conversation.

"'Tis sorry I am to tell ye, but 'twas Doctor Ellard who operated on yer throat and removed yer tonsils. But he's gone back to his regiment."

The sergeant toyed with the cards in his hand. "Looks like...sister...hus-band."

The sergeant's voice grew fainter. Gracie rested her palms on her thighs and leaned close.

He whispered, "Thought doc...his son..."

She struggled to understand but couldn't grasp the last part. With a sigh she leaned back.

Mistaken identity was a common occurrence. Everybody looked like someone else. But the sergeant was so persistent in his belief that Doctor Ellard was another person.

My name is Jason.

She shot to her feet. No! Sergeant Baker suffered from either mistaken identity or the confusion of a fevered dream. Yet…

"Can ye write?"

He nodded.

She swung around and marched down the aisle straight to her table. The solid click of her heels echoed her sense of purpose. She set down the book, picked up her notebook and pencil, and in moments she was back with the sergeant.

That she even considered this only proved how tired she was. There was no logical reason for her brain to even conceive the idea that the note from an unknown boy and a case of mistaken identity from a delirious patient were related in any way.

"Now just to be understanding ye proper," she lowered herself onto the edge of his mattress and passed him the pad and pencil. "The man ye be speaking of, was he tall and clean shaven, with dark brown hair and pale blue eyes?"

Baker nodded.

"Did he have high cheekbones, a bump in the line o' his nose, and a small scar on the left corner o' his chin?"

He shrugged and cocked his head, looking at her oddly.

Heat singed her cheeks. She glanced at the row of seven cards he'd laid out across the blanket, but didn't notice their number or their suit.

Pressing the tip of the pencil against the paper, Sergeant Baker wrote.

Gracie leaned forward and read the words upside down as fast as the sergeant could write them.

Doc looked like my sister's first husband.

"And where be yer home?"

Broken Creek Hollow, Virginia.

"Doctor Ellard cannot be this man." She shook her head. "He be from Philadelphia."

Sergeant Baker scribbled furiously in the notebook while Gracie continued to make her case.

"His grandfather, be the man with the cane, who come here weeks ago. And I saw Doctor Ellard's pocket watch, me own self. Engraved it was, from his mother to his da, with her miniature inside."

He finished writing and shoved the book into her hands, tapping the page with his finger.

Jonathan went to Phil. 25—26 yrs. ago. A doc too.

Gracie stared at the words. She shuddered, that ominous feeling of someone walking over her grave.

That Baker would share this story now was a portentous twist of fate, but there were still gaping holes. She wouldn't even pursue this if it hadn't been for that note, which right now she wished she'd never found.

"But Doctor Ellard knows who he be. 'Tis all a strange coincidence, for 'tis not unusual for one man to look like another."

He held her gaze for a moment then took the book and began writing.

When he passed her the book, she was almost afraid to read the words, as though once she learned the truth there would be no going back.

Jon went to Phil to bring back med supplies. His boy, my nephew went with him. They never came home.

Nausea rolled through her stomach. She glanced up from the paper and met Sergeant Baker's dark brown eyes.

"What was the name o'his son?"

His gaze locked with hers. He whispered, "Jason."

Gracie clamped her hand across her mouth. "Sweet Mary, Jesus, and Joseph," she gasped against her palm.

Like pieces of a jigsaw puzzle, the bits of information spun around in her head faster than she could sort through them. "And how old would the lad be today?"

Sergeant Baker rubbed his chin then shrugged and wrote. *29—30?*

"On yer sainted mother, ye are sure o' this?"

He nodded and wrote. *Doctor looks just like Jonathan.*

"What happened to them?"

Never knew. Thought them dead. Now??? He shrugged.

Trying to make sense of this would drive her to the madhouse. And to what purpose? None of this was her concern. No one but her knew about the rabbit.

If indeed Doctor Ellard had been born Jason, he was Charles now. Speaking of this to him would destroy his life.

She forced a smile and rose. "'Tis quite a tale, to be sure, but likely a coincidence. If he be here now, ye'd see that without yer fever, he'd look to be a different man."

Sergeant Baker frowned. "Maybe," he whispered with a shrug.

Notebook in hand, she returned to her desk in the center of the ward. Four days until she left for Falmouth, and somehow, she wasn't as confident as she'd like to be.

Chapter Ten

"Son-of-a-Goddamn-*bitch*!" Charles wadded the letter into a tight ball and flung it across the tiny hut. It bounced off the log wall and hit the floor. Seething, he snatched the pitcher off the make-shift wash stand and hurled it at the door. With a crash, the pitcher hit the wood and shattered.

He stared at the ruined stoneware, his chest heaving, his heart pounding. The audacity! How dare his grandfather presume to—

The door pushed inward, and Major Dennis stepped inside. Pottery crunched beneath his boot.

"What the hell happened here?" Major Dennis poked at the shattered pitcher with the toe of his boot.

"It broke."

Dennis snorted. He pulled his gum rubber rain blanket over his head and gave it a shake before hanging it from a bent nail in the tent's ridgepole. "Well don't expect me to clean that up or fetch a new one."

Charles said nothing. He merely stepped forward to hunker down and gather the shards. He should have remained calm. Now everyone in the regiment would have another Doctor Ellard story to share around the campfires.

"What's this?" Dennis asked.

Charles pivoted on the balls of his feet.

The major uncurled the wadded up letter, then smoothed it out against his thigh.

"That's mine."

"Looks like you missed the fireplace." Dennis backed away, his gaze focused on the page.

"Give me that." Charles surged to his feet suddenly feeling he was ten years old again and back in boarding school.

"That's mine."

"Finders keepers."

One of the boys tossed Bunzy to a friend.

"Give him back."

"Charles sleeps with a bun-ny."

Bunzy sailed across the room to another boy.

"Charles sleeps with a bun-ny."

The keep-away game continued until Charles was crying and the other boys on his floor were laughing too hard to continue.

Grandfather had always believed his stern reprimands and threats of physical punishment had been the reason Charles had left Bunzy at home after the Christmas holiday.

Dennis swung around, curling into himself, protecting the letter from Charles' grasping fingers as he read aloud.

"Adelaide Mary Ann Emmerson." His laughter could likely be heard three tents over. "Oh ho, a senator's daughter. And her brother has a seat in the House. Impressive."

"Major Dennis, you are an officer and a gentleman. That is a private correspondence."

The major laughed. "Whoa, hold up there. You're going to be married by proxy? Is that still legal?"

Charles made another ineffective grab for the letter. Of course it wasn't legal, and his grandfather damn well knew it. In his usual officious manner, the old man threatened this proxy marriage to remind Charles that he needed to marry and had better set his sights on a suitable wife like Miss Adelaide and not an Irish immigrant not too long off the boat. Another burst of laughter erupted from the man.

"My God, Charles Ellard, married."

Charles snatched back the letter. "I am not married."

Dennis threw himself onto his cot, still chuckling to himself. "Ol' Grandpa plans to marry you off." Laughter rose again from deep inside the man's diaphragm. "And you didn't know anything about it? Have you even a clue what she looks like?"

Charles ripped the letter into tiny pieces.

"You don't, do you?" More laughter. "She could be fifty years old and as big as a cow!"

Calm, Charles reminded himself and tossed the bits of paper into the coals. He clenched his hand around the stick they used as a poker and pushed the bits of paper closer to the reddest embers.

He needed a drink. Ignoring the chuckles from the other cot, Charles dug through his trunk until his fingers brushed the neck of his bottle of Old Crow.

He popped the cork and downed a bracing swallow, not caring if Major Dennis knew he had the forbidden whiskey.

"Is that purely for medicinal purposes, or are you going to share?"

Charles glared at his tent mate and reluctantly passed over the bottle.

Dennis reached out and wrapped his fingers around the neck. "You really don't care about rules, do you?" He tipped the bottle to his lips and took a long swallow. "Wow, this is too good for medicinal whiskey."

"Then don't drink it." Charles snatched the bottle from Dennis, downed another swallow, and returned it to his trunk.

"You're an arrogant ass," the major snapped. "I hope you and Adelaide What's-Her-Name are very happy together."

The fingers of Charles' right hand curled into a fist, tingling to draw back and slam into the major's jaw. Regardless of what everyone believed, Charles did care about rules and procedures. Rules created control amidst chaos. They were vital to both the army and the medical profession. They were vital to him.

In the beginning he loved the organization, the discipline, the challenge of using his skills to make a difference. Now army life and war had become meaningless and futile, like treading water—accomplishing nothing except to keep himself from drowning.

He returned to the broken pitcher and stacked all the smaller pieces inside the concaved portion of the largest wedge.

It wasn't as if he were passing whiskey out to the men. Doctors were allowed to use whiskey in the hospital for medicinal purposes. He wasn't a drunk, and he'd never once taken a sip when he was on duty. He only needed it to keep calm, to keep his temper under control. He'd already been demoted to captain for assaulting that colonel at Aquia Creek. He didn't need any more trouble.

He threw his gum blanket over his head, adjusted his hat, and gathered the broken pitcher. He stepped into the pouring rain and carried the pieces to the trash barrel.

How long before Dennis gossiped and his fictitious marriage became part of the whispers that stopped as he entered a tent? How long before he walked past a group of men and heard the snickers in response to a new joke about Doctor Ellard?

No matter how hard he tried, he just couldn't seem to fit in. Army life had become school all over again.

Would things have been better if he'd been part of a family, learned to engage in lighthearted banter with his siblings instead of relying on joke books filled with anecdotes that apparently weren't funny? Would he have learned to wrestle for fun with brothers instead learning to box so the other boys stopped beating him up every day? And maybe having sisters would have shown him how to talk to women so he didn't end up feeling like an inept fool around Gracie McBride.

Leaving the trash bin behind, he headed to the hospital. Organization, discipline, rules. Control amidst the chaos. His long-legged stride ate up the distance as his boot heels sank into the soft clay where there were no corduroy walkways.

Last week, the President and his family had arrived for a review of the troops. Now the medical department had orders to move the regiment hospitals into one division hospital below Potomac Creek, near the railroad line to Aquia Creek Landing.

As he reached the regimental hospital tent, he stopped on the log walk and stomped off his boots. The afternoon clouds deepened the early evening shadows between the tents.

He glanced down as he had countless times to be sure he'd knocked loose the mud which had oozed over the toes of his boots. What had been red dust the day before, was now, after a day of light showers, red...blood?

Thick, dark red, nearly black as it spread across the cobbles.

His breath caught as his pulse pounded wildly in his ears. His vision narrowed. Darkness loomed in his periphery.

"Captain, are you all right?"

Charles blinked. His heart slowed its wild rhythm. The hospital tent came into focus as did the face of the orderly in front of him. He recognized the man's face but had no idea of the man's name, nor why the corporal stared at him as though expecting a reply.

Unsure how to respond he searched for a nonspecific answer. "Thinking," he said.

The orderly frowned then saluted and entered the tent.

Charles drew a deep breath and released it slowly. He swallowed. Gradually the rigidity eased from his spine, and his shoulders slumped.

The thought of changing dressings and checking wounds sent a chill straight through his bones. Maybe he'd help with some packing at the storehouse, then go back to his quarters and write another letter to Gracie.

He missed that gleam in her eyes when she raised her chin and challenged him. He longed for the warmth of her mouth against his, the strength of her fingers as they dug through the wool of his coat to press into the muscles of his back.

Two orderlies snapped to attention as he entered the supply hut. Boxes and crates surrounded them in piles.

"At ease. What are you men doing?"

The pair exchanged glances then the older of the two corporals stepped forward. "We're loading all these stuffs into those wagons out back. They're going up to the corps hospitals at Potomac Creek. Then we got to restock the division medicine wagons for light march. Two for each division and pack the rest of supplies going with the regiment in the medicine chests for the pack horses."

Charles nodded. "Be sure there are no personal items packed in these wagons which belong to non medical officers."

The orderlies exchanged another quick glance. The corporal spoke again. "Major Balch done told us that. Said only to pack what was on the list."

The pair stared at him, their mouths gaping.

He ignored them and picked up a box of morphine.

"Sir, are you helping us?"

"Yes. I will personally check the bottles of medicines going into our division's wagons."

"Yes, sir." He passed Charles several sheets of paper. "Here's the list what was give to us, for what goes in the Autenrieth medicine wagons."

"Thank you, Corporal." Carefully, he went through the capital operating case, two amputating knives, bone saw, artery and bone forceps, retractors, ligature silk, suture wire. Next, he did the same for the minor operating case as well as his own field case.

"And sir, we're still waitin' on the supplies due from the Sanitary Commission."

"I see. Well until they arrive, carry on. Where are the other officers responsible for accuracy and appropriate paperwork? Are you men responsible for this alone?"

The corporal shrugged. "Can't say, sir, but I hear tell there's a party in Major Balch's tent. They're drinking brandy and eating oysters and sardines on crackers."

Charles stared. "Excuse me?"

"It's a party, sir, cause we're marching in the morning."

A party? Evidently the need for celebratory cakes wasn't exclusive to Gracie McBride. Maybe it was for the best that he'd been excluded. He'd likely say something he'd regret.

"With this downpour, I doubt a fifty-mile train of men, horses, artillery, and wagons will march far in roads little more than sloppy wet clay."

Locating a seat on an empty hardtack box, he reviewed the list the division surgeon-in-chief had given the corporal. The muscles of Charles' forehead tugged together. He withdrew a pencil from his pocket to adjust the quantities and add additional items based on his recollection of the supply lists from Antietam and Fredericksburg. Thirty pounds of candles. No, fifty pounds of candles. Twenty-eight, no, forty-eight pounds of ether, and nine, make that ten pounds of Dover's powder. An ache throbbed behind his eyes, and he took a moment to rub his hand across his forehead before resuming his amended list. Two hundred blankets, one hundred dozen bandages, fifty yards adhesive plaster…

A couple of hours later, he checked through the

Autenreith medicine wagons and replaced any missing surgical instruments.

Twelve surgeon's needles, one mallet, twelve yards suture wire, one artery needle, one chisel, one chain saw.

Though it was late when he returned to his tent, Major Dennis was still absent. Charles shook off his wet garments, grateful for the fire that chased away the chill. Their young aide must have assumed they'd be returning and lit the fire before heading for his own bed. Charles pulled a twig from the bundle of fagots, lit the end, then used it to light the candle which stood in its own wax in the center of the hardtack box they used as a table.

He pulled off his muddy boots and stripped down to his shirt and drawers. Thankfully, the pitcher he bought from the quartermaster had been sent to his tent and filled with fresh water. After a quick wash, he climbed into bed. Using his haversack as his lap desk, he withdrew paper, pen, and ink. He should write to his grandfather, but he was still too furious with the old man.

He opened the ink, filled his pen, and set the bottle on the hardtack box between the beds. He wanted to write to Gracie but had no idea what to include in the letter. She'd yet to respond to his last missive. Perhaps she was so busy she thought of him only in passing. Perhaps he thought about her more than she thought about him.

He reached behind him to adjust his pillow. The thin straw mattress crunched beneath his shifting weight. Mail was notoriously slow, he reminded himself. Until he knew for certain that she wasn't receptive to further communication, she might find news of the President's review of the army exciting. Except Charles hadn't gone. After all, what was there to see among a hundred and thirty thousand men?

Women enjoyed talk of fashion, but he had no idea what sort of dress Mrs. Lincoln wore or even what kind of pony their little boy rode.

Weather was generally considered an appropriate topic for conversation with a lady, and it had rained today. Rather a lot lately. However, the weather patterns here no doubt encompassed Washington, which was only fifty miles away. Most likely, Gracie was also being rained upon.

She might find it interesting that he and the rest of the medical department had been busy moving the division hospitals to Potomac Creek near the railroad line. However, by the time she received his letter, she would have more than likely received at Armory Square, many of the sick and disabled of the division.

He pressed the tip of his pen against the blank sheet of paper. So what should he write? That the regimental surgeon and the whole medical department hated him? That he was lonely? That he was terrified he'd suffer another of his spells? The one at Fredericksburg had nearly caused his heart to stop. What would he do if it happened again? Perhaps he should try harder to focus on other things.

Monday past, thirteen thousand cavalry had moved out, off on some sort of mission. Would she worry if he wrote that now they were all under orders to pack their haversacks with eight days' rations and leave out their clothes?

No, it would be best not to include maudlin

sentiments. After all she was mere woman. Talk of impeding battle might tax her emotions. He would keep the tone of his missive bright and happy.

****

Dear Mrs. McBride,

"A physican, having written out a prescription, enjoined his patient to swallow the whole of it in the morning. The patient understood him literally, swallowed the written prescription, and got well."

I understand some people might find the patient's literal interpretation of the physician's less than specific instruction to be humorous. That the patient also became well, subsequently made the need for the actual medication moot.

I hope you found the brief anecdote to be amusing.

Surg. Chas. P. Ellard, Captain
69th Pennsylvania

****

A smile tugged at the corners of Gracie's mouth. While the joke was mildly amusing, it was the endearing awkwardness of his explanation and his strange need to share it with her that warmed her heart.

Was the telling of these jokes his inept way of trying to charm her? He had kissed her, but she'd spurned his advances. Unless he changed his thinking, to allow more than friendship between them would only lead him on. What she'd had with William had been rare. Despite how much she respected Doctor Ellard, they would never have a relationship like the one she'd shared with William.

She gave her head a shake then refolded the letter and tucked it carefully into one of the inside pockets of her carpet bag.

Lately though, no matter how many times she reiterated to herself that it was William she longed for, there was no denying she still listened for the stride of Doctor Ellard's boot heels on the ward floor. She missed his direct, clinical manner as he dictated his patient notes and the way he looked directly into her eyes.

My name is Jason.

Her smile faded.

She wished she'd never found the note. Now this puzzle would nag at her until she knew the truth of it. Was it even any of her concern? No. What right did she have to become involved in any of this? None.

She slipped on her coat. Her gaze fell on the hat box atop her trunk. Yet, in her mind's eye all she saw was the rabbit. The rabbit and the note.

But didn't Charles at least deserve to have the information so he could decide whether or not to pursue its truth?

Before she could talk herself out of it, she flipped up the clasps, lifted the lid, and withdrew the toy. She studied the silent face as though by concentrating long enough she could elicit some sort of explanation from the rabbit. The ear tipped, but the rolled note kept it upright.

Maybe it was that simple. A bubble of laughter escaped her lips. The note was merely a random scrap of paper, rolled tight by a clever boy or his mother, and placed inside to support the ear and prevent the stitches from tearing free.

But the relief she should have felt for solving the puzzle didn't come. Instead, all she could think about were the desolate words—*Charles is dead. I wish I was too*. What an obscure sentiment to be recorded on a random scrap of paper to then be found and used to fix a toy.

How could any mother have read such a note and not been moved to act? No, the rabbit must have been repaired by the child. This unknown Jason had neatly printed the note and hidden his secret inside the rabbit. But why?

Neatly. Had Charles ever written neatly?

Maybe he hadn't been the boy who'd penned the words. The rabbit was a hand-me-down, and Charles had no idea the note was there.

This whole puzzle had given her a headache. She glanced at the watch pinned to her bodice. She'd think about this later. Right now, she needed to get to the Sanitary Commission supply office, number 244 F Street.

When she got to Falmouth she'd simply ask Doctor Ellard. While her plan seemed straightforward enough, she had no idea what to say or how to say it, because what if it was true?

What right did she have to bring this chaos into his life? But what if it was all her imagination? Likely his explanation would be as simple as a children's game of secret codes and spies. It made more sense than her wild theory of a boy stolen from his parents by a childless couple.

When she returned from Falmouth the new dormitory would be finished. Rain had delayed the construction as well as her trip, but after two days of pleasant weather, the pounding and sawing had resumed in earnest. Tucking the rabbit inside her carpet bag, she gave her tiny room a last goodbye.

****

Charles lowered his hand and knocked on the rough log wall of the quarters for Major Ellis, the surgeon in charge of the II Corps.

"Come in."

Lifting the latch, Charles pushed open the door and stepped down onto the dugout floor of the log and canvas hut. He removed his hat and waited, his black rain poncho dripping onto the dirt floor.

An older man of short stature, the major gestured for Charles to sit on the small camp stool that had been placed in front of a crooked table stacked with papers and ledgers.

He eyed the spindly legs of the stool with skepticism. Not that he was particularly heavy, but the stool looked more suitable for a child than someone with his long legs and arms.

"Thank you, sir, I'll stand."

"Very well." The major rose and reached for a piece of paper, tri-folded into an oblong shape.

A heaviness swelled behind Charles' sternum as an ache rose up through the back of his throat. In his experience pieces of official paper meant either disciplinary action or a transfer.

Suspecting the first, his brain shoved aside the growing sense of dread and quickly organized the events of that day. "Sir, if this is about what happened on Wednesday—"

"Ah, Wednesday." Major Ellis gave his head a resigned shake. "Captain, these surgeons and doctors are your coworkers. Like you, they are here to help these men in any way they can. However, unlike you they cannot memorize pages of medical text at a glance.

You must allow for human error and offer understanding and assistance to those of us with lesser minds, not a fist to the jaw. I would have thought you learned your lesson after Fredericksburg."

"Sir, I did not hit him."

The major sighed and slid his hand through his graying hair. "Semantics."

Charles clenched the hand he held behind his back and pressed his lips together.

He'd heard about the operation, and with nothing else to do, he'd stepped into the surgery tent where Major Balch was performing an amputation at the shoulder joint. Evidently the soldier's horse had slipped in the mud and fallen on him, resulting in a compound fracture of the humerus that had become gangrenous. Assisting Balch was an older civilian doctor who'd been appointed a commission at the start of the war. Charles had stepped close as Balch asked for the man to compress the subclavian artery.

Preoccupied cutting the flaps in the skin, Balch hadn't noticed that the doctor applied his pressure below the clavicle.

Charles stepped closer. "Compression to the artery above the clavicle would be more effective."

The older man's features twisted into a withering scowl. "I am pressing in the correct place, as proved by the name of the artery. *Sub*clavian." He frowned and with a shake of his head, he muttered, "Young upstart."

Balch made the internal flap, and the axillary artery suddenly jetted an enormous spurt of blood. Major Balch fired off five curse words in succession. Charles elbowed the stammering doctor aside and caught the artery in the flap, controlling the hemorrhage.

He hadn't realized until after he and Major Balch had the patient stitched up that the doctor he'd shoved aside had fallen to the floor. The older man hadn't been hurt, but he'd been livid and stomped off to press charges.

"I know your grandfather didn't raise you to be a common street brawler."

Charles gave himself a mental shake and tried to focus on what the major was saying. "Excuse me?"

"I said your grandfather didn't raise you to start fights. Though judging by the shape of your nose, it looks as if you've been in a few."

Charles ignored the comment. The man couldn't have known how many times he'd been beaten up by the boys at school. Instead he focused on the first part of the major's statement. "You know my grandfather, sir?"

"Yes, I was a big supporter of Senator Harrison. Enjoyed many wonderful meals at your grandfather's house. Knew your mother too. Beautiful woman. Such a gentle soul."

"My mother?" Charles stepped closer to the table.

A soft smile spread over the major's face. "Yes, I courted her for a season. Julia was so lovely and soft-spoken. We were not a good match, though. I think I intimidated her, for she became nervous and shy whenever in my presence. Then she met her young banker, Percy Ellard. Eyes only for him, and your grandfather indulged her. Julia was his only child, and he pandered to her every whim. The girl never had to lift a finger. She wanted Percy, so your grandfather made it happen."

"You knew my father too?"

"Not well. Only met him a few times, so I don't remember much. He sure didn't have your mind. Or your height. He may even have been shorter than Julia."

Charles had always assumed that since he didn't resemble his grandfather in appearance, he must take after his father's side of the family. The thought had always given him a little bit of connection with the man he never knew. Now a twinge of sadness poked at his heart.

"Nothing I can tell you that you don't already know."

Charles swallowed the urge to beg. Any tidbit of information would give him some glimpse of the man he knew nothing about.

****

"What did my father look like?"

Grandfather glanced up from the papers spread across his wide desk. "I'm rather busy. Don't you have some school work to do?"

"I've finished, sir. I only thought if you had a moment or two..."

The air in the darkened room seemed to shift, the way it did when the wind changed direction before a storm.

"He was a rather unremarkable man. Plain in his features. Quiet manner." He leveled a steady gaze at Charles, then leaned over and rummaged through the bottom drawer of his desk. A moment later he straightened and held out his hand. An engraved gold disc lay in his palm. A bit of thin chain hung between his fingers and the object gleamed in the lamplight.

"Here. Take it."

Charles stepped forward and lifted the timepiece

from his grandfather's palm. He turned it over and traced the ivy engraved around the circumference. Popping the clasp, he opened it to discover a miniature of his mother and a watch face with roman numerals. The hands had stopped at four twenty-seven and thirteen seconds.

"Take it. I've no use for it. It doesn't even work. Now run along. I'm busy." Ignoring Charles, Grandfather dipped his pen and resumed his work.

Charles took the watch up to his room and sprawled across the bed to examine every minute detail. He imagined his father's hands touching it and winding it every morning before he slipped it into his waistcoat and went off to the bank.

Grandfather had been right. The watch didn't work, but Charles went to the library and read a couple of books on watch repair. The next evening, he took the timepiece apart, spreading the tiny gears and springs on a handkerchief laid over his desk. With Bunzy observing from the corner opposite the inkwell, Charles painstakingly repaired his father's watch.

****

He shifted his hand forward beneath his black gum poncho and felt for the steady ticking through his coat.

"Captain."

Charles blinked, refocusing his attention on the present.

"I received this missive today from Washington." The major unfolded the letter he held in his hand. "Apparently you recently wrote to headquarters detailing numerous cases of scurvy and requested the troops receive more vegetables in their rations." He shifted his gaze to the paper in his hand and read, *"The troops should not have scurvy. Their rations are plentiful and good. Therefore, scurvy does not exist."*

"Of all the pigheaded, asinine—"

"Captain, please curtail your temper."

Charles heaved a breath and crushed his hat brim inside his fist. *Calm. Stay calm.* "I'm sorry, sir. Please forgive my outburst."

"There is nothing to forgive, Captain. Your sentiments are mine exactly. I only wish you had approached me with this issue before you sent your letter. I'm afraid your reputation in Washington is not the best, especially after the incident in December with the stoves."

"Sir, the wounded were lying on the ground with nothing but blankets for warmth."

"I agree with you, Captain. Your frustration with regulations is understandable; however, Washington only remembers that you assaulted a superior officer, and I'm afraid that incident has clouded their judgment in regards to your request."

Charles opened his mouth to argue, but the major held up his hand.

"I received word that supplies from the Sanitary Commission have arrived at Aquia Creek Landing. I am certain they have sent along an adequate amount of vegetables and fruit. It is a constant request by all the doctors.

"I will send my own findings to Washington with regards to the scurvy issue, which will hopefully increase the produce allotted each man's ration."

"Thank you, sir."

"And I'm afraid I have other news."

The major dropped the letter onto the center of his

desk then leaned over to rifle through another pile of papers. He withdrew a second folded sheet of paper and extended it to Charles.

Reluctantly, he accepted it. His stomach clenched as he read the words even as Major Ellis repeated them aloud.

"You are being temporarily reassigned to the First Division. Unfortunately, the rampant illnesses which claimed so many of our boys throughout the winter, take the lives of surgeons as well. They are down two surgeons. Tomorrow, report to Major Triscut of the 61st New York. Pack only your essentials. You may leave your trunk here. Word has it, we will soon be heading across the Rappahannock."

Charles swallowed and dug his fingernails deep into the thick wool-felt brim of his hat.

"And as soon as replacement surgeons can be found, you will be back with us. I am as reluctant to lose you now as I was in December."

"Thank you, sir." Maybe the replacement surgeons would arrive before they received the order to march. He sighed, knowing even if miracles did exist, his oath and skill would compel him to go. If he focused on the wounds, he could do this. He had to. He'd been fine at Antietam. It had been that horrific head wound at Fredericksburg that had triggered one of his spells. He swallowed.

"Shall I pass along a greeting from you in my next correspondence to my grandfather?"

"No need. We keep in touch. And he frequently asks news of you."

Charles nodded. He should have guessed. His grandfather had many friends in high places. At least

Charles could hide in this new unit. And maybe he'd get on better with these doctors. This time he'd keep his medical advice to himself. He'd try anyway.

"That will be all."

Charles turned, put his hat on, and tugging the brim low, he stepped into the rain.

Chapter Eleven

The next morning, after Major Dennis left for the day, Charles began packing. He hadn't said a word to the man about his transfer. If he hadn't told Gracie before he'd left for Falmouth, why would he now tell Dennis? The man would likely celebrate when he returned and found Charles gone.

Wind snapped at the canvas roof, and cold air huffed through the cracks between the roof and the logs. He stuffed in extra socks, rolled a clean shirt inside his blankets, added his shaving and mess kits, his surgical field case, and his bottle of whiskey. It would probably break, but for some reason, he'd rather have that happen than leave it for Major Dennis to drink. He rolled his bedding inside his gum rubber blanket and tied it all together.

At the last minute, he grabbed his notebook. Maybe he'd be able to record information on the initial condition of the wounds he treated in the battlefield for his paper on Pyemia and Surgical Fevers. He might be the only physician who believed laudable pus might not be the good thing they'd been taught. The why of this puzzle would give him something positive to think about during the lull before battle.

He grabbed his gear and headed off to search among the endless rows of log huts for the regimental flag of the 61st New York.

The damp air nipped at his cheeks and nose. Maybe it would rain again. Heavy rain, which would make the roads even muddier than they were now. Then the two-week delay would continue. He could hope, anyway.

He stopped at the hut with Major Triscut's name on the placard nailed to the wall. Squaring his shoulders, he knocked.

"Come."

Charles stepped inside and closed the door. It took a moment for his eyes to adjust to the dark interior. Major Triscut watched him from behind a stack of papers piled precariously around his desk top which was merely a board between two ammunition crates.

Charles set down his gear and pulled off his hat, smacking it against his thigh. He'd gotten his wish on his way over and droplets from his hat dotted the floor and the toes of his muddy boots.

Major Triscut rose and stepped around his desk.

Charles caught the glimpse of a smile behind the wiry hairs of his long salt and pepper goatee. Major Triscut extended his hand. "Captain Ellard."

Charles took a single long step and leaned forward to grasp the offered hand. "Major," he said as the other man slapped his palm against Charles' and gave his hand a quick shake.

"Glad to have you with us. Sadly, we lost Major Church to dysentery and Captain Favor to measles. All this regiment has at the moment are two assistant surgeons. According to the directives Doctor Letterman sent down after Antietam, the regimental hospitals will be combined in the field into one division hospital."

"Yes, sir."

"With these changes the three top surgeons, from all the regiments will be chosen, regardless of rank, to be responsible for surgeries in the field. In the first division, one of those three men will be you. You will also be assigned an assistant surgeon and a third medical officer to organize your patient names and records in the field."

Charles could only manage a quick nod as he squeezed his fingers around his hat brim.

"Now that the sick are being moved to the corps' hospital at Potomac Creek, there isn't much to do but ambulance drill."

"Yes, sir. If you will direct me to my quarters, I'll get settled in."

"You can bunk with Captain Breen. Captain Brooks will be your assistant surgeon. Did you bring your own servant?"

"No. My old tent mate had a boy who served both of us."

"Perhaps that will also work with the young man who serves Captain Breen. Have you a horse?"

"I had one until Fredericksburg, but I was sent to Washington for the winter, and I've no idea what became of him."

"That private of Breen's is excellent with horses. Mention it to him. I'm sure he'll find you a nice mount."

Maybe it was a good thing Charles had accepted the extra money from his grandfather. At this stage of the war, who knew how much a half-way decent horse would cost.

"If you'd like to meet the rest of the brigade surgeons, Major DeLong is making a large bucket of hot punch tonight."

"Thank you, sir, but I prefer to have an early night."

"Good idea. We have our orders. Light march. Two ambulances per brigade and no hospital wagons."

"But sir—"

"Don't fear, Captain. I gave direction that the pack mules belonging to the medical department should be placed at the disposal of the surgeons and that the men from the ambulance squads follow at the rear of the brigade with their stretchers, buckets, and lanterns."

Charles nodded.

"All right, Captain." He stepped around Charles and yelled for his aide who appeared seconds later.

"Martin, show Captain Ellard to Captain Breen's quarters."

"Yes, sir." The corporal opened the narrow, wooden door of the hut and waited for Charles to pass. "Right this way, sir." He stepped up beside him and pointed west.

They walked along streets of cabins that were little more than a cobbled together mix of logs, scrap lumber, and canvas. The quarters for the enlisted men were laid out behind them in the rows of a grid pattern. At the last hut in the row, the corporal stopped.

"Captain, are you in?"

A gust of wind snapped the canvas and molded the rubber fabric of Charles rain poncho against his thighs.

"Captain, I have Major Favor's replacement with me."

When no reply was forthcoming, the corporal opened the door for Charles to enter.

Like his old quarters, the dwelling had a dug out

floor, a fireplace of rock and clay, two cots made from poles and hardtack boxes, and a washstand between the beds.

The corner of a book poked from beneath the pillow of the cot on the right side and neatly folded shirt and uniform pants had been placed on the trunk at the end of the bed as if returned fresh from the laundry.

A blanket had been placed on the bare mattress of the other bed. The trunk of the deceased doctor still stood at the end.

"You can put your gear here." Corporal Martin gestured toward the empty cot. "Reckon they'll be sending Captain Favor's trunk back to Washington soon. Since you don't have yours, I don't suppose there's any big hurry."

"Thank you, Corporal."

"Reckon Captain Breen went to the party. If you want to go, it's three past Major Triscut's quarters."

"No, thank you."

"Right. I'll let Captain Breen's aide know you're here. He'll be by to get hold of anything else you need."

Once the private had gone, Charles tossed his hat onto the trunk, pulled off his poncho, and hung it from a peg near the front door. With a sigh, he shrugged off his pack and set it on the floor near the trunk. He rolled his shoulders and removed his damp overcoat and uniform jacket, leaving him in his shirtsleeves and waistcoat. He spotted a boot jack on the other side of the tent. As he pulled off his muddy footwear, he tugged free his neck cloth. He tossed the length of black silk on top of his jacket and set his boots near the door, hoping the aide would be able to clean them before morning.

He picked up the blanket and set it on another cot. Thinking he'd give the mattress a few shakes to even out the straw before making his bed, he lifted it off the cot. There spread across the wooden bed slats, lay a dozen or so postcards.

Assuming the previous surgeon had forgotten to mail them, Charles gathered them into a neat pile and dropped the mattress back in place. He turned the cards over.

A young lady in her chemise and drawers reclined on a chaise, one foot on the floor, her other leg drawn up, bent at the knee.

Heat seared his cheek bones. The woman's smooth white calves and narrow ankles drew his eye. He imagined wrapping his fingers around her ankle, his thumb brushing back and forth across the thin skin that covered the medial malleolus. Then he'd slide his hand upward, beneath the ruffled cotton, over the smooth curve of her gastrocnemius muscle to the tender skin at the back of her knee.

He slipped that card to the back of the pile and lowered himself to the mattress.

The next photograph presented the side view of a nude woman with one knee bent and resting on the seat of a wing chair. Her forearms lay crossed on the high back as she looked coyly over her shoulder. In the picture, the woman wore her hair up in some sort of loosely gathered knot, but all Charles saw was a long braid of red hair which followed the line of her spine down to the dip just below her waist. Would Gracie's skin be such a smooth ivory? Or would freckles sprinkle across her shoulders the way they dusted her nose and cheekbones?

Beneath her layers of skirts and petticoats would the muscles of her gluteus maximus be round and firm from all the walking she did around the hospital or would she look as this woman did, all soft and pillowy?

The other photographs were more risqué. A naked woman lay on a bed without a footboard, her breasts flat and slid slightly off toward either side of her chest. She wore only her black stockings, her knees drawn up. A soldier in uniform stood at the end of the mattress; his penis jutted from his unbuttoned pants.

Charles' corresponding body part swelled more with each moment he stared. He'd seen pornography before. In a school filled with growing boys, conversations concerning sexuality were inevitable. And though Charles had learned to satisfy his masculine needs without the services of disease-ridden prostitutes, his fantasy woman had never had a clear face. But suddenly Gracie's image had been superimposed over every woman on every card.

Though part of him felt like a voyeuristic cad, another part couldn't get enough. His biological instinct to mate urged him to mollify this consuming desire before Captain Breen returned. Quickly he made up his bed and gathered the post cards for one last look before he stripped off his uniform and doused the light.

Guilt drummed a double-time beat in his ears and screamed for him to throw the cards into the fire and watch the edges curl until the instant they were consumed by flames, but he continued staring, continued imagining.

"Captain?" a young male voice called. "Captain…uh…you have a visitor."

Sonofa—Heat seared his face. He scrambled for a

place to hide the French postcards.

"Captain, are you in there?"

"Uh, yes. Just…just give me a moment."

"Sir, it's commencing to rain again, and your sister has been looking for you."

Sister?

He shoved the cards under his pillow and tugged at the front of his pants. "Uh…Captain Breen isn't here at the moment."

With a quick downward glance, he realized that hadn't quite done the trick. If only there was more time…

"I understand he is at the tent of Major DeLong." He grabbed his long, damp uniform coat, shoved his arms in the sleeves and hastily buttoned it from the bottom up. Captain Breen's sister could wait in here while he cooled his ardor in the rain.

"Come in," he said, and pushed open the door. "You may wait here if you—"

He blinked not sure if she was real or a remnant of his fantasy. She stood outside the cabin, her small frame lost in the rubberized cloth of a gum blanket. On her head, a cavalry officer's hat, and as she lifted her chin to meet his gaze, rain dripped from the brim. Moisture glistened across her nose and cheeks.

"What are you doing here?" he blurted out.

It was the wrong thing to say. He knew it as soon as the words left his mouth, as soon as the corporal frowned.

He opened his mouth to apologize, to make amends before she lit into him for his lack of manners.

Before he could utter a sound, she smiled.

At him.

This had to be a dream. Gracie McBride did not send him smiles like this. Not broad smiles filled with straight white teeth and unabashed joy.

The kind of smiles which lit up her face and brought sparks of gold to her deep brown eyes were saved for Corporal Reid and men like Major Carlton.

He gave his head a slight shake, denying the fantasy.

"'Tis good to see ye, Char-Charles."

Gracie McBride had never used his given name before. Odd that he didn't find more pleasure in hearing the syllables roll from her tongue.

"Mrs. M—"

She cut him off with a severe scowl and a slight shake of her head.

Sister. Right. "Miss," he hastily corrected. "Err, um Gra-Gracie."

Should he invite her in? A single woman alone in a man's quarters? He could prop the door open, but it was pouring. What the hell? This wasn't a Philadelphia drawing room.

"It took me the better part of the day to find ye. Ye might at least offer a word of greeting."

"I apologize." Sister. She was his sister. "Good afternoon, Gracie. It is lovely to see you again." He bowed and held open door. "Do come in. May I take your er…um…wrap?"

"Ye may." She grinned as she stepped through the opening. Her wet skirt brushed the log frame on either side, and she stepped down onto the dug-out floor.

"That will be all, Corporal."

"Yes, sir." The young man saluted and turned away as Charles closed the door behind him.

Gracie whisked off the floppy hat. She gave it a quick shake, scattering droplets across the floor then passed it to him. She lifted the dripping poncho over her head and offered it to his outstretched hand.

"I thought ye were with the 69th Pennsylvania."

"I have been temporarily assigned here to replace one of two surgeons who died of illness."

With her garments in hand, he turned right then left, searching for a place to hang them. He finally settled on a nail in the center support post and set the hat on Foster's trunk. Unsure if the dampness coating his palms was rain or sweat, he wiped his hands down the sides of his coat. His overcoat. He probably should remove it.

He quickly thumbed the buttons through their holes and shrugged out of the garment before he laid it on the trunk beside Gracie's hat.

He'd never spoken to Gracie outside the familiar confines of the hospital and suddenly felt as nervous as he'd been at his first ball.

Now she stood here in his private quarters watching him with a half smile on her face.

He frowned. Did she suddenly find him amusing? Had he forgotten some formulaic piece of social etiquette? He glanced around the space. A chair. A gentleman always offers a lady a chair. "Would you like to sit?"

He turned to grab an empty hard tack crate from the corner. When he swung back, she was perched on the edge of his bed. He stared.

Gracie McBride was sitting in the same place he would sleep. Sitting on the blanket he would wrap around himself for warmth. Sitting in the exact spot he'd been moments ago as he perused French postcards and fantasized about running his hands over her smooth bare skin. Imagined pressing his lips to hers, sucking the thin skin at the base of her throat, running his tongue over her nipples, wondering if they would turn pebbly hard, the way he'd overheard it said between the other men at medical college.

His face flushed with warmth. His mouth went dry. He tried to swallow but didn't have enough saliva. Heat flooded his groin. Perhaps he should not have removed his coat.

He dropped to sit on the wooden box. He thought to cross his legs and place his folded hands in his lap. His knees bumped hers. He leaned back. The crate wobbled. He tried to stabilize his weight, but he overcompensated and tipped over backward in a tangle of arms and legs.

Ears burning, his cheeks on fire, he scrambled to his feet, shoved his hands behind his back, and studied the triple stitched seams in the canvas above his head, terrified if he met her gaze she'd be laughing.

He couldn't bear it if Gracie McBride laughed at him. If she became one of those who stopped talking when he passed by or made sport of him in whispers behind his back.

"Doctor Ellard, I'll have a fair crick in me neck if I have to look up at ye from this great distance. Would ye please sit down? I be feeling like a cat in a room full o' rocking chairs."

He couldn't imagine anything making Gracie McBride nervous, least of all him, but she scooted toward the head of the bed to allow him room. As he moved to join her, he realized there wouldn't be enough space for the width of her skirt without him sitting on it.

She must have recognized the same problem, and at the last moment, she scooted closer to the head of his bed, picking up his pillow to allow more room.

She gasped.

The pillow hung in mid-air. Her face instantly flamed to match the hue of her hair. She slammed the pillow down on top of the post cards at the exact moment he lunged across to claim them.

As he pulled back, his cheek brushed across her breast. The soft mound compressed under the fleeting pressure of his cheekbone. He dropped the cards. They scattered at her feet. Mortified, he bent forward to scoop them up before she could see. His gaze fell on the last card.

A nude woman reclined on chaise. She gazed at the photographer as if he were her lover. Intense longing filled her eyes. The promise of a kiss hovered in the sheen of her parted lips.

He dove for the card and shoved it among those gathered in his hand. Whirling, he tossed them all into the fireplace. When he turned back, Gracie sat perfectly still watching him with the same expression as the woman on the last card.

He blinked, believing for a moment that he had superimposed that woman's expression on Gracie. But as he stepped toward her, the edges of her brown eyes softened. Her chin tipped up. Her lips parted, beckoning.

Didn't she realize she shouldn't look at him like this unless she desired all that had stirred to life inside him? For he ached to know her, all of her, in a way he'd never longed for anyone.

He cleared his throat. "How is Major Carlton?"

A shadow fell across her face, and she frowned. "Major Carlton?"

"Yes, how does he fair getting around with only one leg? Is he adjusting well?"

"Fine, last I saw the man. I've not seen him since…"

"The *John Brooks* departed Washington."

"Ye saw me then." A smile spread across her face and amber highlight brightened her eyes. "I'd come to wish ye well. The rails o'the boat be so crowded with men, I called for ye, but the provost guard would not let me on board."

Her smile faded. "Why did ye not tell me ye were leaving?"

Relief eased the tension is his spine. Maybe Gracie McBride did not care for Major Carlton.

Those earnest brown eyes of hers searched his face, waiting for his answer.

"I…We…were at cross purposes, so frequently I believed…it wouldn't matter to you if I left."

The way she looked at him, her eyes wide, her cheeks pink with cold, her lips moist and slightly parted. Warmth flooded his body, pooling in his groin. Desire swelled inside his pants. He placed one knee on the mattress near her hip, leaned close, and grasped her upper arms.

She gasped but didn't pull away.

He lowered his forehead to rest against the cool dampness at her hairline. The tip of his nose brushed the cold skin of hers. The heat of their breath warmed the air between them.

Her tongue darted out swiping across her lower lip,

drawing him closer.

Even as he wondered why she'd really come, he brushed his lips over hers. Their tender skin was warm and supple beneath his mouth as he pressed light nipping kisses to first her top lip then along her fuller bottom lip. As he'd done before, he explored her mouth, absorbing the texture and taste that was Gracie McBride.

He felt the pull on either side of his waistcoat as her fingers dug into the soft wool. Longing filled her eyes and her lashes fluttered closed.

She softened under the weight of his mouth. Kissed him back. Kissed him as if she wanted him.

Like lightning through storm clouds, desperate longing coursed through his veins urging him to take from her all that he'd denied himself over the years.

His hand slipped to her shoulder, brushing over the twilled cotton to tangle his fingers in the damp tendrils at the back of her neck. He cupped the fine line of her jaw, skimming his thumb over the chilled skin of her cheek.

Her tongue twined with his, and he closed his eyes, savoring the faint taste of coffee and something uniquely Gracie. His thumb traced a line over the curve of her chin, down the line of her throat to the fabric of her collar.

In his mind he saw the postcards, envisioned Gracie naked on the bed beneath him. How would she feel? His fingers popped the first button free, then directly beneath a second, and a third, and a fourth. No more than an inch or two of skin lay exposed beyond the hollow of her throat. How many buttons were on a woman's dress?

There was also a corset. Somewhere beneath her layers of clothing he knew a corset hindered access to her breasts. Were the lacings in the front or the back?

And hoops. Although Gracie's skirts didn't billow and sway as she walked.

But she did wear petticoats with ruffles—scarlet red petticoats. He'd seen that as she'd rolled around on the floor of the ward with that lazy sergeant.

Was there perhaps a book seller in Washington with a volume diagramming the intricacies of ladies clothing?

Gracie moaned softly against his mouth, her fingertips pressing deep into his trapezius.

But as she'd done before, her hands slid down to the center of his chest, and she gently pushed against him.

His heart sank at her rejection. But he was a gentleman and control was his mantra. He would never take more from her than she was willing to give.

He eased back exhaling a soft groan. He shifted most of his weight to the foot which had remained on the floor. Searching her eyes, he waited for the rejection, the reminder that he was not her beloved William. The reminder that he would never be good enough.

He felt a tug at the top of his shirt. A whisper of breath tickled the fine hairs at the base of his throat. When had his top shirt buttons come undone?

Tilting her chin, she met his gaze. A secretive grin tugged at the corners of her mouth.

"It seems, Doctor Ellard, ye have kissed me before I had a chance to touch yer neck cloth. Though 'tis cheating I think, that ye not be wearing one."

Her finger lightly trailed down his skin following the length his shirt opening then slipped free the next button.

He gulped and wrapped his hand around her small wrist, pressing her palms captive against his thudding heart.

"Why are you here, Mrs. McBride?"

She frowned. Her mischievous grin flattened into a tight, uncertain smile. "Doctor Colfax won't let me change dressings or stitch wounds. He be complaining so much, Doctor Bliss thought I be needing time away from me hospital duties, so I've come to distribute supplies with the Sanitary Commission."

He searched every nuance of her expression, but shadows within the tent hid the straight forward honesty he usually found in Gracie's eyes.

The tiny hairs at the back of his collar rose with his sense of foreboding. He released her hand and eased back, rubbing his neck as he sat.

"As you have said, I was not easy to find. So I ask again. Why are you here?"

She exhaled a shuddery breath, sitting up beside him. She glanced down and fingered one of the pleats in her skirt. Pinching the fold line between her fingers, she pressed a crisp three-inch line in the black bombazine.

"I come to…well, the hospital…the patients…they all miss ye. And I…I…"

He studied her face, seeking some clue as to her motive. Though he would have enjoyed the experience of realizing his fantasies with her in his arms, her sudden eager response to his kiss raised doubts. "Why are you here? Is that why you kissed me? To tease me into returning to Washington so I'll support you as you change dressings and stitch wounds?"

"No. Not at all. I have something to say. 'Tis not an easy thing and—"

"Why else would you kiss me? As you have on numerous occasions pointed out, I am not William."

She stilled, and he waited for her response to that cold truth.

She drew a deep breath. Raising her chin, she met his gaze. "Ye are right. Ye are nothing like William. Ye're arrogant and condescending." She inched toward him. "Yer handwriting is barely legible, and ye tell the worst jokes I've heard in me life." Somehow, she'd glided closer.

He swallowed, reminding himself to breathe.

"But ye are brilliant and shy and sweet in yer way." She reached up and grasped his shirt front, tugging him close. "And ye kiss me like William never could."

Lamplight above reflected tiny amber sparks in her brown eyes.

She threw her arms around his neck and captured his mouth with hers.

Chapter Twelve

After a long search in the rain, Gracie had finally found Doctor Ellard's quarters. While he hadn't seemed glad to see her, once she'd seen his face, she'd been helpless to hide her joy.

The postcards had been most unexpected. She'd been disappointed when he tossed them into the fireplace, because once her initial surprise waned the photographs had actually stirred her curiosity.

When his lips touched hers, her knees had gone trembly and weak. Fortunately, she'd been sitting on his bed, the bed where he slept. And once he'd cupped her face so gently in his hands, she was lost.

"I come all this way to...The hospital...the patients...they all miss ye. And I..."

For a moment the barest hint of a smile softened the normal stoicism in his expression. But mistrust immediately overshadowed that rare glimpse of the man behind the doctor.

Whether this man was Charles or Jason, she didn't know. What could she say? At this moment it didn't matter. She was a woman, and she wanted him.

She'd convinced herself she needed to find him because of the note. To learn the solution to a puzzle that had plagued her since the ear of the rabbit had torn. To perhaps give him the family he once said he'd wished for.

But had that only been an excuse? She had no feelings for this man outside their unique doctor-nurse relationship. Did she?

"You've several frown lines furrowing your brow, Mrs. McBride. What causes you to think so seriously?"

"I...um...I'd be pleased to have ye call me Gracie."

Surprise brightened his eyes and softened the usual tension in the muscles of his face. He leaned close and brushed his lips across her mouth and along her jaw.

Then he stiffened as though realizing she hadn't answered his question.

"Come now, Mrs. Mc...Gracie." He raised himself, his forearms braced on either side of her. He searched her face. "Out with it. I've never known you to falter at the line of battle."

She pressed the tip of her finger to his lips. "Later."

But he was not deterred. "You come all this way and suddenly want to kiss me? Forgive me if I have cause to question your motives."

"I...I...happened upon a bit o' information and... I do miss working with ye. I do." She pushed herself up to sit upright, her feet firmly on the floor. What right did she have to say anything? What if she'd misconstrued the facts? Who was she to shatter his life?

"Information? Regarding what?"

"'Tis not important."

"Is it my grandfather? Is he well?"

"Yer grandfather? Aye, as far as I know, he be hale and hearty as ever and no doubt poking at people with his cane."

"Then what has you so tongue-tied? I have no other family."

She gulped and glanced at the wet hem of her skirt, the mud on the toes of her shoes, the planks beneath her feet. The weight of the rabbit inside her pocket grew heavier with each thud of her heart against her breast bone.

He leaned toward her and with one long finger beneath her chin, tilted her head up until their gazes met.

"What's wrong?"

Ducking under his arm as she jumped to her feet, she pushed past him to stand at the foot of his bed.

Her hand slipped between the folds of her skirt, into the large side pocket. For a moment her fingers toyed with the velvety ears as she struggled for words.

Maybe she could show him the rabbit and the note. Not mention Sergeant Baker and his sister. There might be a simple explanation. The toy could have once belonged to another boy.

Turning, she pulled the stuffed animal from her pocket and held it out to him.

He blinked several times before accepting it. "This was in the box from my grandfather. Why did you bring it here?"

"I…" She drew a deep breath. "I do not believe the man to be yer grandfather." She exhaled the words in a rush of air.

His eyes widened. He stepped back, his face pale. "Excuse me?"

She gulped. "I did not intend to find it. 'Twas the beef tea that upset me, and William dying, and me own regrets. I threw it against the wall. The ear tore, and I saw it."

He stared at her intently as though trying to solve a

complex logic puzzle. "Saw it? Saw what? Come now, Mrs. McBride, you are speaking in riddles. Out with it."

"The note."

His brow tugged together forming deep furrows above the bridge of his nose. "What note?"

She pointed to the edges of the hole at the base of the ear.

He glanced down and blinked as though he'd forgotten he held it in his hand.

"Inside."

He stared the rabbit in the face. With his index finger, he touched the frayed bits of thread where the old line of stitches had torn.

"I sewed this when I was very young. I don't recall how it tore."

"Ye may want to sit down, Doctor Ellard."

He looked from the rabbit to her.

"There be a note inside the ear." She clasped her hands in front of her, digging her thumb into her palm. "And I fear the words may give ye a bit o' a shock."

He shook his head and ran his hand around the back of his neck. Drawing a deep breath, he pulled back the fuzzy ear, revealing the tightly rolled paper shoved almost completely into the sawdust which filled the head.

Pulling it free, he tucked the rabbit under his arm then slowly unrolled the yellowed paper.

He stared at the words Gracie knew by heart.

mY nam is JaSon
CharelZ is ded
I wesh I WaS tO

His complexion drained of all color, wan and ghost-like in the shifting shadows of the tent.

236

Unsure what to say, Gracie watched him, waiting for a reaction that didn't seem to come. Instead his features tightened and he rerolled the note.

"I am not amused." He handed her the note and tossed the rabbit on his cot.

She accepted the paper, but watched him warily, waiting for the implication of the words to sink in.

"I expected better of you, Mrs. McBride, than for you to find humor at the expense of another."

She shook her head. "'Tis no prank. Are ye the lad who wrote those words? Are ye Jason?"

His shoulders stiffened. His spine went rigid. He stood so still. What was he thinking? His hands moved behind his back. He exhaled a breath.

"Come," he said moving to pick up her hat and rain poncho. "I will escort you back to..." He turned. "Where did you come from?"

"Potomac Creek. I come with the Sanitary Commission, organizing supplies for the division hospitals."

"But that's five miles from here."

"The corporal borrowed horses for us, but ye sent him away."

He grabbed his boots and with a hard tug and a few stomps, shoved his feet inside. "Remain here."

He spun on his heel, snatched up his hat and poncho, and left the tent.

Gracie exhaled a deep breath. She'd expected a stronger reaction from him. Anger, denial, a simple explanation of some kind. He hadn't said a word, but he'd stared at her as if she'd stabbed him in the back.

His resentment had been so contained, so tightly controlled, she was glad she hadn't shared Sergeant

Baker's story.

A sick lump swelled inside her stomach. Deciding to wait for him outside, she slipped the rubberized gum blanket over her head and added the battered cavalry officer's hat. Her gaze fell on the rabbit laying on the mattress, its blank eyes staring at the canvas roof overhead. Should she take the toy with her or leave it here?

She fingered the note inside her pocket for a moment and listened to the murmurs of male voices passing outside the tent. Removing the rolled paper, she inserted it back in the ear and set the rabbit on Doctor Ellard's pillow. She'd given him the information, whether he pursued it was his decision.

Crossing to the door, it opened before she had a chance to touch it.

A man stepped inside. He wore shoulder straps with the letters M-S, embroidered between his captain's bars and was maybe as old as Callum had been.

If Gracie's emotions hadn't been in such turmoil, the shocked expression on his face would have been comical.

"Can I help you?" he asked, whipping off his hat.

She forced a smile. "I beg yer pardon. I'll be waiting for Doc—me brother outside."

"I'm sorry, but who is your brother?"

She gestured toward the empty bed. "Doctor Charles Ellard."

He nodded. "Good, I was afraid they wouldn't find a replacement before we marched."

"'Twas nice to meet ye, Captain."

"Breen, Roger Breen."

"And I be Mrs. Gracie McBride, a nurse come

238

down from Washington with the Sanitary Commission."

"Well, it's good you had a chance to visit." Dimples appeared in both cheeks when he grinned. "I just heard. We received our orders. We march tomorrow morning."

Outside, beyond the open door, Doctor Ellard hopped down from a small horse-drawn cart.

Gracie said goodbye, and the captain stepped aside so she could pass.

Doctor Ellard gave the captain a brisk nod and handed her up onto the narrow bench seat. Wordlessly, he climbed on beside her and gathered the reins.

The cart lurched and bounced its way through the muddy roadway toward Potomac Creek. Gracie clutched the rough wooden bench to keep from tumbling off. She would have held onto Doctor Ellard's arm, but from the way he'd fixed his gaze straight ahead, with the small muscle at the back of his jaw bunched tight, he radiated an implacable aura.

In the distance loomed the dark oblong shapes of the railcars and the white pyramids of the hospital tents. She glanced at Doctor Ellard, rigid and stoic beside her.

With his gaze fixed on their destination, he said, "You don't like my grandfather because he is too controlling, but you—You wrap your will within a smile and lilting accent, every bit as obstinate as he.

"You decide you don't like the attendants in the ward so you put a purgative in their food. You decide you want cake, and you go behind my back to have the sisters bake it. You decide you know best for my patient and demand I move him away from the door.

"You decide you don't like my family and you

come here with that fabricated note and its slanderous implications.

"I made known my affection for you, yet you play hot and cold with my feelings, perhaps choosing to believe as others do, that I have none.

"My grandfather is right. Miss Adelaide Emmerson will make me the perfect wife. You and I would never suit. This war must have addled my wits to believe otherwise. Good day, Mrs. McBride."

Without giving her a chance to utter a word, not that she could find a single word to utter, he jumped from the cart, handed her down, and drove away, firmly slamming the door on that invisible wall which surrounded him.

Tears burned. Tightness swelled inside her chest as though she'd drawn a deep breath and never released it. She stared after his dark silhouette until it was swallowed by the night. Listening to fading sound of the horse's hooves sucking through the mud, she prayed the sound would change, gradually grow louder as he returned. But only the low murmur of male voices and footsteps of the guards moving around the supply train filled her ears.

She retreated to her quarters. After removing her hat and rain poncho, she pulled off her muddy shoes and stripped down to her petticoat and chemise. Someone had lit a fire in the stove. While it chased the damp from the tent, it did little to ease the chill deep inside.

Curling up beneath her blankets, she stared at the faint orange glow which flickered behind the grate. An ache grew inside her, hollow and empty, leaving her bereft, as if she'd lost him forever.

The pain hurt worse than it had upon learning of Callum and Michael's deaths, cut deeper than it had when William passed, because they had not chosen to leave her. They had not deliberately chosen to shut her out of their lives.

A tear ran across the bridge of her nose and down her cheekbone into her hairline where it joined the moisture of the tears which had gone before, dampening the bleached cotton of her pillow case.

Was he right? Was she too controlling? She didn't mean to be. *'Faugh a Ballagh'* Clear the Way. The motto of the Irish Brigade. Maybe she had more in common with her brothers than she thought. She only tried to do right by the patients. William had liked her spirit. But William was Irish. Doctor Ellard was not.

He'd never mentioned a sweetheart before. She'd assumed he was unattached and interested in her. Had he only kissed her because she was Irish? A nurse? She never should have stepped inside his quarters. Been alone with him. Maybe her behavior had given him the impression she was a loose woman.

She never should have come. He hadn't seemed glad to see her at first. He'd been looking at those postcards. Was that the reason he'd kissed her? Had he been hoping for a quick tumble? He was right. She'd only come to fix what she thought needed fixing. The mystery of his past was not her business.

When she finished her work here at Falmouth, she would return to Washington. She'd tamp down her urge to use the skills William had taught her. She'd refrain from arguing with the doctors and remember her place. Clean, change beds, and write letters. Do not stitch wounds or change catheters.

Tomorrow morning, Doctor Ellard's division would be marching. By tomorrow night he'd be on the other side of the Rappahannock, sleeping in Confederate territory.

Chapter Thirteen

Morning fog rolled across the ground, obscuring the rows of log huts in a misty shroud. Voices murmured indistinct words. Bridles jangled as impatient horses stamped their feet and snorted, the muted sounds carrying through the damp air.

Quiet was the order. With Lee's army camped across the Rappahannock, Hooker didn't want to give the Confederate general any warning that the Army of the Potomac was on the move. The Fifth, Eleventh, and Twelfth Corps had left Falmouth on Monday. They were the farthest from the river and from the sight of Confederate pickets.

Now the Second Corps prepared to march.

"You taking that whole rabbit with you?" Captain Breen chuckled.

Charles shot him a puzzled look. "No." He tossed the toy he'd been holding onto the bed.

"Just wondered, cause most folks only take the foot."

Charles frowned. "This is a merely a toy. If I had a need for good luck, superstition deems it be the foot from an actual rabbit."

Breen burst out laughing. He dropped onto the side of his bed, holding his arm across his abdomen, gasping as he tried to catch his breath.

Ignoring his tent mate, Charles resumed packing.

He hadn't been able to stop thinking about the rabbit since he'd left Gracie last night. Couldn't stop seeing the words every time he closed his eyes.

My name is Jason. Charles is dead.

He checked and rechecked his surgical knapsack.

My name is Jason.

No. I am Charles. Charles Ellard.

Charles is dead.

He walked to the outskirts of camp to check the field packs for the pack mules then slogged through the mud all the way back to his new quarters.

Life had played a cruel joke on him, and the punch line was less than humorous. His name was Charles. Charles Peter Ellard. Named after his father, Peter Ellard. His grandfather was Former State Senator Foster Harrison.

My name is Jason.

How had that note gotten inside the rabbit? The only memory he could conjure, the one which had his stomach twisted into knots, was of him sewing the ear, taking his time with each tiny stitch, making each one exactly the same length as the one before. He'd gotten the needle and thread from…

Danvers. His grandfather's butler at the time. He'd silently held the toy up high so the man could see the torn ear.

But how had the note gotten inside? He concentrated, rubbed his temples forcing himself to focus, to dig deep inside his memories for some hint of how the ear had been torn. Pain stabbed through his head. Remnants of his evening meal churned inside his stomach. Nothing appeared but a black void that made his heart pound.

He couldn't summon a single memory of anything before those moments with Danvers. It was as if his life had begun in that instant, holding Bunzy, staring at the gaping wound between the top of his fuzzy head and the base of his long floppy ear.

My name is Jason.

He winced and rubbed his temple, pressing hard against the pain.

"You feeling all right?"

Breen's inquiry jerked his thoughts back to the present.

"Fine."

He wasn't fine. Why had Gracie shown this to him now? He was heading into battle. He'd have a hard enough time making it through the surgeries and amputations with little food and even less sleep.

Gracie and her damned need to fix things, to make everything better.

****

"Come now, Mrs. McBride you can't cry over all of them."

She sniffed but didn't turn around. "Do not tell me who to cry for."

"You knew that soldier was dying."

"I should have been there…to comfort him so he'd not have to die alone in the dark.…if ye cannot concern yerself with the feelings of yer own brethren, then 'tis ye who will one day die alone in the dark."

****

Breen rolled a pair of woolen socks into a ball. "You probably should have gotten some sleep last night."

Charles shrugged, trying to shake off both the

memories and the looming specter of Fredericksburg.

He squeezed tight his trembling fingers and shoved them behind his back. Calm. As long as he stayed calm, his breathing would be fine. His heart would be fine.

"Richards should be here soon." Breen tugged his pack closed. "With the horses and food." He grinned. "Theirs and ours."

Breen seemed a likeable fellow, inclined to laugh a great deal. Charles did wonder how battle-hardened the man actually was. Would the blood and death ahead of them sour the man's ability to find life amusing?

Charles folded his blankets lengthwise and placed a clean shirt and a second pair of socks on top. He wondered if Breen always rattled on like this or if he was nervous.

"Why is it you don't sound Irish?" Breen asked as he rolled his bedding.

Charles grabbed his knapsack and bedroll and swung around. He hoped Breen was merely nervous. His constant prattle would prove irritating over a prolonged period of time. From the way Charles' skin already crawled, he didn't think he could endure Breen's chatter for much longer.

Breen gathered his gear and stood watching Charles expectantly.

"Your sister's Irish."

Sister. Gracie and her ridiculous lie. "I was adopted." Where the hell had that come from? Bunzy. Between Breen and that damned note, his thoughts were coming and going. Was he adopted? Is that why he remembered lilacs by a back porch? He rubbed his forehead. How would he perform surgery if he couldn't focus?

"I believe I hear Richards with the horses." He ducked through the door putting an end to the conversation.

By ten o'clock the first and third divisions of the second corps were on the move. With the medical department at the rear of the column, Breen rode beside Charles, keeping up a steady stream of questions and comments about Gracie.

"She's a nurse, huh? An admirable quality, volunteering to give aid in that way."

They headed west, following the north side of the Rappahannock.

"Her husband was a doctor, too? Did she also help him with patients?"

At the back of a line miles long, the muddy roads had become a slippery mess of red clay and Charles' horse slid and stumbled several times. Behind them followed the ammunition wagons, the mules double teamed to keep the wheels from bogging down. Next came the rations, then the medical supplies and ambulances.

"So your sister's a widow. How long has it been?"

"Three years." Why Charles had told Breen that Gracie had lost her husband, he could only attribute to a temporary lapse of common sense. All he could think about were the words on that paper. *Charles is dead. Charles is dead.*

"She's a handsome woman. Does she have a beau?"

"Who?"

"Your sister." Subdued laughter ran through Breen's words.

"I don't have a—oh, Gracie." Charles didn't have a

sister, but maybe Jason did. Maybe Jason had brothers too. A real family. Should he try to find the answers?

"No." He gripped the reins tighter. "No, she doesn't have a beau."

Why couldn't Breen treat him as indifferently as the other officers? Why did the man have to be so nice, offering to share his mess, helping him find a horse? Lying to him about Gracie would be so much easier then, although Charles had never been good at perpetuating falsehoods.

After a nine-mile march, word came down through the column to halt. The pontoniers had spent the whole night hauling the bridge trains seven miles through thick forest in the rain, to reach U.S. Ford in time. Now new approaches needed to be cut from the dense woods to the banks on either side of the river. General Couch detailed five hundred infantry men to help clear the trees.

The remaining men rested along the road. Charles and Breen dismounted holding the reins while their horses hungrily nipped short the wet grass and munched the leaves of the surrounding brush.

The sharp popping of gunfire drifted from the southwest.

"What's that?" Breen tensed. His gaze darted around the dense woods on either side of the road.

"Sounds like a skirmish with some Confederate pickets. I only heard a few bursts of rifle fire."

Breen nodded and relaxed his stiffened posture.

Charles didn't want to think about what tomorrow would bring. Nor was he inclined to dwell on that damned note, *My name is Jason*. Charles moved to the back of his horse and checked his saddle bags.

"I have some extra room," he said as he rose to his feet and gathered his reins. "I'm riding back to the medical wagons for some more suture and bandages."

"Why?" Breen asked. "These packs are heavy enough."

Charles stepped into the stirrup and swung his leg over the back of his horse. "Because the ambulances and Autenreiths likely won't be crossing the river."

Breen rolled to his feet. "Are you sure? That doesn't make any sense. We'll need the supplies."

"This is a light march. Ammunition wagons and rations are ahead of the ambulances and medical wagons they did send. But they won't come over until the fighting is done."

"Then can you grab some extra for me?"

Charles gave him a nod then turned his horse and followed the edge of the narrow road, past the rest of the column toward the rear.

****

Shadows lay upon shadows as the fading sunshine filtered through the woods in golden dapples and brought a premature end to the day. By the time Charles and Breen emerged from the trees and moved their horses down the hill, moonlight illuminated the newly cleared shorelines along the Rappahannock.

Ahead, two long columns, Couch's Second Corps and Sickles' Third, stretched like marching ants across the open, over bridges to the opposite shore. Empty pontoon wagons and unused timber littered the wide banks. Horses munched on scattered hay, and engineers slept in hollows carved in the soft sandy soil.

Between the swelled current and the shifting weight of the Second Corps as it crossed, the bridge tipped and wavered so that some men could hardly stand. Charles' horse followed Breen's to the edge of a bridge that was nothing more than tree trunks lashed together over pontoons.

Breen's horse *clomp-clomped* onto the bridge. The long-legged bay Charles rode, lowered his head, his ears pricked forward. He blew huffs of air through his nose but refused to place his hoof onto the first of the lashed timbers.

Charles thumped the animal's sides with his heels, but the gelding wouldn't move. Leaning back in the saddle, he gave the horse a sharp swat on the rump, but the animal stubbornly refused to budge.

The rest of the long column continued forward, their boot heels thudding an irregular cadence against the logs.

Ahead of him on the bridge, Breen stopped and looked back. When the man's laughter rang out, Charles rubbed his aching forehead. His ears burned, and he gave the horse another swat.

Richards rode up beside him leading the pack horse. "Want me to give it a try?" He came up alongside and leaned over to grab the left rein from Charles. Then with a click of his tongue he urged his mount forward as he tugged Charles' horse to the bridge.

The horse stretched his head and neck out as far as they would go, but his white stockinged legs remained firmly on solid ground.

Richard's turned back in his saddle. "Sir, the ammo wagons are coming up close. You want to swap? I'll take your mount and cross him last. I'm betting he won't want to be left behind."

Skin crawling as though a thousand eyes watched, Charles nodded and dismounted, avoiding the gazes of all those men whose snickers reached his ears.

After switching horses, Charles swung into the saddle of the smaller horse dropping the shorter stirrups to ride without them.

"Sir, if you don't mind." Richards passed Charles the lead ropes for two pack mules. "If your horse don't want to go, I might have to swim him across, and I'd hate for all your medicines and instruments to get wet."

"Fine." Charles extended his hand for the rope. At this point he didn't care. He'd drawn too much attention already and only wanted to get on his way, make camp and get something to eat.

Even though Richards' horse wasn't short enough to be considered a pony, the heels of Charles' boots hung low so that he felt as if he was mounted on Toby, the Shetland Pony his grandfather had given him, on whom he'd first learned to ride.

This horse was a plucky little thing, however, and gamely stepped onto the undulating bridge. Head bobbing as he walked, he quickly carried Charles over the wide expanse of murky green water as though he'd done it a hundred times. And as easy as that, Charles was in Confederate territory.

"You have to swim across?" Breen asked as Charles rode up beside him.

Charles frowned. "No. Why?"

"I figured you must have, 'cause it looks like your horse got shrunk." Another burst of laughter erupted from the man.

Charles frowned. "But neither the horse nor I are wet."

Breen's mouth dropped open for a moment. Then he doubled over laughing, slapping his thigh several times. "By God," he sputtered a few moments later. "You're a hell of a lot more fun than stodgy old Bertram Foster."

Charles gave his head a shake unsure if he had inadvertently made a joke or if he had once again become the punch line.

****

They marched into woods, heading south, past empty rifle pits and gun emplacements. Dark seeped into silvery black as evening shadows stretched into moonlit night. They bivouacked at the intersection of Mineral Springs and Ely's Ford roads, where the only cleared area in the dense woods and underbrush belonged to an area farmer. The orange-red glows from hundreds of cook fires lit the clearing as men prepared their rations.

Charles spread his gum blanket beneath the boughs of a hickory tree and eased his aching body against the narrow trunk. Coffee cup in hand, he inhaled the bitter aroma.

Breen, Richards, two other doctors, and their assistant surgeons, sat either cross-legged or reclined around the fire. Richards had taken their hardtack, broken the squares into pieces, and soaked them in the water he'd used to boil the salt pork. He then pan cooked the meat and fried the softened crackers in the grease.

It wasn't oysters and crab, but at least Charles' stomach had stopped rumbling and the pounding that had plagued his head all day eased with each sip of coffee. He set his cup in the grass, arranged his blankets, and using his haversack as a pillow, stretched out on the ground.

He stared through the near-black tangle of branches and leaves to the patches of charcoal night. Around him droned the indistinct murmurs of thousands of men readying for sleep.

My name is Jason.

No. He pinched the bridge of his nose. Think about setting up the hospital tomorrow. Ground with good drainage, water, and straw for the wounded, making do with his field pack until the ambulances and medical wagons came up from the rear.

He could do this. He was a surgeon. He saved lives. He didn't panic. After all tomorrow couldn't be as bad as Antietam or Fredericksburg.

****

"You can do it, sweetie. You're such a smart little boy."

Sitting on her lap, with her arms secure around his waist, he studied each letter on the page of his new book.

"A. In Adam's fall, We sinned all," he painstakingly read.

"That's right."

"B. Thy life to mend, This Book attend."

"That's wonderful, sweetie. Four years old and bright as a new penny."

"C. The Cat doth play, And after slay."

She leaned her face close to his and kissed his cheek. "Mama's so proud of her little Jason."

****

No! My name is Charles.

He jerked upright. Nothing but the snores of a

sleeping army and countless cook fires reduced to coals, like the flickering of a thousand orange fire flies on a summer night.

He wiped the sweat from his brow and lay down again. Fire flies. When had his thoughts ever been so fanciful? Damn, the fighting hadn't even started, and he was already losing control.

Closing his eyes, this time he focused on Gracie McBride and how pretty she'd look wearing something other than black. Maybe dressed in a light purple gown, with her red hair done up fancy.

Auburn. The correct color was auburn.

He imagined her hand in his, her other resting on his shoulder. With his hand cupping her waist they would waltz together at one of the fancy balls his grandfather always forced him to attend. Would she wear her red petticoat?

****

"Sweetie, my dress isn't purple, it's lilac. Like the flowers outside the back door." Gentle fingers threaded through his hair. Her voice was light and happy. He was happy.

****

"Charles...my dar...ling," the woman's voice was thin and trembling. She lay in a big bed, her head turned in his direction. She lifted her chalky white hand. Limp on the blanket a moment ago, she raised it and gestured weakly for him to come closer.

He shook his head. Her damp hair and sunken eyes made her look like a witch. Squeezing Bunzy tight, he backed up.

Something prodded him between his shoulder blades.

"Go see your mother, boy. Give her a kiss."

No! He twisted away from the old man's walking stick.

****

Charles gasped and sat up. His heart pounded. He kicked free from his tangle of blankets. He ran his hand over the smooth ground cloth. Something poked against the rubberized fabric. Groping in the dark, he slid his hand underneath and sifted through the flattened grass.

A small stone. He pulled it out and ran his fingers over it. The circumference about the same size as the tip of Grandfather's cane. For a moment his fingers clenched the cool hardness against his palm then he drew back his arm and hurled it into the trees. He listened but didn't hear it land.

His feet itched with the restless need to walk, to extend his long legs out along the rough road and keep moving until exhaustion drove this whirling turmoil from his head.

But didn't want to be shot by a jumpy picket. He shuddered from a cold that settled deep inside him. Digging through his haversack, he pulled out his bottle of whiskey.

He sat against the tree and sipped savoring the warmth that slid through him. Shadows moved as the pickets changed duty.

Jason.

His name was Jason.

The realization churned the whiskey in his stomach. He downed another swallow and squeezed his eyes closed.

How had this happened to him? He was the same, yet everything was different. God, who was he?

My name is Jason.

Damn Gracie McBride.

The woman who lay dying in the bed hadn't smelled of lilacs or called him, Sweetie. Her cheek had been cold, not warm. She had never been his mother.

The woman had called him Charles that day, and Jason was no more.

The truth left him disoriented, lost in a whirlwind of disconnected thoughts. Maybe it was the whiskey. Either way there was no going back. His life had changed forever.

He must have dozed, for the next thing to pierce his conscious mind was the warble and chirp of birds. Slowly, the trees came alive with their singing, and for those few moments, Charles savored the sense of contentment.

He opened his eyes. Reality.

Richards poked at the coals. Coffee beans roasted in a pan. Beyond him, others stirred in their bedrolls, faint silhouettes in the charcoal gray of pre-dawn. Maintaining the need for quiet, no bugles blew reveille.

Charles rolled to his feet, shoved his bottle into his haversack, and headed into the trees to relieve himself. On the way back, he gathered an armload of sticks for the fire.

While they munched on hard tack and coffee, Major-General Hancock and his aide rode into their area.

Major Triscut walked over to meet him. He fired off a quick salute, and the two talked for a few minutes. Hancock turned his horse, and Major Triscut made way his between campfires and joined them.

Richards passed the major a cup of coffee as he

and the other surgeons listened to their orders.

"Our division will be marching east on Orange Turnpike in an hour," Triscut began. "General Hooker's headquarters are at the brick house at the crossroads. We'll plant our green flag about a mile from there."

"Yes, sir."

"And remember once the wounded start coming in, they will likely be from all divisions as well as the other corps. Treat everyone the same. I don't want the men from our division made a priority for care over any other."

Major Triscut passed Richards the empty coffee cup.

"Captain," he turned to Charles. "I'm grateful for the experience you bring to this division." He leveled a long hard stare on Charles.

Charles met his gaze without flinching. This would not be a repeat of Fredericksburg. He would not have another nervous attack. "We'll be fine, sir."

Major Triscut nodded. "God be with us all, gentlemen."

Charles drew a deep breath. And so it begins. He shoved his hands behind his back, squeezing his fingers tight.

He met Breen's eager gaze with a frown. "You'd best eat up. We march in an hour, and this might be the last meal we have for a while."

****

...twenty-seven, twenty-eight, twenty-nine... Gracie placed the tip of her pencil to the next line in her notebook. *Thirty barrels each*, she wrote. *Bandages, and lint*.

Male voices rumbled from the front of the

warehouse.

"Where you want we should put these?"

"What do you boys have there?" Mr. Bridgerton asked from the counter.

"Bed ticks and pillows."

"Put them over there on those shelves beside the shirts and towels. Mrs. McBride hasn't inventoried that row yet."

Boot heels tromped back and forth across the floor as the men transported their load from the train to the shelves a couple of aisles away.

Gracie finished the section of hospital supplies and turned the corner to count the food stuffs. *Twenty-nine, thirty, thirty-one…* She continued her inventory of the supplies the Sanitary Commission allotted to the II Corps hospitals.…*thirty-two hundred pounds farina.*

"You boys pick up any word on the fighting?" The gravelly voice of Mr. Bridgerton rumbled through the warehouse.

"Naw, just that fighting commenced."

She prayed to God Charles, or rather Jason, would stay safe. Doctor Ellard never actually denied he was Jason, only accused her of trying to control his life. Maybe he'd always known the truth. Maybe he didn't want to be Jason.

Ignoring her crazy thoughts, she focused on her inventory. *Twenty-six hundred pounds condensed milk.* Gracie jotted the total in her notebook and inched her way closer to the conversation.

"I come through The Wilderness back a'fore the war," one of the young men said. "Sure as hell glad I ain't fightin' in that dark, wet, tangled up bramble of hickory and blackjack."

Gracie set her notebook on a shelf next to the cases of wine and cordials. She straightened her apron and marched down the aisle to the front of the warehouse.

Mr. Bridgerton and two privates leaned against a counter that was little more than boards laid across two barrels.

"Have ye any news o' the Sixty-first New York?"

The young men straightened and whipped their kelpies from their heads.

"The Sixty-first?" The younger of the two men rubbed his jaw. "Ain't that part a' General Zook's brigade?"

"Naw, the Sixty-first is Colonel Miles regiment. They's part of Caldwell's brigade, and Hancock's First."

"You sure?"

"Yup. My cousin Marlon's in the Sixty-first." He raised his gaze to Gracie's. "You got kin in that regiment?"

She nodded. "Yes, Captain Charles Ellard. He's a surgeon. Though he should be safe from harm, being at the rear of the fighting."

The young privates exchanged glances then one looked down to study his shoes as the other dug his thumbnail into the counter and ran it along the grain of the wood.

"Ma'am." Mr. Bridgerton leveled his steady gaze on her. "I know he's your brother, but lines of battle change, advances become retreats. Doctors die, too. Pretending they don't, don't make it true."

She squeezed her cold fingers tight and tried to swallow the ache that rose in the back of her throat. First William, then Michael and Callum.

The compulsion to be with him stirred restlessly inside. Though she knew her presence wouldn't actually offer protection, she needed to be with him. Whether for his benefit or her own, she refused to consider. Maybe Doctor Ellard was right. Maybe she did need to be in control, but she couldn't just stay here counting beef stock and fruit.

"Mrs. Anderson says ye be taking a load of supplies to the field hospitals."

"That's right. We're taking a wagon for each division. Most times we can get supplies to the field hospitals before the army." He crossed his arms over his chest and narrowed his eyes suspiciously.

She squared her shoulders and raised her chin. "Good. Then I'll be coming with ye."

He stared at her for several long seconds. "Mrs. Anderson tell you I'm assigned to the first division of the second corps?"

She met his hard glare without flinching. "That she did."

She refused to look away first, nor did he seem inclined to give quarter.

"You do know this is a battlefield. Don't you think you should leave it to the men, and you stay here where you can be more useful?"

"I be a nurse, Mr. Bridgerton. The battlefield 'tis where I can be more useful."

Finally he gave her a long slow nod. "Can you ride a horse?"

"Aye." Though she hadn't ridden since she was a girl in Ireland, as long as she didn't have to ride sidesaddle she'd be fine.

"We pack the wagons on Sunday afternoon and

leave at seven a.m. on Monday. Don't be late."

She turned and marched back down the aisle, her shoes clicked solid and hollow against the plank floor.

She picked up her notebook and pen, staring at the page of blurred numbers and letters. Sweet Mary, Jesus, and Joseph, what was she getting into? Gunfire, shelling, and wounded by the hundreds. She pressed her palms against her churning stomach.

Begorra, if Doctor Ellard had a problem with women working at Armory Square Hospital in Washington, what would he say on Monday?

A grin tugged at the corners of her mouth. She gave her head a shake and pointed her pencil at the first case of wine. *One, two, three...*

Chapter Fourteen

A shell exploded. Then another. The thunderous pounding reverberated through the thick woods around the frame house. Although the dense morning fog had burned off, it had been replaced by thick white smoke which drifted like steam through the impenetrable tangle of trees, obscuring the blue sky and fleecy clouds overhead. The faint taste of sulphur mixed with the coppery scent of warm blood.

The Sixty-first New York, as part of Major-General Hancock's first division, had started the morning by marching east about two miles on the Orange Turnpike.

Charles set to work with the surgeons, assistants, and orderlies to quickly organize a field hospital less than a quarter mile behind Hancock's main battle line.

A never-ending flow of wounded drifted in throughout the day. Some walked, others were carried. From the southeast, shelling pounded incessantly.

"Captain Ellard!" Breen's panicked voice carried across the lawn of the small house. It hadn't taken long for the young man's humorous outlook to wan, and Charles tallied its loss among the other wounds of war.

He stepped back from the makeshift surgical table. "Finish stitching this closed."

Charles' assistant, Doctor Brooks, nodded and removed a needle and thread from his surgical kit.

The patient would be lucky to survive the next forty-eight hours. The entire head of a three-inch shell had torn through the abdominal wall and impacted into the lumbar vertebrae.

With so many wounded he could save, he wasn't even sure what compelled him to try. But the private was barely mature enough to grow a facial hair and his only complaint when Charles checked his wound was that the shell was heavy and gave him colic.

The image of a dying drummer boy had flashed through his mind along with Gracie's naïve declaration that there was always hope.

And rather than having the soldier laid aside with the other mortal wounds, he'd foolishly disregarded his credo to focus only on the injuries. Instead he found himself giving the private's shoulder a squeeze and saying, "You're a brave young man. Your mother must be proud."

He stepped back to allow his assistant surgeon room, wiping his hands on the cleanest corner of his blood-splattered apron. He studied the clumsy technique of his assistant surgeon, tempted to push him aside and stitch the wound himself.

"Captain Ellard," Breen called out again. "I could use your help over here."

In the end, neatness didn't matter, and Brooks needed the practice. At least the private would be comfortable at the last.

Charles strode across the yard to the shade of a large oak tree where Breen had contrived his own makeshift surgery table.

"Captain, I don't know what to do." Breen stepped aside as Charles approached the patient who lay on a door which had been stripped from the house and placed across an end table and sideboard. "I never saw anything like this."

Charles leaned close to the soldier who drifted in and out of consciousness. His face so blackened from powder and smoke, he looked like every other wounded man who lay sprawled over this once pretty lawn.

A shell had taken the soldier's right arm off just below the shoulder, leaving three inches of brachial artery hanging out of the body. Someone had fashioned a tourniquet from a handkerchief and stick, around what remained of the arm.

"Where is Major Andrews?"

Andrews was one of the three surgeons, along with Charles, chosen from the regiments to perform surgery for the division. Breen had been assigned as Andrews' assistant.

"I don't know."

He could have been caught up with a surgical case, found elsewhere, or taken himself back to the brick house at the crossroad.

Dismissing Andrews from further thought, Charles concentrated on the remains of the severed limb.

"Blood loss is substantial. I can ligate this artery and form some sort of flap from the edges of the skin that are left, but these measures are likely too late."

Limbs amputated this close to the body generally had a low survival rate, although amputations done in the field had a higher chance than those performed days later.

Charles set to work as orderlies and assistants moved and talked around them.

"We're falling back to the brick house." Major

Triscut peered at the flap Charles was stitching closed. "We were supposed to hold the line till five, but the Johnny Rebs are pushing our flank. Hancock wanted reinforcements, but Hooker is ordering us back. We'll have to move fast so we don't get overrun. I'll see how many can walk and start them moving. You remain and stabilize as many as you can while I try to find stretcher bearers for the rest."

Charles gave him a quick nod and tied off another stitch.

The other doctors and orderlies moved behind him packing the panniers onto the mules and preparing to first move those men who stood a chance of surviving. Charles waited until every patient had gone before he grabbed his field pack, mounted his horse, and headed down the crowded turnpike to the crossroads where the large two-story brick house stood.

Reserve infantry units filled the wide clearing between the house and the road. A crowd of teamsters and stragglers milled around outside. Officers, staff, and couriers buzzed in and out the front door like bees at a hive. Wounded lay on the lawn and lower veranda.

As Charles dismounted, Richards ran up to take the reins of his horse.

"Why are all these men outside?" Charles snapped as he yanked free his saddlebag field pack. Without waiting for an answer, he strode across the lawn and up the front steps. Crossing the threshold, he found more dirty, bleeding wounded either sitting or lying prone in every available space of the front entry and halls. Carefully, he picked his way through the men toward a room he assumed would be a dining room or parlor. He tugged at one of the pocket handles but the door wouldn't slide.

Cursing under his breath, he stepped back and slammed the bottom of his heel against the lock where the two doors came together.

With a splintering crash the lock broke. He shoved each panel into its corresponding wall pocket and stared. Chairs, tables, armoires, beds, and sofas filled the room.

"Richards!" he bellowed. He swung around and grabbed the first healthy looking man he saw not wearing a surgeon insignia.

"Find some more men and get this furniture out. Empty any room that doesn't have a general in it and move the wounded inside."

"Yes, sir." He fired off a quick salute and dashed for the front door.

Charles stepped over and around the wounded as he made his way to the kitchen at the back of the house. He found Breen kneeling beside a soldier, cutting away his trouser leg.

Charles bent to peer at the bloody knee. "Minié ball?"

"I'm not sure yet."

"The locked rooms are being cleaned out. Find some orderlies and get these men out of here. Where is Captain Brooks?"

"He's with Major Triscut in the sitting room. That's the new surgery."

Charles nodded. "Where is the cook?"

Breen scanned the room. "I believe he said something about fetching water."

"Good. Have him begin preparing soup for these men."

Breen nodded, and Charles turned back into the main portion of the house.

He found the major in the sitting room organizing supplies from the pack mules. Andrews leaned over a patient who lay on a table while orderlies carried in the more severely wounded.

Triscut turned as Charles approached. "Good. You're here. I want you take the worst cases. You're tall, and the piano is a good height for you. That's our amputation table. It's near the window, and the limbs can easily be tossed out of sight for pickup later tonight."

Charles nodded. "I ordered men to clean out the furniture in any of the locked rooms to make room for the patients. Is the family still here?"

"They're in one of the rooms at the back of the house. Some of the neighbors too, trying to escape the shelling. General Hooker and his staff are upstairs."

Charles exchanged his uniform coat for an apron, rolled up his sleeves, and set to work. Without acknowledging any faces, he ignored the pain-filled cries and groans and focused on the wounds.

He tried not to think about the blood that now covered this once beautiful instrument. Its purity as desecrated by this war as these men whose limbs had been destroyed by mortar and shot.

He shoved it all to the back of his mind, wiped his hands, and kept moving.

As the shadows of dusk crept across the room, silvery moonlight lit the clearing beyond the window glass. Grateful for the functionality of the full moon, rather than its beauty, he performed surgery well into the night. He worked until Major Triscut ordered him to take a break.

He wandered outside and spotted Breen and another surgeon by the picket fence. If he hadn't been so exhausted, he might have the energy to pause for a moment and enjoy the night sky.

Instead all he could manage was to sink to the ground and lean against the wooden slats. Resting the back of his head in the space between the pickets, he closed his eyes.

Inside his boots, his socks were wet. Moisture from the morning's heavy dew had seeped through the leather of his boots, chilling his toes. Throughout the day, his sweat added to the dampness soaking the wool. Now his feet were so swollen from standing for nearly twenty hours, he doubted he could even get his boots off to change into dry socks.

His stomach rumbled loud enough for Breen to rouse.

"Was that your stomach?"

Charles grunted.

"Sounds empty."

"I'm not certain. I consumed two hard crackers and a piece of bread at half past three, but since I don't know the rate of my digestion, my stomach contents as yet, may not have been completely absorbed."

Breen chuckled. "You're funny. After all we've seen today and as tired and hungry as you are, you still find a way to make light of our situation."

Charles turned his head. The moon cast a pewter glow across Breen's cheek bones while hiding his eyes in the shadow of his brow. Which made it difficult to discern whether Breen was being facetious. Not that Charles found it easy to read facial expressions, even in broad daylight.

"You find my statement humorous?"

Breen's teeth flashed white as he smiled. "Yeah, you say funny things."

"How is it you perceive my observation of fact to be humorous when no one else would?"

He shrugged. "My mum is English, and she has that same understated sense of humor. I suppose I'm used to it."

Should he tell Breen humor had not been his intent? A low growl rolled through his stomach.

Breen pushed to his feet. "I'll go find you something to eat. It might not be much though, so I hope your rate of digestion remains slow."

He grinned and wove his way between soldiers sleeping across the lawn.

Charles let his eyes drift closed.

"Captain?"

Someone was shaking his shoulder.

"Captain?"

Charles drew a deep breath and blinked. Breen.

"Sorry to wake you, but Major Triscut needs you."

How long had he been asleep? It felt like only minutes. He groaned and pushed to his feet, bracing his hip against the fence for a few moments, giving the muscles in his back time to ease their painful spasms.

Breen passed him a piece of bread and an apple and flashed a quick grin. "Richards swiped 'em from a table for one of the generals."

Saliva pooled in Charles mouth, and he crunched through the apple, snapping off nearly one third of it in that single bite. It was a little dry and pulpy, but he didn't care. He devoured it core and all.

"There's a sergeant with a bullet wound," Breen explained.

Charles folded his slice of bread in half and pushed away from the fence.

"That went in below his left eye and through his mouth."

They hastened toward the house, Breen quick stepping to keep pace with Charles long stride. "Major Triscut says the bullet is lodged at the back of the jaw on the right side. He wants you to extract the ball, because it's lodged against the carotid artery."

The major and two orderlies had laid the patient on the piano. Dried mud splattered his uniform, and powder had blackened his face. Near the man's head sat a block of wood with five augered holes in which five candles stood, casting a flickering light across the bloody distorted face.

Charles bent close. The ball had entered through the side of the cheek, torn through the sinus cavity, taking out several teeth on its way through the roof of the mouth, grazing the tongue and after tearing through several more teeth, had lodged in the bone at the back of the jaw.

He felt the bump of the ball in front of the artery, through which blood appeared to be pumping normally.

The soldier must have lain on the battlefield for a good part of the day, for the blood had clotted and dried.

The man opened his eyes for a moment, met Charles' gaze, and drifted off again.

Charles straightened and stepped back. He ran his hand across his tired eyes and pinched the bridge of his nose. Suture wire, ligature silk, needles, probe, extractor. He checked his surgical kit and glanced up.

Brooks stepped to the head of the patient to administer the anesthesia. He placed the cone over the patient's nose and mouth then pulled the stopper from the bottle of—*Ether!*

"No!" Charles lunged for the table.

The cone ignited over the patient's face as Charles knocked it to the floor with a swipe of his arm that took the bottle from Brooks' hand.

Charles snatched the bottle off the floor and jammed in the stopper, grateful the bottle hadn't broken and created an additional fire. With his free hand he grabbed Captain Brooks by the front of his uniform. "Get away from here." He released the assistant surgeon with a slight shove.

The man stumbled back two steps. "I…I-I'm sorry, sir. I'm so damn tired I forgot it was flammable."

"Your incompetence will go in my report." Charles turned away. "Breen! Cloroform!"

****

"Here you go, Captain." Breen held out a steaming cup of coffee.

Grateful, Charles wrapped his numb fingers around the hot mug. From between his chattering teeth, he managed a brief, "Thank you."

He hunched over the cup for a moment, allowing the fragrant steam to thaw his icy nose.

Breen dropped beside Charles on the back steps of the house, nursing his own cup of coffee. "Damn, it's cold this morning."

Charles sipped the hot liquid, savoring the heat which slid down his throat and eased the trembling in the walls of his stomach.

"What I really miss," Breen said, "is fresh eggs for breakfast. Fried, with a nice thick ham steak. And biscuits." He sniffed and rubbed his nose on his sleeve.

Charles swallowed another mouthful of coffee. Scrambled would be nice, piled between two slices of fresh bread.

Breen tipped back the last of his coffee then peered into the empty cup as though more of the beverage might magically appear. "What happens now?"

Uncertain whether Breen referred to the empty mug or the upcoming surgeries, Charles shrugged. He swallowed the rest of his coffee before it grew too cold to warm him.

"Sure would be great," Breen said, "if we win this one and it puts a stop to the rebellion."

Charles pushed to his feet. He gazed across the mist-shrouded lawn and the rows of canvas covered bodies nearly hidden behind its ghostly veil.

Breen rose beside him. "Yeah," he repeated. "It sure would be great."

****

By midmorning, the sun emerged and chased away the cold, promising a day as pretty as the one before.

Artillery began their battle to the southeast. The bombardment of shelling so constant, Charles no longer heard the resounding booms unless he took a moment to listen.

Wounded drifted in throughout the morning and into the afternoon as the fighting continued.

Charles stepped back as the orderlies grasped the ends of the stretcher and lifted the patient, whose arm he'd just amputated, off the piano and took him to recover in another part of the house.

He turned to a nearby table to rinse his knife and bone saw. But the once clear water which filled the basin had turned the color of burgundy. Its color darker than the blood which dripped from the oil cloth that currently replaced the embroidered silk piano shawl. He rose and searched the room for an orderly.

He shoved the basin at a passing man. "I need clean water."

The young soldier grappled to keep from spilling it. "Yes, sir." He hurried off.

A new patient was lifted onto the table. Charles stepped close to evaluate the wound.

Blood coated the entire side of the man's head and face. The shiny wetness matted his hair and sideburns. It coated his neck crimson, soaked into the collar of his uniform coat, and turned his white shirt to scarlet.

The knife and bone saw Charles held, slipped from his grasp. His heart thudded wildly against his sternum. The pounding reverberated in his head and drowned out the clatter of his instruments hitting the hardwood floor. He gulped short panting gasps of air.

Breathe. There is always a lot of blood with head wounds.

Catching his breath grew more difficult. His vision narrowed so that all he saw was a head split open, bleeding on the cobblestone street. He eased back a step.

"Captain?" Brooks frowned. "What's wrong?"

Charles shook his head and backed away. He ran a sweaty palm down his clammy face as he struggled to breathe.

"Captain, what about the patient?"

"Captain, I got your water."

Spots danced in front of his eyes. He couldn't do this. Not now. He had to get out of here before he passed out, before his heart exploded inside his chest.

He spun on his heels. Lurching to the door, he stumbled over and around the wounded. He staggered his way outside to the back of the house and pressed his shoulders against the wall. Short, panting breaths heaved in and out, as though he'd just out run a Rebel charge. His rubbery knees gave out. As he slid to the ground, his back bumped over the rough bricks.

What was wrong with him? How long could his heart maintain this erratic rhythm before it gave out? It was Fredericksburg all over again.

When this had happened at Armory Square the night the wounded came up from Falmouth, Gracie had been beside him.

For a moment he could almost feel her hand on his back, rubbing up and down, grounding him, slowly relaxing him, driving the irrational panic from his body.

He crossed his arms on his updrawn knees. He dropped his head to his forearms and closed his eyes. Gradually his breathing slowed, easing the tightness in his chest. The boom of artillery resounded through the clearing.

He'd had these attacks frequently when he was a boy, and except for that one time at school, they'd disappeared along with his nightmares as he'd grown older.

In medical school he'd extracted bone fragments from a cadaver with a fractured skull, but he'd felt no irrational panic then.

Were these nervous attacks random, or were they related only to head wounds with blood? Or was there another antecedent? Had the constant shelling caused a disturbance in his mind?

He couldn't think about this anymore, and he couldn't hide back here forever. Someone would find him, and it would be a repeat of Fredericksburg for certain. Rolling to his feet, he headed around the house the opposite way, avoiding the rows of dead. He couldn't face them, or the living right now.

In the front yard another doctor wove his way in and round the wounded who drifted in from the surrounding battle. Behind him trailed his assistant with a notebook and pencil. Head down he busily recorded the name, regiment and wound of each man.

They paid Charles no attention when he passed. Though he didn't know either man beyond their name and rank, he recognized the grim lines etched in their features. Theirs was the bleak task of prioritizing the wounded, separating those who had a chance to be saved from those who would die.

At least Charles didn't have to play God. His role was to fight God for every life placed on the table before him. His jaw clenched with a renewed determination to save as many men as possible, not to abandon any more men to his childish attacks.

Lengthening his stride, he headed for the front steps of the veranda.

From the side, a soldier approached, his left arm held against his body. His face pale beneath the grime, tight lines bracketed his mouth and drew deep furrows across his brow.

"You a doc?"

Without his coat and its medical insignia, the only clue the soldier would've had was the blood staining

Charles' shirt sleeves and apron.

"Yes," Charles replied, his gaze already assessing the arm. No blood. He exhaled a sigh of relief, grateful for the reprieve of taking his bone saw to another limb. He'd come to hate the feel of cutting through bone, hated the way each abrasive stroke shivered all the way up his arm.

No wonder people called him a butcher. Major Carlton had. But it wasn't the doctors. War was the butcher. The surgeons were merely here to salvage what was left.

"I think it's broke, Doc." The private unbuttoned his coat and eased his injured arm from the blue wool sleeve.

Charles cupped the arm with one hand and pushed up the shirt. A large red welt, swollen and bruised, discolored most of the forearm. Charles slid his fingers over and around the heated area searching for a bulge of bone beneath the skin.

"Come inside and I'll—"

"I ain't goin' to let you cut it off!"

Charles glared down at the man. Another who believed him a butcher. "Unless a Minié ball has somehow entered your arm without leaving a scratch and shattered your ulna into bits, I believe a splint and eight-yard bandage will satisfy."

The young soldier released a breath and rubbed the back of his uninjured wrist across his sweaty forehead, smearing through the black of dirt and gunpowder. "Sorry, sir."

"Jason!"

Charles whirled in synchronization with the young private.

Striding toward them, came another grime-covered private carrying a rifle, his focus on the soldier with the broken arm.

"Shit, Jase. Are you all right? That tree limb come down…Thought sure you was a goner."

"Naw, broke my arm is all, and busted my rifle all to hell."

At least the pair seemed to have forgotten Charles. A funny catch tightened the muscles of his chest at his mistake.

Why had he turned at the sound of his name?

No! Not his name. Charles P. Ellard was his name. It was the name inscribed on his medical diploma. Charles P. Ellard was a respected physician. His grandfather was a retired state senator. Charles had merely responded because Jason was on his mind, revived in long forgotten memories.

Regardless, whoever that boy had been, he was long forgotten. Jason was part of a past Charles could never get back, any more than he could get back a mother whose memory was as elusive as the voice in his dreams. He'd best move beyond the tumult Gracie had brought into his life and focus on something productive.

"Private, let's go inside. I need to splint that arm."

The soldier looked up. "Oh sorry, Doc, er…sir."

They'd nearly reached the veranda when, in the lull between artillery booms, the wild shouts of hundreds of voices to the west caught Charles' attention.

"What the hell?" the private asked no one in particular.

From inside the house, a captain from General Hooker's staff, jumped off the porch and jogged past.

Stopping near the intersection, the officer raised his spy glass and focused it on something farther down Orange Plank Road. "My God, here they come!"

A panicked mêlée of soldiers, yelling in a jumbled mix of English and German, surged up the road in a mighty wave of men, crashed through the dense woods on either side and raced into the clearing. Some ran, others rode single and pillion on the horse and mule teams cut loose from supply wagons. Other teams pulled battery wagons and caissons, with more men piled on, clinging to every available inch of space.

Had the Confederates broken through on the army's left flank?

From the house behind him, officers charged past Charles, waving their arms, shouting, "Stand and fight!"

Charles would have been astounded if one man could even hear another, let alone understand the orders.

The panicked division continued its stampede of men, wagons, and cattle. Soldiers raced by without their caps or coats, some men didn't even carry their rifles.

The flood rushed right past the house.

"Holy shit," the private with the broken arm murmured. "They's headed right for Hancock's line. If they don't slow down, they'll be through to the Rebs on the other side."

Charles ushered the soldier inside.

The surgery buzzed with speculation and unanswered questions. Would Hooker be able the stop the Rebel advance? Would they be forced to retreat? How would they move so many wounded out without ambulances?

"We keep working until ordered otherwise," the major announced above the moans and cries of the wounded, over the yelling and shooting outside.

No one even mentioned Charles' hasty departure and prolonged absence.

From outside the open windows, a round of cheers erupted.

"Receive them on your bayonets, boys!" a deep voice cried out. "Receive them on your bayonets!"

The soldier whose arm Charles tried to wrap, wriggled on the chair like a small boy, constantly swinging his attention between the activity outside the window and every person who entered the room.

The lively melody of a regimental band playing *Yankee Doodle* muted some of the outdoor commotion. Charles tied off the bandage around the splint and let the anxious soldier go.

"Ellard!" Major Andrews voice rose above the din. "I could use your help here!"

Charles grabbed his surgical kit and wove his way through the crowded room. Andrews and Breen stood on either side of a table farthest from the piano. A soldier lay with his abdomen torn open from an apparent shell wound, with protrusions of his intestines and omentum.

"I can't get it back," Andrews said. Anxiety raised the pitch of his voice. "I push it in on one side, and as I do, the abdominal muscles spasm and push it all back out at a different angle."

Outside the band moved on to the rousing notes of *The Red, White, and Blue.*

Charles leaned close and studied the fist-sized mass. An image popped into his head of Gracie, her shoulders squared, her brown eyes filled with that familiar amber fire as she declared, *"I stood by William's side during surgeries and passed him instruments. I helped him clean the intestines of a man gored by a bull, before putting it all back inside that man's belly. Me delicate sensibilities did not send me into a swoon then nor will they here."*

A wistful smile tugged at the corner of his mouth. He could benefit right now from her expertise in the matter.

"I want to enlarge the opening," Andrews said, "then with your extra hands we'd have more room to slide it all back inside."

Charles straightened and shook his head. "No."

Andrews stiffened.

Breen, who'd been standing on the other side of the table asked, "Why not? It seems logical."

Charles met Andrew's offended glare. "Sir, you asked for my help. Your suggestion is illogical. What is logical, is the fact that widening the opening will merely allow more of the mass to spill out."

He stepped away from the table and seized the arm of the first soldier he spotted. Tugging him toward the head of the wounded corporal, he said, "Raise up his head and shoulders." He gestured Breen to the end of the table. "Grab his ankles and raise them up high."

With the patient now forming a V, the abdominal muscles relaxed. Charles grabbed a pair of silver spatulas from Andrews' surgical kit and lifted the abdominal walls away from and over the mass. Once the intestine was back in place, he closed the wound with sutures and collodion.

Breen gave a low whistle.

Charles looked up, and Breen grinned.

Andrews gave an indignant huff, then grumbled, "Nice work."

The Star Spangled Banner played outside.

Chapter Fifteen

Much of the fighting ended after dark. Hooker had moved his lines and kept the Rebels at bay. The retreat Charles feared had not come to pass. The wounded, however, limped in or were carried in all night.

During a lull after midnight, Charles had a chance to find some food and catch a few hours of sleep. But early morning artillery batteries soon pounded away at each other to the south, east, and west of the woods. The ground shook through each bombardment, forcing him up and moving at dawn. Shells and canister shot created scattered fires in the dense undergrowth of the surrounding woods. Wind sent the acrid bite of smoke drifting through the open windows.

"Damn shelling's too close," Major Triscut announced as he entered the former sitting room. His gaze honed in on Charles. "We have orders to move the wounded out. I'm going to scout a location and get a new hospital set up. Any ambulatory wounded can start on the road toward the pontoon bridges. You see to the wounded here."

"Yes, sir."

Around them orderlies and hospital staff hurriedly repacked panniers with equipment and supplies.

"Your assistant surgeon, Captain Brooks, will support you. And be careful."

"Yes, sir."

Major Triscut whirled and strode from the room. Charles restocked his field pack while the rest of the medical supplies were loaded onto the mules and horses.

Anything that could be used to transport the wounded was pulled into service: carts, wagons, horses, stretchers, blankets.

The windows rattled as the barrage of artillery drew closer. A resounding bang rocked the house on its foundation. The window glass cracked. Bits of ceiling plaster pelted down like hail on Charles' head and shoulders.

Shouts rang out from the hall.

"We're being shelled!"

"They hit the house!"

"Get the hell out of here!"

"Hooker's been hit!"

Amidst the chaos, more wounded arrived. Those who could walk, didn't stop, but continued down the road. Charles turned away all but the most serious injuries and only then to see them stable enough to endure the move.

Another boom shook the house. Inside its echo, crashed falling brick and timber. The walls cracked. Chunks of ceiling shattered on the floor, covering the surgery with clouds of plaster dust.

"The house is on fire!" someone yelled.

"Get these wounded out of here!" Charles roared, his voice nearly lost in the cacophony of chaos.

He strode into the hall and grabbed the first man he saw by the arm.

"But sir, the house is on fire!" The soldier tried to pull from Charles' grip.

"I don't give a damn if your hair's on fire. Grab one of these wounded!" He shoved the man and sent him stumbling toward an unconscious soldier lying on the floor.

Charles turned and hoisted another man over his shoulder and headed outside. The support column and part of the veranda had been torn away when the house was hit, and he had to maneuver around the damage to get to the front steps. He laid the soldier in the grass, well away from the house, then whirled and raced back in for another.

A wall of orange flames consumed the woods behind the house. From the second story windows, flames stretched up over the brick and licked along the edge of the eaves. Rolling clouds of black billowed upward through gaping holes in the roof, obscuring the sun.

Charles made several trips along with officers and enlisted men who streamed out, bent over, wracked with coughing as they hauled patients to safety.

Brooks dashed back inside, and Charles followed several paces behind.

Coughing, Charles buried his nose in the crook of his elbow. Fire roared as the dry lath snapped and crackled. His eyes stung. Thick smoke filled the foyer with black, absorbing all light and oxygen.

He had to hurry. The floor boards and joists were so dry the house was being consumed like kindling in a forest fire. And if the wind shifted, the wall of flames burning at the edge of the woods would jump the clearing and engulf the house.

"Brooks!" A fit of coughing overtook him, but he bent forward and kept moving. "Brooks! You have to get out of here!"

Where the hell was the man? Didn't he realize any wounded who still remained had most likely succumbed to the inhalation of smoke?

"Help." The faint cry came from somewhere near his feet.

Unable to discern even the outline of a shape on the floor, Charles dropped to his hands and knees, his hand outstretched. Tears ran down his cheeks. He blinked against the burn as well as the futility of trying to see through the rolling blackness.

His fingertips brushed over wool fabric covering the soft form of a body.

"Brooks?" Charles choked out then erupted in a fit of coughing. His inability to draw breath as debilitating now as it was during one of his attacks. He gave the shoulder beneath his hand a shake. "Brooks?"

His lungs screamed for viable air. Coughing, he pulled his shirt up over his nose and mouth, though it probably did little good. Smoke engulfed him like a demon consuming his soul. He could no longer find even a glimpse of daylight. Each way he looked was the same. Which direction led to the front door? Tentacles of panic wrapped around his heart, squeezing tighter with each thud against his chest.

Stop.

Blind terror would get him nowhere.

Think.

When he'd crossed the threshold moments ago, the length of his stride had been shorter, perhaps four feet between the heel of one foot and the toe of the other. How many steps had he taken? Four? Five, before he'd stopped and called for Brooks? Better to overestimate and say six.

When he'd dropped to the floor he'd been facing the rear of the house. Then he'd pivoted to the left about ninety degrees as he groped for the man who'd called for help. If he'd calculated correctly, he only had to turn another ninety degrees and continue straight out the door.

Hoping for the best, he grabbed a fistful of the man's wool coat and crawled, dragging the unconscious man along like small dog dragging home a rabbit.

Blindly reaching out, he swung his arm in an arc, struggling to breathe through the painful hacking which tore from the bottom of his lungs. Finding no obstacles, he crawled forward a few more feet, reached out and crawled again. His throat burned raw. The pressure in his chest squeezed tighter with every second.

He should have felt fresh air by now. Had he miscalculated and crawled farther into the house?

A few moments of smoke-filled breaths, and his hand brushed the wall. Doubt swirled through his mind. No. He had to trust his own judgment. If he'd crawled toward the back he would have encountered the staircase or a doorway into another room. He reminded himself that he had anticipated this. Smoke filled his lungs, suffocating him. Sparkles danced behind his closed eye lids like stars on a moonless night.

From above came a loud cracking. With a splintering crash, something heavy slammed against his shoulder, knocking him flat, pinning him to the floor. Debris pelted down around him. Pain shot across his back, as though a hot knife seared through skin and muscle to his scapula.

Heaving against the weight of what felt like a

burning floor joist, he pushed to his hands and knees. From there he was able to lever the burning timber off his back. Moving onward, he groped through the rubble until he located Brooks. Blindly he resumed his search for the exit.

Air.

A wisp of air brushed across the back of his hand.

Clean, fresh air.

He drew a desperate breath. Coughing wracked his body. The pain in his left shoulder tore at his muscles, but he didn't care. He fumbled along the floor and found the low bump of the door sill.

Relief nearly caused him to collapse right there, but he had just a little farther to go. He grabbed the unconscious man and crawled forward. The planks of the veranda felt wider and rougher than the smooth boards of the floors inside the house. He opened his eyes. Even through smoke, the brilliance of daylight caused him to squeeze them closed again. Tears leaked from the corners and ran down his cheeks.

His fingers curved over the edge of the veranda. He squinted, searching for the front steps.

"Captain!"

He raised his head, ignoring the pain tearing through his shoulder. Someone ran toward him, the blurry form growing more familiar as he blinked back the tears.

"Richards!" he called, his voice so raspy it was barely audible to his ears. Fresh air warred with smoke for space inside his body. A hacking cough tore from the bottom of lungs. Ribs aching, he hung his head like a winded horse, his hair falling forward to brush the floorboards of the porch.

"I have your mount, sir. We have to go. Now!"

Charles pushed to his knees. "Help me with this man."

Richards ran toward him then halted at the bottom of the steps. "Are you all right, sir?"

"I'm fine. I merely need to..." The edge of the veranda tilted. He tried to reach out his hand for balance—

****

The pungent bitterness of smoke filled his nose and coated his tongue. Indistinct voices floated around him. Moaning. Groans and whimpers for water. The soft cries of suffering. Men needed help.

His eyes opened, focusing for a moment on the leafy tangle of branches overhead. From the distance, the synchronized cadence of marching. The jangle of harness. Horses snorted and clip-clopped past. The sharp cracking of rifle fire and the distant thunder of artillery.

The last thing he remembered was pulling Brooks from the burning house.

His left shoulder just plain hurt. He glanced down. His uniform coat and waistcoat were gone. A triangular Esmarch bandage immobilized his arm in a sling. Beneath his ruined shirt he felt the weight of a second bandage wrapped over his shoulder and around his chest.

Using his good hand, he levered himself up and leaned the healthy part of his back against the tree. Pain tore through the burn.

Men, dirty and bloody, unconscious and awake, lay around him. Others sat quietly in small groups. Thick trees and brush surrounded them. On a rise to his right ambulances and soldiers marched past.

Drawing up his knees, he dug his boot heels into the soft peat and pushed, sliding up along the height of the trunk, careful to keep the area of raw burning from rubbing against the bark.

He drew a breath and began coughing. He pulled a handkerchief from his trouser pocket. Pressing the smoke-scented cloth over his mouth, he continued hacking even as he leaned over and braced his hand on his knee to draw breath.

Several long moments later his lungs calmed. He blew his nose. Black smeared the white cloth. He shoved the handkerchief into his pocket and leaned against the trunk, resting the back of his head against the tree.

From the other side of the small clearing, Breen approached, moving carefully around the wounded. He offered Charles a brief smile. "How are you feeling?"

"What"—another spell of hacking overtook him for several seconds—"happened?"

"Richards said you pulled a wounded soldier out of the burning house and collapsed. He put you on your horse and brought you here. You have a pretty deep burn on the back of your shoulder. Took me a while to pick out the pieces of charred wood and bits of cloth. I couldn't find any white paint to cover it so I just wrapped it."

Charles nodded. "How's Brooks?"

Breen gave his head a slight shake. "Haven't seen him."

"Thought I pulled"—he coughed—"him out."

"No, the fellow you saved was a corporal shot in the leg."

"Where's Brooks?"

Breen shrugged. "It puts us down another surgeon. Major Triscut and his assistant, Captain Deaver or is it Weaver, they're leaving with some of the wounded when our division heads to the pontoon bridges. Major Triscut wants to know if you can work." His gaze lingered on Charles' shoulder for a moment.

Charles pushed away from the tree and nodded. "I'm fine. Hardly hurts at all."

"'Cause the major said you can go back with him, and he'll leave Captain Deaver here."

"Deaver is slow and indecisive. When the ambulances start bringing in wounded from the battlefields, he'll stand there wringing his hands until someone tells him what to do."

"They've started sending over the ambulances and medical wagons."

Charles nodded. "I'll need a new assistant."

Breen gestured toward a younger man with a dark beard who stood beside Major Andrews outside the surgery tent. "Captain Morton is still here."

"Good." Charles straightened away from the tree and stumbled along behind Breen, moving around the sea of wounded to the surgery area.

Andrews glanced up from the private lying on the table. "Glad to see you back with us." He cut open the man's bloody coat sleeve and examined the wound, muttering under his breath.

"Damn chaos, moving the wounded in the middle of a retreating army. Back then back and back again."

He wiped away the blood with a piece of cloth. "Bone is fine." He folded a cloth pad over an in-and-out bullet wound and began wrapping an eight-yard bandage around the arm. "Never heard of such a thing. And with only two ambulances. Damn generals."

"Captain Ellard!"

Charles turned. A surgeon from another regiment, notebook in hand, waved for Charles to join him in the area where the names and ranks of the wounded were being processed.

"There's three men over there." The doctor nodded toward a gnarled hickory tree. Two soldiers leaned against the trunk and one man lay between them. "Just walked in from the fighting. The fellow in the middle's got a pretty bad abdominal wound."

Charles nodded and started toward the men. Breen followed alongside, no doubt worried Charles would pass out again. Steadier, but still shaky, he pulled off his sling and passed it to Breen.

"Give this to someone else. Find Richards. Get my field pack and my bedroll. I have a clean shirt rolled inside."

Breen veered off as Charles continued and knelt beside the injured soldier.

He checked the wound but kept his left arm pressed immobile against his abdomen as much as possible. While the actual burn didn't hurt much, the skin around it felt as if were on fire, and moving his rotator cuff muscles was excruciating. Trying to breathe through the pain, he focused on his work.

Gunfire continued through late afternoon. Charles moved from patient to patient by rote, as he and Captain Morton stitched wounds, removed bullets, and bandaged cuts. Major Andrews handled the amputations, with Breen as his assistant.

He'd worked through the pain all afternoon and

evening. The burning in his shoulder was just there, intense and constant.

Now he lay on his right side, his head pillowed on his arm, and tried to sleep. Breen and Major Andrews snored soundly beside him. Exhaustion should have claimed him as easily.

A breeze carried the scent of smoke from the scattered fires which burned in the dense woods and scrub brush. He wondered if he'd ever savor the fresh scent of clean air again.

It had been so long since he'd eaten, his stomach had ceased its rumbling complaints. He closed his eyes and tried to think of something else.

A long rope of red hair, tracing the spine of a smooth white back, dusted with copper-colored freckles. A narrow waist he could grasp in his hands. And hips, hips which spanned the width of a perfect ass. Two firm smooth globes beneath his fingers, soft and pliable as he massaged each muscle. He could almost feel the warmth of her, hear her sigh with pleasure as he traced the cleft between her cheeks to the apex of her thighs, to that warm, moist core—

Damn! His mind was willing, but his body couldn't seem to conjure even a spark of arousal. What was wrong with him?

He rolled onto his stomach, resting his cheek on the back of his right hand. Blades of grass poked at his nose and the corner of his eye, but he couldn't summon enough energy to push them aside.

He sighed.

****

"You have such an active mind."
The voice drifted through his thoughts along with

the sensation of being rocked. He'd been sitting on her lap. She wore a purple dress.

"It's not purple, sweetie. It's lavender, like the lilacs outside the door."

****

He opened his eyes to blackness. Why couldn't he remember?

Was this the same voice that had called him Jason? Had he been the boy who'd written the note? Who was Charles? And damn it, who the hell was he?

Chaos. His entire being was in chaos and it was all the fault of Gracie McBride.

Since sleep eluded him, he might as well check on the wounded. He rolled painfully to his feet.

Chapter Sixteen

"Battlefields ain't no place for a lady." Mr. Bridgerton flicked the reins against the rumps of the bony horses, urging the four-horse team to step up their plodding pace. "You sure you want to do this, Mrs. McBride?"

Despite her forward thinking opinions about a woman's place in this war, Gracie appreciated Mr. Bridgerton's innate sense of chivalry in allowing her to ride his horse alongside the wagon.

She flashed him her most confident smile. "I do."

The wagon wheels on one side, dropped into another rut. Mr. Bridgerton braced his feet on the tool box attached to the front of the wagon and leaned toward the uphill side to keep from tumbling off the narrow seat.

At the pontoon bridges, their long line of canvas-covered wagons was forced to wait for the ambulances and medical wagons to roll across the river.

On the other side, their arduous journey continued as wagons, animals, and soldiers clogged the roadway. The advancing line of ambulances, Army medical wagons, and Sanitary Commission wagons were nearly stalled by the retreating army as it moved around them.

An endless stream of men in blue tromped around the wagons with no more interest than the river gives a rock as it flows around it. Exhaustion dragged their feet. Some limped, others had their arms supported with slings. The grime of sweat, dirt, and gunpowder coated their faces and beards so that they melded into one body of sameness.

Sighting the flag for the first division hospital, Mr. Bridgerton moved their wagon off the road, down the slope into a little hollow surrounded by a forest of dwarf pine, hickory, and scrub oak. Beyond the tree line, daylight had been obscured by dense undergrowth of bramble.

In the clearing, men lay on the ground or sat in scattered clusters beneath the shade of branches green with spring leaves. A small number of soldiers lifted their heads to gaze at the approaching wagon, but most seemed oblivious or too apathetic to care.

"Sweet Mary." Gracie nudged her horse closer to the front of the wagon. "How long have these men been lying on this damp ground?"

"Reckon it depends when they come in from the battlefields." Mister Bridgerton carefully maneuvered the horses around the edge of the clearing and toward the north end where the surgical area had been set up. Two more wagons followed.

"Whoa, boys." He pulled the team to a halt, set the brake, and jumped down.

Gracie slipped her feet from the stirrups, swung her leg over the horse, and slid to the ground. She clutched at the saddle with one hand while hastily shaking out her skirts with the other.

"I'll see if I can find some able bodies to help unload." He took a moment to arch his lower back then, rubbing the area with both hands, he headed toward the hub of doctors, stewards, and orderlies.

Gracie scanned the area for the tall, lanky silhouette of Doctor Ellard. Hundreds of wounded lay on the ground. Their prone bodies filled the entire area between the road and the tree line. For a moment she could only stare, trying to assimilate the image before her.

Their groans and pleas for water nearly overwhelmed her. She drew a deep breath and released it slowly. Find one thing to do and do it.

"Can I take your horse, ma'am?"

Startled, she swung around.

A young soldier stood with his hand extended.

"Thank ye." She pasted on her brightest smile and handed over the reins. "We've gum blankets and tents for the men, if ye've someone free to unload them."

"Yes, ma'am."

"And where might I find yer cook?"

"He's over yon—but—"

"We've beef stock and farina, bread and butter, vegetables and chicken, wine—"

"But ma'am ya got to talk to Major Andrews on how he wants things done."

"And Major Andrews be…"

The young soldier gestured toward the large tent beside a boxy medicine wagon, where Mr. Bridgerton and several men were gathered.

"Thank ye." She flashed him another quick smile and marched over to the surgical area.

Conversation stopped as she approached. Except for Mr. Bridgerton, nearly a dozen men stood staring at her slack jawed.

"Major Andrews?"

A bearded man of average height stepped forward.

Minus his uniform coat, a blood-spattered apron covered his waistcoat. He studied her through dark eyes underscored by deep shadows. A scowl furrowed his brow. "Who are you? And what are you doing in the middle of a damn battlefield?"

"Me name's Gracie McBride, a nurse at Armory Square Hospital. I've come with the Sanitary Commission to distribute supplies."

She shot a quick glance toward Mr. Bridgerton, but he seemed content to watch her flounder.

"If ye have some men to be helping with the unloading of the supplies and give me yer direction as to where to put—"

He shook his head. "I don't know how you got here, miss, but—"

"'Tis Mrs., Mrs. McBride. And I've come to help."

"Help? You're already a hindrance. I'm short surgeons. The one good man I have is wounded. Ambulances are bringing in more wounded as we speak, and you want me to assign the few orderlies I have to help you unload some crates and barrels? Women!"

He glared at Mr. Bridgerton. "Are you the one responsible for bringing her here? I don't need someone to soothe brows and write letters. She'll likely swoon the first time she sees someone brought in with half his head blown off." He ran his blood-stained fingers through his hair. He narrowed his glare on Gracie. "You want your wagon unloaded? Do it yourself."

"I will." She spun on her heels and started back. As she passed Mr. Bridgerton, she was certain she heard him chuckle.

At the back of the wagon, she struggled to push

against the wooden end-gate to ease the pressure as she pulled the pins that held it closed. If only she were a bit taller she'd have better leverage.

Someone stepped up behind her, reaching his big hands over her shoulders as he pushed on the wood panel and easily slipped free the bolts securing either side.

Gracie glanced back.

Mr. Bridgerton grinned down at her. "I reckoned you had enough backbone for this job, or I wouldn't have brought you."

The tension in her spine eased. She smiled up at him.

"Now, what do you want me to haul out first?"

They pulled out bales of wool blankets and gum rubber cloths first, leaving the tents for later. While Mr. Bridgerton lowered barrels of bandages, shirts, and crackers, Gracie filled a bucket with water from the narrow stream which wound through the area. She dropped a dipper in the bucket and with her arms loaded down with ground cloths and blankets, she headed toward the nearest wounded man.

He sat against a tree, his head swathed in white.

"Thank you, ma'am." He passed back the dipper.

"Call me Gracie." She smoothed out the rubberized cloth for him to lie on and passed him a folded blanket before moving to the next man and the next.

Glancing back toward the large white tent, she spotted the familiar form of Doctor Ellard bending over a patient on one of the surgery tables.

Reassured, she continued her ministrations.

She wiped the forehead of an unconscious soldier. Flies crawled across the glistening wet which soaked the front of the man's uniform coat, turning the area from blue to black. Fanning her hand over the man's abdomen, she shooed them away. Carefully, she lifted the limp hand which lay against the wound and eased open the buttons of his coat.

Her nostrils flared at the sharp odors of blood and urine. She pressed the back of her wrist against her nose and lifted his shirt, the white cloth, soaked crimson. A crumpled piece of cloth, soaked with blood, had been compressed against his stomach just above his waist. She tossed it aside. A small hole, to the left of his navel, continued to ooze blood.

From what she could determine, patients whose wounds were mortal were set aside near the woods. Of those remaining, the worst cases were placed in a quiet area near the surgical tent, and so on, down to the minor injuries, which were treated last. But with the steady influx of wounded from the battlefield, the area with the worst cases never seemed to diminish, and the poor man before her would apparently not be seen for some time.

Rising she searched for the men shifting the wounded to and from the surgery area. Spotting a couple of men leaving the surgery area with a litter, she hurried to intercept them before they could pick up the next patient on their list.

"Excuse me." She waved then stepped around the feet of a wounded soldier.

The two men lay their charge in the area with the other recovering patients, then folded the stretcher and met her half way.

"There is a private over there." She gestured toward the man she'd just left. "I fear he's waited so long for tending, that he cannot endure much longer. Can ye not take him next?" She smiled hopefully.

"We ain't s'posed to." The older man gave his beard a thoughtful stroke.

"What's it hurt?" his partner said.

"Thank you." She led them to the unconscious soldier and gave the man's bloody hand a squeeze as they placed him on the stretcher.

She watched them for a moment then knelt beside the man who lay next to him.

His eyes opened.

"Water?" she asked.

He nodded.

She wiped her hands on her apron and scooted around to lift his head and tip the dipper to his mouth.

When he finished, she smoothed out a gum blanket for him to lie on until she had time later to stuff some pine branches and leaves under it.

"That was a nice thing ya done fer that feller."

"Is he a friend?" She helped him slide over, off the damp ground.

"Don't know him, but he ain't made a peep in a while. I figgered he kicked off. Glad you took up fer him."

She shook out a wool blanket and lay it across him. "I'm a nurse. 'Tis what I do."

****

Gracie raised a hand in front of her face and shooed at the swarm of flies buzzing around a pile of bloody bandages and soiled rags outside the back corner of the surgery tent.

With a long stick, she scooped the dirty mess into a barrel. Ignoring the flies, she pushed her forearm against her nose and mouth, doing her best not to gag from the fermenting stench of blood and pus.

Once the dirty rags and bandages had been transferred, she grasped the edge of the barrel with both hands, tipped it on its edge, and began dragging it backward toward the area away from the trees where one of the men was starting a fire.

Her heel came down on what felt like a soft rock as her hind end bumped against something solid. She set the barrel upright and turned.

"By the saints, can ye not look where ye're going?" Her gaze collided with the center of a masculine chest covered by an apron smeared with blood. She looked up, past the spatter, to the achingly familiar face of the man she'd come so far to find.

His posture stiffened. He stared. His Adam's apple worked beneath the thick stubble coating the long column of his throat.

From his stunned expression, she guessed he hadn't known she was here.

She smiled.

The gleam of the setting sun warmed the blue of his eyes with a bit of gold.

"Good evening, Doctor Ellard."

He reached his arm toward her, then dropped it to his side.

For that moment she thought he would pull her close and kiss her in that arrogant way he had about him.

"What are you doing here?" Each word grated deep and raspy, as if sand paper lined his throat.

"Helping." He sounded terrible. She frowned, searching his face. Beneath the grime and thick growth of stubble, his skin was pale. Tight lines bracketed his mouth.

Usually, he assimilated information much more quickly. "I've come with Mr. Bridgerton. We've brought supplies from the Sanitary Commission."

"You don't belong here. Leave your supplies and return to Washington."

"But Doctor, I cannot just go back to Washington. And there be so many wounded. Ye know I can help."

"The battlefield is no place for a woman, even one so valiant as you. Who was your escort?" He cleared his throat with a cough and glanced around. "No doubt another young pup smitten by your smile."

While his backhanded compliments brought a rush of warmth to her cheeks, she would not be put off by his highhanded manner. Planting her hands on her hips, she lifted her chin to meet his gaze. "Here is where I be needed, and here is where I will stay."

"Then return to Falmouth. This is a war, Mrs. McBride. Do you not hear the gunfire? I'm sure you will be just as needed at the division hospital." He drew a breath as though about to say more. Exhaled with another cough then said. "You have introduced enough chaos to my life."

Chaos? Guilt pricked at her conscience. She glanced down and brought her hands together at her waist, pressing her thumb into her palm. "I did not intend to hurt ye."

He heaved a sigh and cleared his throat. "I realize that. However, because of your insatiable need to make everything better, you took my comment about family and turned my life upside down. If the only reason you've come now is to raise more doubts about my identity then take your nursing skills and leave this place. I don't need you."

Though the volume of his words tapered off into little more than a harsh whisper, if he'd punched her in the stomach they couldn't have hurt worse. The back of her throat closed off, and tears stung her eyes.

He sighed and coughed. His features softened.

"I apologize, Mrs. McBride. I fear fatigue and pain have uncensored my tongue. But your tears only serve to prove my point. Women have no place in war. They are too sensitive. They take too much to heart."

Gracie swiped angrily at the wet on her cheeks. "'Tis who I am. I'll not change for you, nor Major Andrews, nor Doctor Colfax, nor—Did ye say pain? Are ye hurt?"

A sheen of sweat glistened on his furrowed brow. The normal tone of his deep voice had grown raspier.

"Colfax? What has that idiot said to you?"

She frowned. Why had he diverted the conversation? "Doctor Colfax said nothing. But he will neither let me change a dressing nor bathe a patient. And no matter how well I do me job, the man makes report of it to Doctor Bliss. 'Tis why he sent me away."

"Sent you all the way to a battlefield in Confederate territory? Come now, Mrs. McBride, are you following me?"

Afraid his astute gaze would see the truth in her eyes, she studied the grass at her feet, the long shiny green blades flattened now by the footsteps of hundreds of soldiers. "At first 'twould appear that way."

"At first? It does appear that way."

"But in Washington, at Falmouth…I be not able to use all William taught me…I need ye."

"You need me?" Skepticism raised his brow.

She lifted her gaze to meet his. The earlier warmth in his eyes had cooled. Uncertain of his mood, she whispered, "I cannot be me without ye."

Vertical creases appeared at the bridge of his nose as his brows pulled toward each other. "Of course you can." He pressed his fist to his mouth and coughed. "My presence is not contingent for your existence."

A laugh burst from her throat, though it may have been a sob.

His scowl deepened. "Come now, Mrs. McBride; you don't need me. Any physician will do." His lips pressed together for a moment, forming a tight line. "Your William, Major Bliss, Major Andrews, even Doctor Colfax, as long as they allow you to utilize your nursing skills the way you believe they ought be utilized." He cleared his throat. "You only think you need me because I currently give you the validation you crave."

Gracie gasped. Her eyes stung. Why was he being so cruel? She swiped the moisture from her lashes. Maybe she had been wrong about his identity. For at this moment he acted more like a younger version of the old man with the cane. Was it not better to learn of him now, before she allowed her fantasy of a life working with him side by side, to completely erase William's memory?

Squaring her shoulders, she reached out with one hand and grasped the edge of the barrel. "Ye are correct. I do not need ye. William was enough o' a man for a lifetime."

He stiffened. His eyes narrowed, but not before she caught the flash of heat in the icy blue. Had he moved closer, or had she?

His gaze locked on her face.

She lifted her chin and searched his features waiting.

The moans of the wounded, the clink and clatter of surgical instruments, faded into the stretching shadows of twilight.

He took a step toward her. With one hand, he grabbed her upper arm and pulled her so close she had to raise up on her toes. To keep her balance, she slipped her hands under his arms and pressed her palms against his shoulders.

He flinched, twisting his shoulder from beneath her hand. She settled her palm against his waist. The sharp scent of smoke permeated his clothing and hair, as though he'd spent too much time in front of a campfire. The heat of his skin radiated through the linen of his shirt, warming her palms.

He leaned down, his face inches from hers. "You yourself said William never kissed you like I do." With that last whisper of breath, his lips crushed against hers.

If he was any other man, she would have pushed away from his assault. But finesse was as foreign to him as his ability to tell a joke or make friends.

The aggressiveness of his kisses reflected the same confidence he showed in his practice of medicine. Decision made, follow through. All others stand aside.

With a sigh she closed her eyes and savored the warmth of his mouth, the smoldering bite of smoke on his tongue. She longed for a taste of the passion which lurked, barely tethered beneath the veneer of an officer and a gentleman. His saliva pooled around her tongue. She swallowed. Her breasts peaked, sensitized to the fabric of her chemise.

Shifting her foot forward, she pressed against him. His body responded. She felt the length of him against her abdomen, through the layers of her petticoats and dress, the layers of his apron, trousers, and drawers.

Oh this man could kiss. She'd come to appreciate his uncompromising, take charge assault on her senses. They aroused a need six years of marriage and William's gentle lovemaking never had.

She longed to finish what they'd started in his tent in Falmouth, to lie naked beneath him like the wanton in his French postcards.

Something inside her chilled. Was that how he saw her? Was that the price she paid for inserting herself in a man's world? Would he kiss Miss Adelaide Emmerson like this, in the open, visible to anyone who should come around the tent?

Twisting away, she stepped back and pressed her finger tips to her lips. "Doctor, ye forget yerself."

He dropped his arm to his side. "As did you." He pressed his other forearm against his waist. "However, as a gentleman, I fear I must once again beg your pardon." He inhaled a breath as if to say more and began to cough.

He pulled a handkerchief from his pocket and pressed it over his nose and mouth.

Concern tugged at her brow. "What have ye done to yerself?"

"I have done nothing." He mumbled into the handkerchief as the coughing eased. "Merely inhaled a bit too much smoke."

"Smoke?"

"Mrs. McBride!"

Gracie whirled toward the voice, praying no one else had seen their kiss. She couldn't be thought of as anything other than a respectable woman. To be perceived as less would undermine what credibility female army nurses had thus far achieved.

One of the stewards gestured toward the fires. "Your fire is ready."

She raised her hand and waved. "I need to be about me duties."

Holding his arm close to his body, he peered over her shoulder at the soiled bandages and rags she was about to drag away.

He straightened and glanced around. "This is not a task for a woman. Assign it to someone else. When the cook has finished, see that the men are fed. I must go. Another ambulance has arrived."

Before she could say a word, he'd spun on his heels and strode back toward the front of the surgery tent.

****

Gracie stifled a yawn and rolled her shoulders against the tightness in her neck. The wounded were settled as best they could manage. Tents had been pitched, and the men were fed and dry.

With one hand she held up the bottom of her apron, forming a pouch. Inside she placed a cloth-wrapped bundle of chicken and soda crackers. Lifting a lantern, Gracie made her way to the surgery tent and shouldered aside the canvas flap.

One of the stewards sat between a barrel of rolled bandages and a small table on which he slid eight-yard lengths of cloth into a bandage roller and turned the crank.

"Have ye seen Doctor Ellard?"

"The captain went out back to get some sleep."

"And where—"

"That way." He pointed toward the rear corner of the tent. "Look for a light near the tree line."

She offered her thanks and ducked back outside.

Moving carefully toward the soft glow of the lantern, she called softly. "Doctor Ellard?"

Two shadowy forms lay on either side of the light. The one on the left rose, his silhouette shorter and broader than she expected. He shrugged into his coat. "Mrs. McBride?"

She moved closer. The man she'd met last week in Doctor Ellard's tent back in Falmouth stepped forward.

He glanced at her apron, the end held close to her waist. "Your brother is sleeping."

Charles lay sprawled on his stomach, his shirt off. One arm was tucked under the haversack he was using as a pillow, his other lay on the ground. His fingers wrapped loosely around the neck of an empty bottle.

She held her lantern close to his sleeping form. "Begorra, what happened to his back?"

"The house we were using as a hospital was shelled and caught fire."

She set her lantern on the ground next to several rolls of bandage and squares of white cloth. Dirty bandages lay in a heap between two field packs. She passed Breen the cloth-wrapped food.

"Smells good," Breen murmured as he unfolded one corner of the linen cloth, raised the bundle to his nose, and inhaled.

Gracie dropped to her knees and leaned over Doctor Ellard's back. With her finger, she lightly traced the area of whitened skin around a burn a bit larger than the spread of her hand.

Raw and red, the burn had seared through his skin, deep into the muscle. A couple dozen blisters rose like angry bubbles across the exposed tissue.

"He was trying to get the wounded out and a burning floor joist fell on him."

"Sweet Mary Jesus."

She picked up the empty whiskey bottle and set it aside.

"I'm afraid he's pretty drunk, but the pain keeps him from sleeping. I recommended Dover's Powder, but he refused. I commandeered that bottle of whiskey and waited until he drank enough to tolerate the torture of having the old stuck-on dressing pulled off. The pain must have been bad because he drank damn near the whole bottle. I think he finally passed out, so I left off bandaging it."

"Me husband, William, swore honey to be the best treatment for a burn. I've a pint jar I be using for me tea. Let me fetch it. Help yerself to the soda crackers and chicken."

"Thank you, ma'am."

Lantern in hand, she rose and hurried off to the Sanitary Commission wagon. She grabbed her bag from under the seat and pulled out her half-pint jar of honey and returned a few minutes later.

Breen jumped to his feet. His small stack of crackers fell to the ground.

She smiled. "Sit, Doctor. Ye are tired as well, and this be a far cry from a proper drawing room."

He grinned and hunkered down to retrieve his spilled crackers from the grass. Crackers in one hand, he sat cross-legged and set the cloth bundle in the hollow. Lifting out a drumstick, he wolfed it down as though it were the finest fare.

Gracie lifted several of the cloth squares from the field pack and lowered herself to the ground close beside Charles. She folded the squares and dipped them into the honey, scooping out a generous amount. Holding it over the burn, she let the honey drizzle across the area, then lay the pad on top.

He lay so quiet and still, her fingers took the liberty of exploring the smooth skin of his bare back, the shape of his shoulders with the few scattered freckles, and the dip of his spine as it trailed beneath the waistband of his trousers. Her hand slid up toward his neck, gently easing around his wounded shoulder. Absently her fingers sifted through the thick dark waves of his hair.

"He's not your brother, is he?"

Gracie yanked her hand to her lap and lifted her gaze to Breen. She shook her head.

She caught a brief flash of white as he smiled. "I did wonder when I met you in Falmouth. I asked him about you, but he never said a word."

Gracie shook her head. "'Tis not his way, to talk of himself." And likely why he hadn't told her of his injury. At times his nature was too stoic for his own good.

Breen held out his hand, offering her some of the crackers.

"Thank ye, but I ate."

"He's a brilliant man, your captain. I'm surprised more of the medical staff don't respect that."

"'Tis both his blessing and his curse, for it separates him from the others, and he's no notion there be a gap."

"Then what happened this morning likely widened it." He threw the chicken bones into the trees. Lying on his side, he propped his head on his hand.

"They brought a soldier in from the field, found insensible near an exploded shell. Major Deavers wanted to bleed and blister the man to restore his humors."

Gracie smiled to herself with a pretty good idea of what would come next. She trailed her hand up and down Doctor Ellard's warm back.

"Your captain said the blisters on his shoulder did nothing to restore his humor and that the doctors of Major Deavers generation were an antiquated group of Rush disciples, with no thought to question the logic behind taking the blood of men who had lost buckets of it already."

Gracie smiled. "He fights hard for the men. In that way we are alike."

Breen chuckled to himself. A few minutes later, his hand slipped from beneath his head. He jerked and rolled onto his back. Soft snores rumbled in the back of his throat.

Gracie leaned over and blew out their lamp then lowered the wick on her own. Darkness swallowed most of the lingering light.

"Gracie?" Doctor Ellard murmured beside her.

"Are ye hungry? I brought ye some food."

"You touched me." His scratchy voice was slurred and muffled against the canvas of his haversack.

"And who were ye thinking 'twas? Captain Breen?"

"Don't go."

Ironic, because since the moment she met him, he'd been telling her to go. Against her better judgment, she shifted closer. Her hip pressed against his.

"Dream of touching you," he mumbled. "Running my hands over your skin."

Heat singed her cheeks. She could almost feel the weight of his hands, his long fingers, roaming over her body. Gooseflesh rippled up her arms and across her shoulders.

"Touch me, Gracie." His softly spoken words slurred against the canvas. "No one's ever touched me like that."

Sweet Mary Jesus, how drunk was he?

She ran her hand up and down the smooth skin of his back, traced the shape of his shoulder, the dip of his spine, and sifted her fingers through his hair. Tenderness swelled inside her, so much deeper than the heat of erotic pleasure she usually felt when he kissed her. Content to sit beside him, pleased she could be the one to give him this.

He sighed.

"I must be going, Doctor."

"Say my name."

"Charles."

"Uh uh. My name's Jason. Charles is dead."

Her hand stilled. Her breath caught for just an instant. "Is that who ye are? Jason?"

"Dun know. 'Member lilacs…an' reading."

The man was definitely drunk.

"Say my name."

Her heartbeat quickened. "Jason," she whispered.

"Ummm. You say it like she…does."

"Who?"

312

"Voice…in my head. Timbre…lilt same."

She had to leave now, while she still could, before she lay down beside him and gathered him close. Maybe this urge to nurture came from not having children. "I best be going."

"No, juss found you."

Was he talking to her or the voice in his head? Was that voice his mother's? "I cannot be spending the night lying between two unmarried men. 'Tis far beyond proper, to be sure."

"Then marry me, Gracie."

She stilled. Her breath caught, and she pressed her finger tips to her lips. No. He was drunk. His eyes weren't even open. None of this was real. For a moment though, she could almost imagine it. A lifetime together, helping people, working side by side as she had with William.

"Marry me, Gracie."

Hope flickered for a moment, that one day this could be real. She'd had a marriage like that once, but she dared not believe it could happen again.

"If I promise to marry ye, doctor, will ye go to sleep and let me off to me bed?"

"Uh uh. Not the doctor. Marry me. Jason."

"Fine. I promise to marry ye."

"Jason."

She leaned over him. "Good night, Jason." She brushed his hair off his forehead and pressed a kiss to his temple.

Rising, she turned away. Holding the lantern in front of her, she stepped forward into the night.

At least in the dark no one could see her tears.

Chapter Seventeen

Rain. Under normal circumstances Gracie would have welcomed a spring shower, savored the fresh scent, and with a light heart enjoyed a walk outside.

Today the soft pelting against canvas tents grew monotonous. The damp air sharpened the pungent miasma of wet horses, earth, blood, and urine. Though she wore a floppy brimmed hat and black poncho, the wet eventually soaked the hem of her skirt and seeped through the leather of her shoes as she moved from tent to tent offering farina and tea to those wounded able to eat.

Her kettles empty, she thought to head back to the cook tent. Instead, compelled by an overwhelming desire to catch even a glimpse of Doctor Ellard, her feet drew her the long way past the surgery tent. The front flaps had been tied back like theater curtains, showcasing the tableau of assistants, doctors, and patients.

She spotted him immediately at the back of the tent.

He leaned over a portable hospital table, focused on the unconscious patient before him. As though he felt her presence, he glanced up and met her gaze for a moment before returning to his work.

She continued on. Did he remember anything of the words spoken between them last night? To be sure, his midnight confessions had been naught but ramblings spoken by a whiskey loosed tongue. 'Twas foolishness to think he meant it when he'd asked her to marry him.

If he had meant it, could she marry him? No matter how strong the physical attraction was between them, would he treat her as William had, fully respecting her as a nurse and as a woman? Right now, in the midst of war, Doctor Ell—Jason, accepted her skills, but if they were to marry would he relegate her to managing a household, with half a dozen children clinging to her apron strings?

She liked the woman she'd become. She felt good about herself. Her life had purpose beyond the norms society dictated for a woman. At least this war had granted her the opportunity to fulfill her destiny. She could never go back to the girl she was before William, or the housemaid she was forced to become after he passed away.

And if Doctor Ellard, if Jason, could not embrace that part of her, they could never wed.

Since she was so near the Sanitary Commission wagons, she decided to grab some extra bandages and lint for her pockets. She set the empty pots in the grass, hiked up her skirts, and climbed inside. Already the barrels of crackers and bandages were almost empty. Crates of shirts and drawers, boxes of chloroform and surgical silk, were all nearly gone. She wiggled sideways between the piles and flipped back the lid of a barrel near the front. She pulled out some bandages and stuffed them into the large pockets of her skirt.

"Ma'am?"

Gracie glanced over her shoulder. A soldier stood

outside. Though the rain had tapered to a light drizzle, he shivered in a rain-soaked uniform. His hair lay flattened to his head, and his dirty face streaked with a pink mixture of rain and blood which trailed into a beard of several day's growth.

"You got any food, ma'am?"

"Ye'd best stop by the cook tent." She closed the lid and made her way through the supplies.

"I did, but he told me I had to wait like everyone else."

She stopped and thought, looking around. "I do not have anything that does not need cooked, except some crackers and applesauce."

"Ma'am, I ain't had nothing to eat in days. I'd eat my shoe leather if I still had my shoes, so whatever you can spare, I'd be obliged."

Shifting a few things around, she uncovered a crate of applesauce and lifted out a jar. From another crate she pulled out a tin of crackers. As she stepped toward the opening, she grabbed a charcoal gray blanket.

He reached out to help her down, and she landed in the mud beside him.

"On me sainted mother, what has happened to yer shoes? I thought ye be jesting about losing them." She shook out the blanket and passed it over.

"Thank you, ma'am." He whipped it around his shoulders like a cape and pulled the wool close beneath his chin. "When I woke up after I got hit, my regiment had pulled back and left me for dead. The Johnny Rebs must have thought I was too, and one of them took my shoes."

Gracie unscrewed the zinc band and wedged a spoon under the edge of the lid.

His gaze fixed on the jar, his tongue whisked away the rain dotting his lips.

Giving the spoon a little twist, the seal broke with a pop. She lifted off the lid, jabbed the spoon into the jar, and passed it to the soldier. "Have ye had one o' the doctors look at yer wound?"

"No, ma'am." He scooped a mouthful and swallowed. "They're all busy. Some ambulances just came in with men who are real bad off, and that's not me."

Gracie pried the lid off the tin of crackers and passed it over. "Ye best go easy now if ye've not eaten."

He grabbed a handful and passed back the tin. "Thank you, ma'am. I feel lots better."

She eyed his dirty face and the open gash across his cheek. "Would ye mind me tending to yer wound? I can clean it up proper, and if it needs a stitch or two, I be a fair hand with a needle."

He shoveled several more spoonfuls into his mouth.

"Ye needn't worry, me husband was a fine doctor, and he had me stitch many a wound in his stead."

He shrugged as he scrapped the bottom of the jar.

Gracie smiled. Though it was empty, he seemed to be hoping to find just a bit more. She took the jar and set it on the end gate of the wagon. "Can ye wait for me now in that first tent there?"

She pointed and he nodded.

"I have surgical silk, but I need to fetch some water and borrow a needle."

Hopefully, Doctor Ellard would not be opposed to loaning her one. The soldier headed for the indicated tent, and Gracie walked back to the surgery.

The raised voices could be heard several yards away.

"This is my patient!" declared the nasally whine of an older man.

"You make that cut," Doctor Ellard's raspy baritone carried through the canvas walls. "The flaps won't be long enough. When the leg swells the stitches will rip out. If he doesn't bleed to death, someone will have to go back and remove the bone higher on the leg just to gain the extra length of skin."

Gracie entered the tent and sidled along the outer wall behind some attendants. Now was probably not a good time to interrupt him for a needle. She should leave, but whether it was the need to be near him, or to be near the surgery, something held her in place.

The older surgeon tossed his bone saw into his amputation case. "You're injured, Captain. The major ordered you to handle minor wounds, not amputations." He scooped up his knives, artery forceps, and sponges and threw them haphazardly into the wooden box. He slammed the lid and gathered the box close. "I shall speak to Major Andrews immediately."

"Do as you will. Just take your saw and your ignorance away from this patient." He looked up. As before, some sixth sense appeared to direct his gaze across the crowd of attendants and assistant surgeon's to lock on Gracie's face.

"Mrs. McBride, lend a hand."

Why he asked for her when he was surrounded by medical professionals she didn't understand. Had he finally come to appreciate the nursing part of her? Except, as she drew closer she saw in his gaze a desperation. A silent plea for an ally amidst the cold condemnation of his peers. And because she needed him to need her, she twisted her way through the crowd to the table.

The soldier lay with his head on a pillow. Most of his face was masked beneath the cloth held by an assistant surgeon to absorb the drops of chloroform. The patient's clothing had been loosened around his neck, chest, and abdomen.

The poor man's lower left leg was a bloody mess. Most of the calf muscle was gone. What remained was a mangle of flesh and bone with bits of tattered uniform, red clay, and blood.

"Canister shot," said the young assistant surgeon from the other side of the table.

Gracie nodded, gulped, and squeezed her fingers together.

The patient's shoe and sock had been removed and his pant leg cut off near his hip. His thigh had already been shaved and the muslin retractor ready in preparation for the surgeon.

She stepped closer, standing beside Doctor Ellard who placed each of his instruments on a small table between them.

Amputating knives, saws, artery forceps, tena cuta, bone forceps. Sponges, threaded curved needles.

He passed her a tourniquet without a word, as though he expected her to know what to do with it.

It had been a long time, but she took a deep breath and drew on the lessons William had taught her.

She positioned the boxy frame behind the retractor, near the groin, so the pad would compress the main artery against the bone. Quickly she slipped the wide band under the thigh, pulled it snug, then buckled it tight. Grasping the top of the screw she twisted and twisted, the pad slowly clamping down on the artery until she could no longer turn the knob.

The amputation knife in his hand, Doctor Ellard grasped a handful of the thigh just above the top of the knee. Next, he pushed his knife into the leg just below his thumb. He slid the blade through the skin until the tip stabbed through below his fingers on the opposite side. He angled the blade upward and around as if he filleted a fish, creating the flap.

He reinserted the knife at the same point but angled below the bone and repeated the procedure so his second skin flap matched the first.

The assistant surgeon, grabbed the ends of the cloth retractor and pulled back, clenching his jaw with the effort to lift the flaps up and hold them back, away from the knife.

Doctor Ellard severed the muscle in the same efficient manner as the skin flaps. He dropped the muscle and tissue into the metal pail under the table.

As he did, Gracie picked up the bone saw and passed it over, accepting the knife from him at the same time.

The saw grasped in his bloody fingers, the back and forth motion rasped through the bone in seconds.

Again she traded—bone forceps for the saw. Sweat beaded his forehead and trailed down his cheek. Tight lines bracketed his pale cheeks above his beard. While he trimmed and smoothed all the irregular edges of bone, Gracie slipped her hand into her pocket and pulled out a square of linen.

Accepting the bone forceps with one hand, she

reached up and quickly blotted the sweat from his face and brow.

He drew a breath. "Remove the retractor."

The assistant surgeon slipped the blood-soaked cloth off the end of the bone and elevated the leg.

Quickly, Gracie drew a deep breath, grasped the amputated limb, and dropped it into the pail. Releasing the breath she held, she stared into the pail. Her emotions at the sight felt as detached as the limb.

Strange to think that seconds ago, the leg had been part of this man. He'd stood on that foot, scratched an itch on his knee, now it was gone. A bit like the sick and wounded patients who came through the hospital. Alive—and then not.

Now that the retractor was out of the way, the main arteries could be seen. Gracie passed Doctor Ellard the artery forceps and sponges.

With the forceps, he drew out the artery. Gracie reached close and took hold of the forceps. Quickly, he separated any nerves away from the artery then tied it off with a silk ligature, leaving a long tail of thread hanging from the knot.

The speed with which he drew out each blood vessel and tied it off was almost mesmerizing. Watching his hands, she could almost forget how much pain he was in.

"Loosen the tourniquet. Not too much."

The assistant surgeon gave the screw a couple of turns. Blood seeped from the apex of the amputated area, though the ligated vessels held.

Doctor Ellard—Jason bent close, a frown marring his sweaty brow. He reached into the wound, trying to find the bleeder.

"Let me." She leaned forward trying to see past his hand. He pulled back, allowing her access.

Warm wet trickled over her hand from a vein which had drawn up inside the remaining thigh muscle. She wiggled her fingers into the muscle and pinched the blood vessel. Then, with her left hand she reached across her body, under her extended arm, and lifted the tenaculum from the tray.

"I almost have it." Still pinching the vein closed, she hooked the blood vessel with the tenaculum and pulled it out.

Needle and thread in hand, Doctor Ellard had it tied off in seconds.

He nodded to the assistant surgeon who loosened the tourniquet a little more. Blood leaked from the lesser arteries.

Ignoring them, he drew a new needle from the chamois cloth on the tray and threaded a new length of silk.

"And what o' these other bleeders?"

"They'll clot or collapse on their own."

The assistant surgeon raised the leg, and Gracie gathered the long lengths of silk thread and divided them to allow them to hang out either side of the skin flaps.

Next she cleaned the stump as the assistant surgeon drew the remaining skin and muscle forward to join the two skin edges.

Sweat beaded over Doctor Ellard's face again, and Gracie wiped him dry then watched as he closed the wound with sutures and adhesive plaster strips, careful to leave spaces for drainage. Gracie packed the wound with cotton to absorb the drainage, holding it in place until Doctor Ellard was able to dress the stump with a Maltese cross of lint spread with cerate. And hanging from either side of the wound were more than twenty silk ligatures.

Gracie exhaled an exhausted breath, more mental fatigue than physical, for the whole procedure had taken only minutes. Two orderlies lifted the litter from the table and carried the patient from the tent.

"Thank ye doctor, for the opportunity to assist ye," she said as she washed her hands in a basin of cold water.

The young assistant surgeon gave her a nod, acknowledging his approval, and passed her a towel.

Doctor Ellard immersed his bone saw and other instruments into a fresh pail of water. "It's what you've been wanting, is it not?" He sloshed them around then pulled them out one by one and wiped them dry on a towel.

"Aye, but—"

"You performed admirably. As well as any assistant surgeon with whom I've yet to operate. You do your William proud."

While she'd waited months to hear such high praise from him, his tone was flat, almost sarcastic. Maybe it was lack of sleep and the pain of his burned shoulder.

"Why do I sense this does not please ye?"

"It does. You've pressured me since March to acknowledge you as a nurse. I do. You are truly as good as any assistant surgeon. You've accomplished all you set out to achieve. You are now free to return to Falmouth and hence to Washington."

"I do not understand."

"Forgive me. What do you not understand?" He lay his bone saw and each instrument precisely inside the green velvet lined case.

"Aye, I be wanting ye to recognize the part of me who is a nurse, but I am a woman also, and from the way ye have kissed me, I thought…"

"Thought what? That we would marry, set up a practice together, like you and William, and go happily into the sunset?"

"I…I…"

"Has it occurred to you that if I am truly not Charles Peter Ellard, then my medical diploma is no longer valid? Would you want to be with me if I were no longer a physician? Because, Mrs. McBride, like you, there are two sides to me as well. Both physician and man. And while you seem to embrace the doctor side of me, you continually reject the man.

"I am not William. I will never be your William. I am however a man, with all the desires and needs of a man. If you cannot embrace that side of me as much as you cling to the doctor I may no longer be, then I would prefer that you take yourself far away before I do or say something I might come to regret."

****

What happened?

Somehow Gracie found herself backed into a corner of the tent watching as doctors, attendants, and patients moved around her in a blur. Numb. That's how it felt. Like that day in March when she was twelve and Callum accidently knocked her into the Charles River. Before he could haul her out, her legs and arms had gone numb. It had taken hours in front of the fire before her insides had stopped shaking.

This time even her insides were numb.

"Ma'am? Ma'am? You'll have to move, please."

She blinked. A young private stood before her, his brow furrowed. Behind him two ambulance attendants with a loaded stretcher between them, waited to place the wounded soldier on the table.

"Sorry," she mumbled and sidled away along the outer edge of the tent. How long had she been standing there? How many people had heard his cruel words? Several men glanced her way. Even Captain Breen sent her a quick apologetic smile. But Doctor Ellard never looked up from his next patient.

Focused on the ground, Gracie slipped out of the tent and hurried across the clearing to the Sanitary Commission wagon. Climbing inside, she slid down between two barrels and drew her knees up, crossing her arms on top and resting her forehead. She felt like a little girl again, hiding in the hold of the Americana, praying her da would come and save her from all the bad.

But her da was back in Boston with her mother and her brother Bryan. Tears welled in her eyes and spilled over her lashes. She wasn't even sure why she cried. For Callum and Michael? For William? For the brave men and boys who lost their lives, in a war that seemed to never end? Or was she crying for herself? For her exhaustive uphill battle to be respected as a nurse?

Was he right? Had she somehow created a fantasy in which life went on as before with Doctor Ellard conveniently replacing William?

Except, he wasn't Charles Ellard. He was Jason. Would his medical degree really be worthless if he accepted the person he was born to be? What would he do if he were no longer able to practice medicine? Would he forsake his birth and keep his diploma? Sweet Mary Jesus, she hadn't thought this through. He was right. She had brought nothing but chaos into his life.

She leaned her head back against the side of the wagon box and swiped the moisture from her cheeks. And what of her future? Would she want to marry Jason if he was no longer a doctor? She'd be hard pressed to find another physician willing to give her a place in his practice.

Last night he'd asked her to marry Jason, but she wasn't even sure who Jason was. Could she sacrifice the nurse side of herself to become his wife?

Sitting here feeling sorry for herself wasn't helping. By the saints, she was a nurse. There was still a war and the poor man with the wounded face waited. She pushed to her feet and climbed out of the wagon.

A couple of ambulances rolled past on their way to unload near the surgery tent.

A loose tendril of hair escaped its bun and blew across her face. With her finger, she looped it behind her ear and made her way back toward the surgery tent to borrow a needle. Maybe she'd ask Captain Breen instead.

Two attendants stood at either end of a litter, holding a wounded soldier, between them. Unconscious, his long legs hung off the end between the arms of the attendant who held the wooden handles.

"Don't know how long this fellow was laying out there, but he looks pretty bad."

"Major?" The ambulance corpsman called to a doctor coming out of the surgery tent.

"What should we do with this one?"

Recognizing the physician Doctor Ellard had shoved aside earlier, Gracie made her way toward them. But an obstacle course of ambulances, horses, and wounded, coming in from the battlefield slowed her progress as she carefully stepped over and around the men.

The doctor leaned over the wounded man, peering closely at his head, then straightened and gave his own a shake. "Nothing to be done. Put him over there with the other mortal wounds."

He turned away, and the ambulance corpsmen carried the soldier to the area assigned for the dying. Gracie altered her course to angle over to where the men were headed. Normally, she wouldn't have followed, but this was the same doctor who had almost bungled the amputation. For all she knew, this was the man who believed in bleeding and purging.

She reached the wounded soldier as the two corporals lifted him onto the ground. They folded the litter in half and left.

Red clay covered a liberal amount of his uniform. Gun powder and a swath of blood disguised his face. Blood matted the man's hair and caked on the side of his neck and collar. Head wounds bled a lot, but this appeared excessive, and still glistened, either from the earlier rain, or because the wound still bled.

The young man's lanky frame triggered a sense of something familiar…something…someone…

She studied the shape of his nose, his forehead, and a mouth which normally spread wide with a smile. Shock dropped Gracie to her knees.

She gasped and cupped her hand over her mouth.

"Sweet Mary Jesus, Robbie." The soft words spilled out in a huff of breath warm against her palm. Tears blurred the image of his face. Hand shaking, she reached out to touch the chilled skin of his cheek.

Robbie. She pushed the stiffened hanks of hair off his forehead. Leaning close, she felt his soft shallow breaths against her cheek. He was still alive, but lying on the ground in a damp uniform, for how long?

She pushed to her feet and snatching up her skirts, ran. She dodged men and horses, jumped over the wounded in her haste to reach the surgery tent and the only man who could save him. She would not lose Robbie too.

He was stitching closed a gash when she found him. Using only his right hand, his assistant aiding him in the process of tying off each knot much like two people knotting a string after wrapping a package.

He glanced up, but said nothing, returning his attention to his long row of stitches. Sweat glistened across his brow. He held himself stiffly as though an invisible board had been strapped to his back. If it were anyone but Robbie, she would have felt guilty for asking him to do more.

Instead she waited, shifting her weight nervously from foot to foot. To keep from ordering him to hurry, she bit down on her lower lip.

"Mrs. McBride." He stepped back from the table allowing his assistant to bandage the wound. He wiped his hands on a linen towel. "You've had time to regroup and have no doubt returned to redouble your effort to convince me of my wrong thinking—"

"'Tis Robbie. He's hurt bad. Ye have to help him."

He pushed his needle through the chamois cloth,

folded over the flaps, and tied it closed. "Robbie?" His brow furrowed. "Robbie? Ah yes, the young puppy, Corporal Reid. Gunshot wound to the left shoulder. Minimal laudable pus. Minimal fever. Interesting case for my paper on—"

"Doctor, ye must come now."

He glanced around the area. He might have been searching for another patient he could claim took priority. He might have been looking for another surgeon who was free to assist her. That way he could avoid spending any more time in her presence.

She didn't care. "Can ye not hurry?"

He blew out an exhausted sigh. "Very well. Lead on."

She whirled on her heels and hastened from the tent. She didn't have to turn around to see if he followed. She felt him behind her, his long legs easily keeping pace as she wove around horses, ambulances, and men, back to the area where Robbie lay.

"Mrs. McBride," he said.

She turned.

He'd stopped at the edge of the area. "I'm not certain you are aware—"

"Aye," she snapped. "I be aware. But I cannot be certain the diagnosis of a doctor ye called a bloody idiot, to be an accurate one."

"I assume you refer to comments I made to Major Deavers? I did not call him a bloody idiot. I merely suggested that medical men of his generation were an antiquated group of Rush disciples. Also, that he had an ignorant knowledge of amputations."

"What does it matter? His diagnosis cannot be trusted, and he be the one who put Robbie here."

Expecting him to follow, she turned and maneuvered around the group of men, some silent, others softly moaning. She dropped to her knees beside Robbie. Reaching out, she carefully lifted hanks of blood-soaked hair away from his wound and brushed it over his ear toward the back of his head.

Black, mud spattered boots and long legs stepped into her periphery. She glanced down at the squared leather toes which brushed the edge of her skirt.

Expecting him to say something, she looked up.

He stood beside her as if frozen. All color had drained from his face. Sweat glistened across his chalky complexion. His hands shook and he curled his fingers into fists.

"Can't." He shook his head. His breath huffed out in short, shallow breaths, like a dog panting on a hot summer day.

Pale and sweaty, he looked as if he were about to collapse from a heart seizure.

"Doctor?" Until this moment, she'd forgotten about his strange reaction to the patient with the head wound at Armory Square. She reached up, intending to wrap her fingers over his fisted hand, but he shook his head, still gasping for breath.

He whirled and stumbled around the wounded, heading for the shadows of the tree line.

She lay her hand against Robbie's cheek and leaned close. "Doctor Ellard is coming to take care o'ye, and ye'll soon be right as rain."

She pushed to her feet, lifted her skirt with both hands, and hurried toward the trees.

He sat with his lower back against the gray, fissured trunk of a scrub oak. Curled forward, his forearms rested on his up drawn knees, his hands clenched into fists.

As she dropped beside him, he seemed unaware of her presence. His breathing rasped in and out, in short wheezing puffs that heaved his chest up and down. Sweat dotted his forehead. His hand pressed against his chest, rubbing the area as if he were in pain.

She rested her hand on his shoulder. He didn't look at her. She wasn't sure he could.

The night of his previous attack at Armory Square, she'd rubbed his back until he calmed.

She slid her hand lower, rubbing in slow circular motions, but it had no effect.

That night he'd been in his shirt sleeves with only the thin cotton between her hand and his back. Today with his waistcoat, and the thick bandage wrapped over his wounded shoulder, could he even feel her hand? Sliding her palm lower, to the curved center of his spine, she continued to create slow circles, hoping the pressure would reach his muscles, but this attack had such a terrible hold on him, she grew desperate to find another way.

Still rubbing his back, she slipped her other hand under his arm, inside the tight space between his knees and chest. She grasped his hand. The heat of his palm warmed her chilled fingers, though he didn't seem aware of their cold.

His heart thudded wildly, his pulse thrumming through the vein at the back of his jaw, as if he'd been running for his life.

When she'd been a little girl on the ship from Ireland, a man had pulled her into a dark corner and lifted her dress. He'd touched her and put her hand against the front of his pants. She'd bitten him and kicked his shin. It had given her enough time to get away. She'd hidden down in the hold, curled into a ball, trying to catch her breath, her heart racing with every creak and groan of the ship. She'd stayed there until her da found her the next day.

But what fear had caused this?

It couldn't be the gruesomeness of the wound. He'd just performed an amputation and tossed the poor man's leg into a pail as if it were no more significant than trimming the crust from a slice of bread.

Her thumb brushed back and forth against his knuckles. His skin cold beneath her touch.

Was it because he knew Robbie? But he hadn't known the soldier at the hospital that night.

"Ye have to breathe slower."

He didn't seem to hear. If anything, his face had grown paler.

She slid the hand on his back up higher, over his collar to the back of his neck. The cords rigid, the muscles hard as stone. She worked her finger tips in small circles from the small bump of bone at the base, into the dark silky hair at the top.

"This cannot be good fer ye, Doctor," she murmured as she tried to massage away the tension.

"Ye have to breathe slower." How could she break through?

"Inhale. Exhale. Please Char—Jason. Breathe with me, Jason. Inhale. Exhale. Breathe. Nice and slow."

Was this what Robbie and others had tried to tell her when she first arrived at Armory Square? That Doctor Ellard had gone crazy at Fredericksburg? Was this what had happened? But this wasn't crazy, this was fear. Mind-numbing, terrifying fear.

There had to be some way to break its hold. She would not lose him too.

"Tell me a joke." The words burst from her lips before she could even think them. "Make me laugh. Ye read the whole book. Please, Ch—Jason, tell me a joke."

She squeezed his hand. "Think. I know ye can do it. Think on the pages ye read. The farmers, gone halves on a pig. The boy crowned king before he could marry. See the words." She continued to rub his back, deep massaging circles. "The physician whose patient ate the prescription and got well. Think on them. See the pages in the book and tell me a joke. Please, Jason."

He closed his eyes. His fingers turned in her palm to squeeze her fingers.

She bit her lip against the strength of his grip, praying she wouldn't cry out.

He rocked, ever so slightly. His eyes still closed.

"A Federal regiment was attacked." He drew several more panting breaths. "By a whole brigade. God, I feel sick."

"Ye can do it. Think on the words o'the joke."

"Unable to withstand such odds...regiment fell back about forty yards..."

The pressure of his fingers around her hand tightened. He leaned toward her.

She slid her hand across his uninjured shoulder and pulled him to her. His head rested against her breast.

"My heart...feels like I'm dying."

"Ye are not dying. I have ye. Now tell me the joke."

"...regiment fell back...losing their flag...to the

enemy."

His struggling breaths drew a spell of harsh coughing from his lungs. "Chest hurts. My head. Feels like...I'm going to pass out."

"Ye will not. I have ye. Now tell me yer joke."

His words mumbled against the bodice of her dress. "Suddenly, a tall Irishman dashed from the ranks and...attacked the squad of Confederates..." He drew several short-winded gasps. "Irishman...felled several with his musket...snatched the flag...and returned...safely to his regiment."

The harsh desperation of his breathing eased with each word he spoke. "The soldier was...surrounded by his comrades who...praised him for his gallantry..."

He raised his head and turned his blue eyes her way. "The hero...cut them short...saying, 'Say no more...about it. I just fetched my whisky flask...which I dropped among the rebels, and I thought...I might as well bring the flag back with it.' "

A laugh burst from Gracie's lips, unbidden, despite her fear for Robbie, despite her worry for this man in her arms. Her light chuckles continued, for several seconds, though she wasn't even sure the joke was that funny.

"You laughed." A spark of wonder lit his eyes. Then with a long-exhausted sigh, the tension in his body slackened, and he relaxed against her.

"Aye. Sweet Mary, 'twas the funniest joke ye've told."

His hand snaked around her waist, and he lifted his head. "Thank you." He released her hand and cupped her face, his long fingers sliding into the hair at the back of her neck as his thumb brush over the sensitive skin of her cheek.

She shivered as warmth pooled in her abdomen. Slowly, she melted into his touch.

He leaned close. Shadow deepened the blue of his eyes as he searched her face.

She brushed the backs of her fingers against the rough stubble which covered his cheeks.

He turned slightly and pressed a kiss to the inside of her wrist. His tongue swiped across the thin skin, before he shifted and pressed his mouth to hers.

She slipped her arms around his neck, kissing him as he eased her onto the ground.

He moved above her, absorbing his own weight with his knees and uninjured forearm.

For those moments, there was no clopping of horse feet, no moans of the wounded, no Robbie. There was only the aching need to be held, to be cherished, to be loved. The yearning to feel the warmth of his bare skin pressed against hers. Her legs tangled with his. She reached down and tugged the bottom of his shirt from the waistband of his pants. Seeking more of him, her hand slid into the hollow at the base of his spine. Her fingertips slid lower, as far as the tightness of the clothing allowed, and brushed over the curve of his buttocks, grazing the top of the crease.

She'd almost forgotten about his burned back, about all those who could turn their way at any moment, and about Robbie.

Poor Robbie. She pressed her hand against Jason's chest, and he rolled off to sit beside her, one knee drawn up on which to rest his arm.

She sat up and brushed at her clothes to keep her trembling fingers occupied. "'Tis not the time," she murmured checking her hair at the back of her head, making sure her bun hadn't come loose. "Ye are a doctor, and I be a nurse."

"Yes." He rolled to his feet. "I'd almost forgotten you'd come looking for a doctor."

He offered his hand. She accepted, and he pulled her up, though the sarcasm in his tone confused her.

"Can ye not come and look at Robbie now?"

He shook his head. "I'm sorry." His hand trembled, and he rubbed it over the back of his neck.

"Even if I could manage to examine the wound without…another…episode, I only have one good hand for a surgery that requires precision."

"I can help. And Captain Breen."

"Gracie, I will need two assistants including you, surgeons who could be using their skills on men who can be saved. Send him to Washington. Let a more capable surgeon operate."

She bit her lip and shook her head. "Please, ye have to come."

"Young men die, Mrs. McBride. You can't fix everything."

"Do ye think I do not know that? Two o' me brothers died at Marye's Heights, the cry o' the Irish Brigade on their lips. I could do nothing to stop their lifeblood from seeping into the mud. William died, calling me name while I searched Boston for someone to come and save him. But this is Robbie, and by the saints I will not stand by and do naught."

"There's nothing I can do. When you pushed aside his hair, did you notice the depression above his ear? A piece of the skull has been pushed into the brain. He requires surgery in a hospital. Not here in the middle of a field."

"But ye have skills and knowledge I've seen in no other."

He shook his head. "Removing tiny pieces of skull is difficult surgery. Regardless, even when performed under optimal conditions, there is a sixty-one percent fatality rate. Assuming the patient survives transportation back to Washington. Even then patients often succumb to secondary brain fever and seizures. Survival is minimal at best. I'm sorry, Gracie. I know you care for the young man, but I can't save them all."

She grabbed his bare forearm, her pinky brushing the soft cotton of his rolled shirt sleeve, and held tight. Desperate, she searched his face. "Doctor. Jason. Ye have to try. Please." Tears clogged her throat. "Robbie is yer brother."

Chapter Eighteen

Brother.

The word slammed into his chest with the impact of an artillery blast, except there was no pain. Only icy numbness. He stared at Gracie, then past her shoulder to the wounded. So many wounded lying on the ground, left to die, alone, in pain, and afraid. Among them his brother.

Beyond, rose the pointed mounds of white tents protecting those who could be saved. What gave him the right, what gave any of them the right to play God? And damn God for forcing him, or any of them, into the chaos and destruction of war with limited knowledge and instruments.

A bird darted across, a black streak against the bleakness before him.

He studied the scene with the same intensity he gave an anatomy drawing in a book. His existence at that moment drifted into the surreal, as if he stood apart from the picture before him and could simply turn back the page to give his life the certainty it held before.

Before Gracie.

Before the chaos.

Fingers pressed heavily into the flesh of his forearm. He looked down. Wide brown eyes stared up at him. Her mouth moved, but oddly he heard nothing. Now she was shaking his arm. Pain pulled at the skin and muscle of the burn on his back. With a jerk, he wrenched his arm away.

"But ye have to come."

He heard that, heard the plea in her soft lilting tone.

"Ye be the only one who can save him."

Him?

Ah, yes. Reid. Head wound. He squeezed his eyes tight and rubbed his good hand over his face.

His brother.

Drawing a deep breath, he studied her features. Shadows underscored her tear-filled eyes. Soot and a streak of mud smeared across those intriguing freckles that dusted her skin.

"Chaos, Mrs. McBride. I specifically asked you not to introduce more chaos to my life. Announcing I have a brother is chaos."

"Aye. And 'tis sorry I am to be telling ye this way, but I did not know Robbie would be here. Please, can we not talk o'this later?"

"May I ask how a note inside my old rabbit led you to this revelation?"

She turned for a moment, back toward the wounded, then sighed and raised her chin to meet his gaze.

"'Twas Robbie's uncle Mark be telling me."

"And who is Uncle Mark?"

"Sergeant Baker. Yer tracheotomy patient." She took two steps back, as if she expected him to maintain the distance and take two steps forward.

He would not be so easily manipulated.

"After ye left, Sergeant Baker wanted to thank ye for saving his life. He insisted yer name be Doctor Reid. That ye looked the image of his old friend and brother-in-law, Jonathan Reid."

Gracie shot a quick glance over her shoulder and inched back another step.

A funny ache settled inside his chest. He rubbed at it and frowned trying to assimilate the information. "I will hear it all. Now."

She flinched at the harshness of his tone.

"Jonathan Reid married Sergeant Baker's sister. She was in the family way with Robbie when Jonathan took their son on a trip to Philadelphia. They never returned. That little boy's name was—Jason."

His whole world tilted as his very existence flipped upside down. The pain in his chest turned to ice. He rubbed harder at the spot as his heart pounded erratically beneath his sternum. He gasped for air, panting for each subsequent breath as he tried to think.

Gracie was beside him, holding his hand, rubbing his back, speaking to him as he tried to breathe.

He tried to slow his breathing. Inhale. Calm. Exhale. Calm. Gracie was speaking. Focus. A brother. He had a family? None of this was real.

In that moment, had no idea who he was, how to feel, or what to think. He only knew he couldn't stand idle any longer. He needed to move, to be busy, to concentrate on something that would consume all his attention. Except, he couldn't think what that would be.

"Please, help Robbie."

My name is Jason. Charles is dead.

A brother.

He had a brother.

He looked deep into her eyes. How the hell could he do this? Operate on such a head wound, in a field hospital, with one good arm, and panic that threatened to consume him at any moment. Remorse tugged down the corners of his mouth.

Why did she have to look at him like that, like a bedraggled puppy shivering in the rain?

He sighed. "All right."

Even as he said the words, even as hope lit a sparkle in her eyes, doubt like an eerie fog, seeped through the recesses of his mind, clouding his usual confidence. There was so much about medicine, about the human body, he didn't understand.

"Find some men with a litter and have him transported to the surgery tent. Then shave that area of his head, mindful not to apply any pressure to that depression in his skull."

Perhaps if all the blood was gone he could manage this.

She smiled. "Thank ye, Doctor."

He nodded and watched her hurry off. She might not want him as a man, but as a doctor she gazed up at him as if he were God's own cousin. What if that idolization was all he'd ever have from her? Could he risk breaking that tenuous connection if another nervous attack like the one at Fredericksburg, sent him running, leaving Robbie to bleed on the table?

Gracie had lost so many, her brothers, her husband, that young drummer boy. Even if he performed the surgery, the probability of survival was slim. If Corporal Reid died, if his own brother died, would she blame him? Would he blame himself? Would that glow of adulation in her eyes darken into hate?

She'd certainly hate him if he didn't try. He'd hate himself if he didn't try.

He held out his hands. Visual conformation of what

he already knew. His hands were shaking.

He curled his fingers into fists and went in search of Richards. He found him at the cook tent and sent him off to locate his field pack.

While he was here, he poured a cup of hot coffee. One of the men had been roasting the beans brought down by the Sanitary Commission, and he'd smelled their charred sweetness all morning.

Whether he told himself he needed a cup to steady his hands or to ease the hollowness in his belly, deep down he knew it was an excuse.

Avoidance was not his way. Shame crept up his spine as he swallowed gulps of the hot brew, and glared at anyone who dared look his way.

Richards strode toward him carrying the field pack.

Somewhat fortified, he tossed the cup in the bin of dirty dishes and pulled the trephine kit—which he hoped he didn't need—from the bottom of his pack.

Trephining, if absolutely necessary, was an outdated surgical procedure, but if he couldn't remove the pieces of bone, he'd be forced to try.

With the box tucked under his arm, he strode toward the surgery tent. No point in procrastinating. In an hour he'd be working on his next patient and the fate of young Corporal Reid, his brother, would be left to God.

Gracie paced outside the surgery tent. She turned as he approached and met his gaze. Though she stopped moving, tension radiated from her body.

Neither said a word as she followed him inside. Robbie's stretcher had been placed on a table toward the back. Someone had covered the young corporal with a sheet. Probably Gracie, so he didn't have to look at the blood-soaked uniform.

Robbie's head had been positioned so his face was turned away and the wound was presented up.

Across the tent, Major Andrews looked up from his patient and frowned. Though his disapproval was obvious, he said nothing.

Jason's instruments had been laid out on the same small table he'd been using all day. He opened the trephine kit and set what he might need beside the scalpels and forceps.

He exhaled a shaky breath and swallowed. He wiped his hands on a square of linen and nodded to Breen, who came to stand on his left side.

With the area shaved clear, two separate wounds were revealed. A long furrow cut across the scalp from an inch above the temple, along the side of the head. Most likely a minié ball, and the source of all the blood.

His pulse thrummed in his ears. He drew a deep breath and exhaled slowly. Focus.

The second wound, the depressed portion of the skull, appeared to be the result of some impact to the head. Irregular in shape. Approximately one inch at the widest point. If he were to speculate, he would presume the first injury caused a fall onto a rock, or judging by the triangular shape, perhaps the corner of his own rifle stock.

Leaning close, he used his fingers to separate the skin of the first. Blood leaked from the wound. The familiar tightness pulled at the muscles across his chest.

Inhale. Exhale. Breathe.

Gracie's hand moved in with sponges to absorb the blood.

The skull appeared intact. No fractures here. Breen

could stitch it closed later.

He shifted his attention to the second wound, the depression above the ear. Surprisingly, the impact of the injury hadn't broken the skin. He lightly brushed his finger around the edges of the irregular shape.

Hoping for the best, he accepted the scalpel Gracie passed him. Using his lightest pressure, he sliced through the skin, making an X which extended beyond the perimeter of the indentation.

Silent in her efficiency, Gracie stood poised with her sponges as Breen reached over and folded back the triangular flaps of skin.

Blood spread out across the cobblestones. A man lay with his head split open.

His heart pounded. Each breath grew more shallow.

A hand squeezed his arm. He glanced down at the pressure and met Gracie's eyes—wide, brown, and trusting. She trusted him to do what needed to be done.

She was emotionally vested in the young corporal, yet she stood calm and composed, not crying or wringing her hands. Could he do no less?

Focus. He drew a deep breath and released it in a long sigh.

Gracie passed him the forceps. "Think of something else," she whispered.

He began lightly picking detached bone splinters from the edges of the depression.

"I didn't understand the humor." So far there was no evidence the fragments had penetrated the dura mater.

"What?"

Tiny, uneven shards of bone had left a jagged edge

around the hole where the piece of skull had been. "Rongeur."

Gracie shook her head.

"Hey's saw," Breen whispered.

Gracie's hand hovered for a moment over two instruments about the size of a toothbrush.

Charles grabbed the smaller one.

"Why is it deemed funny for a man to run back into enemy fire to retrieve something of so little value."

"Are ye speaking o' the joke ye told me?"

"Correct." He smoothed off the jagged edges as Breen cleaned the area with a bone brush.

"'Twas funny because he's Irish."

Along the thin fracture line, a small piece of bone pushed down below the edge of the skull but hadn't broken off completely, so it was impossible to lift out.

He'd hoped this wouldn't be necessary. He'd only done this procedure once and that had been on a cadaver. He raised his head and blew out a sigh.

Breen met his gaze. Understanding filled his brown eyes. He gave a slight nod.

"Trephine."

Either Gracie knew which instrument it was, or she'd made an educated guess, but she silently passed him the T-shaped instrument, pressing the wooden handle against his open palm.

Before beginning, he adjusted the perforator pin, lowering it from the shaft to slightly below the circle of teeth at the bottom of the drum-like cutting head, then locked it in place with a side screw.

Holding the trephine perpendicular to the skull, he centered the pin over the area of bone he needed to remove. Turning the handle, he rotated the cutting head until he'd made a circular groove which stopped short of reaching the membrane which protected the brain. He retracted the pin up into the shaft.

As he set the trephine on the table, Breen brushed away the fine bone dust.

"Elevator."

Gracie searched the table then passed him the thin instrument with the ebony handle.

"Hmm. So an Irishman running through Confederate lines to retrieve his flask is humorous." He slid the elevator between the brain membrane and the piece of bone, then lifted it high enough to grab with the forceps.

Breen chuckled. "That is funny."

"In Gaelic, whiskey is called *uisce beatha,* the water of life. 'Tis a source o'pride. The whiskey we make, and a man's ability to drink it."

Whether the joke was humorous or not, thinking of it had returned his breathing and heartbeat to normal. "Lenticular."

Gracie passed him the slim knife, smooth on the bottom and rough on top. He slipped it between the brain membrane and skull and followed the rim of the hole to even out any rough areas along the underside.

The dura mater showed no bulging or other evidence of hematoma, but evidence of a slow bleed could present itself later. He decided to wrap it well and let the surgeons in Washington either drain it or cover the area with a wax plug or lead plate.

"Let's stitch the first wound and wrap this up with a good thick bandage." Breen threaded the needle and passed it to Jason.

Gracie hovered until Jason stepped away from the

table to wash off his hands.

Without a word she stepped close and slid her arms around his waist, her cheek pressed against his chest, just above his apron. She hugged him tight, but before he thought to wrap his arms around her, she stepped back and looked up, meeting his gaze. "He will be all right now?"

Jason gave his fingers a quick shake and dried his hands on the closest towel.

He hated the expectation in her eyes. Even as the drummer boy lay dying, she'd claimed there was always hope. He could repeat the grim statistics for the survival from a wound like this, but maybe he'd spent too much time with Gracie and her enthusiasm for life, or perhaps it was because this young man, tall and lanky with brown hair and blue eyes was his brother, and he needed that bit of hope for himself, but he shrugged his shoulders and said, "Maybe."

****

Rain pelted down in earnest that evening, thudding against the canvas, washing through the trees.

Gracie had spent as much time as possible that afternoon near Robbie, whispering words of encouragement, holding his hand. Doctor Ellard—it was hard to think of him as Jason Reid—had come by a couple of times to check on him, but he hadn't said much.

Now, kettles in hand, she darted through the rain, from tent to tent, serving beef tea and farina to the men well enough to eat. Once her kettles were empty, she tugged her hat low and dashed toward the cook tent for refills.

"Gracie!"

She skidded to a stop and whirled toward the voice. Captain Breen slogged toward her through the mud. Rain dripped from the brim of his hat and slid shiny and black down his rubberized poncho.

"Captain Ellard asked me to find you."

"Is something wrong?"

He glanced down and smiled sheepishly. "Well, he's been hiding it, but he's been in pain all day."

A rush of guilt seared her cheeks. She'd been so caught up in her worry for Robbie, so afraid he'd pass away alone like Gilbert, she'd hadn't given a thought the burn on Doc—Jason's shoulder. No wonder he'd been so quiet.

"I gave him a bottle of medicinal whiskey, thinking he'd drink in moderation, but he hasn't eaten all day. And well, just so you understand he might be a little…"

"Aye, I understand."

"I wanted to change the bandage, put on some more of that honey you left, but he insists that you do it." He reached for the kettles. "I'll take these back for you."

"Thank ye, but I've a few more tents to feed. I'll be by with something for ye both to eat."

"Don't worry about me. I'm going back on duty. The captain is in our tent. Major Andrews ordered him to get some sleep."

"And where is yer tent?"

"Over in the same spot as last night. Your jar of honey is there and a fresh pile of bandages."

He veered off toward the surgery tent, and she continued slip-sliding through the mud toward the cook tent.

****

"I don't know if you are aware, but I have been writing a treatise on Pyemia and Surgical Fevers."

Doctor Ellard lay on his stomach atop his blankets, raised up on his elbows, writing in a notebook open on the blanket in front of him. His shirt and bandage were off, leaving the burn and his back exposed to the air.

Gracie sat on the canvas cloth spread between and under the two bedrolls inside the small Sibley tent. She set the small pot of farina on his haversack and pulled a stack of crackers wrapped in a clean handkerchief from her pocket.

"No. I did not know that." She pulled off her dripping hat and set it on the ground beside her.

"And what are your thoughts on laudable pus?"

"William said 'twas a good thing, a sign the wound be healing."

"I asked for your thoughts Mrs. McBride. Surely you have made observations, formed opinions of you own, rather than spout parroted versions of your husband's."

She shifted uncertainly and sat back on her heels.

"I do not know. Some patients get better and some do not."

The bottle of whiskey Captain Breen had spoken of lay on its side, securely corked and one-third gone.

Doctor-Jason shot a glance over his shoulder. "I can feel your censorious frown. No. I am not drunk." He turned back to his notebook and his furious scribbling. "Well, maybe a little. I have the right to be. My damn back hurts."

A gust of wind fluttered the untied tent flaps, carrying with it a mist of rain. She swiped the moisture from her cheek. Jason shivered.

"I've brought ye food if ye're hungry."

"Later. What I need you to do is look at the burn now and each evening to come. Take daily notes on the visual condition of the burn, and I will document my symptoms."

He passed her his notebook and pencil.

"I tried viewing it through the use of multiple mirrors but failed to get a look accurate enough to document."

She rose up on her knees and leaned close. "The size o' the burn 'tis the same. The skin around the edge red. Redder closer to the burn."

"Write. How wide is the area? Has the redness spread?"

Hastily she drew a rough sketch and tried to measure using the first joint of her thumb as an approximation of an inch.

"How do the blisters appear? Are there early signs of laudable pus?"

"I cannot say, for I did not count and measure the blisters last night."

"Come now Mrs. McBride, I sense reluctance on your part. Yet, here I present an opportunity to use another aspect of your nursing skills. It is what you want, is it not?"

"'Tis a clear film over the area, like water. Some o' the blisters be larger and maybe there be a few more smaller."

"Count and measure, Mrs. McBride. Document the facts." He reached out and grabbed the bottle by the neck and pulled out the cork. Rolling part way onto one arm, he tipped the bottle to his lips and downed a hefty swallow before slapping down the cork.

"You never gave me your thoughts on laudable pus."

Seventeen tiny blisters. She jotted them down. "Aye, I did. Ye just refuse to accept me answer." She tossed the book on the ground in front of him.

"Now why did ye ask for me? Captain Breen could o' done this and bandaged yer wound, too."

"Because Jason Reid is wounded, and he wants to feel the tender ministrations of Nurse McBride for himself. He wants you to hold his hand and whisper to him in the dark. Lay your hand against his brow and take away the pain."

"Doctor Ellard, I be—"

"Charles Ellard is dead. You know that. You read the note. There is only Jason Reid, and he is not a doctor."

"Ye are drunk, doctor."

"Not a doctor. Just a man."

"Then why are ye writing a paper on pyemia and surgical fevers?"

"Now that, my sweet Gracie is a con-dum-drum, cun-drum-dum. A real goddamn puzzle."

Ignoring him, she reached for the jar of honey Breen had left for her. Without telling him what she was going to do, she scooped some out with a square of linen and lay it over the burn.

"If ye can sit up, I can be wrapping this for ye."

He pushed up onto all fours, wavered for a moment, then sat back on his heels.

"Why are you so anxious to leave? I haven't even gotten a kiss."

"Ye are drunk. I be having patients to see to. And I want to sit with Robbie, in case he wakes."

Folding two linen squares she placed them on top of the honey-soaked pad.

"My brother, Robbie Reid. Robbie Reid is my brother. But you know that. Chaos, Mrs. McBride."

Holding the pad in place she began unrolling an eight-yard bandage around his back and over his shoulder.

"Robbie is in my paper. Or rather his gunshot wound. Minimal laudable pus. Wound healed quickly."

When the length ran out, she picked up another.

"His bed near the door, away from dysentery and gangrene. Lots of fresh air. Even in winter."

"'Tis why ye put Sergeant Baker in that bed."

"Doctor Middleton Goldsmith."

Gracie tied off the end of the bandage. "Who?"

"He wrote a report. Gangrene is caused by miasma on putrid flesh. Treat with bromine or iodine."

"I must be going." She wiped her hands on her apron.

"Bromine and iodine. Rhymes better than mercy and Gracie."

She reached out and snatched the bottle with one hand as she shoved the bowl of farina at him with the other. "Ye best eat something. And no more whiskey."

Without room to stand, she made a less than graceful exit backing out of the tent. Rising, she let the canvas flap fall back in place.

"Gracie, you didn't give me my kiss."

Whirling on her heels she hurried away. Rain splashed down on her head, but she kept walking, for if she returned for her hat, she might never leave that tent.

Chapter Nineteen

"The ambulances will be moving the wounded today." Gracie softly spoke the words to Robbie in the dark gray of early morning. She sat on the ground between his pallet and the next, keeping vigil, holding his hand, being certain he'd not die alone in the dark.

"Ye'll be back at Armory Square in no time, with me and yer uncle Mark. 'Twill be like going home. Won't that be fine. And I've some grand news to share with ye, once ye wake and I can tell ye to yer face."

She gave his hand a squeeze and tucked a strand of hair behind her ear.

A light pressure brushed over her thumb.

She stilled then stared at her hand clasped with his, even though it was merely a silhouette in the dark.

"Robbie?" She scooted closer and rested her other hand on his chest. "Robbie lad, can ye hear me?"

The pressure against her hand grew a little stronger.

"Oh Sweet Mary, thank ye. Thank ye." She squeezed back and gave his chest a quick pat. "Ye're going to be fine, Robbie Reid. Ye're going to be fine."

Relieved, she drew her knees up and rested her head on her arm. When she woke, she found herself slumped against Robbie's pallet. The rain had stopped, and sunlight glistened off the world outside the tent.

She shrugged her shoulders and gave her neck a

quick roll in each direction to ease the kinked muscles. She pushed to her knees and arched her lower back.

She glanced at Robbie. His eyes were open and focused on her. "Top o' the morning to ye Robbie Reid. And how are ye this fine day."

A small smile tugged at the corner of his mouth.

"Would ye like me to fetch ye something to drink?"

He replied with a slow blink of his eyes.

She pushed to her feet. "Ye rest. I'll be back. Ye'll feel better with a bit o' something in yer stomach."

Stepping carefully around the wounded who still slept, she slipped outside and started toward the cook tent. As she rounded the last row of hospital tents, she slammed into Doctor Ellard.

Hot coffee spilled down the bodice of her dress. She swiped at the warm damp fabric. He probably expected her to tell him to look where he was going, but she was too happy. She met his gaze and grinned.

He scowled.

Her smile broadened. "He's awake." Rising onto her tip toes, she put her hand on his shoulder and kissed his cheek. "Thank ye, doctor."

He blinked. His brow furrowed.

She took the tin ware mug from his unresisting fingers. "I'll get ye another cup."

"Wait. Gracie."

She searched his face expectantly, too happy over Robbie's improvement to wonder at the sudden tension in his voice.

He glanced at the sky for a moment then met her gaze. "Why did you kiss me?"

"'Tis because Robbie is awake. Ye saved him."

"And that's why you kissed me?"

"Aye." She smiled. "'Tis a fine clear morning, and Robbie be awake."

"I removed the broken pieces of skull. I have not saved him. There is still the risk of inflammation of the dura mater and a hemorrhage of the brain."

"Ye said as much yesterday. But—"

"I do not want you to kiss me out of gratitude for my surgical skills. I want you to kiss me because you want me."

He ran his hand around the back of his neck then grabbed her shoulders, his clear blue eyes earnestly searching her face.

"You have made it clear from the first, that I respect the part of you that is a nurse. You know I do. You are also aware of my attraction for you.

"However, just as you have two sides, so also do I.

"I appreciate the respect you give me as a physician. I know you crave physical intimacy, but I am not William McBride. I am Jason Reid.

"You have been so busy trying to make me into William that you have no idea of the man I am outside of the hospital. Whatever future you envision between us is not the same one I see.

"Thank you for seeing me through my nervous attacks, for giving me a family, my identity, but this has to end. I wish you well and hope you find the happiness you found with your William."

He leaned close. Slowly his lips pressed to hers. There was none of the usual harshness, the invasion of his tongue, his desperation to claim her. Instead the light pressure of his kiss, the gentle nip of first her bottom lip and then her top, held a sadness she hadn't expected from him.

She reached her hands around his waist, up his back, intending to pull him close and never let go. But he was right. Though she craved intimacy, did it mean she craved him?

His hands slid down her arms and cupped her elbows. Slowly he pulled back. His gaze lingered for a moment, then he turned and walked away. She watched his back until he disappeared behind a tent and was gone.

****

He wove his way between several tents, unaware of any particular destination.

He needed to quit drinking at night. Breen kept pushing those damned Dover's powders, but he didn't want to start taking opiates. Alcohol was better for the pain. Except he couldn't remember half of what happened when he drank. He supposed he had a low tolerance for whiskey. An Irishman he was not. Gracie had come to his tent last night. He remembered that. And laudable pus. Had he actually tried to charm her with a discussion on laudable pus? What the hell was wrong with him?

And he remembered begging her for a kiss.

That specific memory this morning was like a dousing of ice water. Pathetic. That's what he was. Groveling for her affection the same way he'd once groveled for the friendship of the boys at school.

Well he had some pride, and while she might embrace the doctor side of him, she had no idea of who he was as a man. Grandfather was right. They would never suit. Miss Adelaide Emmerson would be the perfect match, someone demure and quiet, who never challenged him. Someone like his mother.

He stopped. Except Julia Harrison Ellard was not his mother. Nothing he knew of his life, of who he was, was real.

My name is Jason
Charles is dead.
My name is Jason.

He had an uncle at the hospital in Washington. Uncle Mark. An uncle and a brother. Robbie. A brother. A real brother.

God, please let the kid make it.

"Captain."

He turned. Major Andrews walked toward him, his large boots slapping against the mud and wet grass.

"Everything all right?"

"Thinking," Jason replied automatically. The response had become his pat answer when he was caught staring into space.

"Good. Well, orders came to start moving the wounded toward the pontoon bridges. Problem is, with all this rain the roads are a mess, which means rough going for these poor boys. River's running high and breaking up the pontoon bridges. It's going to take a while to get everyone across the Rappahannock and on up to Aquia Creek and then to the hospitals in Washington.

"I'm sending you with the wounded and most of the supplies from the brigade wagons. I'll stay here with Captain Breen and follow once we're done. My trick knee is telling me we're in for some more rain. God speed, Captain."

He saluted and spent the morning readying the patients for transport. Using extra blankets, he rolled them and tucked them around Robbie's head and neck to hopefully keep him as still as possible on the journey.

He grabbed a cup of coffee as the ambulances rolled toward the fords. The rest of his day was spent riding back and forth, up and down the ambulance train, helping where he could, rebandaging wounds and stitching wounds that tore open. The cries and moans of the men who endured the harsh jerks and jolts of ambulance travel were not sounds he'd soon forget.

A day and a half in the saddle, and they finally reached the division hospitals on Potomac Creek just before the skies opened up to send more rain pouring down.

Another day of travel on the steamboat and he was back at Armory Square Hospital. He and a good portion of the severely wounded—and Robbie.

He ordered Micah and Harvey to clean up young Reid—it was hard to think of him as his brother—and assign him a bed near the side door next to Sergeant Baker.

Since all his belongings were at Falmouth, he washed at the sink in the bathing room and stopped back at Corporal Reid's bed to make a few notes on his patient card.

From the next bed came a raspy gasp.

"By God, it is you."

He dropped into the chair between the beds. Such a strange sensation, to look at this man, shorter and broader, with light hair, brown eyes, and bandaged throat, and know that as he'd operated, he'd been saving the life of his uncle Mark.

"I begun to think the lady nurse was right and it

was the fever." He swallowed and cleared his throat. "You're the spittin' image of Jonathan. We all thought you was dead. But you're his boy ain't ya? You're Jason."

Jason. He closed his eyes absorbing the sound of his name on someone else's tongue, knowing somehow it felt right.

"The orderlies, the other patients, they call ya Doctor Ellard. A doctor. Don't that beat all. Ya always was a smart little duffer."

A hand landed on Jason's knee and gave it a little squeeze. He opened his eyes. This man was really his uncle. Uncle Mark.

"But why a different name, boy? What happened to ya. What happened to your pa?"

A lump rose in the back of Jason's throat. Unable to find words, he shrugged and shook his head.

"And my nephew, Robbie there. You two worked together and didn't even know you was brothers. Ain't it somethin' the way life works out? Maybe after the war—ya could visit. See your ma. Got a real need for doctors where we live."

Jason looked up as footsteps approached. An orderly he didn't know walked up.

"Excuse me, sir, but Major Bliss wants to see you right away."

Jason nodded and stood. He met the gaze of his uncle Mark and inclined his head. So many thoughts tumbled around in his mind he had no idea what to say.

Instead he followed the young orderly up the aisle.

****

Major Bliss met him in the front office where he stood talking to an older man with black walking stick.

Nausea rolled in Jason's stomach, sending an acidic burn up the back of his throat. It was too soon to deal with his grandfather. He had no idea what to say or think. Hell, he had no idea how he even felt about the man.

"Good afternoon, sir."

His grandfather stepped forward and looked him up and down. "Heard you were wounded. Except for that unkempt beard and your scruffy clothes, you look fine."

"I assure you, sir, I have been injured." And suddenly it was all too much, the hunger, exhaustion, emotional upheaval, and the pain across his shoulder. He longed for a hot bath, a big bowl of soup with some crackers that weren't hard tack, a nice soft bed, and clean sheets.

"Sit down, boy. You look like you're about to swoon."

In two footsteps and two taps of his grandfather's cane, Jason found himself shoved into the nearest chair.

He leaned forward and rested his head in his hands. "I'm fine, sir. Just a little tired."

"Nonsense. You're ill. My cab is out front. You shall recuperate in my hotel room."

Lacking the energy to argue, Jason allowed his grandfather to usher him into the waiting carriage and silently rode through the streets to the National Hotel.

At the front desk, Foster Harrison took charge again, ordering a hot bath sent up to the room with a tureen of chicken soup and two dozen soda crackers.

All his life his grandfather had taken care of him. Grandfather had not been an affectionate man, but he had loved Jason in his own gruff way.

****

Jason slowly came awake. His face buried in a pile of soft pillows, his bladder demanded he leave the comfort of the bed and relieve the aching pressure.

The rustle of a newspaper caught his attention. With a groan he shoved the pillow aside and raised his head. His grandfather sat in a chair near the window, immaculately dressed as usual in his gray morning coat and charcoal trousers.

The drapes had been pulled closed, darkening the room except for a narrow slice of sunlight which cut a golden line across the carpet.

"I'd begun to think you planned to laze away the entire day."

"What time is it?"

"Just past ten. You slept through the entire evening and night. I was about to poke you to see if you were still alive."

He folded his paper and placed it on a small pie crust table. Cane in hand he pushed to standing.

"There is a clean nightshirt and robe at the end of the bed. Fresh water in the pitcher and at the end of the hall is the water closet."

His grandfather made his way to the door, his cane silent across the carpet. I am going to step out and leave you to your ablutions. Please be presentable when I return. God knows what the servants thought when they came to collect the bath last night. You sprawled in all your glory across the bed."

He opened the door, still muttering, "Shameful. Appalling."

The door closed with a soft click.

Jason groaned and tossed back the covers. He hadn't even heard the servants come into the room. Or his grandfather, for that matter. The thought of his horrified expression upon seeing his grandson in the nude brought a smile to his face as he pulled on the night shirt and tied closed the silk robe.

He'd removed the bandage when he'd bathed. He wondered what the burn looked like today. For a moment he longed for Gracie to document the healing and rewrap his burn with her honey.

When he returned to the room, he searched for his clothes, but they were nowhere to be found. No doubt his grandfather had sent them to be cleaned. His stomach rumbled, but there was no food either. Had he eaten all that soup last night?

He walked to the window and pushed back the drapes. On the street and sidewalk below, people and carriages hurried to and fro. Across the road a train pulled away in a huff of steam from the Pennsylvania Depot. Already exhausted, he sat in the chair and picked up the newspaper. A headline of the Union defeat at Chancellorsville and a subsequent article filled most of the front page.

The door opened. His grandfather entered, followed by a bell boy pushing a cart of food. He transferred the tray to a table and pushed the cart back to the door.

Jason rose, lured by the aroma of fresh coffee.

"Eat." Grandfather commanded once the bell boy had left. "I could see every rib and bone in your spine last night."

Coffee, scrambled eggs, thick slices of bread, bacon, and sausage. Jason scooped eggs between two pieces of bread and took a large bite. He sighed. Heaven.

He ate one sandwich and piled on eggs and sausage for another.

His grandfather tracked each movement from across the room.

"Why are you here?" Jason asked taking a bite.

Grandfather lowered himself into the chair by the window. "I received word you had been wounded."

How had he gotten the news so fast? Was he friends with every general in the Union Army?

"You needn't have rushed to my side. I will be fine."

"No grandson of mine is going to recuperate in one of those death houses." He gave his cane a harsh thud against the carpet.

Jason swallowed another mouthful of sandwich. "Thank you for your faith in my ability to have saved one or two of the men I treated during my tenure at Armory Square."

"I do not care for your disrespectful attitude. Was a similar display of insolence the cause of that assault charge and your subsequent demotion?"

"No, Grandfather, I was quite respectful, right until the moment I punched the sanctimonious sonofabitch lieutenant colonel in the face."

"Enough!" His grandfather slammed down the end of his cane so hard Jason wouldn't have been surprised to see it go straight through the floor.

"I will allow some latitude because of the pain you must be in from that burn I saw. However." He raised his walking stick and leveled it in Jason's direction. "I will not tolerate such vulgar language. The army has no doubt corrupted you. I thought I'd raised my grandson to be a gentleman."

Jason rubbed a hand over his face, surprised to feel his fingers trembling. This tumult of emotion was wreaking havoc with his sanity.

"I apologize, sir. That was uncalled for." He poured a cup of coffee. "Would you like a cup?"

Mollified, his grandfather's ruddy complexion faded. "Yes, please. Cream no sugar."

"I remember." Jason rose and passed his grandfather the cup and saucer. Returning to his seat, he poured a cup for himself, black, and took a fortifying swallow.

"Am I your grandson?"

"Excuse me?"

"Am I your grandson?"

"What a ridiculous question. Of course you're my grandson."

Jason swallowed down the rest of the coffee in his cup and moved to sit on the side of the bed, closer to his grandfather.

"I ask because there was a note inside the ear of my old rabbit."

"A note? What note?"

"A note, inside the head, where the ear had been mended, written in a child's hand. It said, 'My name is Jason. Charles is dead. I wish I was too.' "

His grandfather's face washed of all color turning almost sickly gray. Cup and saucer clattering, they nearly fell to the floor before he managed to set them on the small table beside the newspaper.

Jason reached a hand toward his grandfather, afraid he was about to have a heart seizure.

"I used to fear this day would come. That someone would claim you as theirs and take you away. But so many years have passed, only on rare occasions do I ever recall that you are not my blood." His trembling hands grasped the silver head of his walking stick as if it were a life line.

"I did not know your name was Jason. You never talked. You were crying when Cook found you hiding in the bushes in the back garden.

"A Typhus outbreak was sweeping the city. My beautiful Julia was dying, and there was nothing I could do. Would that God had taken me and spared her, but as with the passing of her mother, it was not to be. Peter had already succumbed to the disease and their little boy Charles.

"Julia called for her son daily, but there was nothing I could do except pray for a miracle. God granted it to me when Mrs. White found you dirty and crying, only an alphabet book in your coat pocket, and clutching that damned rabbit.

"I could not leave Julia's side and sent Danvers to the police station to report you'd been found. He returned saying he'd been told the city was full of new orphans because of the sickness and to take me to the closest foundling home that had room.

"Cook fed and bathed you and dressed you in Charles' clothes then brought you to me in Julia's room. Julia saw you and thought you were her little boy. I could not believe the miracle when she rallied. I brought you to her daily, and though for a time she seemed to grow stronger, in the end she passed away.

"By that time I had begun calling you Charles and since you said nothing, I continued. Eventually, I began to think of you as my grandson. You could read and write and were tall enough to fit into Charles' clothes.

But Charles was seven when he died and had lost some of his baby's teeth. But you were younger and did not lose yours until you reached Charles' age of ten.

"I could not send you to school until 'Charles' was twelve, but people thought me overprotective of a sickly child and you were tall and so intelligent you could easily pass for twelve, when you could not have been more than nine."

"I'm not thirty-two?"

His grandfather shook his head. "Perhaps no more than twenty-nine."

Chaos, Mrs. McBride. I specifically asked you not to introduce more chaos to my life.

God, he was only twenty-nine? His life seemed to be spinning out of control.

He slipped to the floor and drew his knees up, draping his forearms on top. "There is a patient at the hospital. He says I look just like my father, his brother-in-law, Jonathan Reid. The man went missing in Philadelphia in thirty-seven with his little boy, Jason."

His grandfather pulled a handkerchief from his pocket and dabbed his rheumy eyes. "What are you going to do?"

Jason shook his head. "I don't know. I don't know who I am. I don't know where I came from or how old I am. But the one thing I knew for certain was that I am a doctor. Now, I'm not even that. My diplomas, my achievement awards belong to Charles Ellard, not Jason Reid."

"I didn't know. You have to believe me." He reached out his hand, his joints swollen with arthritis, his blue veins visible beneath his thin white skin.

Jason reached out and wrapped his fingers around

his grandfather's cold hand. "I believe you."

Tears spilled from his grandfather's faded gray eyes and slid down his papery cheeks. "In my heart you are my grandson. You are my world. I love you. Please, don't leave me."

Chapter Twenty

Fresh paint and new wood filled her senses as she stepped through the door of the new dormitory.

"This is so much more pleasant," Sister Mary said as she showed Gracie to her new room. "Not that I wasn't thankful for our previous accommodations, but the odors at times were indeed difficult to bear. Here we can have our privacy, a chance to chat with other nurses, to support and encourage one another."

Sister Mary moved to the side, and Gracie stepped into her new room.

"There is even a bathing room at the end of the hall. No more sponge baths behind a curtain in a ward full of men. I shall leave you to get settled."

Gracie hadn't thought she would like living away from the ward, but Sister Mary was right, privacy was a nice thing. And a real bath too. She couldn't wait. All of Gracie's belongings had been brought over and aside from solid walls replacing her curtain partition; her space was the same as it had been before. Even her small rag rug lay beside her bed.

She unbuttoned her coat and hung it on a peg behind the door. The light chatter of female voices drifted from down the hall and the lilt of feminine laughter sang out. They'd always had to be so quiet in the wards, so as not to disturb the patients. To now have this little bit of freedom to be themselves would be refreshing.

Her small bedside table with her picture of William was where it had been. She suspected Sister Mary's hand in arranging the room, rather than one of the orderlies.

Her biggest regret was praying to the Father in Heaven that she not conceive a child right away. Her place by William's side assisting him in his medical practice had come to define the woman she'd become. She hadn't wanted to exchange that new found independence for child bearing and motherhood. At least not right away. Naively, she believed there would be plenty of time to start a family.

Now she would never hold William's child close and sing old Irish ballads in the night.

Doctor Ellard's hat box sat in the corner of the new room. She'd thought of him as Doctor Ellard for so long, it was hard to remember his name was Jason Reid. She couldn't imagine how hard this had been for him.

"Chaos, Mrs. McBride."

He'd asked her to call him Jason, as if subconsciously part of him had known all along who he was. As though Charles was merely a façade, controlled and stilted, protecting the vulnerable core that was Jason, the scared little boy who'd written that note and sealed it safely inside the rabbit.

On top of the box was a second parcel wrapped in brown paper. She stepped over and picked it up. It was addressed to her. A frown tugged at her brow as she stared at the postmark and tried to recall who she knew from New York City.

Lumpy and oblong, about six inches wide and eighteen inches long…Drumsticks!

Curse of God on you! Gracie ground her teeth together to keep from screaming. Her frustrated outcry would likely be heard by all through the thin board walls of the new dormitory.

Tears stung her eyes. The dear, sweet lad's drumsticks! How dare that woman send them back!

If Gilbert had been her little boy she would have treasured the drumsticks he'd been so proud of. Cared enough to come to him before he passed away. Cared enough to come and take his body home.

She lowered herself onto her bed and tugged off the string. Unwrapping the brown paper revealed several letters—the very letters she'd written for Gilbert to his mother—wrapped around the lengths of wood. Sweet Mary, Jesus, and Joseph, she wanted to scratch the woman's face off.

She placed the drum sticks on her pillow and unfolded the first letter.

My Dear Mrs. McBride,

I want to say thank you, on behalf of all the families with loved ones fighting in this terrible rebellion, for the care and comfort you give to all our wounded boys.

She glanced at the return address on the back flap of the brown paper wrapping. *Mrs. Lydia Thomas.*

Dread, like a lump of raw bread dough, landed in her stomach solid and heavy.

And thank you for taking care of dear little Gilbert Franklin. He and his mother lived here in my boarding house for nigh onto a year before she passed. I had always wondered what became of Gilbert and suspected he would run away rather than remain in the orphanage. He was a child who always loved an adventure, though I never imagined he would have run to war. Perhaps he wanted to make his mother proud.

The bread dough in her stomach swelled, and she gulped down the wave of nausea that rose up the back of her throat. Hot tears trailed down her cheeks and traced her jawline.

I am returning his drumsticks as you seem to be a woman who will cherish them as much as his mother would have. Maybe you will see them and think of him every now and again.

Sincerely,

Mrs. Lydia Thomas

Gracie grabbed her pillow, hugging tight, the letters in one hand Gilbert's drum sticks in the other. She let the tears fall and muffled her sobs against the feather stuffed bolster.

She cried. For her own selfishness, denying William the children he wanted, the sweet babies she would never hold in her arms. For wronging a woman who had no doubt loved her little boy with all her heart. She cried for Gilbert, sending letters to a mother he no longer had, dying alone in the dark with no one to hold his hand.

Except Doctor Ellard—Jason—had been there, working the puzzle in the night.

What had he said? *Come now, Mrs. McBride you can't cry over all of them.*

Maybe he hadn't cried, but he did care. He just refused to show it.

He'd sat up with Sergeant Baker also, again working the puzzles without a word to anyone, even when he'd berated her for doing the same.

The man who worked puzzles while keeping vigil

beside a dying drummer boy. A man who kept a stuffed rabbit from childhood. A man who had no friends, yet was so desperate to be liked, he told the most horrible jokes.

And in her mind, she'd always thought of him as Doctor Ellard, always called him Doctor Ellard. Had she ever called him Charles?

He was right. She'd never seen him as a man. Knew nothing about him aside from his medical knowledge and his skill as a surgeon.

Her gaze fell on the brown leather hat box filled with toys and books. Curious, she lifted the box from the corner and placed it on the bed. As she sat down beside it, the mattress dipped, and the box tipped against her hip.

She flipped up the clasps and opened the lid. Taking a breath, she peered into his childhood.

Two books took up half the space. Placed on top was a tin soldier holding a guidon. He sat astride a black horse which was mounted on a wheeled platform. Scattered throughout the box were hand-carved spelling blocks, their yellow and blue paint chipped in several places, exposing the wood. Mixed among the alphabet letters were wooden animals, a lion, dog, horse, bear, and tiger. Again the paint worn away from tiny hands wrapped around them in play. From among the animals, she lifted out a weighted leather bag and loosened the gathered top. Marbles. She poured a few into her cupped palm. Each one pristine, without a chip or scratch to mar the clay.

A sense of loneliness engulfed her as she returned the marbles to the bag and tugged the drawstring tight. The animals were worn, but she sensed solitary play.

Had he no friends with whom to share his games, to roll hoops, or build forts?

She'd never known what it was like to grow up alone. She'd always had brothers and sisters to argue with and tease.

"I used to wonder what it would have been like not to be alone, to grow up with parents, and maybe brothers and sisters."

An orphan living in a large empty house with nothing but the echo of a ticking clock. While his grandfather worked in his study, scared Jason Reid crying for his mother, wishing he was dead, alone in his large bedroom, empty except for his books. No wonder he had no idea how to make friends or woo a lady.

And those jokes. Sweet Mary, where had he gotten the notion? A smile tugged at the corner of her mouth. Instead of annoying, the thought of him perusing a volume of humorous anecdotes and choosing just the right one to tell her next, somehow shifted into something sweet and endearing.

Two books lay stacked in the bottom. On top, *The Paragon of Alphabets.* She lifted it out to read the title of the second. *The Life and Strange Surprizing Adventures of Robinson Crusoe.* A children's book and the novel of a lonely man on a deserted island.

She turned to the fly-leaf of Robinson Crusoe.

21 October, 1840
Happy Birthday Grandson #10
Many happy returns.

October twenty-first would see Charles turning thirty-three this fall. Could Sergeant Baker have been mistaken in his belief that his nephew Jason would be no older than thirty?

She set the book aside and opened the alphabet book, the pages warped as though the book had once been wet. On a random page the words, *Tabitha Timid*. A young girl in a pink dress stood at the edge of a bridge, afraid to cross. Another page showed *Wandering Willy*, his walking stick in one hand, his bundle of clothes in the other.

Gracie turned to the beginning of the book.

25 December, 1836

Happy Christmas, my Sweet Boy.

All my love,

Mother

She did some quick calculations, pressing her thumb to the pad of each finger as she counted. Charles would have been six. Jason would have been around three. Was this the mother whose voice he heard in his head?

She returned his possessions to the box. He'd kept the rabbit all these years. Had the toy been his best friend?

He was right, she hadn't known the man, but she should have. He'd been right here all along.

****

She headed to the ward to find him, officially not on duty until tomorrow morning. She hadn't seen him since the field hospital, but she'd returned with the Sanitary Commission a day behind the evacuation of the wounded.

While she had no idea where he was staying, she assumed he'd be by to check on Robbie and maybe talk to his uncle.

Sitting in a chair beside Robbie, Sergeant Baker looked much better than the last time she'd seen him.

"And how is Robbie this morning?"

"He was awake for a while. Had some beef tea and his bed changed. The doctor, young Jason came by to check on him."

"And what did he say?"

"Nothing much. Made some notes on a card and muttered something about a paper." The sergeant frowned. "Not much of a talker, is he?"

"No, 'tis very focused on his patients."

"Reckon he's more sociable when he ain't working."

Gracie almost said no, then asked instead. "Do ye know where he's staying? I've something to discuss with him."

"Said he was going back to the National. He was looking a bit peaked."

"Thank ye," she said and hurried down the aisle.

Tom Halleck jumped up from his seat behind the table. "Mrs. McBride. It's good to have you back."

"Aye, I've had enough o' battlefield nursing to last me a lifetime. Ye can look for me on the ward tomorrow, but first can ye tell me how to get to the National?"

****

Life didn't give out too many second chances. She'd be a fool to let this one slip away.

She knocked on the wide, white door with the gold number five forty-seven. She'd had to tell the desk clerk there was a hospital emergency before he'd reveal the room number for Charles Ellard. As it turned out, the room was in Foster Harrison's name, and she hoped as she knocked again that the old man wouldn't answer the door.

The knob turned, the door pulled inward.

He stood in front of her shirtless, except for the wrapping of a clean white bandage over his chest, and his blue uniform trousers.

Her fingers flew to her mouth, too late to silence her soft gasp. Her gaze dropped to his feet, bare and oddly intimate.

"Gracie?"

"How are ye feeling?" She spotted it then, grasped in the fingers of his lowered hand, a clear glass with a splash of amber liquid.

"Still reeling from the turmoil that is now my life. Thank you." He raised the glass and downed the contents.

He stepped aside and gestured for her to enter. The door closed behind her, and she turned as he refilled his glass from the bottle on the table. "I begin to understand the reason the Irish soldier went back for his flask."

Around the bottle were medical tomes and papers. His report on *Pyemia and Surgical Fevers*.

"I made my grandfather cry."

He scrubbed his hand over his face and heaved a weighted sigh.

She couldn't imagine the old man with the walking stick ever crying, but…

"I have never seen him cry." He shook his head and pinched the bridge of his nose, squeezing his eyes tight for a moment.

Gracie wandered to the window. "Did he tell ye how ye came to live with him?"

"Apparently the cook found me."

Below the bustle of the street mindlessly gave her

something to watch as Jason haltingly repeated the story his grandfather had told.

"Now he's all but tripping over himself to try and please me."

Gracie turned. At least he hadn't yet drunk the whiskey in the glass.

"He had my trunk sent up from Falmouth." He waved at the books and papers and the rabbit sitting on the table beside the chair where Gracie stood.

"Had to see Bunzy and the note for himself."

Gracie reached out to pick up the toy. Lightly, she ran her fingers over the short fuzz of the long ears.

"He's been all over Washington today, contacting people, sending telegrams, as though trying to atone for some great sin."

He lifted a telegram from the corner of the table on which were piled his books and papers. Walking over, he passed it to her.

She set the rabbit on the seat of the wing chair and took the paper.

Jason downed his drink, set the empty glass on the bedside table and lowered himself to sit on the side of the mattress.

"He must have called in a favor with the editor of the Philadelphia Inquirer."

From Article Twelve August 1837 Stop
Unidentified Man Killed Market St By Runaway Freight Wagon Stop
Hope This Helps Stop

Gracie joined him on the bed and passed back the telegram.

He stared at the blunt words one more time and tossed the paper toward the end table where it hovered for a moment then fluttered to the carpet.

"I surmise this is the root of my nervous attacks."

"Ye must have seen yer da killed. A terrible thing for a young lad."

"Explains my aversion to head wounds."

"Aye, and thanks to God's saving grace, yer grandfather found ye."

"He did save me from growing up in an orphanage."

"And he saw to it ye had books and fine schooling to feed that great mind o' yers. Without him ye'd not be a doctor."

"That's what he's doing now." Jason fell back across the coverlet and draped his arm over his eyes.

"Who be doing what?" She squeezed her fingers together in her lap to keep from running her hand over the part of his chest visible around the bandage.

"My grandfather. He's calling in favors, sending telegrams, attempting to have Jefferson Medical College issue me a new diploma."

"'Tis a good thing, yes?"

"Yes."

"Why do ye not sound happy?"

"Chaos, Mrs. McBride. You do recall my feelings on the subject? Instead of calm, my life is in turmoil. I'm exhausted, and my back hurts."

"Then why are ye lying on it?"

"I don't know." He lifted his arm from his eyes, laying it across his chest. "I realize I frequently ask you this question, but why are you here?"

She shifted and turned slightly to better face him. She drew a fortifying breath. "Me mother always says, 'Ye never miss the water 'til the well runs dry.'"

He turned his head and searched her face.

Her heart beat a little faster. She bit down on her lip, waiting.

"Are you saying you miss me?"

"Aye, I miss ye, Jason Reid."

He remained so still, his face so impassive, she had no way to guess what he thought.

Rolling toward her, onto his side, he propped his head in his hand. "What do you miss?"

"I miss yer voice. I miss the sound o' yer boot heels hitting the floor o' the ward. The way yer long legs make a pause between each step. I miss the quiet way ye have about ye as ye care for the men. I miss trying to make out the letters o' that scrawl ye call handwriting."

"Is that it?"

She jumped to her feet and whirled to face him. Her arms crossed in front of her. "Are ye so vain ye need more—"

"Gracie, wait." He grabbed her skirt and pulled. Her knees bumped the edge of his bed, and she fell forward. The spring of the mattress kept her from bruising her face.

Jason grabbed her around the waist and pulled her back close to his chest. "Who do you miss?" he whispered in her ear.

She shivered. Gooseflesh raced up her arms and tightened the nipples of her breasts. Wanting to see his face, she lifted his arm off and scooted from the bed to quickly remove her shoes.

Jason shifted his position so he lay fully on the bed.

She crawled up beside him. "'Tis better now. I can see yer face without needing to tip me head back."

She reached out and lightly ran her finger down the length of his nose. "The bump ye have here." She touched his chin. "Yer scar." She traced an eyebrow.

His eyes dilated.

"Yer clear blue eyes."

Her finger trailed down from his temple along the stubble of his jaw. "I miss the way ye call me Mrs. McBride when ye be annoyed with me and the way ye call me Gracie when ye want me.

"I even miss yer jokes, though I do not know why."

"They were from a book." He pointed toward the battered army trunk under the table. "I assumed they were chosen for publication because they were humorous."

"'Tis like a flower. They all be beautiful, but every person be having a favorite. 'Tis sweet that ye keep trying to find mine." She smiled, a slow, she hoped, seductive smile. Grasping his hand, she raised it to her mouth. Pressing her lips to the smooth skin of his palm, she kissed him.

"I care for ye, Jason Reid. Deeply." When he didn't pull away, she kissed him again. Turning his hand, she placed tiny, nipping kisses along the knuckle of each finger.

She raised her gaze to his face. When had he moved so close? The blue of his eyes darkened and doubt furrowed his brow.

"What of William? You said you could care for no other as much as he."

"'Tis what I believed. Until I took time to really look at the man, Jason Reid." She brought her other hand up to wrap both her hands around his, unwilling to lose the warmth, the tenuous connection between them.

"The man who holds me when I cry. The man who kisses like a charging army claiming a hill."

She lay her hand on his chest. His heart beat softly beneath her palm. Her fingertips trailed over his bandage down his abdomen to the buttons of his trousers.

He lowered his gaze to her hand then captured her hand with his. His slight huff of breath whispered with a mix of desire and uncertainty.

Gracie glanced down and smiled at the swelling mound of his cock beneath the fabric of his trousers. She lifted her gaze to his.

"Nothing between yer skin and mine but me dress, chemise, and petticoat."

His Adam's apple shifted up and down.

"And yer britches."

The thin skin at the base of his throat thrummed with the quick beat of his pulse.

"Is it red?"

"Me petticoat?" She grinned. "I'm thinking ye need to look for yerself."

His hand reached down and raised the hem of her skirt.

"Wait. What o' yer grandfather? When will he be coming back?"

"He was only gone a few minutes before you arrived. He'll probably have dinner with one of his senator friends before he returns. Don't worry, I can be quick."

"Not the words a lass be wanting to hear from her lover." She popped the first button at the top of his trousers.

His fingers sifted through the layers of ruffles.

"Why red?"

"All I be wearing for years is mourning blacks and grays. I love colors. I've green and blue petticoats too."

"How do you feel about lavender?"

"Are ye picking out me petticoats now?"

A faint blush swept across his cheek bones. She slipped free another button then took a moment to run her hand up and down his length.

"No. A dre…" He groaned. "A dress." Rolling over her, he pinned her beneath him and captured her mouth with his. His hand slipped beneath her petticoat and touched her ankle. Slowly his hand moved higher, over her calf to the ruffle at the bottom of her drawers. His fingers slipped beneath the fabric to the tender skin behind her knee.

A soft whimper escaped her throat.

She arched against him. Her fingers working free the last of his buttons then untied the string of his drawers. Hooking her thumbs over the waist of his trousers and drawers, she slid them past his hips.

Eager to touch, she ran her fingertips lightly over his hips and firm muscles of his ass. His hip bones were far too prominent, but she'd lost weight herself since she'd come here. Sliding one hand up his back, she slipped her other hand between their bodies and grasped the solid heat of his length.

His fingers wrapped around her wrist.

"Don't." He pulled her hand away. "Not if you want this to last."

Aching to feel her body next to his, she reached up and helped him work free the twelve buttons of her bodice.

He pressed kisses to the base of her neck. Nipping

and sucking.

She pushed at his shoulders. "Let me up. 'Twill be easier for me to remove the rest o' me clothes."

With a groan, he rolled off her.

Gracie scooted off the bed. She slipped her arms from the sleeves of her bodice and lay it over the back of the wing chair.

"I never imagined watching a woman remove her clothes."

Jason kicked off his pants, letting them fall to the floor. His erection jutted at attention from the dark hair covering his groin. "It's erotic. Better if you remove your corset."

She grinned as she reached behind her to undo the hooks of her skirt. "I do not wear one."

Gracie let her skirt drop to the floor. Slowly, she stepped out of it then picked it up and draped it over the chair.

"You don't?"

"Me bosom be having little to support."

He gulped.

"And 'tis hard to wear leaning over beds, changing dressings and linens." She unfastened her red petticoat with its black embroidered ruffles and let it fall to the floor.

He shifted and groaned.

"I've no crinoline, for nurses cannot be wearing them in the hospital."

She stepped to the bed and lifted her lacy camisole over her head. She let the fabric brush over his thigh as she turned and tossed it in the direction of the chair.

"Gracie." Her name caught in his throat so she could barely hear it.

She propped her foot on the bed near his hip and rolled her stocking slowly down her leg and pulled it off her foot. She did the same with her next stocking then tossed them on top of her petticoat.

"Do ye want me to keep going?"

"Yes." His hands curled into the coverlet clutching fistfuls of fabric. "I've dreamed of seeing you naked."

She reached beneath the length of her chemise and untied her drawers, letting them fall to her feet. The whisper of the cotton over her skin, sent shivers across her flesh and a warmth to her lower abdomen. Her muscles clenched.

Before she climaxed with her own orgasm, she pulled her chemise over her head and stood naked beside the bed.

"Oh God, Gracie, you're so beautiful." He reached out. "Come here."

She climbed on the bed and slowly crawled up the length of him.

With a groan, he wrapped his arms around her and rolled to the other side of the bed, ending with Gracie beneath him. He rained kisses across her face and down her neck as he ran his hand over her shoulder, down her arm, over her hip and belly, up to her breast. Kneading the soft flesh, her nipples peaked, begging for more. His rough, whiskers scratched her face, but she'd discovered pleasure in that aggressive, take-charge essence that was him.

She whimpered and squirmed against him. His erection pressed again her core. Moisture leaked from the tip of his cock.

She clutched his shoulders and tugged him closer, unable to get enough.

Reaching low, she grasped the warmth of his stiffened shaft and guided him to her entrance, moist and ready.

He groaned and pushed into her.

Whimpering, she arched against him then eased back, craving the rhythm of two bodies joined and moving as one.

He responded to her, his thrusts naturally matching her parry as though they'd done this for a life time.

Tension built in Gracie's core, her muscles tensed, her toes curled and her back arched, freezing for one infinite moment before spasm after spasm rocked through her body.

"God, oh God, Jason!" Her fingers dug into his back, careful not to touch the bandaged area of his shoulder.

He pushed into her again and stiffened. A soft groan was the only sound to let her know he'd been caught in his own waves of pleasure.

He started to roll off her, but she wrapped her arms around him. "Stay."

"I love you, Gracie." He murmured against her shoulder as she ran her hands over his back.

He gradually slipped from inside her and dozed for a short time.

They made love again and later lay twined in each other's arms, Gracie, lying with her head on his chest.

"I have compromised you, Mrs. McBride."

She lifted her head and smiled sliding her fingers through the fine hair above the bandage wrapping.

"I fear ye be the one 'twas compromised."

"Perhaps you're right, since I was the virgin."

"Then will ye marry me, Jason Reid?"

His heart beat steady beneath her hand. The smile faded from his lips. "Why?"

"I love ye."

Gracie searched his face but uncertainty clouded his blue eyes. She'd pushed him away so many times it was no wonder he'd eyed her with suspicion. She rolled close to his side and rested her hand over his heart.

"I told ye once if ever I decided to accept the suit of another man, 'twould be someone of a gentle nature, prone to laughter and compassion, who sees me as more than a woman to clean his house and bear his children. Ye are that man, Jason Reid."

"Are you sure, Gracie?"

"Aye. Very sure. I love ye."

"I love you, too."

His hand slid into her hair, cupping the back of her head. Drawing close, his tongue teased her lips.

She kissed him back, savoring every nuance, the warmth of his breath, the security of his arms around her, and the faint taste of whiskey on his tongue.

He pulled back just an inch or so. His thumb brushed over her cheek bone. "Yes."

A sweet smile tugged at the corners of his mouth. "I believe I will marry you."

She wrapped her arms around his neck. "Then if I'm to spend the rest o' me life with a man who can make me laugh, have ye another joke to share, Jason Reid?"

He frowned for a moment then rolled onto his back, bringing her with him, so that she lay sprawled on top of him. Crossing her arms on his chest, she rested her chin on top and watched him.

He stared at the ceiling, as if he first needed to

examine each of the intricate carvings. He drew a breath and recited.

"A patient ordered to take Seidlitz powders, making a grimace at the prescription, the doctor observed, 'It is only the first which is so disagreeable.'

"'Ah then,' said the patient, 'I will begin with the second.' "

A word about the author...

Kathy can't remember a time when she wasn't making up stories and writing them in notebooks. Once her kids were in high school, she joined a writers' group and seriously pursued her craft. Her first short story, *Redemption of a Cavalier* was published in 2007. Since then she has published multiple novels and short stories. She teaches adult classes on fiction writing and is available for workshop presentations.

She enjoys long walks with her dog through the fields and woods near her home. In the winter, she likes to curl up with a good book and one or two of her cats, while the snow blows outside. In between family, work, and animals, she can be found at her computer weaving stories of laughter, heartache, and love for the crazy cast of characters swirling around in her head.

Kathy loves to hear from her readers. You can email her at kathy@kathyotten.com

Thank you for purchasing
this publication of The Wild Rose Press, Inc.

If you enjoyed the story, we would appreciate your
letting others know by leaving a review.

For other wonderful stories,
please visit our on-line bookstore at
www.thewildrosepress.com.

For questions or more information
contact us at
info@thewildrosepress.com.

The Wild Rose Press, Inc.
www.thewildrosepress.com

Stay current with The Wild Rose Press, Inc.

Like us on Facebook

https://www.facebook.com/TheWildRosePress

And Follow us on Twitter
https://twitter.com/WildRosePress